DEAD IS ALL YOU GET

PRAISE FOR DEAD IS ALL YOU GET

"Dave Pulaski carries the novel with his hard edges and slowly softening heart, but his flaws are still impossible to miss. He is far from a noble knight on a white steed, but in this new ugly world, where the living are just as dangerous as the undead, Dave is a perfect protagonist. Hanging on strongly from the first novel is the philosophical bent to Dave —he might be a rugged old drunk with a mean streak, but he leans into the existential musings that being in such a hellscape inspires. There is humor sprinkled throughout the book as well, as some amount of gallows humor is warranted, and Ramirez is adept at keeping his tongue firmly in his cheek."

— SELF-PUBLISHING REVIEW

"*Dead Is All You Get* is cunningly plotted, and the author uses suspense to deepen the quality of horror as he creates scenes that make the reader feel like something could go wrong at any moment. A lot happens in this story, and the pacing is fast and the action intense. The writing is filled with enjoyable and engaging dialogue that enhances the reading experience of this gripping story. Great prose, sophisticated characters, and a very clever plot."

— READERS' FAVORITE

"With *Dead Is All You Get*, it's clear that Ramirez knows his readers will already be familiar with the world he's created, so he's able to really put the pedal to the metal, increasing the scope, tension, and drama of this story, and making for a read that is unputdownable. As pulse racing and action packed as it is thoughtful and moving, *Dead is All You Get* is a superb sequel that builds on the work author Steven Ramirez began in *Tell Me When I'm Dead*, leaving me and I'm sure the majority of readers, hugely excited to see where things will go in Book Three."

— THE BOOKBAG

BOOKS BY STEVEN RAMIREZ

LITERARY FICTION

Let's Get Lost

HELLBORN SERIES

Tell Me When I'm Dead

Dead Is All You Get

Even The Dead Will Bleed

HARD TO KILL SERIES

Brandon's Last Words

Faithless

SARAH GREENE MYSTERIES

The Girl in the Mirror

House of the Shrieking Woman

The Blood She Wore

OTHER BOOKS

Chainsaw Honeymoon

Come As You Are: A Short Novel and Nine Stories

Come As You Are: A Novella

Glass Highway

Los Angeles, CA

stevenramirez.com

Publisher's Note: This is a work of fiction. Names, characters, places, and incidents are a product of the author's imagination. Any opinions expressed belong to the characters and should not be confused with those of the author. Locales and public names are sometimes used for atmospheric purposes. Any resemblance to actual people, living or dead, or businesses, companies, events, institutions, or locales is coincidental.

Dead Is All You Get / Hellborn Series Book 2 / Steven Ramirez. 3rd ed.

Paperback: 978-1-949108-18-7

EPUB: 978-1-949108-19-4

Kindle: 978-1-949108-20-0

Audiobook: 978-1-949108-33-0

Library of Congress Control Number: 2023900370

Edited by Shannon A. Thompson

Cover design by Damonza

To the men and women who serve our country. If the zombie apocalypse ever did come to pass, you'd have our backs.

DEAD IS ALL YOU GET

HELLBORN SERIES BOOK 2

STEVEN RAMIREZ

glass highway

"Just relax, Mr. Jackson. Everything will be all right, but you must relax. You've been a sick man."

— MICHAEL CRICHTON, *THE ANDROMEDA STRAIN*

DEAD IS ALL YOU GET

PART ONE

MISDIRECTION

ONE

It was that guy—the explorer—with the Oxford shirt, skinny jeans, and Tiger shoes. He was the one I worried about because he was wearing Google Glass. I could have gone to Pappy's, but that place was way too crowded. So, I ended up in this greasehole, thinking I was safe.

He came in a little while ago and grabbed a stool at the counter. Sitting in the rear of the restaurant, I choked down a grilled cheese that tasted like burnt cardboard. I didn't want to draw his attention, or he might start recording me.

The locals were fine—or maybe not. Some could have been undead. You wouldn't know right away because they wouldn't be like the ones we encountered when all this began. Lumbering and flat-eyed, coming at you to get a piece of your face or your neck. No, these little beauties would be smart. And they'd only show their true selves after it was too late.

You think I'm crazy, right? It's okay. I call it cautious. Want to know why? Sure, you do. Don't make me tell you. Because to tell you is to remember. And I don't want to relive any of it. The people I lost. The pain I suffered—physical and spiritual. That I'm even alive is a miracle. Yeah, about that...

See, the thing with miracles is you only get one. And they were in short supply during those dark days when we thought we had a way out but didn't. When a few of us—a brave few —banded together to fight the scourge. Not only for ourselves but for the other survivors. God, don't make me tell you.

But you'll insist, like a kid begging for a toy. As if this were a campfire, and you're dying for a good story. *Tell us*, you'll say. And then, you'll needle and cajole and whine and crap till I do. Because foolishly, I'd already begun to recount the facts as I remembered them. How I lost my best friend to a vicious, creeping plague. And how I was a miserable coward who cheated on his wife and left the other woman to die when I might have saved her. And trust me, she needed saving. We all did.

But I didn't stop there. I told you how Tres Marias had become infested by an evil no one could have imagined. Ordinary people turning into grasping things that hungered for the living. Who didn't quit till everything was gray and soulless like them. And how some who remained human—if that's what you want to call them—tried to make slaves of the rest of us in an attempt to reinvent the world in the image of a cool-headed, fork-tongued shoe salesman.

I don't know why I told you those stories. Maybe it was because I'm a drunk, and drunks like to confess. Especially when we're loaded. But I'm not high now. The constant pain keeps me sharp. Somehow, you knew, didn't you? That I would need to purge myself of the writhing pestilence eating out my insides like a gang of guinea worms.

Dead. Not dead. Undead. Doesn't begin to cover it. Because what I learned is that everyone is dead in one way or another. Dead morals, dead conscience, dead heart. We found a few we could trust—people like my wife, Holly, and my friends. But as for the rest of those other suckholes... For them, it was all about the lizard brain that survives any way it can. It makes you adapt, becoming something from a child's night terror. But don't kid yourself—it's not only nature. That lizard brain—our old brain—has an agenda.

For the record, I'm not crazy, but the dead talk to me sometimes. I hear them in my head, asking questions and offering opinions. Mostly, they want to know how I'm doing. Great, I say. Couldn't be better. Driving endlessly without sleep, surviving moment to moment, adrenaline coursing through my veins with every car horn blast. Life is good.

And God? What do I even say to Him? That I'm fallen but want to get better? And that I hope I can be forgiven for all the wrongs—all the bad behavior? That despite the mistakes, I feel like I deserve another chance?

Khalil Gibran wrote, *Doubt is a pain too lonely to know that faith is his twin brother.* At this moment, I'm staring at my twin. But it's through a wall of suffering that makes me doubt he's even there. Yet I continue to look, hoping—praying—I'm not the man I was.

Too much has happened. Death has washed over me like a blood rinse, taking everything that made me a person. It's what you can expect when hell sets up camp and starts barbecuing the townsfolk like Ball Park Franks.

Shit, the explorer was walking over here—coming straight towards me. Probably had to use the toilet. It was too late to get up and slip past him. Anyway, that would make him suspicious. He might turn on his camera and go to town. I had to do something—he was looking right at me now. Thinking fast, I tripped him.

His skinny body went flying, arms windmilling. As he tried to catch himself, his head hit the corner of my table, snapping his headgear in two. There you go—fifteen hundred bucks.

Groaning, he got to his feet and glowered at me. I'd already left money on the table, and when I slid out of the booth, I made sure to crush his glasses with my boot.

"Hey!" he said and tried swinging at my head.

I weaved and gave him a quick jab to the gut, making him double over. Then I walked out of the coffee shop without looking back.

No one tried to stop me. They were too busy gawping at the explorer leaning against the table, holding what was left of his busted cool. All they would remember is some faceless guy wearing a Giants baseball cap.

My truck was parked a few blocks away. I climbed in and headed to the motel, confident no one had followed me.

Time to hit the road again.

It was getting dark. The 5 South was a mess, so I kept to the back roads and stayed within the speed limit. There were a lot of cops around. Maybe they were looking for me. Who knows? I couldn't afford to get pulled over—not in Bakersfield. Not with all those weapons. Still with me?

Telling you this story won't be cathartic because a good part of me has already died in more ways than you could ever know. All that's left now is sorrow—the kind that time doesn't heal because the wound is gangrenous and foul. It stays with you when you rise on an uncertain morning of another damn day. And when you close your eyes at night, the blood-awful screaming is still in your head.

But I haven't convinced you. You don't care that I have

this long road ahead, with bad food and little sleep, the nightmares chasing me like rabid dogs. You want to know everything, even if it means I will die a little more. Don't make me. I'm begging you—I can't.

All right, I'll tell you.

TWO

The horde came from the east, driving us deeper into the forest. Warnick went ahead through the fog, his face grim, like the keynote speaker at a mortician's convention. Springer remained at his side, his finger on the trigger guard of his battle-worn AR-15. Springer—that blond kid from Santa Rosa—was born ready. We had spent so much time together, and I relied on them completely. I hoped I was of some use to them, even though they were US Army trained while I was an amateur who'd learned to kill using an axe, then a gun.

I knew little about Warnick, even though we had fought side by side against the draggers and the Red Militia. What I knew was that he was a man who put his trust in God. Around thirty, he was stocky with a dad body. He'd saved me on many occasions, eventually getting wounded himself. And with his worn, blood-stained Bible, he showed me the power of faith.

Springer was someone I knew even less about. He seemed too young to have experienced anything. And speaking of miracles, I think he was one. Shot in the neck to almost dead on the street, yet somehow surviving. He made it to our base and revealed the location where I was held captive by the Red Militia, halfway to dead myself. So many debts to repay.

High in the trees, a crow cawed plaintively but didn't give away our position. My heart thudded like a punch press on Red Bull. I turned to Holly, who stood behind me with our adopted daughter Griffin. Greta, her ears forward, watched them as they paraded through the mist like bent robots. The German shepherd's black-and-tan face was alert, her body tense and ready. If they attacked us, she would tear at them. Unable to kill them because they were already dead, she would hobble them long enough for us to escape.

I almost lost Holly—not because of the craven stupidity of infidelity, although that would have been enough for any woman. No, it was because, in my old life, I had demonstrated a cowardice she couldn't fathom. I could've saved Missy Soldado—that adulterous young thing—from my friend Jim before he savaged her. Instead, I chose to hide.

In the months following, I fought my way back to my wife, crawling on my belly—a legless dog—eating my own shit every inch of the way. And somehow, I made her mine again. With her fine blonde hair and hypnotic green eyes, she didn't just pick me up—she made me right. I had fallen away from everything that mattered, and she brought me back. I may have owed others my life, but I owed her my soul. When I confessed this to her in a moment of sentimentality, her response was so Holly. *No charge.*

And there was Griffin, the trembling teenager we had rescued from her violent, predatory stepfather—that piece of shit Travis Golightly. She'd lost her younger brother, Kyle, to the insanity of the Red Militia. Frightened and withdrawn when we met, she had grown into a fighter who knew how to handle a weapon. When it came to draggers, she was no-nonsense. The girl was a badass, and we cherished her. These four—and the dog—were my family now.

The other guards in our squad remained scattered among the trees, watching and waiting. Like Warnick and Springer, they were used to fighting human combatants bent on blowing themselves up at military checkpoints seven thousand miles away. Now, these American warriors fought monsters made of rotting flesh, with mealy skin and doll's eyes that looked but didn't see. Who wanted only to devour the warm meat of alive humans.

We had come here to rendezvous with Evie Champagne, the intrepid news reporter. Together, we hoped to find answers to the mystery of the contagion that ravaged Tres Marias, the town where I grew up. Though other towns had seen evidence of the plague, it originated here.

Evie had hinted that Robbin-Sear, a secretive company hidden in the forest, was the key. And so, three vehicles set out in the cold early morning to find the truth. We'd already parked miles out and hiked in. Not knowing whether the facility was heavily guarded, we didn't want to announce our arrival. If all went as planned, the reporter and her faithful cameraman would be waiting.

But they never showed. Believing they were in trouble, Warnick decided to search for them in the forest. We ended up in this desolate place where dead and dying trees loomed like gray ghosts in mourning. Well over a mile from our vehicles, we heard the unmistakable sound. Not marching. Not walking. *Dragging.*

I couldn't make them out through the fog, but I knew they were there. The only way out of this was to get to higher ground. The horde would pass, never knowing a free meal had been within reach. But then, they began to emerge from the mist. Was it a coincidence, or had they tracked us?

No choice now—we ran.

THREE

We saw them in the sketchy patches of sunlight that broke through the trees. Hundreds. Lurching and ravenous, they moved like blood-soaked puppets on guy wires. Where had they come from?

Standing on a narrow deer trail, I watched as the draggers in front took charge. I'd witnessed this phenomenon only once at Staples when Missy ordered my manager, Fred Lumpkin, to kill me. And what it meant was incomprehensible and chilling. They had learned to organize.

Blood pounded in my ears. Hot streaks of red lightning danced across my eyes. I took Holly's trembling hand, trying not to show fear. But as we retreated into the darkness of an October morning, I knew this might be the end. It figured. We had come all this way through what I believed was the worst of it. Since July, when the nightmare began.

You always think that, right—the worst is over? But it never is. There's always another dangerous corner, another circle of hell. By rights, we should have been dead long ago. Maybe now we would be. What if, in trying to get to the truth of what happened to our town, we ended up dying alone out here? Taking our unanswered questions with us?

That stupid, nagging crow had followed us. Joined by others, it cawed, taunting us endlessly. *Death ain't pretty. We'll begin with the eyes.*

With one hand on her weapon, Griffin looked scared. And why not? She was a kid—a lanky fifteen-year-old who might lose her life any second. What teenager thinks about that? But it was our world now—an insane universe where things that shouldn't walk did. Brushing the light-brown hair from her dirt-smudged face, my wife gave her a smile.

"We'll be okay," she said.

The girl nodded and gripped her weapon even tighter. All of us knew we couldn't stay out in the open. The only problem was they were close. Any move we made now, they were bound to see.

Using short, piercing chirps, two undead commanders directed their murderous legion down and across—towards us. Like Fred, the others did as they were told. I touched Warnick's arm. He turned to Springer and pointed north, his eyes like agate marbles. Then he signaled us to stop. Something had gotten the horde's attention, and they began moving away. If we could make it to the upper ridge, we'd be home free.

Silently, we made our way over the pine needles and fallen branches. The others had already gone ahead and were no longer visible in the mist. We were twelve in all—couldn't spare any more. The rest were at the Arkon building, protecting civilians. Dammit, but we could have used them now.

Relentlessly, the horde traveled north like they were late for the train. None were freshly dead. Many looked like they'd been part of a Japanese tour group. Even in death, they stuck together. They were all ages too. Some were missing limbs, and others had lost ears and noses. The worst were the children, slack and gray-eyed, their small arms flopping uselessly —their tiny, undernourished grunts signaling a crippling desire to feed. Suddenly, Griffin yelped.

"Sorry, sorry."

Holly grabbed her hand. "What was it?"

"Something on the ground. I— It was crawling on my foot."

Kneeling, I took a quick look. "Maybe a gopher snake. They're harmless."

The dog approached the spot to investigate. As I pulled her away, an all-too-familiar sound echoed through the forest. It was a bone-chilling prelude to a mauling. A clarion call telling us we were finished. It was a death shriek, and it meant only one thing.

They had seen us.

FOUR

T he horde descended like a swarm of locusts. Griffin, Holly, and I sprinted ahead. Warnick and Springer remained behind, covering us with a line of suppressive fire. Before the draggers could recover, the guards rejoined us.

Soon they were after us again. A plague of fast-moving creatures drunk with bloodlust. We could have stood our ground, but there were too many.

"Keep moving!" I said.

I made sure the women were ahead of me. If it came down to it, I would stay and fight to save them. My lungs searing, I pointed at a fire road. The draggers hadn't lost sight of us and ran full-out as if sprung from a starting gate.

Leaping like stags to either side of the road, the undead commanders split their followers evenly. I realized almost too late what they were up to. My friend saw it too and ordered us to take cover among the trees. Tirelessly, the hostiles closed in from either side. And that's when I knew I was right. They were herding us like sheep.

"Get Holly and Griffin out of here!" Warnick said and radioed the other guards.

I pushed the women ahead, and we ran for our lives. Meanwhile, the commanders barked unintelligible orders at their murderous troops. The guards fired at an oncoming column, going for the knees instead of the head. The ones in front fell, temporarily stopping the others from advancing. But the fallen continued to crawl towards us, grinning with anticipation.

More guards returned to assist us. Someone lobbed a grenade, taking out a leader. Its rancid body blew apart like bad sausage. The horde scattered. As the mist cleared, I spotted the crest of the hill. Something hovered in the sky—a drone! If we could reach the top, we might have a chance. When I looked back, the guards were holding their own.

We continued to climb, straining under our weapons and backpacks. Halfway up, I stopped. Another commander went down in a stream of rapid fire that tore off its face. As it fell, its hands grasping air, the leaderless horde fanned out. I was faster than my wife and, afraid of losing her, forced myself to slow down.

"Dave!"

Griffin had fallen and lay halfway up the road on the forest floor, holding her ankle. The horde was quickly approaching. Seeing them, she screamed. Holly and I hurried down the steep incline, losing our balance as we slipped on the pine needles.

A dragger—a middle-aged woman with painted-on eyebrows—grabbed her foot and, yanking it, opened its mouth like a trapdoor. Baring her teeth, Greta went after the attacker. Its eyeballs spinning, it clung to the girl while the German shepherd tore at its hands and neck.

Griffin held the dog by the collar as Springer mag-dumped

the hostile, turning its skull into a black, smoking crater. I unslung my axe and hacked off the arm, the still-grasping claw clinging to the girl's ankle as she kicked at it.

"Get it off me!"

Prying off the lifeless meat hook, the spidery gray flesh felt cold in my hands. I checked her ankle. The skin wasn't broken—thank God. My wife and I helped her up. We continued up the road with Griffin limping along.

A few minutes more, and we were at the top with the others. As we made our way down, I heard Tom Petty's "American Girl" blasting out of the sky like high-pitched thunder. I couldn't believe what I was seeing.

Black Dragon guards on bright red ATVs streamed across the valley like angry wasps. The noise from their vehicles was deafening. They shot past us onto the fire road and engaged the oncoming horde. Using AR-15s, they mowed down the draggers. Then more guards armed with shotguns blasted the hostiles' heads to sawdust.

The tops of the trees swayed. Dust and pine needles churned all around us as helicopters with the Black Dragon logo circled the area—one pounding out the rock song through its PA system. The lead chopper set down in a clearing below, its blades beating.

A tall, uniformed African American man jumped out and waved to us. He was around fifty, with short graying hair and a clean-shaven face. His only weapon was a sidearm.

Joyfully, Holly embraced Griffin. "It's the damn cavalry!"

"We need to get you out of here," he said when he was close enough. "This dog coming too?"

He didn't need to ask. The girl had already led Greta to the aircraft. Once we were aboard, the helicopter ascended, and we were away. Below, I watched the ATVs plow through the horde, taking them out by the dozens.

When my wife tugged at my sleeve, I turned to find Evie Champagne, the reporter we had come to meet. She stared at me with haunted eyes. The last time we saw her was with her cameraman over a VTC connection in the Arkon building. I could still picture their wooden faces on the large TV monitor as unseen hostiles closed in on them.

Looking shell-shocked, she shivered under a gray patient blanket. I wasn't sure I would ever see her again after that videoconference when draggers had overrun their building. We had gotten so used to watching her on the local news, going to places she shouldn't, and digging up story after story as the outbreak spread. Now, even with her tangled hair and clothes in disarray, her powerful presence filled the cabin. Before I could ask about her cameraman, she leaned forward and spoke into my ear over the noise.

"Glad you made it," she said. "I have so much to tell you."

FIVE

We flew over residential streets where draggers wandered like hungry ghosts in a perpetual twilight of damnation. Eventually, we landed on the high school football field. Outside the fence, Humvees and LMTVs—Light Medium Tactical Vehicles—with the Black Dragon logo patrolled the neighborhood. Hundreds of security guards watched over the campus. Each wore a helmet and body armor and carried a rifle.

The few hostiles who managed to get close to the school pressed against the chain link, hoping for a quick bite. Guards patrolling the fence on ATVs took them out with bayonets to the head. I imagined they would burn the bodies in pits like all the others we'd seen since summer. But something was different. I no longer smelled the foul, greasy smoke that used to hang in the air.

Disembarking, we made our way to the gate. There were no signs of the horde we had escaped from only a week earlier. We'd mounted a full assault on the Red Militia and rescued Griffin from her stepfather. That day, the group's leader, Ormand Ferry, died screaming as hungry draggers tore him to pieces like pulled pork.

I felt like I was in a dream. After weeks and months of running and hiding, we were actually safe. Black Dragon had finally sent in badly needed reinforcements and regained control. Instead of a wasteland, the high school had become a secure, organized command center.

As we traversed the newly cut grass, workers in overalls patched and painted the bullet-scarred buildings. Others replaced outdoor lights and tended the greenery that dotted the campus. I would have said our surroundings were idyllic if we weren't in the middle of an outbreak.

A guard approached Warnick and Springer, telling them something I couldn't make out. Then all three headed for the administration building while we followed our escort. Up ahead, a row of large trailers stood in the rear parking lot. Civilians waited in line in front of each.

"What are those?" I said to the guard.

"Mobile medical units. We're testing everyone for the virus."

Holly did a double-take. "Wait, there's a test?"

Never missing an opportunity for a story, Evie brushed past us. "What happens if they're infected?"

"We transfer them to an isolation facility."

I side-eyed the others. "Where?"

"That's classified. Now, look. We need to—"

The reporter grabbed his arm. "Not so fast. What if someone tests negative?"

Exasperated, he pointed at the gym. "We find them a place in our evac center, okay?"

When Black Dragon first arrived, they converted the gymnasium into a shelter. But it all went sideways when someone forgot to secure the doors. As the horde attacked, the building became a charnel house.

Ignoring the guard, I broke away and headed for the entrance. The doors were open, and bright lights shone inside. The interior was clean and smelled of disinfectant. There were coffee stations on either side in front of the bleachers. A sea of army surplus cots and blankets stood in neat rows. Civilians sat at round banquet tables, playing card games and chatting. The people were all ages and included children, some of whom belly-laughed their way through Twister and Chicken Limbo. Guards kept watch along the perimeter.

I remembered searching for my wife here. We were separated then, and I didn't know whether she was alive or dead. I recalled Mrs. Hough, an old neighbor whose mind had faded and who I'd tried to help. Like all the others, she was lost to the horde.

Holly joined me, slipping her arm through mine.

"It's like it never happened," I said.

I ran my fingers down the freshly painted doors. No sign of blood. Far off, I recognized Eddie Greeley, the owner of Happier Times, the local ice skating rink. That was where I almost died at the hands of the previous Black Dragon supervisor, Chavez, in a twisted ice follies version of sudden death. Eddie looked frail—at least he was alive. When he saw me, he waved. I started towards him, but our annoying escort took my arm.

"You can't be in here until you've been tested," he said.

Inside, a little boy let out a scream that sent shards of glass raking my spine. A guard ran to where he was playing with the other kids. As his mother hugged him, the boy pointed a trembling finger at the bleachers.

Dropping to his knees, the guard laid down his weapon

and peered underneath. Then he signaled everyone to move back. Another guard joined him. The first one said something, and his partner ran off, returning with a shoebox.

The first guard reached in and pulled something out. Before anyone could see, he placed it in the box. His partner walked it out of the building. He tried getting past me, but I blocked him and opened the box. Inside, there was a severed hand, gray and desiccated.

"Satisfied?" he said.

Our escort walked us to the front of the line at an MMU. Holly instructed Greta to wait outside. Wearing the disappointed look only a dog can manage, she lay near the steps, resting her head on her paws. A young girl tried petting her, but her mother stopped her and led her away.

Inside, there was an impressive array of medical equipment and electronics. A physician's assistant guided us to the workstations, where they began performing a series of standard tests—the kind you'd expect during a routine physical. After our exams, phlebotomists drew vials of blood from each of us.

"I heard you guys identified the virus," I said.

"Wonderful, isn't it?"

"But there's no vaccine, right?"

The phlebotomist gave me a professional smile. Through sheer luck and God's good grace, I didn't think any of us were infected, but I worried about the possibility. The thought frightened me. As I waited for the others, I walked to where Evie was sitting. Her bare arm was extended as her phlebotomist drew blood.

"Where did they pick you up?" I said.

"Along a fire road."

"Thanks for alerting the troops. Hey, did you guys ever make it to—"

Ignoring me, she turned to the health worker. "I can't wait to take a hot shower."

I stopped a passing physician's assistant. "How long before we know the results?"

"Couple of hours."

"What about communications?"

"Cell service is down, I'm afraid."

"Internet?"

"Tits-up." Then to the reporter, "Pardon my—"

"Trust me," she said, smiling. "I've heard so much worse."

SIX

After the exams, we walked over to the administration building, where the gray-haired man who had rescued us waited with Warnick and Springer.

"Kelly Pederman," he said. "I'm the new supervisor."

I shook his hand. "I guess you heard about Chavez."

Clearing his throat, he side-eyed my friend. "That was a tragic loss."

"Yeah, tragic." I looked at Warnick, whose face was like smooth stone.

"We should have the results of your tests shortly. In the meantime, I'd like to extend what hospitality we can. Anyone hungry?"

They led us into a conference room on the first floor. Greta accompanied us, remaining close to Griffin.

"Why don't you try being nice for a change?" Holly said as we took our seats.

Evie sat across from me. When we made eye contact, she nodded in agreement. Shortly after, they brought us actual food—not the MREs we'd come to loathe. We had a choice of

McDonald's Egg McMuffin sandwiches or pancakes with bacon. And there was plenty of coffee and orange juice.

The girl tossed a slice of bacon to Greta. "I've been craving McDonald's."

"I'll catch up with you folks in a bit," the supervisor said.

On his way out, he instructed another guard to bring a bowl of water for the dog. It bugged me how Warnick was behaving. I felt something was up but let it go.

"Where's your partner in crime?" I said to the reporter.

Her eyes were distant, as if she were struggling against the memory traces of a bad dream. "Jeff didn't make it."

My wife put down her food. "Aw, man."

"If it wasn't for him, I'd be dead. He was a stand-up guy, you know? Never complained, no matter how bad it got. And trust me, I'm no picnic when things don't go my way."

I gave her a smile. "Sounds like a great guy."

"He was—the best."

As we ate our breakfast, I stole another glance at Evie. There were so many questions I wanted to ask her, but this wasn't the time. It was apparent she didn't trust these people. On the other hand, they were the authorities. Why not trust them? Or was I being naive?

I couldn't help wondering if she thought there was some rogue element at work—like Chavez. Even with my suspicious nature, though, I didn't think so. Kelly Pederman seemed all right to me. Then again, I wasn't a reporter with gut instincts. How else could this woman have survived so long without any weapons?

"Is there any hope?"

"There's always hope," she said. "It's what gets me up in the morning. That and a good story."

. . .

After our meal, we relaxed as best we could in our leatherette chairs. As soon as I closed my eyes, vivid images of the past few weeks played through my brain like a glitchy slideshow without music.

There I was, skating on the ice at Happier Times, desperate to avoid Missy. She had been reduced to a hungry skeleton with skin like leather. Hell-bent on revenge, she pursued me as crazed guards hooted and whistled from the bleachers...

Off the ice, Chavez lay dying in a dark pool of blood, his skull crushed by a pipe wrench...

In a dim conference room, a security guard named Barnes whimpered in a corner, his leg chewed to shit. Hurtling towards eternal undeadness...

Like a red tide, armies of the undead surged through the streets of Tres Marias, backlit by the angry roaring fire pits brimming with burning bodies...

I saw everything that had gone wrong since that first night when my friend Jim died in my car but wouldn't stay dead. And his enormous dog Perro, bloody and rabid, panting in the cold night air—waiting for me...

And finally, Nina Zimmer's baby daughter, Evan, gurgling and happy. Her bright little face warmed me, reminding me there might be something to hope for after all.

When I opened my eyes, the supervisor was standing in the doorway holding a pile of manila envelopes. Smiling, he handed out our test results.

"I'm happy to report you're all clean. It's pretty unusual, considering what you've been through."

"What happens now?" I said.

"Warnick and Springer have been given new assignments."

I shot my friend a look and got nothing back. Didn't they understand that we were not only a unit but a family?

"We fought together," I said. "Saved lives."

Pederman gave me a patient look. "I understand how you feel, Dave, but it's a new day. Everything has to change."

Now Holly looked nervous. "Where will you send us, though? It's not like we can go home."

"Mrs. Pulaski…"

"Holly."

"There's something I'd like to discuss with you and your husband in my office."

"Sure, but I don't want to leave Griffin."

My wife was already on her feet in that power stance I knew so well. Even the reporter seemed impressed by her fearlessness.

"I'll be fine," the girl said, embarrassed.

Warnick got up and took the seat next to her. "Springer and I aren't going anywhere."

Holly relented. As the supervisor led us out of the conference room, she looked back at Griffin. She seemed relaxed, drinking her juice and stroking Greta's head. We continued down the hall to the principal's office. I tried not to think about all the times I'd ended up in there.

"This can't be good," I said.

SEVEN

Pederman closed the door and sat at the principal's desk.

"Have a seat," he said.

I remembered this room—the smell of stale coffee and Mennen Skin Bracer. On the wall, the framed photos of countless school functions and awards banquets. Back then, the principal would begin every visit with those same words. *Have a seat.*

In one photo, my old teacher shook the winning student's hand at the science fair. Irwin Landry was younger then, but with those familiar steely blue eyes, hawk nose, and shock of white hair. It still hurt, remembering how he died—a bullet to the brain.

The last time I was here, the principal warned me I might not graduate. He told me my mother had called him, expressing her concern. Her illness had advanced to the point where she rarely left her bed. Yet she never stopped pressuring me to succeed at something. And now the principal was doing it. *Let's get those grades up, huh? You don't want to disappoint your mother.* I thought he was a prick, and I hated him. But his approach worked.

And so, with my dying mother as a witness, I managed to squeak by and get the cap and gown. Though my parents were long dead, that was at least one regret in a pile of failures I wouldn't have to live with.

"What's this about?" I said.

The supervisor looked me in the eye. "Considering everything that's happened, I get that you don't trust me. But I'm confident I can earn that trust."

Holly gripped the edge of the desk. "Are we in trouble?"

Pederman laughed. "Far from it. Did either of you serve in the military? I couldn't find anything in the files."

"No," I said. "Why?"

"For a couple of civilians, you've proven to be more than capable under fire. After reviewing the organization, I've made a few adjustments. Some guards have been reassigned, but I believe we're stronger now. I'm sure you've noticed the change."

He waited for us to agree. My wife and I looked at each other, unsure of where this was going.

"How were you able to turn things around so fast?" I said.

"Most of us are ex-military, and we know how to get the job done."

He came around the desk and took a seat in front of us. Though it felt awkward, he had my attention.

"I'd like you both to consider joining Black Dragon Security."

Holly looked stunned. "Wait, what?"

The supervisor laughed again. I thought of Warnick and realized he and Springer must have had something to do with this.

"I'm prepared to make each of you a generous offer right

now. We're one of the few companies that provide a full pension. And the medical is awesome." He was looking at my wife. "And we have a robust bonus structure."

I couldn't help myself—I laughed, which annoyed Pederman. "Excuse me, but this is unexpected."

"I understand—it's a big step. Why don't you think it over?"

He walked us out of the office, his manner decidedly cooler—possibly resentful. And why not? The guy had put serious money on the table, and I'd crapped all over it. But like a pro, he shook our hands.

"I've already set up quarters for you and the girl," he said.

After my misstep, I felt bad asking, but I had to. "What about Evie?"

"The reporter?"

"She's also part of our group."

"I admire your loyalty," he said. "I'll see what I can do."

When we reentered the conference room, Springer and a young Latino guard attempted to teach Griffin how to play Texas Hold'em. Though she wasn't trying to be funny, these guys couldn't stop laughing. Warnick sat by himself, reading his Bible.

Holly turned to me, half-smiling. "I think you pissed him off."

"You know me," I said and joined the game.

They'd set up a series of trailers across the campus to accommodate management and the medical staff. Pederman arranged to provide one for our family.

"Who's paying for all this?" I said.

Ignoring me, Holly began exploring. "This is incredible. They even stocked the fridge."

Griffin pointed at the bathroom. "Shower time!"

My wife narrowed her eyes. "Not if I get there first."

They raced to the bathroom. But with her long legs, the girl had the obvious advantage.

"Too bad, Mom," she said. "But you lose."

While Griffin showered, Holly and I brought in our few belongings and stored them. They had confiscated our weapons except for my axe. I had relied on it since the start of the outbreak. With it, I'd destroyed Missy and countless other draggers. Blood-stained, it was like an old friend. I found a utility closet at the rear of the trailer and set the weapon against the wall.

My wife and I sat at the dinette and opened our test results. I already knew we were fine, but seeing the proof gave me a huge feeling of relief. The computer printout confirmed my white blood cell count was normal. I didn't have high cholesterol and wasn't at risk for diabetes. When I asked Holly about hers, she slid the paper into the envelope and smiled wistfully.

"All good," she said.

We decided to take a walk. I felt safer than we had in months. They had reinforced the fence surrounding the school, and guards patrolled the grounds. Whenever a dragger appeared, they would quickly dispatch it. I didn't know what they did with the bodies—there were no open pits smoldering with human meat.

Warnick and Springer had returned to the Arkon building, our former command center. Their orders were to coordinate the evacuation of the remaining civilians. There was a rumor that Black Dragon had taken over apartment buildings around town. They planned to convert them into temporary living quarters. Like the school, these sites would be heavily guarded.

"Tell me," I said. "Can you see yourself wearing a Black Dragon uniform?"

"Not sure. It isn't like we're new to this kind of work." She seemed distant and thoughtful. "Besides, we don't have jobs. At some point, life will return to normal, and we'll need money."

"That reminds me. We have a mortgage on a house that's uninhabitable. And what about our old jobs?"

"I couldn't go back to Staples."

"Me neither. And Griffin?"

"She stays with us, no matter what."

"Agreed. But if we're working for Black Dragon, we can't come and go as we please. What's she supposed to do all day?"

"I don't know. Attend high school?"

In a matter of hours, we had gone from elation at being rescued to worrying about our future. I knew Holly wasn't mad at me. We were at a crossroads, no longer volunteer guards but ordinary citizens without guns. And with a teenager to look after. I changed the subject.

"I want to find out what Evie knows about the outbreak."

"If they can stop it, what does it matter?"

"I need to know."

"Why?"

In the distance, guards loaded dead draggers onto a flatbed truck. "Because of Jim. He's a part of this—I know he is."

"You'd better discuss it with Warnick first. We've been given a chance, and I don't want to blow it."

"Don't let all this fool you," I said. "The nightmare isn't over."

•   •   •

That night I dreamt about my dead friend Jim. Clean-shaven, he wore fresh clothes and a new pair of Nikes.

"Thanks for the awesome funeral," he said.

"I did the best I could." I took his hand, which was smooth and wound-free. "Jim, I wish I could—"

"Forget it, dude. Not your fault."

"How've you been?"

"Can't complain. Hey, I want to show you something."

As he swung open the gate to the field, I noticed the reddish gash that ringed his neck. Suddenly, I relived the impact of the car crash that had sent my friend through the windshield and into the night, where I lost him forever. Now I was back on that dark forest road.

"Jim!" I said. "Come on, man, this isn't funny."

Something moved in the distance. It was my friend waving at me. "Hurry up, lard ass!"

He seemed impossibly far away. I struggled to reach him, but my leg hurt where Travis had beaten me. When I finally caught up, Jim led me to his dog, Perro. The beast lay in the road, hardly breathing. Steam rose off his body like a red mist. He looked smaller than I remembered. Emaciated. Harmless.

"They had no right to take him," my friend said. "No right at all."

He receded into the darkness, his dying dog in his arms. Perro was a puppy now. I tried waving, but my arm throbbed where I had been shot while rescuing Griffin.

"Don't go! You have to tell me what happened!"

"No time," he said. "Dream faster."

EIGHT

olly and I were anxious to learn what happened at the Arkon building. And when Warnick and Springer returned, we ambushed them as they hurried to the administration building.

"How are Nina and her baby?" I said to my friend.

"Fine."

Warnick moved briskly, not bothering to make eye contact. I wondered if there was something they weren't telling me.

My wife ran alongside, with Greta trotting beside her. "And the others?"

"All fine. We're evacuating them in the morning."

I'd had enough and grabbed my friend's arm. "Slow down, dammit. Hey, come on. What's going on?"

"Can't talk now. We have a meeting."

I side-eyed Springer, who shrugged. "Dude, really? A meeting?"

He and Springer headed up the steps to the front entrance and sailed past the guard. Pederman was in the foyer, speaking to an aide. Holly and I tried following, but the stony-faced guard blocked us. Greta snapped at him before my wife could pull her away.

"Sitz!" she said. The dog obeyed. "Braves Mädchen."

"We're part of this team," I said to the guard.

I looked past him at the supervisor. He continued his conversation as another guard on the inside closed the door in our faces. I grabbed the door handle and pushed.

"Warnick? What the hell?"

My friend glanced back, embarrassed. Springer pretended we weren't there. Incredulous, we watched as the men I trusted with my life follow Pederman to the conference room.

"You need to leave now," the outside guard said.

I felt like an ass. Stomping down the steps, I kicked over a trash receptacle and marched to our trailer. Holly and the dog followed at a safe distance.

"That ungrateful sonofabitch," I said.

Fuming, I sat on our sofa as the women made sandwiches. "We helped save all those people. This is Pederman's doing. What gives him the right to cut us out like we're some kind of...of outsiders?"

Holly looked at the girl and sighed. "You don't get it."

"Okay, what don't I get? This guy's another Black Dragon stooge."

"No, he's not."

"And he's turned Warnick and Springer against us."

"That's not what happened." She handed me a plate.

"Why are you disagreeing with me? You saw!"

"Lower your voice. Don't you see? He's sending us a message."

I took an angry bite of my sandwich. "I've got a message for him."

As I got to my feet, my wife came at me with a butter knife. "David Michael Pulaski, sit down. Or, so help me, I will remove a testicle."

I froze mid-stride and turned to Griffin. She wore an expression of polite sympathy—the kind of look you gave a puppy who'd had an accident on the carpet. Red-faced, I groaned and sank onto a seat cushion.

The girl headed for the door. "Going to eat outside."

"No, honey," Holly said. "This concerns you too."

Griffin sat beside me and stroked Greta's head. My wife paced like a head coach before the big game.

I let my anger dissipate. "So, what am I missing?"

"Pederman is forcing our hand. He offered us those positions, and he expects us to take them."

"But what does that have to do with—"

"Think about it. He warned us that everything has to change. And that means you, me, and Griffin are civilians now."

"But—"

"Who cares if we saved all those people? That's ancient history. Unless we join Black Dragon, we're out."

"Wait," the girl said. "They want to, like, hire you guys?"

"We were planning to tell you."

"What happens to me?"

Holly stroked her hair. "We're not going anywhere, no matter what happens—I promise."

I looked out the window at two passing guards. "Let me get this straight. Unless we sign up, he's leaving us to fend for ourselves. Like the rest of those rubes in the gym?"

"Pretty much."

Though I knew she was right, I was pissed off. *I admire your loyalty.* The supervisor had said that too. What a load of crap. But what made me angrier was that my wife had put it together so easily when all I could see was betrayal. She had always possessed a better mind than me. And once again, I was getting schooled.

"Let me ask you something," I said. "How did you figure all this out? I mean, I'm not exactly stupid."

I turned to Griffin for confirmation. She pretended to notice a flea on the dog's ear. Holly rested her head on my knee.

"Don't try to think like a woman. It'll only give you a headache."

"Shit, I suck."

"It's not your fault."

"I'm an idiot."

She hugged me, probably more out of pity. "No, you're a guy."

Great. More evidence to prove that women were wise and men were clueless. Alert the media. I desperately needed a comeback, but I had nothing.

Kissing my wife's hand, I headed for the door. "I need to talk to Warnick."

"I don't think he can help you. Don't forget, he works for Pederman now."

"Fine. I'll talk to Evie."

"Wait," she said. "We're coming with."

NINE

Evie interviewed a physician assistant outside an MMU, her notebook in hand. I almost didn't recognize her. Though her clean clothes fit well enough, they weren't the tailored jacket, pencil skirt, and stilettos we were used to seeing.

"We need to talk," I said as Holly and Griffin looked on hopefully.

"Thanks for your time." She shook the interviewee's hand and waited as he headed into the MMU. Then to me, "Not here."

"Where? There are guards all over the campus."

"I know a place," the girl said.

We made our way around the administration building, past the shed where her gangrenous stepfather had dragged her. I could still hear her screams. Like the rest of the school, the area had been renovated. The ground was swept, and flowers were planted along the pathway leading to the common area.

She led us to a basement entrance at the rear of the building. Handing Greta's leash to my wife, she trotted down the few concrete steps while we kept an eye out for guards. The entrance was locked. She rammed her shoulder into the door and, springing it, went in.

"Griffin, how did you know about this place?" Holly said when we were inside.

The girl's voice sounded low and afraid. "This was where Travis kept me locked up."

I took her hand. "We don't have to do this."

"No, I want to."

As my eyes adjusted to the darkness, I could make out dusty gray metal racks of junk—old homecoming dance decorations, pep rally banners, and discarded furniture. Griffin froze.

"You okay?" my wife said, putting her arm around her.

"I need a minute."

A pair of police handcuffs hung from a metal rack. On the floor lay an overturned gray plastic bucket. A shudder ran through me as I imagined her trapped in here, at the mercy of a sex offender. Forced to pee in a pail. The scene brought back painful memories of me being held prisoner and beaten mercilessly. But I was a grown man, capable of moving past it. How could anyone expect a teenager to forget?

With the grace of an angel, Griffin made her way to a sturdy metal table and chairs. The dog sat next to her, her eyes alert.

"Who's this Travis?" Evie said.

Grimly, I looked at her. "Travis Golightly—her stepfather. He's dead."

"Sounds to me like the girl caught a break." She touched Griffin's shoulder. "Listen to me, kid. For years, my dad terrorized my mother and...hurt me, which is why I left home at sixteen. It is what it is. Best to move on."

I wasn't sure the girl needed to hear the raw, bitter truth.

When I looked at Holly, I could see her anger rising. Griffin nodded meekly. Maybe she'd found a kindred spirit.

"I still have nightmares," she said.

The reporter's voice was softer now. And like an unjudging mother, she took the girl's hands.

"I was lucky enough to find good people who were interested in helping me. Not wanting anything in return other than my promise to better myself. They made all the difference in my life. I'll tell you about them one day."

"Thanks, Evie."

Weak light filtered in through the dirty basement windows like distant starlight. The stern expression on the reporter's face melted like new-fallen snow, leaving the careworn lines of worry that come from the wrong kind of life experience.

She was an attractive woman—older in person—and damaged in so many ways over the years. It made sense that she was fearless, having suffered at the hands of whatever demons had possessed her father to destroy her childhood. She was a dark survivor who had not only found a way to live but discovered in herself something that could make a real difference in the world.

"So, formal introductions," I said. "Dave Pulaski and my wife, Holly. And this is Griffin Sparrow."

The reporter looked around the table. "You all know me. Hell, everybody knows me—Evie Champagne. As you can see, somewhat worse for wear. If you have a problem with the wardrobe, talk to my producer."

"Did you get any information from that PA?"

"I've interviewed a bunch of people. No one knows anything, and Black Dragon isn't talking."

"Speaking of which, what's happening with the cell service?"

"Helluva mystery. No one can explain it, nor can they tell us why the landlines don't work. Or the internet. My guess is it's intentional."

"When we were on that video call, you wrote down *Robbin-Sear Industries*," my wife said. "Who are they? And what do they have to do with the outbreak?"

The reporter gave Greta a pat on the head. Outside, children laughed as they ran past while anxious parents called to them. When she turned to us, her eyes were fixed on something intangible—a dangerous secret.

"You have to understand. The evidence I've collected is sketchy. But I know in my gut I'm right. Robbin-Sear is responsible for everything."

Holly started to say something, then lowered her voice to a whisper. "You mean, the virus? The draggers? All of it? How do you know?"

"Because it's happened before," Evie said.

TEN

We sat there, stunned. Holly moved closer to me, as if the words Evie uttered had the power to harm us. The reporter gave us a minute.

"When I found out the truth, it knocked me on my ass," she said. "But it's true. And I intend to prove it."

I decided to challenge her. "You realize what you're saying—"

"I know. Look, being a reporter is hard. Most of your time is spent chasing leads, doing research, putting the pieces together until you have a verifiable story. Every once in a while, you get lucky—I mean, really lucky. I live for those moments."

The way her eyes sparkled told me she was born for this. I wished she was back on television—it was where she belonged.

"Before I became a reporter, I was a researcher at the *San Francisco Chronicle*. A friend of mine, Rudy Moritz, could see I was good and asked me to help him with some research. The Associated Press reported on an event in a remote village in Guatemala near Jacaltenango. There were maybe a hundred people living there, most of them elderly. Practically everyone had come down with a strange illness. The symptoms were similar to what you saw in Tres Marias in the early days. People wandering the streets, eyes blank, gibbering like idiots."

"The jimmies," I said.

"Exactly. At first, the doctors thought it was hantavirus or Ebola. Rudy has a medical background and convinced our editor to let him fly down there to investigate. Meanwhile, I dug into public records and spoke to immunologists. I explored every angle—tainted water, drugs, sick animals. Nothing seemed to fit. Then one day, Rudy called me on his satellite phone. He'd seen a group of Americans hanging around. They claimed to be from some NGO. You can guess who they worked for."

"Robbin-Sear," my wife said.

"Smart girl. Like me, Rudy was persistent and got an interview with the person in charge. He claimed they were there as observers. My friend could smell the bullshit, but he played along in order to get more information."

I was on the edge of my seat. "And?"

"The next day, the Ministry of Public Health and Welfare got Rudy expelled from the country. The local police confiscated his notes, camera, computer—everything. As a result, he was unable to write the story."

"What happened to the old people?" Griffin said.

Evie stared at the floor. "They never said—*officially*. Rudy had made friends with a Catholic aid worker while he was down there, and they stayed in touch. She told my friend that everyone died."

"And the bodies?" I said.

"Cremated."

"Tell us about Tres Marias."

The reporter laid out everything for us. She and her cameraman had covered the story from the beginning, getting what information they could from the locals. No luck talking to Black Dragon, though. Understandable, considering the town was on lockdown.

At the start of the outbreak, people began coming down with the jimmies. At the time, it was thought they'd gotten bit by animals or other humans—no one was sure. After the first group died off, the hordes began appearing. People turned by the hundreds, becoming flesh-eaters that hunted the innocent. And the more who got bit, the bigger the hordes. No one had any clue that something similar had happened outside the country.

"Then Black Dragon rolled into town," Evie said. "The first thing they did was burn the bodies. I interviewed Ormand Ferry. He insisted the whole episode was a government cover-up. I thought he was another conspiracy nutjob."

Soon, it became too dangerous to be out in the open, so she and Jeff went into hiding. A break came when their news van nearly collided with another vehicle traveling in the opposite direction. A scientist from Robbin-Sear was driving—Larry Evans.

"He was pretty keyed up if you ask me," she said.

They pulled over to make sure no one was injured. Seeing the company name on the van, the reporter connected the dots. I pictured her on the side of the road, working the scientist like a ventriloquist dummy.

Robbin-Sear was a privately funded bioscience technology company. They were under contract—he wouldn't say to whom—to develop a vaccine to inoculate American troops serving overseas. He insisted he didn't know anything about the outbreak. But Evie pushed hard. That's when Larry referred her to his boss.

"After that meeting, I tried getting more information," she said. "But by then, Black Dragon had quarantined the town. Even if we'd wanted to, there was no way for Jeff and me to get out. The evac center was overrun, and we needed a place to hole up. We got lucky when we discovered that office building."

"How long were you there?" Holly said.

"Weeks. Seemed like forever. We had electricity and running water. Jeff, God bless him, got us food—whatever he could scavenge. We found the VTC equipment in a conference room. Jeff tried calling out. He must've worked on it for days, but no one was on the receiving end. It was a total accident that we connected with you guys."

"And then the draggers broke in," I said.

"They were downstairs. We barely made it out."

"And you headed straight for Robbin-Sear?"

"We managed to get out of the city—away from the Red Militia—and into the forest. By then, it was dark, so we slept in the van. We intended to drive to the facility in the morning, hoping you guys would meet us."

"But you were attacked."

"I think it was the same horde that found you. Jeff held them off so I could get away. I ran and ran. When I reached the top of a ridge, I looked down and..." She stopped and took a long, ragged breath. "Jeff never had a chance."

"Oh, Evie..." my wife said.

"When I saw the helicopters, I waved my jacket at them like a crazy woman. Fortunately, it was red, and they spotted me. I suspected you guys might be nearby and asked them to search for more survivors. You know the rest."

"It doesn't make sense," I said. "How could a private company do that without anyone finding out? Unless... You think the government is involved?"

The reporter gave me a wry smile. "History is full of examples of the US testing modified viruses and experimental vaccines on its citizens. I'll give you one. In 1994, Senator John D. Rockefeller released a report stating that for fifty years, the Department of Defense experimented on military personnel."

"Okay, sure, but that was—"

"You tell me. What's to stop these guys from sacrificing a few isolated villagers in a country nobody gives a shit about?"

"But this is California."

"In 1951, the DOD began open-air tests in this country using disease-producing bacteria and viruses. That little experiment continued through 1969."

It was all too much. I wasn't the most optimistic guy. But what she was suggesting was diabolical. I got to my feet and started pacing when I ran into a giant cobweb. I swatted it away as the women gaped at me.

"I'm kind of with Dave on this," Holly said. "How can you be sure the two events are related?"

Evie lowered her voice. "Because the person Rudy met in Guatemala is the same man who runs the lab here. He was the one Larry Evans mentioned. Guy by the name of Bob Creasy."

Blanching, I sank into my chair. My wife laid her hand on my arm. When I looked up, everyone was staring at me.

"Dear God," I said. "I know him."

ELEVEN

Thoughts of Jim and his dog swirled in my head. It couldn't have been a coincidence that Creasy was on that lonely highway.

"I was in a car accident last July," I said. "My friend was with me—we were in the forest. I must've blacked out. When I came to, he was gone. Bob Creasy showed up and gave me a ride."

Evie's expression was intense. "What was he doing out there?"

"That's the weird part—I don't know. I was glad he showed up, though. Jim's dog Perro was wandering the roads. I'm pretty sure he was rabid, and Creasy was trying to catch him. But the dog escaped. On the way back, he kept asking if I got bit."

"That is weird."

"I read something once about the Department of Defense," Holly said. "They were building a special facility to manufacture vaccines—I forget where. Maybe these guys are tied to the government."

"And it turns out that an ex-DOD official is now the COO of Robbin-Sear. Kind of cozy, no?"

Griffin's mouth fell open. "Holy shit."

My hands felt clammy. "I can't help thinking Jim got mixed up with them somehow."

"What makes you say that?" the reporter said.

"Because at the beginning of the outbreak, he got bit. Anyway, he's dead now."

My wife tugged at my sleeve. "When Creasy picked you up, didn't you say he had other dogs in the van?"

"That's right, I forgot. And he was pissed off that Perro had gotten away."

"I don't get it. Why would a government research facility care about one rabid dog?"

The girl cleared her throat. "I know this sounds crazy. But what if they made him sick?"

Evie turned to her with a kind smile. "Go on."

"My stepdad used to meet with these Red Militia guys at the house, right? Me and my brother Kyle weren't allowed to hang around. After they'd been drinking awhile, they got loud. We heard them talking about this big conspiracy. Medical experiments and stuff. What if someone infected Perro?"

I remembered my dream. In it, Jim had tried telling me they'd done something to his dog.

"My friend didn't get bit by a human," I said. "I know because I saw the autopsy photos. To Griffin's point, Perro could have been given the virus. If he escaped, he would've gone straight home to Jim."

Holly wasn't buying it. "Then why didn't people get rabies instead of whatever the hell this is?"

"What I want to know is how Black Dragon figures into all this. Wouldn't the governor declare an emergency and send in the National Guard?"

"True," the reporter said. "Remember the LA riots in '92?"

"I was a toddler, so. Okay, Black Dragon—a private security company—shows up. Who made the call?"

"Another mystery. We need to get inside that facility on Old Orchard Road. That's where the truth lies."

So much for that. We were civilians with no resources. And no weapons. Maybe there was a way she could find out on her own.

"I was thinking," my wife said. "If we join Black Dragon, we might be in a better position to help Evie."

"I need to talk to Warnick first. He's the only one I trust."

"I don't think that's going to happen. You saw how they've been acting."

Holly was right. Everything pointed to Pederman and his damn offer. Unless we agreed to join up, he would keep us out of the loop. Being part of their operation would give us access to communications and, more importantly, intelligence. It was the only way.

"Why do I feel like I'm going to regret this?" I said.

"We'd like to speak to the supervisor," I said to the guard at the administration building entrance.

"What's this concerning?"

"Tell him we're ready to talk."

The guard radioed someone who escorted my wife and me inside. We were told to wait in the foyer. After twenty minutes, another guard walked us into Pederman's office. The supervisor and Warnick greeted us. Two uniforms in clear plastic garment bags hung on the coat rack, and there were two shoeboxes on the floor.

"How did you know?" I said.

Pederman side-eyed my friend. "Let's say we were hopeful."

Warnick extended his hand warmly to each of us. I hadn't seen him this happy since someone piped in Weezer's greatest hits in the cafeteria during lunch.

"Welcome to the team," he said.

The supervisor handed each of us a packet. "First, we need you to fill out some paperwork. Once everything has been processed, we'll issue you weapons. I'm going to San Francisco to meet with HR. Someone will be onsite tomorrow to walk you through the employment contracts and review your benefits packages."

"No signing bonus?" I said, skimming the documents. For the record, I was totally kidding.

"I'm authorized to offer each of you twenty-five thousand dollars. Of course, it'll be grossed up to cover the taxes."

Holly's jaw dropped. "Oh my gosh!"

"I think you're going to like working for us."

"Can't wait to get started," I said.

Pederman snapped his fingers. "Oh, I almost forgot. Because of the unusual nature of the events over the past few months, we'll need to interview you and take statements."

"You mean, like a deposition?"

"Nothing to worry about. We're trying to gather all the information we can about what happened over the summer. Sooner or later, there'll be an official investigation and possible lawsuits. We're getting our ducks in a row."

Okay, now I was worried. My wife and I had done things —questionable things—to survive.

"And we won't be charged with anything?" I said.

"Absolutely not. If it makes you feel any better, Warnick and Springer have already vouched for your character. Frankly, their version makes you guys look like heroes."

That wasn't a word I would've used to describe me. Maybe this was the right decision after all.

Walking to our trailer, I breathed in the crisp fall air. The sky was clear, and other than the sounds of the ATVs patrolling the fences, all was quiet. Far off on the outdoor basketball courts, a group of men and teenage boys played a pickup game. All of it reminded me of how things used to be. Before walking in, Holly stopped and took my hand.

"Thanks for doing this," she said.

"I get the feeling you want it."

"I do. But not for the reasons you think."

"That's code for something. Are you messing with me again?"

Laughing, she pressed her head against my chest. I kissed the top of her head. When she looked up, her eyes were glistening.

"No, honey," she said. "It's just that, well... I'm pregnant."

TWELVE

A hammer to the side of my head would have been less jarring. I didn't know whether to laugh or cry. I don't usually weave—unless I'm drunk—but I tilted back as Holly reached for my arm.

"Easy, cowboy," she said.

We found a shady spot under an oak tree. A squirrel observed us from halfway up the light-brown trunk, chittering and flicking its tail. I felt nothing but love for the animal as I drew my wife next to me. Neither of us wanted to be the first to speak, so we played the staring game. In a few seconds, I blinked.

"Do-over," I said.

"Not a chance."

It was surreal, us sitting there—the sun breaking through white billowy clouds, while not fifty yards away, two groaning draggers pressed up against the chain-link fence as if eavesdropping. We were between worlds—the sane and the insane. And our choices were pulling us towards the former. But that other dangerous dimension was never far away.

Somehow, Greta had gotten out of the trailer and found

us. Whining, she lay at our feet and waited for one of us to stroke her neck. Some guard dog.

Holly took my hand. "I didn't mean to spring it on you like that. I was pretty sure, but the tests confirmed it."

"I wondered why you were acting all weird. How far along?"

"A few weeks. I'm still getting used to the idea. Are you upset?"

"No, I'm… Everything is so crazy. I mean, we're safe now. But can we have that kind of life again?"

A young guard hopped off her ATV and skewered the leering draggers through the head with her bayonet. It was deliberate and routine, like picking up trash in a public park. She wiped her blade on the grass and radioed someone—the cleanup crew, probably.

My wife stroked my beard. "Life is always going to be hard. And we'll be dead someday. But we have to live the best we can."

"Circle of life?"

"Pretty much," she said.

Maybe it was the effects of the killing and the blood and the suffering. Or the glimmer of a future where we might be happy again. Whatever it was, I choked up. We'd been through so much together, Holly and me—barely surviving. Seeing friends and comrades killed. Experiencing the worst of humanity. And sometimes, the best. Each of us lost a part of ourselves, yet somehow we became stronger.

How could anyone do this alone? There were so many people out there with no one to help them. And plenty who wanted to cause harm. There's an old French proverb—God always helps fools, lovers, and drunkards. I could attest to the last one. In my drinking days, I was on that lonely, godforsaken road, miraculously surviving from one bender to the next. Without my wife, my luck surely would have run out.

"I'm a pussy," I said, wiping away the tears.

"You're not."

She rubbed my shoulders and pulled me close. I could smell her fragrant hair, the scent of her skin. Then, she kissed me.

"I will always love you, David Michael Pulaski. Promise me you'll never forget."

They were words I would take to my grave.

We returned to our trailer, Holly holding my hand, Greta bounding ahead like a puppy. I thought of our baby. Would it have a chance? I knew she would be an awesome mother, but what about me? I could barely take care of myself. How would I ever measure up? *For starters, stay sober.* Good advice. Especially since there was always another nightmare waiting around the corner.

When we told Griffin, she squealed with joy. Though she had grown into a formidable fighter in her own right, she was filled with the tenderness and hope only the young can possess—the perfect big sister.

"When will you know if it's a boy or a girl?" she said.

Holly laughed. "It'll be a while."

"Can I name it? Pleeeez? Say yes."

"What?" I said. "Griffin Jr.?"

She giggled, then became serious. "Or Kyle?"

"After your brother? Very cool."

The girl's face darkened. "They're not gonna send you out on, like, dangerous missions, are they?"

"Hey, I'm not crippled," my wife said. "I still got some moves."

She pretended to round a corner, aiming an imaginary weapon. Sneaking up from behind, I poked her in the ribs, and she yelped. I loved that she was so ticklish.

She scowled. "Oh, you did not just do that."

Now everyone was tickling everyone as Greta barked and spun in circles. A knock at the door put a full stop to the hilarity. It was Warnick. I shook his hand and waved him inside.

"Thank you for what you did," I said. "For both of us. It means a lot."

He seemed uncomfortable. Reading the room, Griffin excused herself and took the dog for a walk. Holly and I sat on the sofa as our friend paced, fingering two manila envelopes in his sweaty hands. I had never seen him so edgy.

"Warnick, will you calm down? You're making me nervous."

"I know you're anxious to find out what caused the outbreak," he said. "But you should forget about it and accept whatever assignment Pederman—"

Before he could finish, I was on my feet. "Look. We're happy to be good soldiers and all, but someone needs to look into this—"

"No, they don't! Your job now is to do as you're told."

Forget pins dropping. You could have heard atoms rearranging themselves in the atmosphere.

THIRTEEN

For as long as I had known Warnick, I couldn't recall a single time when he raised his voice to me. Holly and I stood like statues in a park. Our friend rubbed his face, surprised at his own outburst. My wife got a soda from the refrigerator.

"Anyone want anything?" she said.

I looked at my friend. "Warnick?"

"You have to understand. We have a mission."

"So I've heard."

"Really? What is it?"

Groaning, I closed my eyes and pinched my nose to make me sound nasal. "To make the town safe so the regular authorities can take over."

"Correct. And it's important we focus on that—and only that."

"Can I ask you a question? Did something happen?"

He crossed to the refrigerator and looked at Holly. When she nodded, he grabbed an orange soda. He drank deeply and rubbed the back of his neck. Whatever was weighing on him had me concerned. My wife offered us the sofa.

Finishing his drink, he stared out the window. He looked tired.

"This operation has gone way beyond what I thought it would be," he said.

Holly grabbed a chair and sat across from us. "How did you end up working for Black Dragon? Did they recruit you?"

"Me and my brother were serving in Afghanistan."

"A brother?" I said. "Younger or older?"

"Older."

"Is he a Weezer fan too?"

"He gave me my faith. Someday, I'll tell you what my life was like before that."

"Where is he now?" my wife said.

Our friend crushed his soda can. "He was stationed at a COP—combat outpost—and went on patrol in a village, searching for Taliban. Got killed by an IED."

"Dude…" I said.

"Anyway, shortly after, I finished my tour."

"What were you doing?"

"Training ANA forces—Afghan National Army. I was getting ready to come home when the Black Dragon recruiters visited our base. They were signing up soldiers like crazy. Chavez, Estrada, and I said yes. I had no other job prospects, so I figured, why not?"

Their first mission was to remain in Afghanistan, providing private security for various Afghan leaders. Warlords mostly, who were supposedly friendly with the US. They appointed Chavez supervisor, and unlike his command in Tres Marias, he handled the assignment beautifully.

They hadn't seen any combat till one day when the Taliban sent in a suicide bomber—a kid on a scooter. He showed up at a warlord's home, pretending to make a delivery. Warnick and Estrada were almost killed in the blast.

Chavez nearly died when more Taliban began shooting up the place. After recuperating in the hospital, all three were sent home to Black Dragon's regional office. They were assigned light duty till they could recover. Then, Tres Marias happened.

"We weren't even in San Francisco three months," my friend said.

It all fit—why Chavez had gone over the edge and why Estrada had followed him. Somewhere along the way, the supervisor must have lost it over there. Maybe it was because he'd almost died. Or he was already heading into madness madness—the kind of lunacy that was irresistible to others. But not Warnick.

"Everything fell apart," he said. "Chavez and his people—you saw it."

I could never forget those dangerous days. My friend was our guiding light. He kept us going even when things were at their worst. But he seemed different now. Something had gotten to him. He squeezed the already-flattened can even tighter and set it aside.

"It didn't have to be this way," he said.

"What do you mean?"

A knock at the door startled me. Holly answered it and found one of Pederman's aides.

"Is Warnick here?" she said.

My friend got to his feet. "I'm prepping them for the meeting with HR."

"Pederman wants to see you asap."

"Tell him I'll be right there."

After she left, Warnick stood by the door and handed us each an envelope. I was anxious to hear more, but he was in a hurry.

"Report to the administration building tomorrow at 0900

sharp. Your assignments are in those envelopes, assuming everything goes well."

I took him aside. "There's something you're not telling us."

"Stick to the mission," he said and walked out.

I wandered the campus looking for Evie. When I asked the guards if they had seen her, they claimed total ignorance. Frustrated, I headed for our trailer, where I found Holly fixing dinner. Griffin sat on the sofa, reading a school library book. The dog lay curled up at her feet.

"What are you reading?" I said.

"*The Catcher in the Rye.*"

"How is Holden Caufield these days?"

"I don't get it. Why is he, like, so depressed all the time?"

I hesitated to say anything. Hell with it. "His brother died."

"Oh." She closed the book and put it aside.

"Did you find Evie?" my wife said.

"No one's seen her."

"Maybe she left the command center."

"She would've said something."

I got out placemats, flatware, and napkins and arranged them on the table. "I'm worried about Warnick. Okay, you have this little woman who tells you stuff, right? What's she saying now?"

"I got nothin'."

I spotted Springer walking past our window and bolted out the front door. When he saw me, he hurried away.

"Springer, wait up!"

He stopped and fingered the belt clip on his holster. "Oh hey, Dave. S'up?"

"What the hell is going on around here?"

"I have no idea what you mean."

"Cut the crap, Calvin. Warnick is acting all weird. I can't find Evie. There's a lot of stupid shit that somebody needs to explain."

"It might be your imagination."

"Don't even try to gaslight me—I need answers. Where can we talk?"

Glancing around, he lowered his voice. "I'm not supposed to."

"Come on, we've been through too much. Throw me a bone."

He waited a beat. "The maintenance shed. Midnight."

Walking away like he didn't know me, he vanished around a corner. Then Griffin appeared.

"What's up with him?"

"I think we're being watched," I said.

FOURTEEN

Alone, I waited near the entrance to the maintenance shed. I'd forgotten a jacket and shivered in the cold October wind. Shadows played along the walls. I imagined draggers coming for me out of the darkness.

A crunching noise startled me, and I tensed. Expecting to see Springer, I stepped into the glow of a floodlight hanging off the side of the building. A lone figure approached—Warnick. I was about to greet him when he shushed me.

"Inside," he said.

He eased open the metal door, and we went in. We didn't turn on the lights, instead feeling our way along the wall. Moonlight shone through a window, casting a luminous pool in the center of the oil-stained floor. We stood close to one another so we could speak softly.

"Are you going to yell at me again?"

Ignoring me, he glanced at the closed door. "You shouldn't be asking all these questions. I thought I made that clear."

"Listen to me. We agreed to sign on like you and Pederman wanted. We'll do our jobs. But I need to find out what happened to Jim. And I won't stop till I know."

I looked into my friend's eyes. There was something he wanted to tell me—I could feel it. My wife and I hadn't shared our news with anyone except Griffin. I decided now was the time.

"Holly's pregnant," I said.

He didn't react at first. "All the more reason to keep a low profile. Congrats, by the way."

"You want me to stand down. But dude, you know me—I'm not going to do that. So you might as well come clean."

He paced for a while, then stared at something across the room. By now, our eyes had adjusted to the darkness. Metal folding chairs were stacked against the wall. We grabbed a couple and sat across from each other.

"I don't have the answers you're looking for," he said.

"That's okay. Tell me what you know."

"This is strictly confidential. If you breathe a word—"

"Lips sealed."

"Yesterday morning, I was in the administration building doing paperwork. The walls are pretty thin. Someone was interviewing Evie in the office next to me."

"That was her deposition, right?"

"It sounded more like an interrogation. The guy asked her all kinds of questions about her reporting during the outbreak. What she'd seen. Places she'd gone. The people she'd interviewed. He wanted to know how she'd survived all this time on her own. And he demanded that she turn over all the footage her cameraman had shot."

"I'm pretty sure she had nothing with her when Black Dragon picked us up."

"I think you're right. She wasn't even carrying a purse."

"Did she sound scared?"

He considered the question. "You know Evie—she played along. Kept her answers very general. She talked about the close calls she and Jeff had with draggers and how they'd hidden from the Red Militia. Nothing specific. She told him all the footage was lost when the draggers killed Jeff."

"All they would need to do is track down the van."

"That's exactly what this person suggested. He mentioned sending the cops to locate the vehicle."

"Did he mention Robbin-Sear?"

"No. But he asked her if she had any thoughts on how the outbreak might've started or how far she thought it had spread. She said she assumed it was a virus and that she'd heard it was detected as far north as Mt. Shasta."

"Shit, everybody knows that."

"Right. Like I said, she played along."

Something struck the door. Warnick went to check it out. He waited a moment, then cracked open the door and peeked outside. After a beat, he returned.

"Must've been the wind," he said.

"So our supervisor is interrogating civilians now?"

"That's just it—Pederman's in San Francisco. Anyway, he let her go. Said he might ask her to come in again if he had more questions."

"Are you planning to tell Pederman?"

"You bet. I'm guessing he has no idea someone is using his offices to interrogate civilians."

"Maybe the guy works for Black Dragon. You know, some higher-up who blew into town."

My friend stood and checked behind him as if someone else might be in the room. I had never seen him so paranoid.

"My door was open. When he walked past, I saw him briefly. Stocky guy with red hair. Had on a really nice suit. I remembered seeing him before when you and I were on patrol."

"Wait, are you telling me—"

"Yes," Warnick said. "It was the mayor."

PART TWO

SHOCK TREATMENT

FIFTEEN

Dressed for work, I fastened the last button on my shirt. Holly stood in the tiny bathroom, arranging her hair in a military bun as Greta sat in the doorway, fascinated.

"Griffin, get up," she said. "It's almost nine."

The TV in the kitchenette blasted *The Lazy Man's Lunch* throughout the trailer. Connie McBride was the hottest thing going on the Food Network. The show was hosted by a burly, Red Sox-loving ex-maintenance worker from South Boston. Sporting a permanent five o'clock shadow, he appealed to every talentless tool desperate for a quick meal on the cheap.

"So whadda we got here?" he said, rummaging through the kitchen cabinets. "Triscuits... Tabasco... McCormick Paprika... Ooh! Kraft Grated Parmesan."

He set these on the counter and comically stuck his head inside the refrigerator. When he spoke, his voice was muffled.

"Oscar Mayer hot dogs!"

With the skills of a good-natured line cook, he laid out a dozen crackers on a plate, cut up the dogs, and delicately placed a slice on each cracker. Then he sprinkled the whole business with cheese, paprika, and a few squirts of Tabasco.

"Almost there."

He microwaved the plate for fifteen seconds. When it was done, he added a sprig of parsley and held up the food for all to see. Smiling into the camera, he delivered his trademark line.

"And there's your lunch."

"Holly, do you have any bars?" I said.

She gave me a morning kiss. "Nope."

"No internet and no cell service. How are we getting television?"

"Griffin, for cryin' out loud."

My wife whispered something to Greta. The dog bounded over to the girl's bed and, throwing her paws on top of her, began licking her face.

"Ew, Greta!"

Holly gave me a satisfied smile. "Do these pants make me look fat?"

Wisely, I dodged the question. "How did you get the dog to do that?"

"She's a girl, so we're on the same page. Also, Ram taught me all the German commands, remember?"

"I hope you're not planning to use those on me."

"Only one, I promise. *Braver Hund.*"

"What does that mean? And it better not be—"

"Good dog," she said and bolted out the door before I could catch her.

The guard said nothing as we entered the administration building, wearing our new uniforms. We headed for Pederman's office, where we found the supervisor with another man. The stranger was in his fifties, with thinning gray hair, corn-fed jowls that were too red, and a bulbous nose dotted with burst blood vessels. Judging by his waistband size, I guessed he liked his beer.

"Walt Freeman," he said, shaking my hand.

Pederman joined us. "Walt is the new deputy mayor."

One time on patrol, I saw this guy getting out of a black Escalade in front of City Hall. Now it made sense.

"The mayor wasn't available?" I said.

He side-eyed the supervisor. "With so many depositions to get through, he and I are tag-teaming. Do you know the mayor?"

"Not personally."

"Why don't we get started?" Pederman said.

In the conference room, an attractive, full-figured woman with reddish-brown hair, huge brown eyes, and red lips sat at the table before an open laptop. I also remembered seeing her at City Hall.

"This is Becky, my assistant," Walt said.

As we took seats, the deputy mayor hefted a clear plastic storage box from the floor and set it on the table. Judging by its contents, a lot of people must have testified. Despite the supervisor's assurances, I worried they were gathering evidence to make arrests. He pointed at a device on the table.

"I must advise you that we're recording the interview."

He reached into the box, and scanning the files, grabbed one and opened it. Inside were around a dozen typed pages. My chest tightened at the thought of telling this guy anything about what I had done over these past months.

"I'm sure you're aware that Mr. Warnick and Mr. Springer have already given their depositions," he said. "Don't be nervous. With so many dead from the, uh... the unpleasant-ness, we're trying to gather as much information as possible."

Unpleasantness. I thought about how I'd blasted Fred Lumpkin's head to confetti with a cop's .44. Come to think of it, that was pretty unpleasant.

Walt made a note. "Since you're married, we'll combine your depositions. Dave, we'll start with you. When did you first encounter the sickness?"

"You mean, when did I notice it?"

"When did you knowingly come in contact with a person or persons exhibiting symptoms?"

"July 5th. We used to call it the jimmies."

He glanced at his assistant. "That's pretty specific."

"I'll never forget the date. It was the night my friend Jim Stanley came to see me. He was drunk. I was giving him a ride home when we got into a car accident. The way he looked and acted made me think he was infected."

Despite my earlier misgivings, I told them everything—how Holly left me and went to Mt. Shasta to be with her mother. And later, when they went missing, and I searched for them. Along the way, I met Ben and Aaron Marino and my high school teacher, Irwin Landry. We decided to stick together. When we returned to Tres Marias, I managed to locate my wife. But her mother was dead.

We moved to Ram Chakravarthy's compound to wait it out. Warnick and other Black Dragon guards stayed with us for protection. After the Red Militia destroyed our compound, we left. By then, Griffin Sparrow had joined us. She and Holly escaped an ambush on the streets. But Chavez's people took the rest of us prisoner and forced us to compete in death matches with draggers in a dilapidated ice rink.

"What happened to Enrique Chavez?" the deputy mayor said.

"I think you know."

Unfazed, he referred to the file. "Ormand Ferry abducted you, is that right?"

"I don't want to talk about that."

"Okay, son. I understand."

I ended my story with our attack on the Red Militia at the high school and how we rescued the girl from her deranged stepfather.

"What happened to Ormand Ferry?" he said.

"The draggers got him."

"Since July, how many would you say you've killed? An estimate is fine."

"Humans?" I glanced at my wife, then Pederman. "Other than the Red Militia, none."

It took better than two hours for Walt to depose Holly and me. I didn't know about her, but I was wrung out. The deputy mayor stopped recording.

"I think we have everything we need," he said. "Appreciate your cooperation."

"Thanks, guys," the supervisor said to us. "It can't have been easy reliving all that."

Walt began putting the papers into the storage box. He was shorter than me and, up close, smelled like cologne and sweaty shoe leather.

"Where is all this information going?" I said.

"Good question. Like-uh-said, it'll be placed in an archive, along with everything else we've collected—papers, audio recordings, video, and so forth. If any government agency needs access, we can provide it. Nice meeting you both."

After he and his assistant left the room, Pederman closed the door. Smiling, he placed a hand on each of our shoulders. I could tell he was proud. My head hurt bad. And I desperately wanted a drink.

"You did great," he said. "Now comes the fun part."

SIXTEEN

After lunch, Holly and I returned to Pederman's office. We found him chatting with a fiftyish-looking woman who wore a gray suit and black high heels. Her brown hair was pulled back in a short ponytail. I guessed she had arrived from San Francisco.

"Ah, here they are," the supervisor said. "Miriam, I'd like you to meet Dave and Holly Pulaski."

The woman extended her hand. "Miriam Cantrell, Senior Director of Human Capital. It's a real pleasure. Let's use the conference room so I can go over everything with you and answer any questions. Are you excited?"

I noticed the director looking at my wife as we walked. Was she judging her now?

"Honestly, Kelly," she said when we arrived.

Pederman looked surprised. "What did I do?"

"You gave this poor girl a man's shirt. Oh, my gosh, and those pants." Then to my wife, "Don't worry, hon. I anticipated this and brought along some women's uniforms for you to choose from. I'm guessing size zero?"

"That's right," Holly said, blushing.

It took a little over an hour to complete the paperwork and review the salary and benefits information. Miriam took my wife into another room to try on uniforms. When they returned, even I could tell the difference.

The director thanked us and excused herself, explaining that she needed to return to San Francisco. I wondered how people could come and go so freely when there was a quarantine.

"How's life in San Francisco?" I said.

Miriam knew what I meant and side-eyed the supervisor. "We haven't seen any signs of the virus, thank goodness, which means the quarantine is working. Now, who's taking me back?"

"One of my people will drive you," Pederman said. "I'll walk you out."

"Thanks, Kelly." She extended her hand to Holly and me. "Welcome to Black Dragon Security."

When we were alone, my wife poked me in the ribs. "Did you see how she was dressed?"

"Um…"

"Burberry suit? Manolo Blahnik shoes?"

"I have no idea what you just said."

"She's paid very well."

"Hey, I meant to ask. What are they doing about your uniform when you—"

"Blow up like the Goodyear Blimp? We talked about that. When the time comes, they'll issue me maternity wear."

I laughed. "Picturing you in stretchy pants and packing an AR-15 is—"

"Careful, buster. Pregnant women are known to be volatile."

"Have I told you how beautiful you are?"

"Nice save."

As we sat leafing through our employment packets, Holly squeezed my hand. I didn't need to ask why she was scared. I'd already shared with her the details of Evie's interrogation.

"I have this feeling," she said. "It's like, I want us to be happy. Make a life for our baby. But I'm worried about what's gonna happen. And it's bigger than Evie."

"I feel the same."

"You asked me about my little woman. I lied when I said she wasn't telling me anything. She definitely is. There's something very dangerous going on."

"Which makes me wonder why we're doing this?"

"Because it's better than the alternative. We've already lived life on the streets. And I don't wanna go back, especially not with Griffin and the baby. I've been thinking..."

"Uh-oh."

She elbowed me. "Shut up. Every night, I pray for a normal life. What if, when that happens, we start over somewhere else? San Francisco, maybe. You know, the four of us? If we stay with Black Dragon, we'll have more than enough money."

"I love the idea. But it's hard for me to imagine life ever being normal again."

"That's where faith comes in."

"Tell you what. Let's promise each other we'll do what we have to. But I still need to find out what happened in Tres Marias."

"Dave, can't we—"

"I owe it to Jim."

"Okay, I promise."

"I love you," I said.

We were about to kiss when the supervisor walked in carrying two black hard-shell cases. "Welcome aboard, guys.

You are officially entitled to your Black Dragon-issue weapons."

He set the cases on the conference table and snapped one open, revealing a brand-new Glock 17 pistol, speed loader, and two magazines. Adrenalin had me wired, and I took a breath before reaching for the weapon.

"See the quartermaster to pick up your holsters and extra mags," he said. "Holly, this gun is a little larger than what you're probably used to. But I think you'll come to appreciate its firepower."

She opened her case and removed the weapon. "This is gonna sound weird, but it's beautiful."

He shook our hands. "I just wanted to say how pleased I am to have you on my team."

"Mr. Pederman," I said, "I'm curious about people coming and going. I mean, with the quarantine and all."

"There is a protocol. We need special permission from the mayor, but we're permitted to make trips outside when warranted."

"What about people coming in?"

"Same deal. I'm late for another meeting. See you both soon. Again, congratulations."

When the supervisor left, we took each other's hands and stared at the hard-shell cases.

"I never thought a gun would get me this excited," she said.

"Careful, sista. You're married."

"As Chuck would have it."

Mrs. Malaprop was back.

SEVENTEEN

Holly and I spent the afternoon doing target practice, followed by a CrossFit workout in a weight training room just off the gym. The session nearly killed me, considering my bad shoulder and leg. When we were done, I was drenched and sore as hell.

"What is this?" I said. "Basic training?"

"Lightweight."

When we got outside, Evie was waiting for us, wearing a backpack and hiking boots.

"Hey!" my wife said. "Where have you been?"

"Nice uniforms. Listen, I'm glad I found you. I'm heading out."

I came down the steps, and the three of us started walking. There were guards and civilians everywhere, and we had to keep our conversation discreet.

"We heard the mayor interrogated you," I said.

"Interesting guy. I'd keep an eye on him if I were you."

I checked my watch. It was nearly five and getting dark. I was starving and suggested we walk over to the cafeteria.

Inside, dozens of guards and civilians ate at long tables.

We found an empty spot in the rear by the entrance to the kitchen. The reporter picked at her salad while Holly and I chowed down on pasta and bread.

"Where will you go?" I said.

"I'll find a place for the night. Tomorrow, I'm heading out to Robbin-Sear. I want to interview Bob Creasy. Hell, there might even be an Emmy in it for me."

I didn't like it—way too dangerous. "I think you should stay here with us."

"I can't." She leaned in, her voice a whisper. "It's not safe."

"Aren't you worried about the draggers?" my wife said.

"I'll be careful. Besides, after my meeting with the mayor, I'm convinced there are other forces at work."

I had been thinking that too. "Care to elaborate?"

"Better not." Then she brightened. "Come with me. It'll be an adventure."

We looked at each other guiltily. I wanted to say yes, but I knew how Holly felt. Though we hadn't given up on solving the mystery of the virus, we needed to be careful. And that meant keeping a low profile.

"We can't," I said.

Evie shrugged it off and gave my wife an appraising look. "What made you decide to work for Black Dragon? I didn't picture you as the law-and-order type."

"I'm pregnant. And, well, we need the money."

"Blessings. And I don't blame you. I might've done the same in your shoes. No worries. You never know—maybe our paths will cross again."

As she rose from the table, I saw the disappointment on her face. I wanted to say something to let her know we were on her side. Instead, I gave her some lame advice.

"Stay safe," I said.

Outside, the reporter touched my shoulder. "By the way, an old friend of yours asked me to say hi."

"Most of my friends are dead."

"He mentioned that if you ever needed ammo for that bullpup, he's got plenty."

"Wait, you know Guthrie?"

Instead of answering, she walked away, raising a defiant fist.

Landry's friend Guthrie Manson was a lifesaver in the early days of the outbreak. He'd equipped us with a lot of powerful weapons, including a light shotgun known as a bullpup. We found him living in the forest with his wife, Caramel, and their two sons. I was relieved to hear they were alive, growing marijuana and holding their own against the draggers—and anyone else who might threaten them. What I couldn't figure out, though, was how Evie had connected with them. Damn, she was good.

I took Holly's hand. "I never thought I'd hear that name again."

"I'd love to meet him sometime."

"Like Evie said, you never know."

We watched our friend fade into the twilight of an uncertain tomorrow. I wondered what the reporter would find out there. On the way to the trailer, Warnick flagged us down.

"Have you guys seen Evie?" he said.

I side-eyed my wife. "Have you checked her trailer?"

"She's not there. Someone thought they saw her walking along the fence, wearing a backpack."

I felt bad withholding the truth. But ever since her comment about the mayor, I thought it best to keep my mouth shut.

"Wish we could help," I said.

I wasn't sure he bought it. People had seen the reporter

with us at dinner. Eventually, the news would get back to my friend. Whatever. Delaying the inevitable would at least give her a head start.

Halfway home, Holly stopped. "I don't like that we lied to him. He's our friend."

"I know. But if we'd said something, the guards would prevent her from leaving."

"Did she look worried to you?"

"More like scared," I said.

EIGHTEEN

We found Griffin sitting on our trailer steps with the young Latino guard she had played cards with the day we arrived. He was a good-looking kid—bigger than I remembered. I noticed he didn't carry a gun. When the girl saw us, she stood.

"Hey, Griffin," I said.

"Um... You remember Fabian Lopez? Fabian, these are my..."

My wife extended her hand, and they shook. "Holly and Dave."

"Glad to meet you—officially. I hope you don't mind I stopped by. I wanted to say hi to Griffin."

"Thought it was time for another poker lesson?" I said. "Fabian, is it?" I knew damn well what his name was. "How old are you, son?"

Turning crimson, the girl gave me the stink eye, but I held my ground.

"Nineteen, sir."

"I didn't know Black Dragon hired so young. I noticed you don't carry a weapon."

"I'm an intern. Haven't earned the right, I guess."

"Would you like to come in for a soda?" my wife said.

I didn't like her encouraging the boy and was relieved by his response.

"Naw, I gotta get back."

"Okay then," I said.

He walked away with his head down. "See you around, Griffin."

Inside our trailer, the girl went off on me. "I can't believe you embarrassed me like that. He was just being friendly."

"I'm sure that's all it was."

Holly tried intervening. "Dave, you didn't have to be so hard on him. I thought he was polite." Then to Griffin, "I like him."

"Okay, so he's a nice guy," I said. "But he's nineteen, Griffin. You're fifteen. Am I the only one around here who can do the math?"

"I hate you!" she said and stormed out, taking the dog with her.

Folding her arms, my wife pursed her lips and stared at me.

"What?"

"I agree he's a little old, but—"

"The last thing that girl needs is some swinging dick hanging around."

"I was going to say that she's a young woman. Maybe you should lighten up. This kinda stuff is bound to happen."

"Not on my watch."

"Aw, man," she said, laughing. "You're jealous."

"What?" Why was my voice suddenly so high? "No, I'm not."

"Yes, you are."

"Holly, I hope you're not suggesting..."

"No—shit, no. What I mean is you're jealous the way a father would be if another guy even looked at his daughter."

"That's crazy talk."

"Fine, have it your way."

I followed her as she began tidying up the trailer. "There's a difference between jealousy and concern, you know."

"Whatever you say, dear."

"I'm going for a walk."

It was cold out—and dark. I wandered the grounds, trying to dissect my feelings about the girl we had come to think of as our own. Could my wife be right? Before I could dig any deeper, I saw Springer crossing the campus with a stack of files.

"Hey, wait up!"

As he stopped to greet me, everything slid from his hands. I helped him pick up the papers and noticed a requisition for more arms and equipment.

"Let me ask you something," I said. "What do you think about a fifteen-year-old girl hanging out with an older guy?"

"Dude, I'm the wrong person to ask. Me, I'm looking for a girl with long legs and a short memory."

"Can you be serious for one minute? I'm talking about Griffin."

"I figured. And Lopez, right?"

"He might be okay and all, but..."

"He's a guy. And you want to protect her."

"What's wrong with that?"

"Okay, so if she was eighteen, and he was twenty-two, would you have a problem?"

"That's different."

"Why?"

"Because she's fifteen—not eighteen. There are laws..."

"I get it. But fifteen ain't what it used to be. Besides, he knows you carry a gun, right? I have to go."

"Thanks, Springer," I said.

Getting advice from Springer was like asking Taco Bell if chimichangas were good for you. He had a point, though. I had gotten the feeling that Fabian was afraid of me. Good.

Continuing across campus, I found the girl sitting with Greta under an oak tree. She was pulling up blades of grass and arranging them in piles. Seeing her made me realize Holly was right. When the dog saw me, she bounded over.

"I'd like to apologize," I said and sat beside her.

She refused to meet my eyes. "That was so embarrassing."

"I know." I patted the dog's head. "But my heart was in the right place."

"We were just talking." She turned to me, her face defiant, tear streaks on her cheeks.

"I was only trying to protect you."

"I know." She mashed the little grass piles.

"Tell me something about him."

"He's from Salinas. His parents came from Mexico as teenagers. When he was a baby, they picked fruit and vegetables. They own a little grocery store now. Oh, and he's a writer. He hasn't published anything yet..."

"You sure know a lot about him. What kind of stuff does he write?"

"I don't know. Stories about his childhood, I guess."

"Do you like him?"

"He's nice. I mean, I'm not, like, in love with him or anything. We're friends."

"Anyway, I'll try to behave. But you have to promise me you won't do anything stupid."

She looked at me like I'd arrived on the midnight bus from Mars. "You're unbelievable. You know my history."

She picked up a dead leaf and ran her slender index finger over the delicate veins. Watching her, I wished her stepfather could die all over again.

"I lost my innocence a long time ago."

"That wasn't your fault. It was taken from you. Griffin, look at me. In my eyes—in Holly's eyes—you're an innocent girl, And you deserve all the respect in the world."

She gave me a hug. I felt her tears on my shoulder as I stroked her hair.

"And if Fabian or any other guy tries to hurt you, you tell me."

"Okay. Dave?"

Maybe it was how she looked at me. But at that moment, she no longer seemed like the kid I remembered. That tall girl with the heavy eyeliner and black nail polish who'd come to us looking for protection. What I saw was a woman, with her sandy hair in a ponytail, minimal makeup, and the kind of poise a royal would appreciate. Or at least one trained to handle a military-grade weapon.

"Thanks for caring about me."

She smiled in a way that tore me up. I got to my feet, groaning over my sore muscles.

"No problemo," I said and walked away.

NINETEEN

The news was all over the campus—Evie Champagne was dead.

Warnick showed up at our trailer, looking sleep deprived. Inside, he laid into me. Fortunately, Griffin was off somewhere with Greta. Holly was on the sofa, her legs tucked beneath her. I plopped down next to her and took her hand.

"Why didn't you tell me you'd seen her?" my friend said.

"What difference would it have made?"

"For starters, she wouldn't be dead."

"Debatable. What happened—draggers?"

"She was shot in the head. A squad found her in an alley not too far from here."

My wife was near tears. "But who would do that?"

"Someone who didn't want her asking a lot of questions," I said, glaring at Warnick. "We can't let this lie. Right?"

I hadn't meant to take my anger out on my friend. But at that moment, he represented everything that was wrong with the program. First Chavez, now Pederman. I didn't trust anyone, and it made me gutsick.

"I already spoke to Pederman about it."

"Yeah, I'm sure that helped."

"Can you not be a dick for one minute? He agreed to let me look into it."

"You mean *really* look?"

Holly sprang to her feet. "Dave, give the man a chance—jeez!" Then to Warnick, "What about the police? Maybe they can help."

"Yeah, about that. The entire force has been replaced. And now Pederman doesn't want them involved. He wouldn't say why."

A chilling sadness came over me like December in Seattle. We'd spent so long battling evil forces in the town. And let's not forget the hordes. Evie had been the one bright spot in a cesspool of black rot. She'd given us a way to make sense of things. And now she was gone.

"Where's the body?" I said.

"In the hospital morgue. We're waiting for the autopsy."

"Any idea who's performing it?"

"A Dr. Fallow."

"Isaac Fallow?"

"They brought him down from San Francisco today. He might already be over there."

"Let's go," I said and grabbed my gun.

The hospital was on lockdown, with Humvees parked outside and Black Dragon guards posted at the exits. The building itself had sustained only minor damage. Without comment, those covering the emergency room doors let us pass.

Inside, hospital staff and maintenance crews were visible everywhere. This was unlike the deserted scene we had found after my rescue from the brewery. Warnick was leaking blood from a gunshot wound, and I was towing a badly injured leg.

We rode the elevator down to the morgue. The last time I was here was to identify Jim's body with a Homicide detective. Missy had split his head open with an axe after he came after us in the forest. I didn't like thinking about who I was back then—a coward who'd left my ex-mistress to die at the hands of a dragger.

I was still a suspect in Jim's death, and I wondered if the police would ever get around to arresting me. The episode seemed like a million years ago. Meanwhile, I was headed down a dark river of blood to a new seething terror. And its calling card was a dead reporter.

The waiting room was clean and pleasant, with nice furniture and artificial plants. A chirpy attendant wearing fresh scrubs greeted us.

"Dr. Fallow has already begun the autopsy," he said.

Warnick moved past Holly and me. "He's expecting us."

The attendant used his card key to admit us to a room labeled Conference Room—Private, which turned out to be the autopsy room. The interior was brightly lit. Four large tables stood in a single row, each with a sink and surgical equipment. Over each table hung a microphone operated by pedals. Despite the acute presence of death, the room smelled antiseptic and, surprisingly, a little musty.

I recognized the doctor standing at the farthest table, recording an observation. As my friend and I headed over, Holly hesitated.

I took her hand. "You okay?"

"Go ahead, I'll catch up."

"Isaac?" I said, barely containing my excitement.

Dr. Isaac Fallow was the medical examiner in Tres Marias

and a family practice physician. He had known me my whole life and was a dear friend. We'd last seen each other when the outbreak started. Before the quarantine, he left for San Francisco to search for answers. I wondered if he had made any progress.

"Can't shake your hand," he said. Then to Warnick, "I hope you're taking good care of my boy."

The guard gave him a cryptic smile. "He's a handful."

"Don't I know it."

Keeping my emotions in check, I tried to see Evie as nothing more than a corpse. It shouldn't have been that hard after everything I'd been through. But even in death, her authority and confidence shone through—something her killer couldn't take away. Then the glow vanished when Isaac removed the top half of her skull with an oscillating saw.

He traced the bullet's path to the hole in her forehead. The sweet smell of brain tissue got to me. *It's just meat.* Turning to Holly, I found her seated by the door, her head between her legs. I was surprised at her squeamishness, considering the number of draggers she had dispatched.

"Dave, I can't tell you how happy I am you survived," the doctor said. "You're working for Black Dragon now?"

"It's all Warnick's fault. Oh yeah, that's Holly over there."

He waved to her. "You've got a good man."

"I know." She got up and opened the door. "Think I'll wait outside."

Isaac separated the folds of the brain with his thumbs. "Manner of death is homicide. Judging from the body's condition, I'm guessing it happened before midnight. There are no bites and no signs of disease. I was told the guards who found her didn't recover the bullet. But from what I can see, it was a fairly large caliber—at least 9mm."

My friend took a closer look. "How did they do it?"

"There were bruises on both knees. It looks like she was forced to kneel on the ground. The shooter was behind her, standing between four and six feet away."

"Sounds like an execution," I said.

TWENTY

Instead of returning to the command center, we decided to hang out in the cafeteria till Isaac completed the autopsy. The food service wasn't fully operational yet, and we had to settle for coffee and snacks. It was good to see doctors, nurses, and orderlies milling around. One more sign that a normal life might be within reach.

I thought about what Holly and I had discussed. Would it be possible to start over someplace else? Ignoring her donut, she rubbed her temples.

"Still not feeling better?" I said. "Want me to see if I can find some ibuprofen?"

"No, I'm good. I can't understand why that affected me so much."

"Blame it on the pregnancy." Then to Warnick, "I've been thinking about Evie. Anyone in Black Dragon could've killed her. All of us carry 9mm weapons."

"So do the cops."

"Okay. But how do you know that patrol didn't do it themselves?"

"Because we have a record of when they went out. It was

early morning. When they found her, the body was already covered in blowflies."

"Maybe another patrol got to her first."

My friend scoffed. "You keep wanting this to be about Black Dragon. You work for us now, remember?"

"I know, but—"

"Every patrol takes a different sector. These guys just happened to go down that alley. End of story."

"I'm not trying to blame our guys. But with everything we went through…"

"I get it. But I'm pretty sure Black Dragon didn't do this."

"That leaves the question—who wanted her dead?"

My wife ran her hand over my beard. "You could use a shave." Then to Warnick, "What happens to the draggers' bodies after they're terminated?"

I laughed. "That was random."

"It's been bothering me. We haven't seen any fire pits since we got here."

My friend stood. "Want me to show you?"

He led us to the rear of the hospital, where we discovered three gigantic gray boxes resembling shipping containers with chimneys. I couldn't believe my eyes.

What the…"

"Mobile incinerators," he said.

A forklift carried a pile of bodies to the units, where guards in hazmat suits tossed them inside one by one. A separate crew shoveled debris from the ash pits and poured it into red hazardous waste bags, which were loaded onto trucks for disposal.

"What do they do with the ashes?" I said.

Unconcerned, Warnick continued watching the operation. "Landfill."

Clean and efficient. Pederman was right—things were getting better.

It was time to go inside. We rode the elevator to the administrator's office. I noticed Holly looking at my friend. From her expression, I knew her little woman was at it again. This was going to be good.

"Warnick?" she said. "These incinerators are everywhere, right?"

"Uh-huh."

"What's to stop someone from tossing in an extra body or two—say, a murder victim?"

His eyes bored into her. "Nothing, I guess."

"After they killed Evie, why didn't they get rid of the evidence?"

Something had been nagging me about the reporter's death. Once again, she beat me to it. I felt like an idiot who was late to the party.

"Remember that time we found Yang's head in the forest?" I said. "And I was sure it was Chavez who left it there?"

My friend peered at me. "I don't get the connection."

"Whoever killed Evie wanted us to find her."

It was clear he was resisting the obvious. When he turned to my wife for confirmation, she gave him a nod.

"Definitely a warning," she said.

We waited for Isaac in the administrator's office. After a few minutes, he walked in and, taking a seat, folded his pale, liver-spotted hands. The man looked exhausted.

"This is your office now?" I said. "What happened to Dr. Vale?"

"She left before the quarantine. After the incident with

that other patient—I think it broke her. Anyway, I've finished the autopsy, and it's as I suspected. Someone shot Evie Champagne execution style. It happened sometime during the night, but not in the alley. Her body was moved there."

"For us to find."

"What happens after you write your report?" Warnick said.

"I have to file it with the coroner's office and send copies to the police department. It's officially a homicide case."

"Have you learned anything new about the virus?" I said.

"I met with a group of immunologists from UCSF. They developed the blood test that detects the virus. They're currently working on a vaccine."

"Any idea how it all got started?" Holly said.

"No. And the CDC was no help, which continues to baffle me."

After saying our goodbyes, I shook Isaac's hand. "You planning to stick around?"

"You bet. People still need doctors."

In the parking lot, we climbed into our vehicle. I sat in front with my friend. He was about to start the engine when I covered his hand.

"We need to go to Old Orchard Road."

"Robbin-Sear?"

He pushed away my hand and started the engine. After we exited the parking lot, he sighed—something he did a lot when I was around. Then he pulled over.

"We can't walk in there asking questions about the virus," he said.

That was exactly what I wanted to do, but he was right. "Look, we're investigating Evie's murder. And we know she met with them. We're just following a lead."

When I glanced at my wife, she was smiling. Gripping the steering wheel, Warnick rolled his eyes.

"Okay, I'll agree to it. But I need more people."

Holly touched my shoulder. "What about Griffin? We might be gone awhile."

"I can't let her come with us. Too much liability."

Now I scoffed. "She can take down draggers as well as any of us, and you know it."

"She's not permitted to carry a weapon."

"I'll stay with her," my wife said.

He shook his head. "Negative. I need you with me on this."

She batted her eyelashes at him. "Warnick, I'm flattered."

"I'll assign someone to look after Griffin. There's this female guard I know."

"Okay, but I need to meet her first."

"I'll ask her to report to your trailer," he said. "You'll like her, I promise."

TWENTY-ONE

A tall African American woman showed up at our door. She was in her late twenties and wore a perfectly pressed uniform. We had already told Griffin what was happening. Though unhappy about the situation, she accepted it.

"I'm Erzen," the woman said. "May I come in?"

I shook her hand. "Of course. Is that your first or last name?"

Her raised eyebrow warned me to stand down. The others came over to meet her.

"Um, my wife, Holly," I said. "And this is Griffin."

Erzen gave the girl a warm smile. "How are you, Griffin? I understand you've seen combat."

"Yes." The girl averted her eyes, embarrassed by the attention.

"No need to be nervous—I'm not here to ruin your life. Here's how this works. You'll check in with me before each meal. You can usually find me in the administration building. I'll stop by the trailer once at 2000 hours. That's curfew, young lady, and I expect you to be home. Are we clear?"

"Yes, ma'am."

I had never heard Griffin call anyone *ma'am*. Or *sir*, for that matter. I was beginning to like Erzen.

"Looks like we're good, then," the guard said. "See you at lunch."

Though she had a tough exterior, the woman struck me as caring. In some ways, she reminded me of Warnick. I could see why he chose her for the assignment. After she had gone, the girl looked at us imploringly.

"Can't I come with you?" she said.

I hated being the bad guy. "You'll be safe here."

"But what if you get into trouble?"

"All the more reason."

I hadn't meant to sound harsh. I thought we could move past this, but then I saw the tears welling in her eyes. Holly noticed them too, and brushed the hair away from her face.

"Honey, what's wrong?" my wife said.

"Why did they have to kill Evie?"

Holly and I exchanged a look. At this point, anything I said would sound awkward, so I left it to my wife. She walked Griffin over to the sofa. The girl's tears flowed freely, reminding me that *I* hadn't fully processed the reporter's death.

"I won't lie to you," Holly said. "These are dangerous times. We don't know who killed Evie—that's what we're going to find out. But we can't let anything happen to you, honey."

"I can handle myself."

"I know you can. But we work for Black Dragon now. And that means there are rules."

She hugged Griffin like a daughter. "It still hurts me when I remember how we almost lost you. Dave and I will be fine. You have to trust us. Do you think you can do that?"

The girl wiped away her tears with her sleeve. "Uh-huh."

"This is for the best." My wife nudged me to say something.

"At least Erzen is nice," I said.

Griffin stared at the floor, her shoulders slumped. "I guess."

I felt bad for the girl as we joined Warnick and the others outside. Days earlier, she was a vital, functioning part of our team. I promised myself we would find a way to let her join us. Holly must have noticed my distress and took my hand.

"We did the right thing," she said.

There were six of us in the Humvee. Warnick drove, with Springer riding shotgun. It was like old times, except for the new guys, whose names I hadn't bothered to learn. They sat on either side of Holly and me. A good night's sleep had been a rare commodity lately, and before I knew it, I'd drifted off.

In my dream, Evie ran through a white mist—she was following someone. I couldn't make out the person, but it was a man, short and stocky. When he turned around, I recognized Walt Freeman.

Startling, I opened my eyes and peered out the windows. We had entered the forest.

"Did we hit something?" I said.

My friend glanced at me in the rearview mirror. "Pothole."

My wife leaned against me, her head on my shoulder. Rubbing her eyes, she sat up and looked around.

"Where are we?"

It was early afternoon, and the temperature had dropped. A heavy mist clung to the forest floor like a diaphanous blanket, and it was difficult to make out details among the trees.

Springer fiddled with his phone, though there was no cell service.

Warnick glanced at the map on his lap. "I think we might be close."

If I had to guess, I would have said we were somewhere to the east. The trees were less dense here. Someone had erected miles of fence hewn from logs. There were no markers, but they'd mounted lights on the trees. I couldn't imagine there being any night traffic, so why light the way?

Up ahead stood a series of low, unmarked buildings surrounded by a fence similar to the one Ram Chakravarthy had around his compound. Inside there was a small, unmanned guard station. The gate was on wheels. My friend parked along the road, and we got out.

We studied the fence, afraid to touch it in case it was electrified. A sign read PROSPECT CORRECTIONAL FACILITY.

"Interesting cover," I said.

Holly pointed at a dead raccoon lying next to the fence, its fur singed. A woman's scream came out of the forest. We returned to our vehicle and grabbed our rifles. If we encountered a horde, we would double back and drive away to safety.

My wife and I stayed with Warnick and Springer while the other two guards split off. We cut a path through trees that thinned into a clearing. A man and woman ran towards us. Each had on blue jeans and a dark insulated vest. Both wore glasses and carried backpacks. The man had a catchpole.

Ignoring us, they crossed the road to the facility. The man opened the gate using a remote control and waved everyone inside. Instead of joining us, my friend returned to the Humvee. Then, from out of the mist, a dragger pack appeared. They were dressed as tourists, forest rangers, and Black Dragon guards.

"Hurry!" the woman said.

Warnick pulled into the yard, and the man closed the gates. Holly raised her weapon, but he pushed down her arm. Snarling, the draggers grabbed the electrified fence, did a crazy dance, and fell away. Incapable of learning their lesson, they repeated the exercise till they eventually tired of it and wandered off.

The main building had no windows. There were security cameras mounted on the roof. I expected to see dogs, but none came. If this was Robbin-Sear, they had done an excellent job of masking its identity. Anyone passing wouldn't have given the place a second thought.

The front door opened, and another man in his forties stepped into the afternoon light. Disheveled, wan, and unshaven, he wore a long-sleeve shirt and jeans. His hands were trembling. He squinted at us with dilated pupils. His curly black hair was overgrown, and his black horn-rimmed glasses practically slid off the end of his nose. He smelled ripe. As we moved in to greet him, an oppressive dread welled up in my gut.

It was Bob Creasy.

TWENTY-TWO

Blocking the entrance, Creasy glowered at his colleagues.

"You're trespassing," he said to us.

Warnick displayed his ID and pushed past. The reception area was small and nondescript. There was a side table with a visitor's log and a cup filled with ballpoint pens—nothing else. A corridor led to the rest of the building.

Creasy took the couple aside. "What possessed you to let them in here?"

"We were almost killed," the man said. Then to us, "I'm Dr. Larry Evans. This is my wife, Dr. Judith Evans. So glad we didn't have to engage those things. We can usually handle one or two, but..."

My friend instructed the other two guards to wait outside. Ignoring Creasy, he addressed Larry. "What were you doing in the forest?"

The scientist's eyes darted to his colleague. "Research."

Creasy seemed edgy and unfocused—different from the way I remembered him. He looked as if he hadn't slept in weeks. And he had lost a lot of weight. With a scowl, he got between his people and us.

"I'm afraid I'm going to have to ask you to—"

"Do you remember me?" I said as Holly reached for my hand.

Warnick rolled his eyes. "I thought we agreed—"

"It's fine." I gave my wife a reassuring smile. Then to Creasy, "We've met before."

He squinted at me as if the light hurt his eyes.

"A few months ago, you picked me up on the highway. It was night, and I was injured. You asked if a dog had bitten me."

Scratching at the backs of his arms, he shot a questioning look at the scientists. "I dropped you at the police station."

"That's right."

"We need to ask you some questions," my friend said.

"Not allowed."

"Talk to them, Bob," Larry said. "This has already gone too far."

"Shut your mouth."

Judith sighed. "He's right. We shouldn't get involved."

Warnick put on his best smile. "We're conducting an investigation and would greatly appreciate your cooperation."

The couple side-eyed each other. His jaw set, the man led us into a break room, where we found a few tables and chairs. A coffee machine and a microwave oven sat on the counter next to a refrigerator.

"This isn't a good idea," the woman said to her husband.

Creasy lingered in the doorway, then crossed to the sink for a glass of water. My friend whispered something to Springer, and the guard took off.

Judith pointed vaguely. "There's coffee and tea."

Creasy eyed us suspiciously as he drank. "What is it you want?"

"A news reporter named Evie Champagne was murdered recently," Warnick said.

Startled, Larry turned to his wife. "She's dead?"

I glanced at Creasy to gauge his reaction. Though he seemed unfazed, his eyes shifted from me to his colleagues.

"Did you know her?" I said.

Avoiding eye contact, he set down his glass. "Only from the news."

"She was investigating Robbin-Sear," my friend said. Then to the man, "She told us she met with you."

Creasy gave his colleague a warning look. "She was lying."

Larry slammed his palm on the table. "Dammit, Bob!" Then to us, "It's true, I spoke with her."

"She and my husband had a near miss on a back road," Judith said a little too fast. "That was it."

He nodded. "She asked me a lot of questions, but I didn't tell her anything."

"Any idea who might've wanted her dead?" Warnick said.

"Of course not."

"Did she ever visit this facility?"

"No," Creasy said. "That would be trespassing, like what you're doing now. It's unfortunate that a woman was shot, but that doesn't—"

"No one mentioned anything about her being shot," Holly said.

A violent look passed over his face like a poisonous cloud. "I'm not going to be a part of this. You people have no idea what you're toying with."

The minute he was gone, I felt the tension ease.

"Is he okay?" my wife said.

The woman shook her head. "He's been under a terrible strain since the outbreak. We all have."

"What's his role?" my friend said.

"He's the project lead."

"And what exactly *is* the project?" I said.

Larry took his wife's hand. "That's classified."

"As scientists, you must know what happened in Tres Marias, right?"

"I warned you," someone said.

Creasy stood in the doorway, pointing a handgun at us.

Judith gasped. "Bob, what are you doing?"

As we scrambled to our feet, I stood in front of Holly and raised my weapon. Licking his lips, the project lead blinked at us. I thought he might have the jimmies, which meant that any second he could lose control of his trigger finger. Raising his handgun, Warnick drew a bead on his head.

"Drop your weapon," my friend said.

"Don't you see? We have to finish this—it's all that matters now!"

All of a sudden, Springer was in the doorway. Moving swiftly, he brought down the butt of his rifle, making a dull thwack. Grabbing his head, Creasy collapsed with a groan. As he hit the floor, his glasses went flying. The guard retrieved the handgun and joined us while the scientists tended to their unconscious colleague.

"You saw," Springer said. "I had to do it."

TWENTY-THREE

Creasy lay on a bed in the building's sleeping quarters with a bandaged head. His breathing sounded like a toy train whistle. Judith rolled up his sleeve, revealing a lost highway of black needle marks. She sterilized the skin with an alcohol-soaked cotton ball. Reaching for a syringe, she found a serviceable vein and administered an injection.

"What are you giving him?" I said.

"Librium. Enough to keep him under for several hours."

Larry walked in and motioned for us to follow him. "I locked up the gun. We should be safe now."

Springer stared at the patient. "Shouldn't somebody keep an eye on him?"

"Trust me," Judith said. "He's out."

They led us to an executive conference room on the opposite side of the building. The others avoided eye contact as we took our seats. They had seen the marks on the project lead's arm and didn't want to talk about it. So I did.

"Creasy's a heroin addict."

Larry side-eyed his wife. "Morphine, actually."

"He steals it from the dispensary," Judith said. "We're not sure how long he's been using."

Her husband laid his hands on the table and gave us an apologetic look. "We don't have any other information for you, so."

"We're the ruling authority in Tres Marias," Warnick said. "If we decide to launch an official investigation, it would mean search warrants, interrogations—the works. I want to know why Evie Champagne was so interested in what you're doing here. Can you help us?"

I admired the way he handled the situation. Pleasant but firm. Me, I would've held a gun to their heads.

"Could you excuse us for a minute?" Larry said.

After they left, Springer used the opportunity to join the other guards outside. The scientists argued in the hallway. Judith raised her voice. Her husband said something under his breath, and she quieted down. Then they returned to the conference room.

"We'd like to cooperate," Larry said. "But we need assurances that we'll be protected from prosecution."

His wife sat quietly, fingering the zipper on her vest. Then, "Please understand. We're taking a huge risk. If it gets out that we leaked classified information, the company could take legal action."

Her husband took her hand. "We could go to prison."

"Everyone in the chain of command will know you cooperated," my friend said. "You have my word."

The man removed his glasses and pinched the top of his nose. "I don't even know where to begin. The project was already in full swing when Jude and I arrived."

"Where are all the other scientists?" Holly said.

"Originally, there were twelve of us, plus Bob. Most of the

staff left when the outbreak happened. All we know is they were transferred to another facility."

That got my attention. "Where?"

"No idea. They've kept us out of the loop." He glanced at the door as if expecting someone. "We'll tell you what we know."

The scientist explained that Robbin-Sear was a privately held bioscience technology company founded in 1990 by two former government scientists, Dr. John Robbin and Dr. William Sear. They were headquartered in Virginia. After incorporation, they were awarded a Department of Defense contract to provide vaccines to our troops during the Gulf War.

"In the beginning, the company produced vaccines for Hepatitis A and B, typhoid, and malaria," Judith said. "Soon, we began manufacturing drugs to protect against chemical and biological agents."

Over the years, the firm continued to provide these vaccine-manufacturing services for the DOD. As far as these scientists knew, there were no other customers. When Larry and his wife were hired, the company had been looking for a way to inoculate soldiers against PTSD.

"They'd been experimenting for years," he said. "Most of the research was focused on various combinations of drugs to suppress the fear response in the amygdala. The team theorized that if soldiers were unafraid, they would act more rationally when confronted with danger. Also, they wouldn't suffer the typical aftereffects."

"Of course, there was a problem," Judith said. "We would essentially be creating an army of drug addicts."

She and her husband had published a research paper on controlling the brain using a viral delivery mechanism. They built a computer model demonstrating that a virus laced with a nonaddictive drug could act similarly to security software on top of an operating system. When applied to the amygdala, the result would be a reduction in the fear reaction without any side effects. Soldiers would, in essence, remain unaffected by the events they experienced during prolonged periods of combat. And later, there would be no sleep loss, nightmares, or violent bursts of anger.

Someone at Robbin-Sear read the paper and asked the scientists to join the team in Tres Marias. After reviewing their computer model, all drug-related research was halted. And the team focused on developing a new super-drug.

"That was six years ago," Larry said. "We kept searching for the right virus to modify. But no matter what we tried, it would always kill the host."

Holly gave me a worried look. "What kind of host?"

"We experimented exclusively on animals—mice mostly."

"Not humans?" Warnick said.

Judith squirmed. "Human trials were years away."

"What about Guatemala?" I said. "Everyone died."

The scientists looked at each other, stunned that we knew about the tragedy near Jacaltenango.

"I swear to you," Larry said. "We had nothing to do with that."

TWENTY-FOUR

Holly and I had neglected to tell Warnick about the outbreak in that little Guatemalan village. And as he glowered at me, I wished we had.

"You may not have been there," I said. "But Bob Creasy was."

Larry blanched. "You have to believe us. We didn't find out until after he returned."

My friend made a few notes. "Right now, I'm interested in what happened in Tres Marias."

Judith explained that she had made a breakthrough. She found that if they combined the drug with a genetically modified rabies variant, they could target the brain.

"That was exciting," her husband said. "Once we could control the delivery mechanism, we could move to the next phase."

"Which was..."

"Induce fear in a test subject and measure the response."

"And how did you do that?" I said.

"We have a machine."

"Why rabies?" my wife said.

Judith smiled, which was all kinds of creepy given the circumstances. "Most viruses travel through the bloodstream, but rabies is different. It can bypass the BBB via the central nervous system."

"*BBB?*"

"Blood-brain barrier. Rabies binds to receptors on the test subject's nerve endings. With the right dose, we can reach the brain."

Her husband joined in. "Once we were satisfied the process worked, we experimented on dogs while continuing to refine the virus to achieve the desired results."

"But one of the animals escaped," I said.

"H-how did you know?"

"Because he belonged to a friend of mine."

I dug out my phone and flipped through the photos till I found one of Perro playing at home in his yard. I showed it to Larry.

"I'm pretty sure this is the dog," he said. "We saw him running through the woods—no tag and no collar. We assumed he was a stray and picked him up."

"And you deliberately infected him."

Holly raised her hand. "I thought most dogs were vaccinated against rabies."

"Not Perro. As far as I know, Jim never took him to the vet." Then to the scientists, "But what about the others? Some of those dogs must've gotten their shots."

The man was about to say something when his wife cut him off. "Since we modified the virus, a vaccine would have little effect."

"So, what went wrong?" Warnick said.

"This particular subject reacted to the treatment in a way we hadn't anticipated. He became incredibly strong. After only a few hours, he overpowered us and escaped the facility.

We searched for a week. He was highly contagious, and we were afraid he might infect someone."

"I went out every day," Larry said. "I found your friend wandering along a fire road, drunk as a skunk. He was looking for his dog too. When he described the animal, I knew it was the one we were searching for. I offered to give him a ride home. On the way, we saw Perro."

"Did you try to catch him?"

"Your friend got out and walked up to him. The dog bit him on the hand. I tried trapping him, but he got away."

"What about Jim?" I said.

"I told him I'd help him find his dog. It was a lie, but I couldn't leave him there—he was infected. So I brought him here."

"And how long did you keep him?"

"I can check the record, but I'm pretty sure it was about a week."

I could barely contain my rage. "Did you experiment on my friend?"

Warnick raised a warning hand. I already knew the answer, but I wanted them to admit what they had done.

"We, um, we used the machine," Judith said. "But it wasn't our idea."

Her husband put a comforting arm around her. "Bob made the call. He said it was an opportunity to fast-track the project."

I wanted to strangle these two, then burn the place to the ground. Instead, I got up and stood against the wall.

"We noticed that, like the dog, your friend's strength had increased," she said. "We tranquilized him in case he became violent."

Larry turned to Warnick. "Bob decided to move him to the

other facility. The last time Jude or I saw the patient was when we put him in the van. Later, we learned he'd escaped."

"Do you remember what day that was?"

"No, but it was in early July."

Sinking into a chair, I took my wife's hand. "July 5th. It all makes sense now. Jim must've wandered home and gotten drunk. Then he made his way to our house."

"And we know the rest," Warnick said. "Between the dog and your friend, others became sick. Then everything spiraled out of control."

Judith's eyes glistened. "We tried to stop it."

I glared at the scientists. "Why does the virus make the victims undead?"

The man reacted as if I'd slapped him. "That's not... We never intended to— The whole point was to make it so soldiers would look and behave normally."

"Technically, they shouldn't have died," the woman said. "But..."

Warnick was laser-focused on her now. "But what?"

"The virus is mutating faster than anything we've ever encountered. What you're seeing now—this undead effect— is not what we designed."

Larry patted his wife's hand. "And I'm afraid we don't know how to stop it."

I came around the table and grabbed his arm. "Jim was patient zero, wasn't he?"

The scientists exchanged troubled glances. They didn't say anything, and the seconds felt like minutes. Then...

"Not exactly," Judith said.

TWENTY-FIVE

The scientists walked us to a stairwell at the rear of the building. We headed downstairs to an alcove with a steel door. Swiping his badge, Larry opened it and ushered us through. Inside, there was a massive lab with tables filled with microscopes, computers, and other electronic equipment. An entire wall was stacked with large cages containing barking dogs. Next to those were smaller ones with laboratory mice.

The rear third of the lab was walled off in plexiglass. There was a mantrap in the center. Larry explained that it required two codes to get in—one for each door. Inside the secure area was a third scientist in a filthy, bloodstained lab coat. It was hard to tell his age, with his ravaged face and one eye swollen shut. He sat on a stool, peering into a microscope with his good eye. The scientist gazed at him with a gloomy expression.

"That's Dr. Royce."

"What happened to him?" I said.

"He got bit trying to stop Perro from escaping."

I moved closer and peered through the plexiglass. "Did he turn?"

"I'm afraid I don't understand."

"For shit's sake, is he undead?"

"He's *infected*," Judith said, giving me the stink eye. "Which is why he's in isolation."

They were in denial over what they'd unleashed. This guy was a dragger, pure and simple. Still, it was strange he wasn't attacking the plexiglass.

"What's he doing?" Holly said.

Judith approached the barrier. "Continuing the work he started before the accident."

I side-eyed Warnick. "Are you saying he's rational?"

"We're not sure. We've been treating him with a second-generation virus. So far, he appears to be going through the motions."

Larry pressed a button and spoke into the intercom. "Dr. Royce? There are some people I'd like you to meet. Can you stop what you're doing and come over here?"

Either the dragger didn't hear or didn't care. Instead, he flicked his hand at his head as if swatting away a gnat.

Larry slumped his shoulders. "That's one of the side effects. We think it may cause a kind of buzzing in the brain, which tricks the ears into thinking there are flies."

"Can he talk?" my friend said.

"A bit. But his mind wanders when he's away from the microscope."

Near the scientist, there was a dark pool on the floor. I recognized it as black vomit, an early symptom of the draggers we first encountered. When I pressed up against the plexiglass, I broke Royce's concentration. He stared at me with flat eyes, his jaws working menacingly. Larry laid a hand on my shoulder and guided me away.

"You told us you didn't know how to stop this," I said. "What are you doing now?"

"Studying how the virus mutates. That's why we were in the forest trying to capture specimens."

"We call them draggers."

"I'll try to remember that," he said.

Larry escorted us outside while his wife went to check on Creasy. It had turned cold, and the darkening sky threatened rain. There were draggers at the fence, trying to get in. Springer and the other guards bayoneted them through the head so we could leave.

The scientist made a face. "Can't you leave us one or two for our research?"

"I'm not putting my people at risk," Warnick said. Then to the rest of us, "Let's roll."

Judith came running out of the building. "I can't find Bob. Larry, I'm worried."

The automatic lights clicked on as the last of the daylight left us. My friend signaled us to leave.

"Are you going to report this?" she said.

"I have to let the supervisor know. But we're treating this as highly confidential."

Larry opened the gate. We were already in the Humvee when two police cruisers appeared at a crest in the road, approaching fast.

"Now what?" Holly said.

The vehicles stopped in front of the gate, blocking us. Two officers emerged from the first cruiser and stood on either side of the Humvee, their hands on their holsters. Another cop exited the second car and approached our driver's side.

He was young, with steel-gray eyes and jet-black hair. His nameplate read HANNITY.

"I need you to exit the vehicle," he said.

We did as he asked. As I climbed out, a fourth cop emerged from the other cruiser. He was around sixty—large and out of shape—with short, curly gray hair and dispassionate blue eyes. Two silver bars decorated each shoulder. He was the new police captain.

The superior made his way around our vehicle and stopped in front of me, giving me no room to maneuver. His nameplate read O'BRIEN.

"David Pulaski," he said. "You're under arrest."

Though his manner was vicious, his face betrayed no emotion. He smelled faintly of bourbon and cigarettes—a walking cliché.

Defiant, my wife took my hand. "What's this about?"

"Mrs. Pulaski? Your husband is an accessory to the murder of James Stanley."

O'Brien never moved or looked away as Hannity handcuffed me and recited my rights like the Pledge of Allegiance.

"Warnick, do something!" she said.

"I don't think I can."

O'Brien gave him the smile of a predator. "Correct."

They placed me into the backseat of the second cruiser, and we were off. Through the rear window, I observed everyone getting smaller. Gripping Warnick's arm, Holly said something. No one made a move to leave the premises.

I had convinced myself that the outbreak had rendered my past null and void. Just like all those draggers we put down. But another truth continued to nag at me, and it refused to let me alone.

Because, deep down, I had known all along this day would come.

TWENTY-SIX

I spent the night in jail—a first for me. And although I was certain Warnick and the others had followed me, they weren't allowed inside. Knowing Holly, she would exhaust every avenue. In the end, it was no good when you were dealing with a hardass like O'Brien.

As Hannity led me through to the holding cell, I passed through a front office bursting with activity. Twenty or thirty cops—all strangers—sat at desks, up to their necks in paperwork. It was bedlam, and the jokes were flying.

Entering the large cell, I found I wasn't the only occupant. A teenager wearing a Billabong T-shirt and distressed jeans sat sulking at the end of a long bench. Tattoos covered his forearms, and his ears were gauged.

"What are you in for?" I said. "Fine, don't tell me."

"B and E. Not like there's anything left worth stealing."

After a couple hours, the cop showed up again with MREs and water. Just like old times.

"I guess a lawyer is out of the question," I said. "What happened to the former captain?"

"Red Militia got him."

I gave the kid a *watch this* look. "You guys aren't from around here, are you?"

"They brought us up from LA."

"No outbreak down there?"

"Stop asking so many damn questions, Pulaski."

Hannity left us for the night. I ripped open my MRE and stared at the off-color beef franks that real soldiers liked referring to as *five fingers of death*. The beans didn't look any better. Not hungry, I set aside the package. Taking a swallow of water, I lay down at the other end of the bench.

The kid had heated his food, and soon, the cell was filled with the odor of suspect hot dogs and bean gravy. After he finished his MRE, he zeroed in on mine. Rolling my eyes, I waved at it. Watching him eat, I wondered about his future. I doubted he would come back with me to the command center. And the thought of him being left on the streets to fend for himself... How long could he last out there?

"Where did they pick you up?" I said.

"Some random street. I don't get it. Since when is it a crime to look for food? It's not like anybody's living in those houses anymore."

"See any draggers?"

"What?"

"You know, the infected."

"Oh, the tweaks?" He laughed, revealing two or three beans stuck to his teeth. "Me and my homie—well, he's dead. Anyways, we used to dump gasoline on 'em, then light 'em up. It was sick, I swear. It's like they're too stupid to know they're on fire. So fun..."

At first, the kid hadn't wanted to talk to me. Now, he wouldn't shut up. I closed my eyes and tried ignoring his colorful stories of life on the streets. Eventually, he quieted down. Outside, I heard Black Dragon LMTVs patrolling the neighborhood. The sound comforted me.

Sometime after midnight, a different cop came to check on us. After he left, I drifted off to bursts of intermittent gunfire and death shrieks. All night, bizarre dreams haunted me. The last one was the worst.

I was in the lab at Robbin-Sear, naked and strapped to an operating table. Dr. Royce came at me with an oversize scalpel, his head twitching like he'd been tased. Starting just below my Adam's apple, he made a precise vertical incision down the length of my torso.

My skin was dry and rubbery, and there wasn't any blood. He stopped and considered my case for a moment. Then, reaching deep inside me, he pulled up Perro's head. It snapped and snarled as it was forced to leave my body. Seeing it, I screamed.

When I looked up, Jim was beside me, holding the dog in his arms. The wet fetal animal dripped with the gore from my mutilated insides. The gash around my friend's neck pulsed with wriggling kidney worms. He smiled at me with bean teeth.

"It had to come out eventually," he said.

TWENTY-SEVEN

After a breakfast of coffee and store-bought donuts, Hannity walked me outside, where a police cruiser was waiting. O'Brien sat in the front passenger seat. I didn't like the way he smiled. They'd handcuffed me, and I needed help getting into the backseat.

"Where are we going?" I said. "And what's going to happen to that kid you're holding?"

The police captain leered. "I'd be more worried about your future."

In minutes, we arrived at a sprawling house on a hill overlooking the valley. The estate was vast, with no sign of draggers. A wrought-iron gate fronted the long, curving driveway. A stone pillar stood on either side, with a security camera mounted on each. As our vehicle approached, the gates opened automatically.

The house was impressive but not overdone. Not that I would know. I was surprised there was anyone with money left in Tres Marias. Maybe a wealthy benefactor had heard about the injustice and posted my bail. Unlikely.

After we parked, O'Brien got out and, taking my arm,

walked me to the front door while Hannity remained behind the wheel. The police captain rang the bell. Soon, a Latina housekeeper answered. When she saw us, her eyes got huge, and she let us in.

The foyer was minimalist and elegant, with recessed lighting and a tile floor. There was a staircase with a polished banister. The housekeeper brought us into the ultramodern kitchen. O'Brien released my arm and took a step back.

"What now?" I said.

He ignored me. Looking out the French doors, I saw the mayor in blue jeans and a yellow golf shirt. What the hell? He was on a massive lawn, playing touch football with two pudgy boys who were maybe seven and nine. Around my height, he had wiry red hair and a ruddy complexion. His body was broad and amorphous, having gone from muscular high school jock to flabby politician.

A slim, pretty blonde in her mid-thirties entered the kitchen, dressed in a pink cashmere sweater and dove-gray pants. Seeing a stranger in handcuffs, she startled. Not having showered, I was pretty ripe and felt bad for her. To her credit, she made the best of it and introduced herself as the mayor's wife.

Outside, she said something to her husband. He tossed the football to his older son and jogged to the house, only stopping to pull up a weed.

"You wanted me to bring him right over," the cop said, feigning humility as the mayor walked in.

He gave me a once-over and led us into his study, which was tastefully decorated, no doubt by the missus. The walls were covered with framed photos of his family.

Sheer white curtains hung over the French doors. Outside, the boys played as their mother relaxed on the patio, drinking coffee from a china cup. It was hard to comprehend that beyond the gates was a town under siege.

"Close the door," the mayor said.

O'Brien complied, then urged me over to the desk so our host could inspect me. He flicked a finger at the cop.

"I don't think we need those handcuffs." Then to me, "You're not planning to run away, are you?"

I'd never actually met this guy. Six years earlier, he was elected after a bitter campaign between him and the affable, long-time "Mayor Bob," who had recently suffered a stroke. The poor old guy had had no intention of leaving office even though he talked like Carl from *Caddyshack*.

Mayor Bob's opponent, this ginger-haired upstart, was a successful real estate developer who had a hankering for politics. During the campaign, he promised us state redevelopment funds courtesy of his close ties to Sacramento. Since the people were tired of the current do-nothing mayor, the challenger won the election handily.

"You can wait outside," the mayor said as if O'Brien were the gardener. "Mr. Pulaski and I have business to discuss."

TWENTY-EIGHT

When we were alone, the mayor waved at a chair. I wasn't exactly clean and worried I would soil his wife's expensive fabric. Rubbing my wrists, I sat while he opened a mini fridge and grabbed a beer.

"Can I offer you something?" he said.

"I'm fine. What's this about?"

"Oh, the arrest? It's like this. Just because we're under quarantine doesn't mean criminals are free to roam the streets."

I was a criminal now? He opened the middle drawer of his antique desk and pulled out a dark green file folder. I recognized the coffee stain. This was the evidence Detective Van Gundy had collected on me. I wished I could burn it.

"Seems you're the subject of a murder investigation."

"Am I going back to jail?"

"We'll see. I wanted a chance to talk to you first. Now, I won't lie to you. It's chaos around here. We don't even have a police chief, for shit's sake."

"Why not promote O'Brien? He seems nice."

"Yeah...O'Brien." He rolled his eyes. "Anyway, there's

more to me than real estate. I'm also a lawyer, and I've decided to pitch in to get a handle on the backlog."

I waited while he scanned the file, but it was all for show. He had studied it way before I got here, and he already knew what he would do. If this was his way of building suspense, it wasn't working. I'd seen better play-acting at dinner theater.

"You last spoke to Detective Van Gundy in the summer, that right?" he said, running his finger down the page.

"There wasn't enough evidence to connect me to anyone's death."

"You married, Dave?"

I loved the way lawyers asked questions they already knew the answer to. "Yes."

"Then why were you seeing Melyssa Soldado?"

It always came down to that—the stain on my life that wouldn't come out. I hated my past—what I'd done to Holly. And I thought when I destroyed the monster Missy had become, this sordid business would be over and done with. Hearing her name spoken by a stranger made me sick. It conjured up her image. Not the rasping dragger she had become, but the sex-starved girl I refused to save even as she begged for her life.

"I had an affair," I said.

"Your wife know?"

"I told her everything."

He sighed like a soap opera actor in closeup. "Marriage is hard, you know? We go in with the best of intentions, but sometimes we mess up." Was he talking about me—or him? "Is that what happened? Did you mess up?"

"I cheated."

"You're Catholic, right? Confession will put you on the right track."

It was an odd comment. I scanned the room and saw a

photo of the mayor wearing a Knights of Columbus uniform, complete with the hat and ceremonial sword.

"And James Stanley? How does he fit in?"

"He was my best friend."

"Was he also screwing the girl? Is that why he's dead?"

"He didn't even know her."

"Interesting. That's not what you told the detective."

"I lied."

"I see. No double-teaming the little Mexican, then?"

If I'd had a gun, I would have shot him in the face.

"How did Mr. Stanley die?"

Though my instinct was to avoid the truth, I was finished with lying and told this fat clown what happened that day.

"Jim attacked us in the forest. He'd turned and—"

"*Turned?*"

"He was carrying the virus."

"You're saying he died, then—"

"That's right. He chased us through the forest. At first, I tried helping Missy, but she fell. I panicked and hid inside a ranger station."

"Where was she?"

"Outside. With him."

"And you didn't try to save her?"

My mouth tasted like copper, and I realized I'd bitten the inside of my cheek. He took a swallow of beer and leaned back.

"That's pretty cold," he said, laughing. "I'll bet she was screaming too. *Dave, help me. Help me, Dave.* Am I right?"

"Something like that."

"What happened next?"

"She killed him with an axe and ran away. Eventually, she turned too."

He set aside the beer. Stretching, he got up and gazed out the French doors. I waited for more mayorly advice.

"That sucks. All in all, not a good day for Melyssa Soldado." He opened the doors. "Let's take a walk."

He led me through to the patio. When his wife saw us, she gathered the boys and took them inside through the kitchen. We made our way to a meticulously maintained garden. He looked straight ahead as we walked.

"I'll be straight with you," he said. "I think I have enough evidence to go to trial. I can prove that, by your own admission, you were with James Stanley and Melyssa Soldado at the time of Stanley's death."

He picked something off his shirt. "I might not get a conviction on second-degree murder, but I'm confident I can get the jury to find you guilty on an accessory to murder charge. I'll paint the picture as romantic in nature. I'm sure jealousy will come into play. And I might suggest something kinky. Juries are suckers for that."

He looked at me without emotion. "How's that sound?"

Rage boiled in me like hot lead. The mayor bent down and picked a few brown petals off his prized camellias. I wanted to stomp on his fat neck and beat him senseless using one of his kids. Closing my eyes, I tried to focus.

"What are you after?"

He straightened, and brushing himself off, got up in my grill. I could smell the beer on his breath and wished I had one.

"Stay out of my business," he said.

"And what business is that?"

He backhanded me across the face, his class ring busting open my lip. The stinging sensation made my eyes water. It took me a second to regroup.

"I don't have time for your games, Pulaski. Stay out of my

way, or you'll be saying goodbye to that pretty little wife of yours."

"Leave her out of it!"

"A lot of people are going to be arrested soon. Wait and see. And we'll process them as fast as we can. I have every intention of making your case a priority."

"There's no evidence."

He laughed. "Don't be an asshole. It's like I said, everyone's pitching in. Who knows? I might have to step in later and comfort Holly. The boys at the police station tell me she's a looker."

He noticed my balled-up fist and smiled with small, pointy teeth. His devilish orange eyes gleamed like jewels in firelight.

"Go ahead and take a swing," he said. "That's all I need to seal the deal."

He looked past me. When I turned around, Hannity was walking towards us.

"We'll keep Mr. Pulaski under surveillance," the mayor said, cleaning his ring with a handkerchief. "Give him a ride to the high school. I'm sure they miss him."

As I followed the cop, the fat bastard called to me. I wanted to keep walking, but I stopped.

"What we discussed goes for your friends too," he said.

Instead of returning me to the police vehicle, Hannity escorted me through a side door into the detached garage. Inside, it was dark and cold. When the lights came on, O'Brien was standing between a silver Volvo Cross Country and a candy-apple-red Audi R8.

"Hold him," the police captain said.

The other cop grabbed my upper arms from behind and thrust his foot between mine. As O'Brien moved in, I prepared myself.

"We want to make sure you don't forget what the mayor told you," he said.

Winding up, he hit me in the solar plexus, and the air went out of me. I would have collapsed if I hadn't been propped up. Then he hit me again. And again. I lost count of how many times because I blacked out.

When I came to, my abdomen was on fire, and the police captain was gone. Hannity tried getting me to my feet. I made it as far as my knees and vomited. The pain shot straight up through the top of my head. He got me to stand and helped me outside into the waiting police cruiser. I collapsed on the backseat and shut my eyes.

"That didn't go the way I thought," he said. "I was sure he wanted us to kill you."

TWENTY-NINE

Hannity eyed me in the rearview mirror. I avoided his gaze. As we exited the gates, he started in.

"You gotta understand," he said. "The mayor has a lot on his plate, what with everyone breathing down his neck. Then there's the feds and Black Dragon. He wants what's best for the community, is all."

"So, I should keep my mouth shut."

"Do like the rest of us and help get this town back on its feet."

"Easy for you to say. You guys aren't even from around here. So what, was LA having a fire sale? Who are all those cops?"

He bristled. "A community is a community."

"Can I ask you something? Did you ever lose anyone close?"

He shifted in his seat. "My sister. Drunk driver."

"We lost a lot of people too—good people. And now I come to find out the mayor might be involved. Doesn't that piss you off?"

The cop drove us past the command center guard station

and pulled up in front of the administration building. Craning his neck, he glared at me.

"Sure, it pisses me off. But I keep my head down—it's the only way to survive. The sooner you learn that, the better."

Opening my door, he handed me my gun and holster. Wavering from the pain, I gazed at the campus—the people coming and going, the kids playing. This was a community, and it was beginning to thrive. Priorities—it was all about the priorities. I felt lost.

Holly and Warnick were waiting for me when I arrived at our trailer. Griffin was out, probably with Fabian.

"Are you okay?" my wife said. She touched my swollen lip. "What happened?"

Gently, I moved away her hand. "It's nothing—I'm fine."

"No, you're not."

Inside, I found the sofa and sank into it, groaning from my injuries. Holly was insistent and unbuttoned my shirt. She gasped at the massive red-and-purple bruises blossoming around my abdomen.

"What did they do to you?"

"Taught me a lesson, apparently."

My friend was uncomfortable. "Pederman wants to see you. I'll tell him you're not up to it."

"It's okay, I'll go."

"I'm coming with you," my wife said. "You might want to shower first."

We met Pederman in the conference room. He wasn't all that happy to see the three of us.

"I thought this was a *private* meeting," he said.

Holly eased me into a chair and side-eyed Warnick. "This concerns us too."

Rubbing the back of his neck, the supervisor looked at me with a mixture of sympathy and disappointment. I noticed the dark green folder on the table. The mayor hadn't wasted any time giving him the police report.

"Looks like they roughed you up," he said. "I intend to file a complaint. Why didn't you tell me about the murder investigation?"

"Because I was never charged. I didn't think you needed to know."

"Does this mean he'll lose his job?" my wife said.

Pederman sank into a chair and massaged his eyes. "The background check never turned up anything, so I think you're fine. But, dammit, I need you to be straight with me. Any other secrets I should know about?"

"I'm a recovering alcoholic. Actually, that's not a secret."

As the supervisor digested the news, Holly squeezed my hand.

"You wouldn't be the first," he said.

"Mr. Pederman, what's Black Dragon's relationship with the mayor?"

"He signed the contract to bring us in."

"Is he involved in the day-to-day?"

"Walt Freeman is my contact. I'm required to file a weekly status report. Why?"

"Because the mayor is up to something. I knew it the minute I sat down with him."

My friend had been standing the whole time and sat next to the supervisor. "Are you going to let us continue investigating Evie's death?"

"The police are better equipped to handle it."

I scoffed. "They'll bury it."

Annoyed, Pederman turned to Warnick for confirmation.

He nodded. "We know it was Creasy who called the cops."

"Which is why they grabbed Dave so quickly," my wife said.

The supervisor flung the report across the room. "I hate this cloak-and-dagger bullshit." Then to my friend, "How many people do you need to continue your investigation?"

"Our squad should be enough."

"Okay, I'll give you a little more time. And Warnick, I expect results. We have other priorities. Like getting Tres Marias ready to turn over to civilian control."

Pederman stopped me at the door on my way out and laid a hand on my shoulder. "How bad did they hurt you, son?"

"I'll live," I said.

We sat under a tree outside our trailer—Holly, Warnick, Springer, and me. The ibuprofen hadn't kicked in yet, and my midsection throbbed.

"Are we to assume the mayor's in bed with Robbin-Sear?" my friend said.

My wife slipped her arm through mine. "Why not? It could be something as simple as money."

I touched my lip and winced. "He warned me not to investigate."

Grunting, Springer stood. "Screw him. Let's find out everything we can about the operation."

I would've agreed with him if I had been alone in this. But the mayor hadn't only threatened me. And there was no telling what he might do to Holly. I was reluctant to let the others know my decision because they were counting on me. But they were my friends, and I owed it to them.

"I'm out," I said.

Springer slammed his open palm on the tree trunk. "Dude, no."

As much as I hated the mayor, I was scared of him. And I would do everything in my power to keep the sonofabitch away from my family. If that meant staying silent, then so be it.

"This guy's not only a sleazy politician," I said. "He's dangerous. And don't forget, the cops work for him."

Standing, I took my wife's hand. She rested her head against me. I felt shitty betraying everyone, but what was I supposed to do?

"You sure this is what you want?" Warnick said.

"He threatened Holly."

"Guess I'm out too," she said.

I took my friend's arm. "Do what you have to. But the mayor's warning applies to everyone."

Springer cackled. "Shit, that tool ain't got nothin' on me. What do you say, Warnick? Do we keep going?"

"Let's stand down," he said. "For now."

Holly and I sat on our sofa. Half-asleep, I felt her small hand stroking my hair. A few minutes later, Griffin walked in with Greta. Seeing me, she gave me a hug.

"Easy," I said.

"Are you hurt? Want me to stick around?"

"I'm okay."

"Um, would it be all right if I met Fabian in the cafeteria?"

"You're asking our permission?"

"It's fine," my wife said. "Don't be too long."

"I won't. Come on, Greta." When the dog wouldn't budge, the girl rolled her eyes. "Hier!"

Pricking her ears, Greta obeyed. Griffin seemed happy, which made me feel better.

"Am I doing the right thing?" I said when we were alone.

"Shit, I don't know. What exactly did he say about me?"

"Never mind. But his meaning was clear. I feel like I'm letting everyone down—especially Jim. To think I was the one who wanted to get to the truth. But I can't lose you—or the baby."

"You won't."

Leaning back, I closed my eyes. My entire being was in turmoil. Holly laid her head on my chest.

"What do you do when you don't know what's right?" I said.

"You pray."

"It's been so long."

"Hang on."

She went into our bedroom. When she returned, she was holding her rosary. Sitting beside me, she showed me the little white crucifix.

"Time to bring out the big guns," she said.

THIRTY

Two yellow school buses pulled into the command center parking lot. Inside were the civilians from the Arkon building we'd rescued only weeks earlier. Warnick and Springer handled the paperwork. Holly, Griffin, and I lined up the arrivals for their medical exams. When Fabian showed up to assist, I nodded.

Nina Zimmer stepped off a bus with her daughter, Evan. She seemed happy and, when she saw us, hurried over to give us warm hugs.

"Welcome to civilization," I said.

"It's so great to see you guys. Hey, I love the uniforms."

"Evan!" My wife reached for the baby. "Can I hold her?"

"Here you go. My arms are tired."

"She's so cute," the girl said.

Seeing Holly with the baby made me realize I'd made the right decision. There was nothing more important than family. Wherever Evie and Jim were, I hoped they would understand.

"We've got a trailer for you and the baby," I said.

Nina took in her surroundings and walked between us. "This place looks great. I can't believe how clean it is."

My wife snuggled Evan. "And the showers are amazing."

The women laughed as we headed to an MMU. We waited while they tested Nina and her daughter. When the exams were done, I grabbed their few belongings and led everyone to the trailer. Holly insisted on carrying Evan, who gazed into her eyes and pulled her nose.

"What's life like on the other side of town?" I said.

"Not so good. We lost Ed Riley. Everyone else is doing fine, but a few have been sick. There's a woman—I forget her name. She has diabetes. And when her feet turned black, they rushed her to the hospital."

"Oh. And this little one?"

Nina smiled and reached for her baby. "Somehow, she's been managing through all this. And she's put on weight."

"Here we are," I said. "Home sweet home."

Nina gazed at her trailer, a smaller version of ours. I trotted ahead and held the door open. The interior looked comfy. In addition to the kitchen, there were two bedrooms. The second one contained a crib. She cried when she saw the pile of brand-new toys on the floor. My wife squeezed her shoulder and guided her to the living room sofa, where they sat.

"I can't thank you guys enough," Nina said. "For everything. Dave, if you hadn't shown up at Walmart..."

"All part of the service. Why don't you get some rest? There's food and fresh water in the fridge and baby formula and diapers in the cupboard."

As we exited, Nina embraced Holly and kissed my cheek. I felt good about what we'd done for the baby and her. It was a rare bright spot in a miasma of suffering. As we headed back, my wife fake-punched my arm.

"She's kinda sweet on you, bub."

"Don't start with me," I said.

After lunch, Warnick stopped by to give us our new assignments. We were scheduled to go into the neighborhoods, searching houses and clearing out draggers. If we found any survivors, we would bring them to the command center for testing.

"I wanna come with you guys," Griffin said.

Holly frowned. "No, sweetie. It's not allowed."

"But I'm good."

"Yeah, you are," I tried high-fiving her, but she wasn't having it. "Stay here and make sure the new arrivals have everything they need."

"Fine," she said.

If it had been up to me, I would have brought the girl along. She was an important member of the team, and I missed her company.

"You're coming with, right, Warnick?" my wife said.

"It'll be you two, Springer, and me."

"As per usual," I said.

"There are some areas we haven't gotten to yet. We're not sure what we're going to find. I'll warn you, though. It might be a little sketchy."

I side-eyed Holly. "Are you sure you're up for this?"

"Even pregnant, I'm way better than you."

Griffin giggled and pointed. "Burn!"

"Shut up," I said, though I knew my wife was right.

THIRTY-ONE

We drove across town to a neighborhood near the 5 freeway, wearing body armor and helmets. I hadn't been this close to the city limits in ages and didn't know what to expect. Barriers blocked the freeway exits and entrances. LMTVs were parked along the sides, and guards with AR-15s made sure no one got in or out. A Black Dragon helicopter did a low flyover, its occupants also armed.

Warnick stopped at a cul-de-sac entrance and parked the Humvee. We surveyed the street, looking for signs of life. A police cruiser appeared, and my stomach twisted into a knot. I sneaked a look at the driver, who was at the police station when they booked me. He didn't recognize me as he drove past.

"Are we doing a house-to-house or what?" I said.

My friend checked his weapon. "Affirmative. Looks like our guys came by here before."

"How can you tell?" Holly said.

Springer pointed his rifle at a stop sign. On it was a sticker with the familiar Black Dragon logo. I noticed those same stickers on several of the houses' front doors.

Warnick started walking away. "We can skip this street."

I joined Springer. "So, are these searches random?"

"They are. We mark them off as we go."

Thinking I saw something, I peered at a front window. "What if squatters move in after we've been here?"

"I suppose we could make a second pass," Warnick said. "But right now, too many other places on the grid need our attention."

We headed over one street. There was no sticker on the stop sign, so we walked in. Another sign read DEAD END.

I smirked at my wife. "Sounds about right."

She jabbed me in the ribs. "Where's that positive attitude, homie?"

We approached the first residence, a small ranch house with faded tan paint and a crabgrass lawn. A chain-link fence ran the length of the property. As we got closer, I thought I heard whimpering. Now, the sound of frantic barking. Behind the gate, a mixed-breed dog jumped and, pressing its paws against the fence, whined hopefully. The poor animal's ribs were visible, but he was alert and friendly.

"Hi, boy," Holly said, approaching the fence.

Warnick moved in ahead of her. "Step aside."

As she backed away, he pointed his weapon at the animal, who looked at us with trusting eyes.

"What are you doing?" she said.

"We have orders to eliminate all dogs."

Furious, she stepped in front of him. Rolling his eyes, he looked to me for support.

"You are not killing that animal. Look at him—he's harmless."

She crouched next to the fence to get a better look. With a pained expression, my friend lowered his weapon.

"You don't understand."

Springer groaned. "If another squad finds him, they will shoot him."

Scowling, my wife pivoted. "Does that mean you're going to shoot Greta too?"

"She doesn't have rabies. And besides, she's one of ours."

"Well, that's a relief. Why can't this dog be tested?"

"Because we don't have the resources." Warnick sighed. "Now move away from the fence, so I can do my job."

"What if he tests negative?" I said. "Who's going to care for him?"

Incredulous, she stared at the three haters. I felt like a dick for not taking her side, but my friend was right. There were probably hundreds of abandoned animals all over town. Springer laid his hand on her shoulder.

"Way it is, Holly. We can kill the animal now or wait for someone else to do it. Either way, he's dead."

"You guys are crazy," she said.

She stomped off to the next house. In another beat, I was standing on the porch with her. A gunshot echoed in the street. The dog yipped and howled till the second bullet silenced it.

My wife looked straight ahead. "Would you have done it?"

"I guess if they ordered me to. You?"

"I don't know. Helluva way to make a living."

I peered through the window. "Doesn't look like there's anyone inside."

"Guess we better go in," she said.

There was a profound sadness in her voice, but at least she'd pulled herself together. Even if we had saved the animal, it would end up in a shelter with all the other dogs and cats, only to be put down later. I didn't want to say we did it a favor, but we might have reduced its suffering a little.

Holly tried the front door—it was unlocked. Warnick and

Springer had crossed to the house opposite us and disappeared inside. I nodded to my wife, and we entered, our weapons up. It felt weird walking into someone else's home unannounced. The interior was dusty and unkempt, with worn furniture and peeling paint. It might have been a bank repo that no one had gotten around to renovating.

The house was quiet as we made our way cautiously from one section to the next. At the rear, we found a baby's room, freshly painted. A blond wood crib with the price tag still on it stood in a corner by the window. Next to it, a matching dresser and changing table. A used rocking chair sat in another corner. There was a *Sesame Street* mobile on the floor next to a toolbox. Near a pile of new, unopened toys lay a blood-spattered stuffed bear.

I wanted to say something to Holly but held her instead. After seeing that room, it seemed hard for her to enter the other houses, yet she soldiered on. Everything looked the same. Lives abandoned. The invisible ghosts of families watching helplessly as looters cleaned them out. Eventually, the thieves would be dead too. Or already were, their spirits having joined those of their victims.

We never did find anything on that godforsaken street.

THIRTY-TWO

At the start of the outbreak, Holly and I and a group of survivors had gone to Royal Ranch Market to stock up on supplies. As we pulled into the parking lot, I thought of Landry, Ben, and his son Aaron—all dead now. And I wondered what had become of the family who owned the store.

The boards we had put up over the windows to repair the damage from looters were still in place. Parking close, we headed to the front door, which was locked. I tried to see inside. The lights were off, and the place looked deserted.

A crash echoed, the sound like metal hitting concrete. Something moved through the shadows—an animal? Or maybe a person.

"It might be a raccoon," I said.

Warnick peered through the glass. "Or a survivor."

Springer pointed his index finger at the building like a gun and pretended to fire. "Or a dragger."

My wife walked to the side of the building. "Only one way to find out, gentlemen."

"Shouldn't we take a vote?" I said, hurrying after her.

Drawing our weapons, we made our way around to the rear to look for another way in. There was a small loading dock, which faced an alley. Beyond that lay a weed patch with trash scattered here and there. We walked the length of the whitewashed wall, passing blood spray several feet wide. No sign of any human remains. The only door was up a short flight of stairs.

"Springer, can you pick a lock?" my friend said.

"Maybe in my dreams."

A metal ladder bolted to the wall led to a gravel roof. One by one, we climbed up. Leaves and other debris were strewn everywhere. Missing patches of gravel exposed ripped, sunbaked tarpaper. But the view was good. I spotted a dragger pack off in the distance, wandering the streets. Another patrol would dispatch them. Springer found a galvanized hatch in the middle of the roof. The hasp was missing a lock. Warnick pulled open the hatch and looked down.

"Anything?" I said.

"Too dark."

He removed a small flashlight from his shirt pocket and directed the beam inside.

I sidled next to him, trying to see. "How far down is it, do you think? My leg's not a hundred percent."

Springer stretched his arms and cracked his neck. "I can get down there."

He removed his helmet and handed it to me. Giving us one of his wiseass Springer smiles, he climbed into the hole.

"Careful," Holly said.

We waited to make sure he would be okay. Peering down, he got his bearings and let himself drop, which was followed by a miserable groan.

"Are you okay?" my friend said.

"Fell on my ass."

"Gomer."

A beam of light appeared in the darkness—Springer's flashlight. When we were sure he was all right, we climbed off the roof and waited on the loading dock. Inside, there was a scuffling noise. On edge, we raised our weapons. A moment later, the door flew open, and Springer gave us an embarrassed grin.

"What happened?" Warnick said.

"I tripped."

It took us a few minutes to find the light panel. I expected to see nothing but rotting produce and dry goods. But when my friend hit the switch, I froze.

Seven or eight draggers stood before us, their weak eyes blinking at the lights. Their slavering mouths masticated the air, and their fingers extended, ready to grab us. Warnick moved into the lead position and shot two through the head. That was our cue. We spread out and put down the advancing dragger pack one by one. The last one lurched at Springer.

"Whoa!"

Before it could bite him, my friend shot it through the eye. Shuddering, it fell, twitching into stillness.

"I hate surprises," Warnick said.

I let out a relieved laugh. "Remind me never to throw you a birthday party."

We took a moment to catch our breath, then checked out the room. Boxes of paper supplies and cleaning products were stacked in neat rows. Along one wall, there was a massive freezer unit. A low hum told us it was working.

My friend signaled Springer. "Better check it out."

The guard trotted over and pulled on the large metal handle. The door swung open, and a burst of ice-cold air covered us in mist.

"Oh, no," my wife said as the fog cleared.

Sides of beef and pork hung from rows of hooks. In one section, there were shelves of ice cream and frozen dinners. A young man wearing a gray North Face jacket and gloves perched against a side wall. His hair, eyebrows, and eyelashes were dusted with frost, and his skin was blue gray. Crouching, Warnick examined him.

"He picked a bad place to hide." My friend felt his neck for a pulse. "I'm not getting anything. Dave, give me a hand."

"Maybe we're not too late," Holly said.

Warnick and I dragged the man out and laid him on his back. I joined the others as my friend continued checking for signs of life. Shaking his head, he looked up at us.

"We'll get someone from the hospital to pick him up. Let's check the rest of the store."

"Wait," I said. "What if he got bit?"

Impatient, Warnick laid down his weapon and drew closer. He unzipped the man's jacket and checked for blood. Removing both gloves, he examined the hands. Immediately, I noticed the torn skin and telltale teeth marks.

Suddenly, the eyes flew open. Scooting away, my friend reached for his weapon. The dragger blinked slowly and began mewling. Before I could react, a bullet tore through its head. I pivoted as my wife lowered her gun.

"I don't like surprises either," she said.

A shuffling noise got my attention. I ran to the swinging doors leading to the store's main floor and peered through a yellowed plastic window. Then, I turned to the others.

"We're not alone."

Splitting up, we made our way up and down the aisles, no longer visible to one another. I hurried past the produce section, gagging on the smell of decaying fruit and vegetables. Slivers of daylight bled through gaps in the boarded-up windows. Holly called from another part of the store.

"Over here!"

I found her in the meat section, pointing her weapon at a female dragger—a young Latina. It was on its knees in front of the display case, devouring the last of the expired meat. I moved next to my wife as Warnick and Springer joined us.

The creature turned, its mouth dripping with blood, and stared at us. The eyes were alive with an iridescent purple glow. It got to its feet and straightened its spine with excruciating effort. I waited for the inevitable death shriek, but it never came. And it made no move to attack us. My friend pointed his weapon as it raised its trembling hands in protest.

"Espera," it said.

PART THREE

CONSPIRACY THEORY

THIRTY-THREE

We were spellbound. Why didn't the dragger try to bite us like all the others? Instead, it stared, wavering and weak. Its eyes pleading, and its arms outstretched. *Wait*, it had said in Spanish.

Holly turned to me with glistening eyes. "I don't understand. Isn't she one of them?"

"We have to help her."

Warnick still hadn't lowered his weapon. "I don't know…"

"She isn't a dog," my wife said.

We backed off as the wretch inched forward. Like Dr. Royce, she swatted at imaginary flies. Then, collapsing, she wept. This was no dragger. At last, my friend put down his gun and turned to Springer.

"Go to the Humvee and bring whatever you can find to immobilize her."

"On it."

Moments later, the guard returned with a coil of nylon rope and handed it to Warnick. She snapped viciously as they approached her

"How do we keep her from biting us?" Springer said.

I looked around. Then, "Hang on."

Hurrying to the produce section, I found burlap sacks filled with potatoes. Quickly, I emptied one and brought it back. Warnick and Springer had already bound the woman's hands and feet as she struggled on the floor.

I handed Springer the sack, and he threw it over her head, which further enraged her. Mewling, she tried twisting free. Holly found a roll of duct tape, and we secured the bag loosely around her neck so she could breathe.

"We'll have to carry her," my friend said.

I moved towards her. "Let me try."

Warnick and Springer helped me get the woman to her feet. As I bent over, they draped the squirming body over my shoulders. Gripping her arms and legs, I headed into the storage area. My friend waited at the exit, holding the door open. The woman was small—around Holly's height—and didn't weigh much. But having to fight her as I made my way to the Humvee took its toll. By the time I reached our vehicle on the other side of the building, I was exhausted and in pain.

Springer cleared a space in the rear of the Humvee. He and Warnick helped me get the woman inside. As she continued to struggle, we closed the door and headed out. When we radioed the command center, someone instructed us to proceed to an unmarked warehouse off the main highway. Dr. Isaac Fallow would meet us there. None of us had any idea what to expect.

The fence-enclosed building was protected by Black Dragon guards. There were LMTVs and Humvees parked nearby. A guard shack stood behind the closed gate. I recalled this used to be a bicycle factory that had gone bust in the nineties.

Someone in the guard shack hit a button, and the gate

rolled sideways so we could continue through. Hospital orderlies were waiting with a gurney. We unloaded the patient, who they secured with leather straps. We followed everyone inside.

The interior was vast, with rows of plexiglass cells—many containing patients. The enclosures were big enough to accommodate a cot and a chemical toilet. Electric pumps at the end of each row vented fresh air into the units.

"What is this place?" Springer said.

The orderlies wheeled the woman down an end row to the rear of the facility. Following them, we passed other cells housing patients in various stages of the disease, although none seemed violent.

Stopping in front of a cell, the orderlies removed the woman from the gurney and placed her inside. One stepped out as the other cut the ropes binding her arms and legs. While he pulled the sack from her head, the first returned, holding a cattle prod.

Reacting to the bright lights, she turned away. When she lurched forward, the armed orderly zapped her once. Screeching, she pulled away and fell onto the cot. They waited till she stopped moving, then locked her in.

Isaac approached us from around the corner, accompanied by a man and woman in their thirties. All were dressed in medical lab coats. The guy was lean and around my height, with blond pompadour hair, dense eyebrows, and pale blue eyes. His partner was tiny—shorter than Holly—with shoulder-length straight blonde hair in a ponytail and those same eyes. Both wore an expression of intellectual disdain.

"Thanks, fellas," the doctor said to the orderlies. Then to us, "Good to see you again. This is Dr. Bud Vollmer and Dr. Nancy Vollmer."

"Are you two related?" my wife said.

On cue, they rolled their eyes. Isaac smiled at their reaction.

"They're fraternal twins."

"The Vollmer twins?" Springer said to me on the sly. "What are the odds?" Then on my nonreaction, "Dude, *Time Cop*?"

The doctor cleared his throat. "Bud and Nancy are immunologists. I brought them down from UCSF to try to make sense of all this. They were part of the team that developed the blood test. We hope what they learn here will help them create a vaccine."

"Any idea when that might be?" I said.

Bud observed the patient and wrote something on the chart. "You can't rush genius. But I'm sure you have nothing to worry about."

"What did you say to me?"

Holly grabbed my arm before I could teach this tool a lesson.

"I understand the patient spoke," Isaac said.

He watched as she explored her surroundings. The researchers looked at her with the same fixed gaze.

"One word that we could make out," Warnick said. "After that, it was a lot of gibberish. She's not exhibiting the same symptoms as the others we've seen. And there's something weird going on with her eyes."

I approached the enclosure to get a better look. "I don't think she got bit."

Nancy studied me with a sly smile, her arms folded. "Said the pretend doctor."

"What do you mean?" my wife said, ignoring her. "How else could this have happened?"

My friend looked at me, irritated at my spot diagnosis. "So you think she was deliberately infected?"

The twins seemed to enjoy this while Isaac remained serious.

"You said it yourself. Her symptoms are different. Remember the draggers we encountered in the forest before we were rescued?"

"Draggers?" Nancy said, nudging her brother.

"That's what we've been seeing since all this started. This woman is carrying another form of the virus."

"And how do you know this, Dr. Nick?" Bud said.

Though I appreciated *The Simpsons* reference, I wanted to pimp-slap this clown. The doctor got between us.

"There's an easy way to find out," he said. "We'll test her."

After Isaac left, Bud smirked at me, arrogant as hell. "You people need to do whatever it is you do and let the real scientists do their job."

I'd had enough. "And you should bite me."

"Oh, are we doing this?" he said, tossing the chart aside.

Warnick grabbed my arm. "We don't have time for this shit."

Springer helped pull me away and, looking past me, glared comically at Bud.

"Trust me, Sheldon," he said. "You don't wanna mess with this guy. He'll kick your bony ass into next week."

THIRTY-FOUR

Isaac returned with a needle and syringe, several vials, and the cattle prod. He handed the device to Bud and instructed the twins on how to proceed. On the doctor's signal, they opened the door and waited for him to enter.

Using the cattle prod, Bud immobilized the woman. Then he and Isaac held her down while Nancy searched for a vein. When she had drawn enough blood, they released the patient, and everyone got out.

I approached the doctor. "How long before we know?"

"A couple of hours. I suggest you return to your base. I'll stop by later with the results."

On our way out, a commotion erupted. A patient in a nearby cell thrashed violently, exhibiting the classic symptoms. Despite what the Vollmer twins thought of me, I knew the score—this guy had turned. Then, he let out a chilling death shriek.

Immediately, a series of bright blue lights flashed sequentially along the top of the cell. An orderly appeared, followed by two Black Dragon guards, one carrying a cattle prod. The other held a futuristic ray gun that reminded me of an old 1950s sci-fi movie.

"Whadda ya think, Doc?" a guard said.

Isaac took a moment to assess the patient. After conferring with his colleagues, he lowered his head. The guard with the cattle prod flicked a finger at the orderly, who unlocked the cell door. Mercilessly, the guard zapped the man, attacking different parts of his body. Though the repeated assaults enraged him, the electric shocks had the desired effect.

Weaving, he evacuated his bowels and collapsed on the cot. The second guard rushed in and pressed the ray gun against the dazed victim's forehead. Then he squeezed the trigger. A scorching, high-pitched whine assaulted my ears, and the man stopped moving. Nancy handed her brother a medical kit. After recording the patient's temperature, he took blood and spinal fluid samples as orderlies moved in to dispose of the body.

"What did they do to him?" Holly said, covering her nose.

Bud stepped out of the cell, ignoring the other patients' horrified stares. "Pulsed Neurofrequency Device, courtesy of Clayborn Electronics."

His sister followed him. Was she *smiling*? "Kills the subject by inducing catastrophic instability in the brain's neural circuits."

"So, a brain blaster," Springer said, his eyes huge. "Remind me never to stay in this hotel."

Outside, we shook hands with the doctor while avoiding his weirdo friends. I wondered how often they had used the ray gun. From the look on his face, the situation had taken its toll.

"How many patients are in there?" Warnick said.

Isaac sighed. "Over three hundred, and we're taking in more every day."

At the command center, the four of us sat in the conference room, waiting for Pederman to say something. Finding a dragger that didn't behave like the others was big news, not to be shared with just anyone.

"Doesn't make any sense," he said. "A dragger who can talk? I need to report this. Warnick?"

"You might want to wait until the results come back. We should have all the facts."

Springer spun his phone on the table. "We don't trust the mayor. There, I said it."

My friend side-eyed him. "Dr. Fallow is performing tests on the woman now. We should at least—"

A knock at the door interrupted him. It was Erzen. Sticking her head in, she addressed the supervisor.

"A patrol found another family holed up at the Pine Nut Motel at the edge of town."

"What kind of shape are they in?"

"No one got bit, as far as we can tell. We brought them in a little while ago. They're being processed now."

"Thanks, Erzen," Pederman said. "Keep me posted." Then to Warnick, "Okay, you've got twenty-four hours. After that, we're out of compliance."

Holly stopped the supervisor on his way out. "Can I ask you something unrelated? I wanted to see about assigning Griffin to our squad."

"Not possible."

"But she's battle-tested. Ask Warnick and Springer."

"She's awesome in combat," my friend said. "And she knows how to handle a gun."

"Federal law prohibits anyone under eighteen from carrying a weapon."

Erzen overheard us and stepped into the room. "Actually, there is no federal law stating a minimum age for long guns. And there are exceptions for handguns." Could that be true?

"Where did you come across this information?" Pederman said.

"As you know, I've been looking after the girl. I took the liberty of doing some research in the library."

She pulled a folded-up piece of paper from her shirt pocket and read from it. *"Federal law provides exceptions for the temporary transfer and possession of handguns and handgun ammunition for specified activities, including employ- ment, ranching, farming, target practice, and hunting."*

The supervisor read the words and laughed. "I'll be damned."

"I don't know about ranching," Springer said, scratching his ear.

Warnick gave us one of his rare smiles. "I think we could argue for target practice and hunting draggers. And if you brought her on as an intern, there's your employment requirement."

In solidarity, my wife moved next to Erzen. "Seriously, we need her on our team."

"I would have to agree," the guard said. "She's very mature for her age."

Pederman rubbed his eyes and reread the paper. "You guys are killing me. But...it makes sense. I'll start by fast- tracking her employment and signing her up for target prac- tice. If—*if*—she passes our test, I'll issue her a weapon."

Outside on the steps, Holly gave Erzen a hug. "This means a lot to us. Thank you."

"My pleasure."

"Erzen, I'm curious," I said. "Why did you do it?"

"Griffin shows a lot of promise. She reminds me of myself at that age. And besides, I think a young woman should be able to protect herself. Don't you?"

"I can't wait to tell her," Holly said.

THIRTY-FIVE

Fabian found Holly, Griffin, and me in the cafeteria eating a late lunch of meatloaf that looked as if it had come from an episode of *The Lazy Man's Lunch*. For days, the girl had moped around the campus. Now, she was bubbly.

"Did you hear the news?" she said.

"I did. Congrats, güera." Then to my wife and me, "Dr. Fallow is here. They're waiting for you in the conference room."

The kid left before I could question him. On the way out, I touched Griffin's arm.

"What did he call you?"

She blushed. *"Güera."*

Holly looked suspicious. "What does it mean?"

"White girl. But he's not making fun of me."

I might have rolled my eyes. "Right."

"He has a cousin who's blonde, and the family always calls her that."

"Whatever you say. Güera."

"You're such a jerk," she said, laughing.

When we entered the conference room, we found Isaac chatting with Pederman and Warnick. Thankfully, he hadn't brought the Vollmer twins.

"I'm afraid I can't explain these results," the doctor said. "We found evidence of the virus. But it's like you said, Dave. It appears there are marked differences in the morphology. The number and arrangement of the capsomeres, for instance."

"I hope you're going to explain this in layman's terms," the supervisor said good-naturedly.

"Viruses fall into classifications based on their structure or *morphology*. By looking closely at how they're constructed, we can tell if they're different, even within the same family."

"And this one is different?" my wife said.

"It has many characteristics of the other virus, but it's unique. And here's something else. From what I've observed in the patient, this strain doesn't appear to affect the speech area of the brain. Which leads me to believe she may be capable of rational thought."

"That sounds like Dr. Royce," Warnick said to me. Then to Isaac, "We went to Robbin-Sear to investigate Evie's murder. The scientists showed us their colleague, who was infected."

"They gave him a new form of the virus," I said. "He continues to work, but not very well."

"Interesting." The doctor thrummed his fingers on the table. "Is he violent?"

"He has this weird tic. He swats at flies that aren't there. The girl was doing the same thing when we found her."

"Yes, I've noticed that." Isaac turned to Pederman. "Dave suggested that she was given the virus. If that's true, then we have a different problem on our hands."

Everyone waited for me to say something. Though I had

no data to back me up, I knew I was right. The Latina we found wandering in that market was a test subject.

"They must've done it sometime after Dr. Royce was treated."

"Dave," my friend said. "I know where you're going with this, but I think you're wrong."

"Not about this."

"It can't be. They could never get away with it."

"Warnick, where have you been? They are getting away with it."

"Will someone tell me what in hell you two are talking about?" the supervisor said.

Judging by the doctor's expression, he had come to the same conclusion as me.

"Robbin-Sear is conducting human trials," I said.

The room erupted, with everyone talking at once. It was as if I'd thrown a live grenade into the middle of the conversation.

"You can't be serious," Pederman said. "Why was that woman in the store? Wouldn't they want to keep her under observation?"

"I don't know."

"Tres Marias as a giant test lab? I can't accept that."

"Mr. Pederman, history is full of examples. Evie told us about the Rockefeller Report. For years, the DOD experimented on military personnel."

"Sure, but they weren't civilians."

"Okay, how about this? And I can thank my old high school science teacher. Tuskegee."

Holly and Warnick blanched. Isaac lowered his eyes. The supervisor wrung his hands, and when he finally spoke, his voice was almost a whisper.

"But that was— It was a long time ago."

"I don't understand," Griffin said. "What's Tuskegee?"

The doctor glanced at Pederman before answering. "In 1932 in Alabama, the Tuskegee Institute conducted an experiment to study the effects of untreated syphilis in men. The program was run by the US Public Health Service."

"They used black sharecroppers," the supervisor said. "No informed consent. The program ran for forty years."

"But they eventually cured them, right? Once they had a drug?"

I gave the girl a sad smile. "They did not. And by 1940, everyone knew that penicillin would have cured those men."

"Oh. Shit."

My friend gave me an accusing look. "So, who's behind this?"

"I think you know."

Pederman leaned forward, his hands flat on the table. "The mayor?"

"Why not? He warned me to stay out of his business."

"Sure, but—"

"Let me ask you something," I said. "When the outbreak happened, why wasn't a state of emergency declared and the National Guard called in? Wouldn't that be the normal procedure? Who ever heard of bringing in a private security company?"

"I'll admit, I've wondered that myself."

"The more I think about it, the more I'm convinced there's a conspiracy behind the outbreak."

"And Black Dragon is part of it?" the supervisor said.

"I don't know—maybe."

"What does that mean?" my wife said.

I regretted opening this can of worms because it meant I was starting to give a shit again. "I don't have the answers.

But it seems suspicious that this entire operation is being run without outside oversight."

"What about the mayor?" Pederman said.

"What about him? A reporter is dead after he interrogated her."

"Sounds to me like you want to be part of our inquiry."

"I..."

Holly squeezed my hand. "I'll be right there with you."

"Me too," Warnick said.

I ignored everyone else and focused on my wife. This was about her and me, and Griffin and the baby.

"What about the mayor's warning? Aren't you scared of what they might do to us?"

She gave me a smile. "It can't be any worse than what we've been through."

I looked at Warnick. He was the reason all of us were alive. If anything happened to me, I had no doubt he would protect my family from the mayor, even if it meant risking his own life.

"I can't believe I'm saying this," I said. "I'm in." Then to the supervisor, "But I have to ask. How much do you know about Black Dragon? The company, I mean."

"We used to be privately held. In 2011, we were acquired by Baseborn Identity Research."

The name didn't ring a bell. "I wish we could get on the internet. What happened to the communications?"

"I can answer that. Everything's blocked."

"What?" my friend said. "Why?"

"It's part of the quarantine protocol. The news media has been trying for weeks to get in here. A total blackout is in place."

"Who gave the order?"

Pederman looked around the room. "The mayor," he said.

.   .   .

Outside, I walked Isaac to his car. Everyone else had taken off. Distracted, I wondered what the mayor might do if he knew what we were planning.

"Have you got a minute?" he said.

"What is it?"

"I'm not sure who to tell. Can you stop by the isolation facility tomorrow?"

"I think we're scheduled to patrol the neighborhoods. Maybe we could take a detour. I'll ask Warnick."

He seemed skeptical. "Can he be trusted?"

"I trust him with my life."

"That's good enough for me. I'll see you in the morning. Oh, and this is on a need-to-know basis. Capisce?"

"Understood," I said.

He drove off without looking back. I felt the heavy, cloying weight of lies bearing down on me and wondered if I'd made the right decision. Warnick trotted down the administration building steps and clapped me on the shoulder.

"I realize that was a tough decision for you," he said.

I decided not to tell him yet about the doctor's request. "Thanks. Hey, if anything were to happen to me, you'd—"

"You should know by now, I've got your back. Ready to go out there?"

I gazed around the campus. It seemed like such an idyllic place, with children playing and guards keeping everyone safe. But I couldn't shake the feeling that something horrible awaited us beyond the fence.

"Yeah," I said. "Ready for whatever."

THIRTY-SIX

Somehow, I'd convinced Warnick to go along with Isaac's plan. Now we were on our way to the isolation facility. Though his instinct was to tell Pederman everything, I begged him to wait.

"He's the supervisor and has a right to know," he said.

"Dr. Fallow insisted. Besides, Pederman authorized this investigation. Look, we're gathering more facts. Once we know everything, we can make our report."

"I don't like it."

"How about a little faith?"

The look he gave me put an end to the conversation. Springer had been assigned to another detail, so I rode shotgun while Holly sat behind me. As our Humvee approached the isolation facility, the guard opened the gate.

We entered through the front doors unescorted and headed across the expanse of smooth concrete, passing depressed-looking patients. Their sad eyes followed us. It might have been my imagination, but there seemed to be fewer than last time. The doctor met us halfway and acknowledged my friend with a nod.

"We're not sure how to explain this," Isaac said. "You three will have to judge for yourselves."

He led us to the cell that held the Latina we had rescued from the Royal Ranch Market. The Vollmer twins were already there. They weren't happy to see us.

"Here to dispense more medical wisdom?" Bud said, smirking.

This asshole was asking for it. Before I could respond, the doctor raised a warning hand.

"Knock it off, Bud. These people are conducting an investigation. And you're to extend them every courtesy."

"Sure thing, Dr. Fallow."

The twin stepped aside so we could get a better look. I expected to find the patient in the state I was familiar with—animal-eyed and lusting after human flesh. But when I saw her, I stopped cold.

She sat quietly in a plastic chair, wearing a thin white cotton patient gown printed with a field of lilacs. Freshly bathed, her damp hair was tied back, revealing a lovely face. As she sipped liquid through a flexible straw, I realized my wife and I had met her before at the Royal Ranch Market, where she'd worked as a checker. Holly moved closer and gave her an encouraging smile.

"I don't understand," she said. "Isn't she infected?"

Isaac joined her. "She is—the blood tests confirm it."

"She's carrying the virus," Bud said. "But her symptoms seem to have subsided."

I approached the cell to get a better look at her arms and legs. "I guess she didn't get bit after all."

As I turned to face the twins, they stared at their shoes. Meekly, Nancy nodded. I wasn't about to give up my moment of glory and cupped my hand around my ear.

"What? I didn't get that."

Tensing, the chastened researcher cleared her throat and said, "No, she wasn't."

My wife rolled her eyes at me. "Okay, we're all very impressed, Dr. Nick."

"Do you think we could talk to her?" Warnick said.

The researchers exchanged a look, then Nancy answered for them. "She's coherent, but I don't think she speaks much English."

"And we're not sure how stable she is," Bud said, his ears bright red.

A couple hundred thousand in school loans—my ears would be red too. I glanced at a chart sitting in a clear acrylic holder mounted on the cell. A white plastic label ran along the top. Printed on it was a bar code, followed by a name—ARIEL.

"Is that her name?"

"We don't know," the doctor said. "I thought it would be better to refer to her as a person."

My friend squinted at the label. "Lion of God."

"Someone knows his Scripture."

"How long has she been like this?" Holly said.

Isaac grabbed the chart and flipped through it. "Since last night. She was already responding to treatment yesterday afternoon, which is why I asked you to come. We've got her on antibiotics. Her recovery is nothing short of miraculous."

"Wait," I said. "Are you telling me this generation of the virus can be treated with medication?"

Bud scowled. "That's not what we're saying at all. There is no cure. We're using antibiotics to treat any secondary infections."

The doctor gave the woman a fatherly smile. "We don't yet know how the virus works, but it seems to have gone into remission."

Nancy took the chart from Isaac and scanned it. Though she was the size of a Barbie doll, she spoke with authority.

"We plan to try a modified vaccination series using HRIG—human rabies immunoglobulin."

A noise from inside the cell got our attention. Ariel's cup lay on the floor, the thick yellowish liquid pooling near her foot. She seemed agitated, muttering in Spanish and swatting at flies.

The doctor pressed his hand to the plexiglass as if to calm her. "She still has these episodes. Eight or ten a day. But they pass quickly."

"When we found her, she was eating raw meat," Warnick said. Then to Nancy, "What are you feeding her now?"

"A high protein liquid supplement."

Bud pointed at the IV. "Also, she's getting the standard electrolyte therapy. Chloride, gluconate, magnesium, phosphate, and potassium."

Isaac signaled a passing orderly, who came over immediately. "Our number one priority is keeping her stable. It's all we can do at this point."

The woman shielded her eyes from the lights as the orderly cleaned up the spill. After he left, she mewled and stared through us like we weren't even there.

"This isn't over for her," I said.

THIRTY-SEVEN

The coffee tasted like ass water. I pushed aside the cup and took a seat with the others.

"What's the story with the other patients?" I said.

Isaac side-eyed his colleagues. "They're not improving. Keep in mind the virus they carry is different from Ariel's. The morphology is much closer to what we first encountered during the summer."

"And you've got them on the same treatment program?"

"Yes, but the results are negligible."

I needed more. "Then how is this new virus different?"

Balling his fists, Bud glared at me. "We don't know yet."

"We're all on the same side," Warnick said. Then to the doctor, "How many have you lost?"

Hesitating, he exchanged another pained look with the Vollmer twins. No one wanted to answer the question.

"More than sixty percent."

"Dear Lord," Holly said.

Forgetting myself, I took a swig of coffee and made a face.

"Isaac, when you examined Ariel, did you find any needle marks?"

"We did. There was bruising on her upper left arm and numerous puncture wounds. It appears she was repeatedly injected."

"Any timeframe on that?" my friend said.

Bud shook his head. "Hard to say. The virus continues to mutate. And without a detailed medical history, there's no baseline."

"We've charted her progress since she got here," his sister said. "Taking blood every eight hours."

"What do the results tell you?" I said.

"I think it's better if we show you."

She retrieved a laptop from the credenza and connected it to a ceiling-mounted projector. While we waited for the image to appear on the white wall, I flicked off the lights.

"I built a computer model showing how Ariel's virus is evolving," the researcher said.

An animation showed a graph on a dark background. A cluster of spiky little balls appeared in the lower left-hand corner. Quickly, they began multiplying and traveled across the chart, growing in size. I expected the virus to fill the screen, but it leveled off.

"Based on our research, we know the virus travels up the spinal cord to the brain, where it remains. As the infection spreads, all brain activity falls under its control. As you know, in earlier strains, this condition created what you refer to as *undead*."

Bud interjected. "In Ariel's case, the virus has taken over as expected. And it allows her to function within a limited range."

"But there are glitches," I said.

"Yes. Those incidents when she appears to be swatting at flies and so forth."

"It's almost like the virus is trying to hide."

"That's exactly what it's doing," the doctor said.

Warnick switched on the lights. Isaac looked old, like the years had caught up with him in a cruel procession of dangerous living.

I turned to my friend. "We need to interview her."

"Maybe we can find someone who speaks Spanish. But that would mean bringing them into the situation."

"We have to risk it. Who can we trust?"

My wife tugged at my sleeve. "What about Fabian?"

"What? He's a kid."

"Who speaks fluent Spanish. And I'm sure we can trust him."

"Who's Fabian?" the doctor said.

Warnick cleared his throat. "A Black Dragon intern. He's a good guy. And Holly's right—we can trust him."

I narrowed my eyes at him. "I can't believe you like this idea."

"Who do you suggest?"

"I suppose this is your little woman talking."

"I defer to Holly's."

Flattered, my wife arched her eyebrows at me. I was pretty sure my lack of enthusiasm came across loud and clear. Still, what choice did we have?

"Fabian it is then," I said.

It's not like I hated the kid. I just didn't want to give him another reason to get close to us. Maybe I was too protective of my family. But it was how we'd survived all this time. Why did I have to flunk high school Spanish?

The aroma of Mexican food filled the air as Holly and I approached our trailer. I hadn't eaten, and my stomach growled obscenely.

"Hello?" my wife said.

Greta saw us and trotted over, wagging her tail. Fabian and Griffin sat at the dinette, finishing their lunch. When the girl belched, her friend laughed, and she punched his arm.

Holly patted the dog's head and walked over. "That smells so good."

"Griffin was tired of the cafeteria food," Fabian said.

My wife stood next to them and took a whiff. "Are those chicken enchiladas?"

"It's his mom's recipe," the girl said, wiping her mouth with a napkin.

The Latino showed Holly the foil pan sitting on the kitchen counter. There were a half-dozen more enchiladas and containers of rice and beans.

"They let me use the cafeteria kitchen. Have some—there's plenty."

"You don't have to tell me twice," my wife said and loaded up a plate. "Dave, come on."

I grabbed a soda from the refrigerator. "Not really hungry."

Though the conversation was pleasant, I brooded. I remembered what Holly had said about me being jealous. The truth was we needed this kid's help.

"How's the target practice going?" I said to Griffin.

Erzen had arranged for the interns to train together. I didn't like it, but it was the only way we could legitimately get the girl back in the squad. She ran to her bed and brought me a silhouette shooting target. Nearly all the shots were centered in the head.

"Wow, these are kill shots."

"She's better than me," Fabian said.

When they'd finished eating, he began clearing everything away.

"Leave it," I said. "We need to talk."

"Am I in trouble?"

I gave him a smile. "Look, I know what you think. But I don't dislike you." Then to Griffin, "Can you take Greta for a walk?"

"Seriously? You're making me leave right now?"

"This is Black Dragon business."

"Fabian's my friend. We don't keep secrets."

"Oh, boy."

"Griffin is family," my wife said. "And she's an intern now." Then to the girl, "You can stay."

We explained the situation, emphasizing that they couldn't breathe a word to anyone. I wondered what kind of a person the kid was—whether he valued his job over friendship. That worry evaporated in an instant, making me admire him in spite of myself.

"What do you need me to do?" he said.

THIRTY-EIGHT

In the late afternoon, we returned to the isolation facility with Griffin and Fabian. Getting permission to bring them along had been easier than I thought. We told Pederman the patient only spoke Spanish, and Dr. Fallow requested our assistance. When the supervisor asked why the girl needed to be there, we assured him this was a milk run and that the experience would do her good.

The teenagers were nervous standing outside the facility with Holly, Warnick, and me.

"The patients are infected," my wife said. "But they're people like you and me."

My friend gave them handguns and holsters. "They're contagious, so watch yourselves."

Griffin stared at her shoes. "Maybe I should wait out here."

"Don't be like that, güera," her friend said. "Show 'em what you got."

The Vollmer twins led us to an examination room with dimmed lights. Ariel lay on a stainless steel table, wearing wrist and ankle restraints. An IV ran into one arm, and light from the patient monitors shone on her anxious face.

"What's that on her wrist?" Holly said.

Nancy pointed. "Heart rate monitor. Connects wirelessly to that screen over there."

Isaac hovered over his patient and, checking her pupils with a medical penlight, side-eyed me. "Decided to bring the whole family?"

Clearing my throat, I gave him a sheepish smile.

"We've given her a mild sedative," he said. Then to the Latino, "Are you our translator?"

"Yes, sir. Fabian Lopez."

"Warnick will tell you what to ask her. It's imperative you translate everything she says word for word. Is that clear?"

The doctor switched on a voice recorder and nodded to the researchers, who stood ready with pads and pens. When the Latino caught Ariel's expression, he swallowed and touched her hand.

"Me llamo Fabian Lopez," he said. "Quiero hacerle algunas preguntas. ¿Me entiendes?"

"Sí. Ya estoy lista."

"Gracias." Then to my friend, "She'll answer your questions."

The interview took twenty minutes, and the Latino dutifully reported the woman's responses. There were disturbing gaps in her memory, especially regarding her name and where she was from. Her story unfolded in a patchwork of harrowing recollections. Conjuring my high school Spanish, I did my best to follow along.

Ariel had been hiding in an apartment building not far from the market. There was food, electricity, and running water. She couldn't remember how long she'd been alone—everyone else had fled.

One night, a van pulled into the parking lot. Three men entered the building and searched it. Two were police officers. When Warnick pressed her, she said they were wearing uniforms. As they searched floor by floor, she hid in the laundry room.

A cop discovered her and dragged her out. Outside, they tied her up and threw her into the van. When they opened the doors again, she was in the forest. Though most details were sketchy, she remembered the electrified fence. They took her inside and put her in a cell similar to the ones at the isolation facility.

Ariel vaguely recalled experiments. Over several days, a man in a white coat strapped her to a table and injected her with something that made her sick. Each time, he waited for her to react. Several times, she vomited.

"Sangre negra," she said. *Black blood.*

Fading in and out of consciousness, she had no idea how long she was in that place. Every day, her interrogator asked her the same questions in Spanish—her name, where she lived, and the names of her friends and relatives. At first, she answered correctly. But as time went on, she could no longer remember. Soon, she forgot her own name.

My friend asked her to describe the man. She said he was the same person who had invaded the apartment building and called him *asustadizo*—skittish. Also, he wore glasses with black frames and smelled bad.

"Bob Creasy," I said.

Ariel didn't know how she ended up at the market. All she could remember was waking up inside. When she opened her eyes, she was surrounded by draggers, which she called *los no muertos.* Though they left her alone, she tried escaping, but she was too weak.

The young man we found in the freezer was a cart pusher

named Luis and had gotten bit earlier. She tried looking after him, but it was too late. Just before he turned, she locked him in the freezer. That was the last thing she remembered till we showed up.

Thanking Fabian, Isaac took the twins aside. "This is not how you run a controlled experiment. Why did they release her? Bud?"

"Nancy and I discussed this earlier. Their methods are sloppy and random."

His sister glanced at the patient and shook her head. "Maybe they're tracking her."

The doctor took out his penlight and rechecked Ariel's pupils. "Hey, look at this."

The medical team watched the patient's face. When I inched closer to see, something made my blood freeze. Her eyes alternated between brown and glowing purple. With each cycle, her expression changed from a young, timid woman to something reptilian. Bud checked the heart rate monitor, which beeped frantically.

"Her pulse is over one-eighty and climbing."

"What's happening?" Griffin said, terrified.

As Isaac leaned in to get a better look, Ariel's head snapped up, and she let out a menacing hiss. Panicked, I pulled him away. An ominous stretching noise was followed by a pop as a wrist restraint tore open. Warnick grabbed the interns and pushed them out of the room. When he returned, he was gripping his weapon.

The Latina flailed violently on the table, mewling and snapping. Isaac and the researchers were frozen with fear. Grabbing our guns, Holly and I moved to the wall.

"Is there anything you can do?" my friend said.

When the medical team didn't respond, he ordered them to get out. Now, only the guards were left. We aimed our weapons at Ariel, none wanting to pull the trigger. Then the other wrist restraint broke.

Encouraged, she tore viciously at her ankle straps. With a grunt, she burst her bonds and stood on the examination table. Sizing us up, her predator gaze landed on my wife. I squeezed the trigger.

The round caught her in the chest. Ignoring her wound, she leaped off and bolted to the exit. We kept shooting, but the bullets didn't stop her. So I went after her.

Before I could reach the hallway, a gunshot rang out. A bullet had torn through Ariel's forehead, spraying blood and brain everywhere. In her final moments, her eyes turned brown again.

"Dios," she said and fell dead.

Griffin lowered her weapon. Her friend stood beside her, his lips moving but not saying anything. As the others joined us, Holly took the girl's hand and held her close.

Gazing at the body, I wanted to scream my rage. That poor, innocent girl didn't deserve this. Like all the others, she'd gotten caught up in some ruthless program with an agenda no one understood.

"We have to tell Pederman," Warnick said.

THIRTY-NINE

Seeing Ariel alive only hours earlier had given me hope there might be a way out of the crisis. But her death showed us that hope was an illusion. Like all the others, she had turned. We tried reaching Pederman by radio, but he was unavailable. So we arranged to transport the body to the hospital morgue, where Isaac would perform the autopsy.

On the way to the command center, Griffin insisted she did what she had to. No one disagreed. Considering the circumstances, she was holding up well. Fabian, not so much. He was a sensitive kid who had no business on the front lines. And in more dangerous circumstances, he might be a liability.

After dropping off the interns, Holly, Warnick, and I joined the doctor in the autopsy room. He photographed and X-rayed the corpse, took vitreous fluid from the eyes, and drew blood. Then he used a reciprocating saw to open the skull and examine the brain.

He worked quietly, only speaking to record his observations. It amazed me how a family physician who'd brought countless babies into the world—including me—could so ruthlessly cut into a cadaver and marvel at its dark secrets.

Though my wife was squeamish, she kept her feelings under control. Taking her hand, I reminded her of the new life she carried inside her. She seemed grateful for the support and made herself watch, like she owed it to Ariel.

There's something otherworldly about an autopsy. Watching organs being weighed and examined—the same pieces inside you—brings on an overwhelming sense of loss. It's as if you, the observer, are reduced to nothingness. And though there was no life in this corpse, there could be at the whim of a lethal virus nobody understood, least of all its unhinged creators.

I'd seen draggers in various states of decay, missing limbs —even half their faces. And yet they walked, hell-bent on only one thing—feeding. What kept this girl from getting up and leaving the room?

Finally, Isaac laid down his bloody scalpel and removed his gloves. Something about Ariel had surprised him—I could see it in his eyes.

"What is it, Doc?" my friend said.

"This patient was human when she died."

I remembered what Nancy had said at the isolation facility. *Maybe they're tracking her.*

"Could Robbin-Sear have planted a device in her?" I said.

His eyes widening with recognition, he examined the hands and feet. He turned her head from side to side, then peered behind her ear.

"I see a small scar."

Grabbing a scalpel, he made an incision and used forceps to remove something. We gathered around as he held it up to the light. It was capsule shaped—about an inch long—made of clear glass and filled with electronics. I noticed a lighted magnifier on a tray and held it over the device. Next to a serial number were printed the words CLAYBORN ELEC-TRONICS. Shit—the same people who'd invented that sci-fi stun gun.

"Nancy was right," Holly said.

Isaac sat behind the desk in his office, warming his hands around a mug of coffee. We waited for him to say something.

"From my experience, everyone who carries the virus eventually turns. But not Ariel. Maybe if we'd let her live…"

"You saw what happened," Warnick said. "Now what?"

"The Vollmer twins aren't making much progress. Not their fault. It's a difficult problem, and they don't have access to the data." The doctor leaned back and rubbed his tired eyes. "I think it makes sense to contact Robbin-Sear to see if they'll share their research."

"The mayor won't like that," I said.

"He doesn't have a choice. We need a vaccine."

Though my friend gave assurances he could arrange everything, I was skeptical. The mayor was dangerous. Once he got wind of our plan, he would shut us down like an unwanted marriage proposal. As we headed for the door, Holly became faint and almost fell. I caught her and eased her into a chair.

"Autopsy get to you?" I said. "Or is it the baby?"

Concerned, Isaac came over. "She's pregnant?"

"Several weeks along. I meant to tell you."

He took my wife's hand. "I assume you're not under a doctor's care. I'll examine you myself, young lady."

Knowing that he would look after my pregnant wife comforted me, but I couldn't shake the dread over what his hands had touched only minutes earlier.

. . .

Warnick and I waited in Isaac's office. I was tense, imagining horrible scenarios involving Holly and our child. Meanwhile, my friend tried radioing Pederman again but couldn't reach him. Eventually, Warnick tracked down Erzen. A little while later, the doctor returned with my wife, who was smiling.

"Everything's A-OK," he said and gave me a wink.

"What about the fainting?"

"Nothing to worry about. Her heart is pumping more blood now, and her blood pressure's going down. That can of course cause lightheadedness. Eventually, her body will stabilize. I prescribed some vitamins. You can pick them up from the hospital pharmacy."

The relief I felt was overwhelming. "Thanks, Isaac. With everything going on…"

"No need to explain." Then to Holly, "I want to see you again in four weeks."

My eyes misting, I took her hand. "You scared me."

She touched my cheek. "I'm fine."

A rapping on the doorframe got our attention. It was the supervisor.

"Am I interrupting?"

"Perfect timing," the doctor said.

We spent the next few minutes updating Pederman on the incident at the isolation facility. Instead of congratulating us on a job well done, he gave us a butt-reaming.

"When I gave you guys the go-ahead to investigate, I didn't mean keeping me out of the loop."

Isaac interrupted him. "It's my fault, Kelly."

The supervisor ignored him and glared at my friend. "What if Griffin or Fabian had been injured? We're supposed to work as a team."

"It won't happen again," Warnick said, taking it in stride.

His anger spent, Pederman exhaled. "There's something I need you to look into. A number of our people have gone missing the past few days."

"How many?"

"So far, twenty I can't account for."

"Do you think the draggers got them?" I said.

"Possibly."

My friend got to his feet. "I'm on it. Send me their photo IDs."

"Roger. Start with the checkpoints. And be careful—we're having problems there."

"What kind of problems?" the doctor said.

The supervisor closed the door. "Outsiders have been attempting to get in to see their friends and loved ones. The situation is becoming critical."

Warnick side-eyed my wife and me. "Do you need all of us out there?"

"I do. But the mayor is concerned about our ability to control the situation. He reached out to me directly. I advised him to let us do our job."

"Does this mean he's getting off my case?" I said.

"You're part of a murder investigation, remember? He's trying to make this town safe."

"Is that why he ordered O'Brien to beat me up?"

"I called the mayor on that. He promised to rein in the police captain. I think we need to put that behind us for the good of the town."

I felt my lip where Hizzoner had belted me. "Hey, I'm all about turning the page."

Holly's expression said it all. I was lying my ass off.

FORTY

Warnick filled Pederman in on Isaac's suggestion to collaborate with Robbin-Sear. Surprisingly, the supervisor seemed open to it.

"And how would that work?" he said to the doctor.

"The immunologists are more or less stuck. I thought if we combined forces..."

"That's what I was thinking." Then to us, "I want you guys to get over there asap. I'll make a call so they can be ready when you arrive."

"What about the mayor?" I said.

"I'll take full responsibility." Pederman smiled. "Why the worried look, Dave? I thought this was what you wanted."

He was right, but there was no way I would let my wife be a part of it. "Fine, but I'd like Holly to stay behind on this one."

She gripped the arms of her chair, her mouth open. "There is nothing wrong with me. Tell him, Isaac."

I admired her sense of commitment. But I was afraid for her too. When I turned to the doctor, I saw some fatherly advice headed my way.

"She's in her first trimester. And she's probably in better shape than you."

"I don't care—I don't like it."

"Too bad." To underscore the point, she stuck her tongue out at me.

"Real mature," I said.

The supervisor's radio crackled. Giving us an apologetic look, he stepped outside. When he returned, his mouth was a thin, hard line.

"There's a group of armed civilians trying to breach the checkpoint. We're expecting casualties. Doc, you might want to alert the hospital staff."

"What about Robbin-Sear?"

"Right now, this is priority one," Pederman said.

At the command center, we loaded up on weapons and ammo. When we reached the flash point—a freeway exit on the edge of town—we found ourselves in the middle of a standoff.

A hundred heavily armed civilians waved their weapons at us. Behind them, burning tires created a pall of toxic black smoke. Black Dragon helicopters, equipped with Browning M2 .50-caliber machine guns, hovered overhead. Inside, the gunners awaited their orders as they trained their weapons on the intruders.

A voice over a helicopter's PA system ordered them to lay down their weapons. No one paid attention. Instead, they pushed against the concrete barriers, screaming obscenities. Someone hurled a Molotov cocktail at a guard, striking his shield. Overreacting, he shot the hostile in the arm. Enraged, the others overran the checkpoint.

I climbed out of our vehicle and took cover behind it with

the others. Holly looked at me with frightened eyes and, knowing what I was thinking, patted my arm as if to reassure me.

"Pray," she said.

I saw Springer across from me at the other end of the checkpoint. Behind me, Pederman called out orders. I grabbed Warnick's radio and yelled into it.

"Do we wound them or…"

The supervisor shook his head. Meanwhile, the intruders were getting closer. His voice came back loud and clear.

"Shoot to kill, son," he said.

My friend nodded grimly. This wasn't easy for him—or me. All I'd ever killed were draggers and Red Militia. These were *civilians*. Still, they would have no trouble taking our lives. Putting aside my feelings, I focused on the angry faces of the approaching mob.

A Black Dragon squad emerged from the vehicle next to ours as more gunfire erupted. In response, a helicopter gunner fired his autocannon on the attackers, cutting them to shreds. A man's detached legs stood for only a moment, then toppled like pick-up sticks.

"I'm going to help Springer," Warnick said. "You guys stay here and defend your position." This was happening, and nothing could change that now.

"Are you ready?" I said.

My wife stared past me. Then, "Dave!"

A horde had broken through the trees, attracted by the gunfire. As I turned back, two men carrying shields made from scrap iron rushed us. Holly and I fired at them. But the bullets ricocheted off the metal, pinging loudly.

"Why won't they fall down?" she said.

"Aim low!"

"Roger that."

My wife sprayed a stream of bullets at their boots. The men fell in a heap in front of her, screaming and cursing. I took out as many draggers as I could. But most got past me and, with vicious precision, went after guards and civilians alike.

Warnick and Springer came to assist, dodging fire as they ran. The creatures moved fast—faster than I'd ever seen. Those we missed attacked the nearest humans, tearing out their throats and luxuriating in the gore. The unfortunate victims fell, squirting blood and shivering into death. Predictably, they rose to join the others and infect more of the living.

While the gunners focused on the horde, I did as Holly had advised and prayed. But I was afraid it wouldn't be enough. The right hand gives, but the left hand takes.

FORTY-ONE

Springer lobbed a grenade into the horde. The explosion was deafening and sent blobs of decaying flesh everywhere. As the draggers regrouped, Pederman gave the signal, and everyone fell back, including the intruders. A helicopter swooped in and shredded the remaining hostiles with the M2. Those who hadn't been blown to shit rose from the carnage. Guards and civilians alike finished them off.

Holly lay on her back, covered in dirt. Frantic, I checked her over. She gave me a thumbs-up.

"Thought I'd lost you," I said and held her close.

Several feet away, an injured civilian around my age lay whimpering. When he raised his hand to get our attention, I noticed the wedding ring.

"We just wanted to see our families," he said, delirious.

Getting to her feet, my wife tossed her backpack on the ground and dug through it. She handed me a bunch of white plastic ties. I rolled the bleeding man onto his stomach and tied his hands behind him.

"You're under arrest," I said.

When the other guards saw what we were doing, they joined us and, grabbing fistfuls of ties, saw to the other wounded. Eventually, the shooting stopped, and all was quiet —except for the wailing of the injured and the angry beating of helicopter blades. The ambulances arrived to transport the injured to the hospital. Smiling, Pederman approached Holly.

"That was some quick thinking," he said.

For the next hour, we walked the area, checking the twisted, motionless bodies for pulses and sending rounds through their heads so they wouldn't reanimate. Surprisingly, we had lost only a handful of guards. But many more civilians lay dead or wounded.

After dropping the injured at the hospital, the ambulances returned to pick up more. It took us till evening to clear the area. Other guards stayed behind to reinforce the barricade. The bodies—human and dragger—were loaded onto flatbed trucks and taken to the incinerators.

The night was black and cold. My body was numb as I helped Holly into a Humvee. Warnick's radio crackled—it was the supervisor. We gathered around to listen.

"We're not done, boys and girls," he said. "Over."

Side-eyeing Springer, my friend brought the radio up to his face. "What have you got? Over."

"A drone spotted two men in the forest. We think they're civilians trying to make their way into town."

Before he could finish, a Black Dragon helicopter swooped in low, its blazing spotlight cutting a stark, burning-white path through the dense trees. Farther away, bands of light from another helicopter pierced the darkness.

"I'm west of you guys. Take your squad into the forest, and let's catch these numbnuts."

"On our way. Warnick out." Then to us. "This is where we earn our pay."

Springer slung his rifle over his shoulder. "We get paid?"

Using my thumb, I removed the dirt from my wife's face. "You okay?"

"Outstanding," she said.

Though we were beyond exhausted, we replenished our ammo and grabbed flashlights.

We had walked for nearly a mile when the crunching of branches alerted us. Something moved in the darkness. We shone our lights on the approaching figure. It was a dragger wearing a blood-stained Starbucks apron. Its filmy eyes took us in, blinking into the light beams. Holly started to raise her weapon when my friend stopped her.

"Bayonets," he said.

After we signed on, they trained us to use the Ontario 490 M9 Bayonet. The blade was deadly sharp. I had almost sliced open my hand while attaching it to my AR-15. Of all the weapons I'd used, this was my least favorite. We secured the blades and stood in a line as the hostile approached, black drool dripping from its gaping mouth. Then, more appeared.

"Spread out," Warnick said.

These past months, I'd encountered draggers with varying degrees of what could loosely be called intelligence. These were the slow and stupid kind. Arranging ourselves, we went to work. A creature missing an ear let out a hair-raising death shriek. As it came at me, I knifed it in the head.

When you run your blade through a dragger's skull, there's a delay as you pull it out. Too long, and another one could be on you, gnawing at your neck. The groaning sound they made was chilling. And the rancid smell of leaking brains sickened me.

Within seconds, they lay in front of us like fallen trees.

Using our flashlights, we scanned the perimeter. My beam caught the shiny eyes of something lurking in the darkness—a deer.

Over the next mile, we saw nothing and heard only the sounds of the nighttime forest—crickets, frogs, and the occasional great horned owl. I remembered my time with Jim trekking through the woods at night. Drunk. Macho. For us, the forest had never been a place of fear. It was our home. Now, I felt only dread.

In a clearing up ahead, dark shapes swayed rhythmically in a half-circle. Lowering our flashlights, we slowed and kept our voices to a whisper. Eight Black Dragon guards stared at something on the ground.

"What's wrong with this picture?" Springer said.

A full moon shone coldly through the tree branches. We killed the flashlights and waited for our eyes to adjust.

"Hey!" my friend said, using his command voice.

Instead of turning, they continued to rock to the sounds of imaginary music. A man let out a bloodcurdling scream.

"Somebody help me!"

A steady crunching got our attention. It sounded like teeth tearing through gristle. Then, more screaming as we jogged over. Even after everything I'd witnessed in this unending Grand Guignol of a nightmare, what I saw made me want to scream. Splitting up, we rounded the tree and faced the guards.

A frightened man lay against the trunk, bleeding from his side. Beside him, another man—or what was left of him—straddled the ground, his thighs tied off with tourniquets made from rifle slings. His legs were reduced to reddish bone—the flesh picked clean. His face was a frozen grimace as he shuddered into unconsciousness. The guards serenely chewed the meat they'd carved off the civilian's legs. And though they appeared normal, their eyes glowed an eerie purple.

"How is this happening?" my wife said.

Warnick raised his rifle, and we followed his lead. A hostile whose mouth dripped blood snarled at us. We put them down with shots to the head. The lingering odor of blood and gunpowder hung thick in the air. Springer removed a pack of photos from his pocket and showed one to my friend.

The injured man shivered from shock as we examined his partner, who was too far gone to be saved. He'd lost a massive amount of blood, and there was no way he would make it back alive. Springer and I dragged the survivor away from his dying friend.

"J-just...end it," the survivor said. "Please. Can you end it for him?"

Springer granted the request with a bullet to the unconscious man's head. Holly treated the survivor's wound using a QuikClot bandage.

"I need to know if you got bit," Warnick said, examining the survivor's arms.

"No—I swear."

"Can you walk?"

He nodded fiercely and got to his feet, biting down on the pain. He had lost a lot of blood as well. I hoped he would make it.

"You have to believe me—I didn't shoot anyone!"

"Who was your friend?" I said.

"Kevin. He was just a guy I knew."

My friend radioed Pederman, who instructed us to proceed to another clearing, where a helicopter would pick us up.

"I've got you." I threw the man's arm around my shoulder. "What's your name?"

He barely managed to answer. "Steve Zimmer."

"What were you doing out here?" Holly said.

"Trying to get home to my wife."

I kept him talking so he wouldn't pass out. "What's your wife's name?"

"Nina. I-I have a daughter. Evan, she's…"

Warnick and Springer walked ahead, discussing something I couldn't make out. I turned to Holly as tears rolled down her cheeks.

"Everything's going to be fine," I said. "Your wife and baby are safe."

FORTY-TWO

A helicopter flew us to the hospital, where they treated Steve Zimmer and the rest of the wounded. Pederman met us with an update. He'd just come from an emergency meeting with the mayor, who had ordered the trespassers to be expelled. And although they'd broken the law, the police didn't have the resources to handle the caseload.

Contrary to what the mayor had preached about law and order, he agreed to let everyone go, providing they never set foot in Tres Marias again. However, they could be arrested and charged at a later date. He didn't comment on the dead civilians.

After returning to the command center, Holly and I gave Nina the news about her husband. At first, she couldn't comprehend what we were saying. My wife explained that Steve had risked his life to be with her and the baby. That's when she broke down and insisted on going to the hospital, which wasn't permitted. We promised to keep her informed. But we didn't tell her he would be sent away as soon as he could walk.

. . .

It was after midnight when Holly and I arrived at our trailer, spent and aching. Images of those monstrous guards in the forest haunted me. What they did confirmed a suspicion that had nagged at me ever since we learned about Ariel. Robbin-Sear had made significant progress with the virus. And now, the test subjects appeared almost human.

Erzen greeted us as we walked in, looking fresh and alert. Not bothering to get up, Greta lay on the floor, wagging her tail.

"Griffin's asleep," the guard said.

My wife gave her a hug. "Thanks so much for looking after her."

"Heard it was pretty bad out there."

"Lots of casualties," I said.

Erzen set out sandwiches and sodas while we put away our weapons. The woman was a treasure.

"I'm heading out. Radio me if you need anything."

Holly followed our new friend to the door, where they spoke briefly. I only caught the last part of what my wife said.

"....how much longer I can do this."

"You'll be fine," the guard said. "Word on the street is you're a real ass-kicker."

Laughing, Holly hugged her again. Though she hadn't gone with us, Erzen sounded like she knew exactly what we'd been through. She never talked about herself. But I recognized in her eyes a familiarity with the darker alleyways of life. After she left, we sat at the dinette and ate our sandwiches.

"Of everything that's happened to us, this was the worst," my wife said. "What about Nina's husband?"

"They won't let him stay. Listen, I've decided to help him."

"How?"

"Too tired," I said. "We'll talk in the morning."

In the darkness of our bedroom, Holly found my hand and held it close to her heart. I felt the gentle beating against my palm. Thinking about the tiny life growing inside her, I marveled that the two of us would become three. The steady rhythm relaxed me, and soon I was out, holding my wife close. In the few short hours we slept, I was mercifully spared any dreams.

An urgent knocking cut through my foggy brain like a sharpened bayonet. It was Springer. Pederman was waiting for us in the administration building. I rubbed my burning eyes and gazed at the gray early light.

"What time is it?" I said.

"After seven."

"Give us a few minutes to shower and dress."

The sky was dark with clouds. I saw Erzen in the distance heading our way. Twenty minutes later, Holly and I followed Springer across the parking lot through a light rain.

"Get any sleep?" I said.

He yawned. "Most times, I can't tell if I'm asleep or awake."

"What were you and Warnick discussing last night when we left the clearing?"

"Those guards we shot were among the ones reported missing."

"Are you sure?"

"We have their photo IDs, remember?"

"Right," I said. "And thanks, by the way."

"For what?"

"Ruining our morning."

The mood was somber as we passed guards and civilians. Word of yesterday's incident had spread. It reminded everyone that the terror and violence of the outbreak were far from over. Fabian trotted down the administration building steps as we went up.

"It's pretty intense in there," he said. "They sent me to get coffee." Then to me, "Is Griffin okay?"

I bristled. "She's fine."

When he was gone, my wife said, "I wish you'd make an effort."

"He needs a hobby."

"Looks to me like he has one," Springer said.

Pederman, Warnick, and Walt Freeman were waiting in the conference room. Becky sat next to the deputy mayor, ready to take notes on her laptop. Everyone wore expressions that reminded me of those giant Easter Island heads—dark and inscrutable.

"Take a seat, guys," the supervisor said.

FORTY-THREE

I didn't know what was coming, and Warnick's expression betrayed nothing. Springer, Holly, and I took our seats. On the table, manila folders stamped SERIOUS INCIDENT REPORT in red block letters awaited us. Flipping open mine, I skimmed the first page. It was a checklist.

My eye caught one item—Photos of Disturbing Scene— and I realized what this meeting was about. The mayor hadn't mentioned the civilian casualties the previous night because he wanted his response nice and official.

The deputy mayor flicked his forefinger at Becky, who began typing. Welcome to small-town politics. We were about to get a good old-fashioned cornholing.

"First of all," he said, "I want to offer everyone my condolences on the casualties your firm sustained. After reading Mr. Pederman's account of the events, I can only conclude that you were under serious attack."

We waited for the supervisor to say something, but he declined.

"That said, there were also an unacceptable number of civilian casualties. Mistakes that could've been avoided had you been in better control of your people. The mayor has asked me to conduct an investigation. Kelly, I've incorporated your report into a new draft. And once we're finished, what you see will become the final report."

"Walt," Pederman said, "I can assure you we followed procedure to the letter. As you pointed out, my people were under fire."

"That may be. But there was a high loss of life. Like-uh-said, we must abide by the rules. Now, the mayor has been in touch with your leadership in Pittsburgh."

"I thought all communication was down," I said.

He barely acknowledged me. "We have a secure channel." Then to the supervisor, "They recommend you be relieved until the investigation is complete."

I was on my feet before he finished. "You can't—"

"Dave, sit down," Pederman said. Then to the deputy mayor, "If that's the case, who's in charge now?"

Walt stood, yanking his belt over his generous gut. Ten pounds of shit in a five-pound sack. I would've laughed if we weren't getting our asses handed to us.

"Until further notice, Black Dragon will report directly to Captain O'Brien."

Springer pushed away from the table in disgust. "What? No way."

"You can't be serious," I said. "The cops?"

Now the supervisor was on his feet. "Dave, for the love of—"

"This is bullshit, and you know it. What about the separation of church and state?"

"This isn't a joke, son," the deputy mayor said, his ears

reddening. "Ladies and gentlemen, I'll contact you with any more questions. In the meantime, I need each of you to read the report carefully to ensure everyone agrees that nothing has been left out, so on and so forth. If you feel there's a discrepancy, come and see me. You have until end-of-day."

After the Grand Inquisitor and his minion had gone, we took our seats. I regretted my outburst—not because I wasn't right, but because my behavior had reflected poorly on our supervisor.

"I could've handled that better," I said.

Pederman ignored me and flipped open his copy of the report. Surprisingly calm, his eyes met mine. "Never mind. He's doing his job."

"But how is this going to work with the police in charge?"

"We don't have a choice," Warnick said. "I suggest we make the best of it."

Fabian returned from the cafeteria carrying a plastic tray of to-go cups. "I had to wait for them to make a fresh pot. Wha'd I miss?"

"They sawed off our nuts with a plastic knife," Springer said.

My wife gave him the stink eye. "Speak for yourself."

"Oh, right. They sawed off *my* nuts and fed them to these guys."

I scanned the report while the Latino handed out the coffees. For the supervisor's part, he had been thorough and, from what I could see, factual and impartial. He hadn't tried to whitewash our actions or overstate what the civilians—not to mention the dragger horde—had done to us. He had, however, left out something important.

"There's no mention of the guards we found in the forest," I said.

"I included them in the list of Black Dragon casualties." Pederman reached over and took my copy. Going around the table, he collected the rest.

"But I thought we were supposed to—"

"We're not contesting anything. End of discussion."

"Okay. Can I bring up something else? It's about the guy we rescued in the forest. What's going to happen to him?"

"Once he's released from the hospital, he'll be escorted to a checkpoint along with the other civilians. We've already arranged private transportation."

"But his wife and baby are here," Holly said. "Can't he stay with them?"

"I don't think so. And anyway, I'm no longer in charge."

"Well then, can they go with him?" I said.

"Afraid not. It would violate the quarantine."

"They've been tested, and they don't carry the virus."

"Dave, I appreciate what you're trying to do for that family, but our orders are to keep everyone who was quarantined in and everyone else out."

Sighing, I turned to my wife. "We tried."

"I can't believe you caved like that," she said when we were outside. "It's not like you."

"Don't worry—I have a Plan B. I'm going to see Isaac."

"What for?"

"To get Steve Zimmer a doctor's note."

"Mind if I come with?" my friend said.

"Warnick, the last thing you need is to get involved in one of my dumbass schemes."

"There are worse things."

"Like what?" Holly said.

Springer laughed. "Like being crushed to death by Walt Freeman's gut."

"It would make an awesome steamroller against a horde, though."

I would've laughed too, but I was working out what to say to the doctor. I needed to keep it simple and practiced in my head.

Isaac, I need you to lie about a patient.

FORTY-FOUR

Isaac stared at me like I'd asked him to help me bury a body. Holly and Warnick hung back, letting me take the brunt of the doctor's ire.

"You want me to falsify an official medical record?" he said.

"Only a little. I was hoping you could *bend* the truth."

"Nina's baby needs her father," my wife said.

I touched his arm. "The only way for him to avoid being expelled is for you to—"

"I know." Sighing like the dead, he returned to his desk and plopped into the chair. "You'd like me to say he's sick."

Holly gave him a little girl smile. "Can't you give him a disease?"

"Like what?"

"Something that'll make it so he can stay at the command center, but not fatal."

He sank back and closed his eyes. I knew he'd been working long hours and didn't need someone else making demands on his time. He flipped open Steve Zimmer's chart.

"Okay, let's see. We gave him a transfusion the night he

was admitted. Looks like he ate breakfast. And he's responding well to the antibiotics. Seems he had a nightmare. Hmm…"

"What is it?" I said.

"White blood cell count's a little high. Probably due to an infection."

He pored over the chart, then returned to the first page. When he looked up, he was smiling.

"Elevated white blood count could indicate something serious such as an autoimmune disorder or even leukemia. Keeping him under observation is at the doctor's discretion."

"So you wouldn't have to lie," my friend said. "I'm good with that."

"You know what, so am I. He's due to be released this afternoon. I'll see to it he's moved to the command center." He winked at my wife. "And I'll continue to monitor his progress."

Holly high-fived him. "Awesome!"

He turned to Warnick. "We still need to connect the Vollmer twins with those scientists. I realize your reporting structure has changed, but if we wait any longer…"

"Understood. I'll figure out something."

"Any change to those isolation facility patients?" I said to Isaac.

"We've lost most of them. And it's getting more dangerous to continue with the remaining few."

"So, no more like Ariel."

"She was the only one."

My wife took my hand. "Maybe not."

We told the doctor about the guards we'd encountered in the forest. As an experienced medical examiner, he had seen every kind of death. Yet he blanched when we described what they'd done to Steve Zimmer's friend.

"I'd like to confront the people responsible."

"You have my vote," I said.

At the command center, Holly, Griffin, and I waited with Nina for the ambulance to arrive. Greta sat at attention. The vehicle stopped briefly at the guard station and pulled in front of the administration building. Nina tensed. She held Evan close and faced her forward so she could see her daddy for the first time in months.

A paramedic jumped out and opened the rear doors. Steve Zimmer lay on a gurney, looking weak and wearing borrowed clothes. Another paramedic helped him sit up. They assisted him as he climbed down from the ambulance.

I wanted to interrogate the patient—to learn what was happening outside our town. Instead, I focused on the situation. I didn't know what would become of this family, but I was happy for them. Thrilled that in this black parade, they'd found each other again.

"Forgive me," Steve said as he held his wife and kissed his daughter.

"Don't ever leave us again."

"I won't—I promise."

With Steve in a wheelchair, we made our way to Nina's trailer. He was in a lot of pain, but he seemed happy. Inside, he sat on the sofa and waited for his wife to place the baby in his arms.

"Hey, Peanut," he said, tears running down his cheeks. "I missed you so much." Then to my wife and me, "I can't begin to thank you."

I shook his hand. "We'll come by later with some more clothes. Oh, I almost forgot." I handed Nina a plastic bag of medications. "Follow the instructions. There are pills to help him sleep. You can take him to any MMU to get his bandages changed and pick up more fluids."

She followed us outside, where Griffin waited with the dog. "Thank you so much. I never thought I'd see him again."

"He's a good man," I said. "You and Evan are everything to him."

"I won't forget you guys for as long as I live." She held Holly like a long-lost sister.

There weren't many good days like this, and I wanted to cherish them.

Holly, Griffin, and I ate in the trailer. The TV droned in the background, tuned to a hockey game between the Sharks and the Kings. I wasn't sure if it was live or prerecorded. Though I loved watching, I was distracted. In the final few seconds of the third period, the Sharks won by a single point.

"Slapshot, and he scores!" the Sharks-friendly announcer said.

The fans went through the roof. The sound of the cheering took me back to my hockey days. Maybe someday, when all this was over, I would pick up a stick again. My wife laid down her fork and took my hand.

"It's hard, you know?" she said.

I knew what she was talking about. Images of the battle we'd engaged in—the worst ever—flashed through my mind, along with the menacing groans of the draggers and the cries of the people we had to shoot.

We weren't guards, not really. Though we had fought to survive all these months, something was different. I could see it in Holly's expression.

"I want to attend Mass," she said. "And I'd like you to come with me."

"You mean now?"

"Tomorrow morning. Will you do it?"

"I don't know. It's been a long time..."

"I need this, Dave. We both do."

"You're not going to make me go to Confession, are you?"

She smiled. "Baby steps."

The girl watched us, saying nothing. There was a look of longing on her face—something I hadn't noticed before.

"Can I come?" she said.

My wife stroked her arm. "Oh, honey. Of course, you can. Are you Catholic?"

"I'm not anything. I've never even been inside a church. It's just that, what happened to Ariel... When I..."

"You don't need to explain. And you'll like it, I promise. It's comforting."

"That's what I was thinking," I said.

But it was a lie. At that moment, I had dread on my mind. The kind that overtakes you when you recall your past sins.

And I had a boatload.

FORTY-FIVE

On Sunday, we attended the only Mass of the day. The mayor had arranged for school buses to transport Catholics staying at the command center to St. Monica's, a few blocks away. I drove Holly and Griffin separately and parked on the street, leaving Greta inside to wait.

Armed Black Dragon guards stood outside the granite structure. I recognized many and acknowledged them as we walked up the steps. Though my wife had gotten me into the habit of praying, I was uncomfortable being here. It wasn't that I wanted to avoid God, but I felt dirty—especially after the violence at the checkpoint. How do you begin to ask forgiveness for taking the life of someone who's trying to kill you? Despite my feelings, I put on my best smile for the girl, who was excited to be part of the sacred mystery.

Inside, a surprising number of families filled the cherry-wood pews. Glowing colored light streamed through the beautiful, undamaged stained glass windows. During the outbreak, it seemed like everyone had died. But here was proof of the living—mothers and fathers, boys and girls, and the elderly.

Holly had asked if she could make her Confession and entered the sacristy. What would she tell the priest? I wondered. *Father, I killed.* Stepping into the pew with Griffin, I noticed other Black Dragon guards, Fabian among them. Minutes later, my wife joined us. She looked happy.

The Mass began with the Sign of the Cross. The celebrant was the elderly priest who had comforted Holly at the start of the outbreak. Cringing, I remembered how I'd gone off on him. Now, I was grateful he had survived. I wondered how he continued to keep the church safe, a place of refuge.

In here, there was no blood, no violence. But there was sadness. All around me, people dried their tears. Was this what being saved looked like? When I turned to see how the girl was doing, I noticed her eyes glistening. Mine stayed dry.

When it was time for Communion, my wife left the pew. I didn't want to go. Griffin wasn't sure what was happening, but she seemed caught up in the ritual and followed. How could a girl without any religion be so drawn to Catholicism while someone like me, raised in the faith, was nearly immune to it?

"I can't," I said.

Holly frowned. "I want you to get a blessing."

Stepping into the aisle, she gently crossed the girl's arms over her chest and waited for me to do the same. As we neared the altar, a small group of elderly men and women sang "Softly and Tenderly Jesus is Calling." There were so many—people like me who'd seen and done unspeakable things. Still, in the end, there was forgiveness. At least, that's what the Good Book said.

I gazed at the Italian crucifix on the wall, aware of how the weeks and months of fighting had deadened me. I hardly knew myself. My temper—legendary to begin with—had gotten worse, especially when we weren't in combat. Constantly wary, I slept little. And I kept my weapon close. My worst fear was losing everyone I loved in a flash of violence. At any time of the day or night, I would experience what could best be described as a panic attack. Other times, I felt depressed.

Having never served in the military, I wasn't sure if what I was experiencing was PTSD. But I knew I was happiest with a gun in my hand. Was that a sin? And it wasn't about killing people. I needed to keep my family safe. If I had to choose between a gun and a crucifix, I'd take the weapon every time.

My wife bowed and put her hands out to receive the Eucharist. A part of me wanted that too. It was a vague longing I hadn't known was in me. Imitating the others, Griffin bowed and stood before the priest.

"May the power of Jesus Christ keep you safe always," he said, making the Sign of the Cross on her forehead with his thumb.

That simple gesture made her cry. Embarrassed, she followed Holly to our pew. When it was my turn, I lowered my head and, only half-listening, waited for a textbook blessing for the damned.

"May the Holy Spirit descend upon you," he said. "And may He help you accept what must be."

Raising my head, I stared at him as if he'd slapped me. Then, disoriented, I returned to join the others. With her eyes closed, my wife prayed. The girl stood beside her, head lowered, stealing glances at those around her. After the final blessing, we exited the church. There wasn't any singing now. Good thing—it would have been wrong.

The best music was silence.

FORTY-SIX

Holly and Griffin walked down the steps arm-in-arm. Nearby, the priest chatted with the parents of two small children. The strange blessing he had given troubled me. Putting it out of my mind, I joined my family.

"That made me feel so special," the girl said. "Like my life matters."

My wife patted her hand. "Grows on you, huh?"

I opened the car door for Holly. "Feel better?"

"A lot. Thanks for coming."

Fabian marched past us, giving Griffin a quick hello. The women stared with their mouths open as he climbed into a Humvee with other guards.

"Okay. So what was that?" my wife said, narrowing her eyes at me.

"He's a busy guy."

"I think he's scared of you."

"I'm sure I don't know what you're talking about," I said.

I'd planned on returning to the command center. But before I could make the turn, Holly touched my hand.

"Can we take a detour?" she said.

"Sure. Where to?"

"Turn right up here."

I did as she asked. After a couple miles, I guessed what she was up to and, my stomach roiling, gave her a concerned look.

"Are you sure?"

"Where are we going?" the girl said from the backseat.

"You'll see," I said, my hands tight on the wheel.

I turned onto the familiar street and parked across from our house—the last place I ever wanted to see. At some point, we would have to resume making payments or let the property slip into foreclosure. Still carrying the horrible memories of my last visit, I preferred to walk away.

Once the quarantine was lifted, the bean counters from the banks and insurance companies would arrive. So many residents had died and left behind cars and houses. I supposed everything, including our property, would be tidied up and sold at auction.

"This is where we used to live," my wife said.

We remained in the Humvee, staring at the dilapidated mess that was our home. When I last saw it, the inside was stained with the blood and entrails of animals Missy had killed to impress me. Most of the windows were broken. The stucco walls were spray-painted with profane slogans. The front door was missing, and the fence was in ruins. Our people must have missed this street because there were no Black Dragon stickers.

I took Holly's arm before she could open her door. "I don't think we should go in."

Defiant, she climbed out and stared at me. "Coming?"

Griffin got out and signaled the dog, who followed. "You heard the lady."

We walked up the short driveway to the entrance. Even from outside, the smell was overpowering—rotting meat and wet fur. Decaying animal matter lay strewn across the living room carpet, along with leaves and branches.

My wife closed her eyes and, taking a breath, went in. Whining, Greta followed her. I had an overwhelming urge to wait outside, but I didn't want the women to be surprised by a dragger pack.

"It's, like, really gross in here," the girl said.

The dog sniffed the debris as we made our way through the living room into the kitchen. Our beloved teapot sat on the counter, the spout in pieces. Why would anyone do that? Spoiled food covered the floor, mixed with raccoon droppings.

Undaunted, Holly continued her inspection. She picked up a discarded tea towel with an image of a rabbit on one side. The inscription read *Some bunny loves you.*

Upstairs wasn't any better. Though there was no blood, the carpet was filthy. All the master bedroom furniture was missing. A wood picture frame lay on the floor. Griffin picked it up and handed it to my wife. It was a wedding photo taken outside St. Monica's. She held it in both hands, staring at the relic like it was something precious but foreign.

"Aw," the girl said. "That's such a pretty dress."

Holly gave her a sad smile and approached our closet. Both floor-length mirrors were shattered, and broken glass crunched under our feet. I helped my wife force open the door.

All the clothes were gone—even the shoes. Boxes lay scattered everywhere, most of them empty except for a few CDs. But one remained on the top shelf. I grabbed the cream-colored box and gave it to Holly. Behind the clear plastic window was her wedding dress. Incredibly, it was untouched.

My wife left the room, carrying the photo and box. At the

top of the stairs, she stopped. She walked into the spare bedroom we'd planned to turn into a baby's room long before she was ever pregnant. It was the only place in the house that was unaffected. I recalled finding her there one morning, daydreaming, as I rushed off to convince Missy to leave me alone. Another time, another me.

After leaving the house, Greta let out a low growl. Two slow draggers dressed as sheriff's deputies limped towards us. The dog, ears pointed forward, stood alert. I unholstered my weapon. But instead of aiming, I handed it to Griffin. Surprised, she stared at me.

"Are you sure?" she said.

She turned to Holly, who nodded her approval. After checking the loaded chamber indicator, the girl fired at the hostiles, striking each in the head. They dropped in the street in a heap. My wife gave Greta a command, and trotting over, the dog sniffed the bodies.

"Easy peasy," I said and took back my gun.

FORTY-SEVEN

I had planned for us to grab lunch in the command center cafeteria. But Holly was still upset and returned to the trailer with Griffin. As I headed over alone, Springer flagged me down.

"Where've you guys been?" he said. "Dr. Fallow came by, insisting that we visit the self-harm farm."

"Robbin-Sear? What did Pederman say?"

"He's not in charge, remember?"

"Where's Warnick?"

"In the administration building."

I found my friend sitting in an office, combing through reports.

"Hey," I said. "So when are we going?"

"We're not. And before you lose it again, you need to listen. Isaac went directly to Captain O'Brien."

"Shit. And I'm guessing he said no."

"Correct."

"Did he at least give a reason?"

"Until the investigation is concluded, we are not to get involved with Robbin-Sear. Under any circumstances."

"I don't see what one has to do with the other. Never mind. Pederman must've given you some advice."

He pretended to ignore me. Then, "He said to wait."

"But time is running out." I could tell from his body language he knew I was right. "Warnick?"

"Let's hope the Vollmer twins come up with something."

"Not good enough."

He shoved the papers aside and rubbed his eyes. "And here we go."

"We can't just sit here and hope everything works out for the best."

"I can't believe I'm asking this. What exactly did you have in mind?"

"Ever heard of a stakeout?" I said.

Warnick, Springer, and I sat in our Humvee, chomping on beef jerky. Our vehicle was hidden among the trees along the road leading to Robbin-Sear. Though it was a long shot, we hoped we would spot Larry or Judith.

"Any more Dew?" I said.

Springer tossed me another can. "Keep drinking that, and you'll pee like a horse with a UTI."

A biting wind ripped through the forest under a lead-colored sky. Thunder rumbled, and the first few raindrops hit our windshield. In a few minutes, a drizzle became a downpour.

My friend read his Bible while Springer played a game on his phone. I kept watch, my weapon lying in my lap. There was movement up ahead—draggers, drenched and wandering down the road like a shadow parade. They passed us, unaware of our vehicle.

Sometime later, I heard the sound of an engine. I grabbed

my weapon and jumped out. Inching my way to the road, I kept to the brush. A van approached, heading towards the research facility. I recognized Judith in the front passenger seat and, waving my arms, ran through the mud and leaves into the middle of the road.

Larry was behind the wheel. I could barely make him out behind the beating windshield wipers. He slowed and pulled off to the side. I stuck two fingers in my mouth and let out a sharp whistle. The others came running, carrying their rifles. Wary, the couple got out to meet us. We had to practically shout over the rain and thunder.

"Thanks for stopping," I said.

Larry glanced up and down the road. "What are you guys doing out here?"

My friend approached him. "We need your help."

We explained the situation. Though the scientists appreciated the urgency, they seemed reluctant to get involved.

"We were instructed not to meet with anyone outside the company," Judith said, shivering from the cold.

I grabbed her husband's arm, making him wince. "There was a time when you guys wanted to help us. What changed?"

He pulled free. "We can't talk about it."

Like idiots on a fool's errand, we stood there getting soaked. I was about to say something when Warnick got in Larry's face.

"We know you've been injecting people with the virus," he said.

Judith inched closer to her husband. "No, we—"

"You kidnapped our people and turned them into something grotesque."

"It wasn't us, it was Bob. He—"

"It's time to end this sick experiment," I said.

My gut told me they were good people caught up in a bad situation. Nevertheless, they were also responsible. Larry looked at his wife, who shook her head. Then, he turned to my friend.

"How would we do this?" he said.

"We'll return with our medical team tomorrow morning. Dr. Fallow feels that if you work together, you might be able to stop the—"

"Stop it?"

Judith grabbed her husband's hand. "If Bob finds out— We never wanted this. Larry?"

"I don't know…"

I'd had enough and grabbed him by the shoulders. "It's time to do the right thing."

"I'm not sure what that is anymore," he said and walked away.

FORTY-EIGHT

The sky was clear as Warnick and I rode out to Robbin-Sear, with Springer driving Isaac and the Vollmer twins in a second Humvee. The previous night, Larry had contacted a Black Dragon patrol with a message for my friend. He and Judith had decided to cooperate. There was a good chance I would be arrested again, and I didn't want Holly mixed up in it. So she agreed to stay behind.

The scientists waited at the entrance while we parked on the road and walked in. They stood close together, holding hands and avoiding eye contact as our team met them. After introductions, Warnick cut to the chase.

"Does Creasy know?" he said.

Judith reddened. "We didn't have a choice."

He took us aside. "What do we think?"

"Creasy may have already called the cops," I said. "Isaac?"

"So they arrest us. I say we proceed."

Bud and Nancy seconded him. As the scientists walked us into the building, Warnick pulled Springer aside.

"Stay here and keep an eye out."

"Hooah."

"We'll share our research with you," Larry said. "But I must warn you. What we're doing is dangerous."

I thought Isaac might lose his shit. "No more dangerous than what you people have done to this town. What in hell were you thinking?"

"Let's stay focused," Warnick said.

They led us to a conference room, where we learned that the code name for the latest generation of the virus was RS-6160. I was lost as Larry and Judith tag-teamed, walking us through everything they'd done. Their lack of emotion astonished me as they described their experiments in clinical terms—things that had resulted in the deaths of thousands. When they were finished, the Vollmer twins—equally dispassionate—shared their work.

Finally, when Bud asked to see the virus, Larry told him all the samples were stored offsite. Instead, we spent the rest of the time looking at computer simulations. Two hours later, after everyone had finished geeking out, we moved on to Ariel's case. Judith seemed surprised to learn we'd taken their patient.

"We witnessed a profound change in her," Isaac said. "During my examination, her irises changed color, and she became violent. She tore through her restraints and tried to attack us."

Judith touched her husband's arm. "I'd like to examine her." Then to the doctor, "Is she at the isolation facility?"

"She's dead." He handed her a file. "This is a copy of my autopsy report. I'd like to see the lab now."

They took us downstairs to the laboratory, where Dr. Royce worked behind the plexiglass wall. All the animals were gone.

"How's he holding up?" Warnick said.

Judith observed her colleague with sadness. "He no longer sleeps. We look after his nutrition."

"What does he eat?" I said.

They led us to a stainless steel refrigerator. She opened it, revealing stacks of raw, bloody steaks. The sight of all that meat made me hungry.

"It's the only food he's interested in," she said.

Isaac laid a hand on Larry's shoulder. "Let's continue."

"As I mentioned, we don't keep virus samples here. But I can show you some recent histological stains."

Our medical team spent the next half-hour peering through microscopes while Royce swatted at flies. Warnick decided it would be best to get out of their way. We were about to leave when Nancy turned to Judith.

"You engineered the virus here?" she said.

"We've been focused on it for the better part of two years."

"And how long have you been working on a vaccine?" Bud said.

Larry seemed surprised. "Vaccine? We're not."

Grabbing his arm, I made him face me. "Are you kidding me right now?"

"Let go of me."

"We thought you wanted to help," Warnick said.

He stared at the floor. "We didn't mean to mislead you. The experiment is at a critical stage, and..."

Before he could finish, Bob Creasy walked in, accompanied by two cops. The project lead's skin was pasty, his pupils like pinpoints. And like any junkie, he wiped at a runny nose.

"What my colleague is trying to say is we've nearly perfected the virus," he said.

Glowering, the doctor confronted him. "Are you responsible for this madness?"

"I'm in charge of the project, yes. And you're trespassing."

Then, like a conductor, he raised a finger. The cops drew their guns.

"Weapons on the floor," one said.

I glanced at Warnick. There was a slim chance we could outgun them, but innocent people might die. His expression told me he'd come to the same conclusion. Reluctantly, we obeyed.

"Is this some kind of joke?" Isaac said.

The second cop smiled viciously. "No joke."

With dead eyes, he shot the doctor. I caught him as he fell and eased him to the floor. Blind with rage, I looked up to find Bud and Nancy staring like mannequins trapped in a tableau of twin horror.

"You were warned, Pulaski," Creasy said. "But you couldn't leave it alone. Did you really think you could stop this?"

He signaled his team to join him. They did so meekly. Seeing all the blood, Judith burst into tears. Gripping Isaac's hand, I glared at our betrayers.

"You never intended to help us," I said to her and pointed at the project lead. "You're no better than this sociopath."

Unbothered by the insult, Creasy gave the cops a final order on his way out. His tone was dismissive.

"Kill them all," he said.

FORTY-NINE

Isaac lay on the floor, groaning in pain. One cop pointed his weapon at the Vollmer twins while the other covered Warnick and me. I was grateful Holly wasn't here. As I closed my eyes, I wished I could've said goodbye.

Gunfire echoed outside, momentarily distracting the aggressors. Leaving the doctor, we scrambled behind a counter and hid. I could see the room reflected in the plexiglass. Two more gunshots, and the twins fell dead.

The cops moved to either side of the doorway and returned fire. Meanwhile, we worked our way backwards, one aisle at a time, till we reached the wall. Behind us, there was a supply closet. We crawled inside.

Warnick flicked on his flashlight. Silently, I began searching for something we could use as a weapon. There was a metal shelving unit bolted to the wall. On the bottom shelf sat gallon plastic jugs of hydrochloric acid. I grabbed one. He spotted a box of glass beakers and passed two to me.

With trembling hands, I unscrewed the cap and carefully filled both containers. When a drop hit my skin, I bit down on a scream and, wiping off the burning poison, replaced the cap. Outside, shouting and more gunfire.

Approaching footsteps now. My friend switched off his flashlight and reached for the door handle. Each of us clutched a beaker. A band of white light shone along the bottom, broken by a shadow. We waited. Then…

"Warnick! Pulaski!" It was Pederman.

As the door swung open, we found the supervisor, Springer, and several other guards with their guns drawn. Behind them, the two cops lay dead. Pointing at the beakers, Pederman squinted at me.

"What the hell is that?"

"Desperation. How did you know we were here?"

"I'm starting to think like you—God help me." Then to my friend, "I thought I was clear about keeping me in the loop."

Meekly, I raised my hand. "It's all my fault. We—"

"Save it." He gazed around the room. When he saw Royce behind the plexiglass, he addressed the other guards. "Get that man out of there."

Warnick set the beakers on a counter. "You don't want to do that. Any more cops out there?"

"The place was deserted when we arrived. Isaac's bleeding pretty bad—he needs surgery."

Kneeling, I examined the doctor. His pulse was weak, but it was there as blood leaked from his side in a growing pool. Though I knew what to do, I couldn't move. Still conscious, he gripped my arm.

"Need… Apply pressure."

Warnick was beside me now. "Use the heel of your hand and press down."

As I followed his instruction, I could feel Isaac's life draining away.

"The Vollmer twins?" he said.

The guard shook his head. Then to the others, "I need a medic kit!"

Springer left the room. When he returned, he was carrying a backpack and dumped the contents on the floor. Warnick grabbed the paramedic shears and cut open Isaac's shirt. After dousing his hands in Betadine, he used his fingers and a Kelly clamp to probe the wound. Then he slid his hand under the patient.

"There's an exit wound," he said.

I handed him a box of QuikClot bandages. He ripped open the packaging and applied one to the front and rear. As he worked on the patient, an explosion sent us reeling. My ears rang. It took me a minute to get my bearings.

"What was that?" I said.

The supervisor peered out the doorway, his weapon raised. "Came from upstairs. Sounded like a grenade. We need to move. Warnick, how much longer?"

Another explosion knocked us off our feet. Soon, thick white smoke filled the room, burning my eyes and throat. I thought I would suffocate.

"CS gas!" Pederman said, coughing.

A high-pitched alarm sounded, and white emergency lights flashed through the haze. The fire sprinkler system activated, drenching us as Springer and my friend carried the doctor towards the door.

Everything happened so fast—I couldn't see the others now. Suddenly, I was alone. Someone called my name from far away. Coughing, I tried to answer and struggled to my feet. The murky shape of a man appeared from out of the fog. When he saw me, he grinned, his flat eyes alive with hunger.

It was Dr. Royce.

FIFTY

Royce slapped his head, trying to get at the flies that plagued him. In an instant, his eyes glowed iridescent purple. Then he lurched at me, slavering like a hungry ghost. I shoved him away, my lungs burning. When I tried calling for help, no words came out.

The noxious fumes had no effect on my attacker, and he easily overpowered me. I dropped to the floor and tried rolling away. Grabbing my ankle, he pulled me in like a rag doll. I kicked straight up and broke his nose with a sickening crunch, and he lost his grip.

Through stinging tears, I saw the beakers on the counter. I scrambled backwards, and getting to my feet, hurled acid at the murderous scientist. An acrid plume of smoke shrouded him. His face and neck sizzled as the flesh melted away like hot wax, exposing muscle and bone. With his eyelids burned off, Royce lunged again.

An AR-15 lay on the ground a few feet away. As I went for it, another explosion sent me to the floor. Now he was on me again, dragging me ever closer to his chomping bare teeth in a horror-show mouth with no lips. I reached for the gun. Soon,

I felt the barrel. In another beat, the weapon was in my hands, and I shot him in the face. Wailing, he fell against the counter.

Outside, smoking CS gas canisters lay at the bottom of the stairs. After making my way up, I climbed over dead cops and wandered the corridors till I found Warnick and Springer tending to Isaac. When the doctor saw me, he smiled and reached for my hand.

"Glad you made it," he said in a weak voice. "Think I'm finished."

"What do you know? You're a patient."

The alarm and flashing lights were disorienting, but at least the sprinklers had caused the smoke to dissipate. Pederman and another Black Dragon squad joined us.

"Thought we lost you, Pulaski," the supervisor said. "Bad news. More cops are waiting for us outside. We have to surrender."

My gut told me giving up was a death sentence. But what choice did we have? Springer and I helped Isaac to his feet, and we made our way to the reception area. Everyone laid their weapons on the floor. Pederman cracked open the door.

"Hold your fire!" he said. "We're unarmed, and we're coming out!"

He swung open the door. Outside, police cruisers filled the yard. Armed cops wearing protective gear crouched behind open car doors, their weapons trained on us. Hanging back, Springer and I shielded the doctor. There were eight other guards. The supervisor stepped aside, and four advanced, their hands in the air.

A torrent of gunfire cut them down like matchsticks, despite their body armor. Pederman took a round in the arm. As bullets rained down on us, we pulled the remaining guards inside and secured the front door. I found a QuikClot bandage and treated the supervisor's arm.

"So much for surrendering," I said. Then to Pederman, "Why can't we radio for a helicopter?"

"No good. We're too far from the command center."

Isaac grabbed my arm. "We need that research…"

When he passed out, my friend placed his fingers on the carotid artery.

Springer shook his head. "I don't think he's gonna make it."

Furious, I shoved him against the wall. "He'll make it!"

"Knock it off and see if you can find the research," the supervisor said, nursing his arm.

Springer and I made our way along the corridor. On the way, he apologized. We returned to the lab downstairs, where we grabbed as many external hard drives as we could carry.

Upstairs, we found the others in the infirmary. The doctor lay on an examination table. While Warnick looked after him, I found a refrigerator and flung open the door. On the shelves lay thick plastic bags filled with blood. I grabbed what I needed and returned to the exam room.

"In case we can't reach the hospital," I said.

Springer searched the cabinets, where he found needles, syringes, and rubber tourniquets. We loaded everything into a backpack and placed the blood in a plastic cooler. Then we covered the bags with ice from the freezer. My friend threw the hard drives into another bag and looked at me.

"Are you sure that's the right blood type?"

"He's the same as me. O positive."

Springer clapped me on the back. "Dude, how do you even know that?"

"Trust me."

When I was a kid, a drunk clipped my bike with his car. The impact sent me into a wall. I remember spitting up a lot of blood. The surgeon managed to stop the internal bleeding, and I remained in the hospital for a week. That's when I learned Isaac had donated blood—O positive.

Warnick lifted the patient's eyelid and felt his neck. "I'm barely getting a pulse."

I stood in the doorway and checked the corridor. "There's got to be a way out of here. What about through the rear?"

A guard raised his hand. "The fence goes all the way around. And there's no rear gate."

"We need more firepower," Pederman said.

I wracked my brain. This was a research facility—not an armory. Yet the last time we were here, Creasy had gotten ahold of a gun. These guys were under contract with the DoD. Maybe they had more weapons for protection. I signaled Springer and two other guards. We did a quick search of the floor. At the rear, we found a room marked SUPPLIES. The door was locked.

"What do you think?" I said to Springer.

"I don't." He kicked open the door.

Inside we found an impressive weapons cache—AR-15s and an assortment of handguns, shotguns, and rifles. And three MilKor M32 MGL grenade launchers—enough for a small war. Springer held his head in his hands.

"Boys, I think I'm in love."

I grabbed a crowbar and opened a wood ammunition box, where I found a steel case. Inside were twenty black nylon bandoliers, each holding six 40 mm grenades. We carried the weapons and ammo into the infirmary. Isaac had regained consciousness, and my friend continued to monitor him. When the supervisor saw us, he struggled to his feet.

"Looks like you've been busy. Pulaski, I know I'll regret this, but how do you propose we get out of here?"

"Through the front door," I said.

FIFTY-ONE

Isaac fought to stay conscious as we waited in the reception area for Pederman's orders. The supervisor had listened to my lame-ass Butch and Sundance plan and nixed it—rightly. Unlike me, he and the others had seen actual combat. And what they came up with was way smarter.

Our mission was to get past the gate to our Humvees and head for the hospital. The only way to do that was to make sure someone covered us as we exited the building. So, he stationed three guards on the roof—each with a grenade launcher.

"What do you see up there? Over," Pederman said into the radio.

A voice came back. "Looks like they're waiting for us to make a move. Oh, and we got draggers approaching at twelve o'clock. Over."

"How far?"

"Half a klick."

"Okay. On my command. And remember, one grenade per vehicle. Pederman out."

Rubbing the sweat from his forehead, he looked at each of us. Then, he closed his eyes. As he opened them, he brought the radio up to his face.

"Fire!"

Outside, earsplitting explosions, with people screaming and the staccato of erratic gunfire. Waiting a beat, Warnick opened the door and began firing. Springer and I got the doctor to his feet as everyone prepared to advance.

Six police cruisers, each with a blown-out windshield, burned hot from the inside. More grenades destroyed the other vehicles and sent the cops scattering. Panicking, they opened the gate and ran outside, where the draggers were already waiting. Forgetting about us, they opened fire.

The supervisor raised his good arm. "Everyone ready?"

On his signal, we hurried past the wreckage to our vehicles, carrying our supplies. Our people on the roof covered us with their rifles. The Humvees were now within reach. The others surrounded Isaac and me as I helped him to a vehicle.

The guard in front of me fell, shot through the neck. Someone on the roof took out the shooter hiding behind the guard station. When it was safe, I eased the doctor into a Humvee and leaned him against the backseat. All I could do now was wait for Pederman, Warnick, and Springer.

When we were all together, Warnick started the engine and gunned it as draggers devoured the remaining cops. Our plan called for the guards on the roof to get to their vehicles and return to the command center. They'd have their work cut out for them. With the dead police officers, the dragger pack had swelled.

It started raining, making the road slick. Lightning lit up the sky as thunder came up from the east. The supervisor rode in front with Warnick. Springer sat in the backseat with Isaac and me. I thought we were home free, but I was wrong. Around a mile from the research facility, two black Escalades with government plates came out of nowhere and began pursuing us.

"Who are those guys?" Warnick said.

Pederman craned his neck. "We'd better get off this road. Dave, what do we have in the back?"

Getting closer, our pursuers began firing at us. As bullets glanced off the rear window, I climbed over the seat and dug through the supplies.

"More guns. We should've brought a grenade launcher. Wait—we have grenades."

"Figure something out," the supervisor said. "And fast."

I grabbed one and tapped Springer on the shoulder. "Keep Isaac stable."

"You got it, boss."

Clutching the deadly device, I pulled the pin. I thought of Holly as I flung open the door and tossed the grenade. My timing was shitty. The device bounced on the road and to the side as the vehicles shot past it. The resulting explosion caused them to veer but didn't do any real damage.

There were two agents in each vehicle—one driving and the other with a shotgun. We hit a bump, and I nearly fell out. Recovering, I ducked inside and closed the door as buckshot peppered the rear of our Humvee.

My heart racing, I armed another grenade and threw it. The Escalades accelerated, with the lead vehicle trying to ram us. The driver was a nondescript man in a gray suit and sunglasses. His partner was a woman dressed the same. The grenade exploded well behind the second vehicle.

"Dammit! How long is the delay?"

"Five seconds," Springer said. "Wait— Yeah, five."

I reached for another grenade and released the spoon—

but I didn't throw it. One thousand…two thousand…three thousand. I tossed it.

The device bounced once and exploded under the lead vehicle, lifting it in the air and sending it into the path of the second, which it crushed. A ball of flame shot up from the mangled frames of both cars. As we pulled away, I couldn't believe that worked and high-fived Springer. Pederman turned around, grinning with pride.

"Nice work, Pulaski," he said.

Warnick slowed as we approached a fire road. "Better hang on to something."

He made a sharp turn and burst through the locked gate. We continued north into the forest.

I studied the landscape through the window. Something about our surroundings seemed familiar. "I know this road. It'll take us north towards Mt. Shasta."

"Where are we going?" my friend said.

"To the only safe house I know."

For forty-five minutes we cruised slowly under the darkening canopy of trees as rain poured down.

"Okay, see that road up ahead?" I said. "Make a right and go slow."

We followed the path, where it dead-ended in a large clearing, its edges outlined by a circle of rocks. In the center stood an impressive concrete birdbath—the goddess Diana, with a dead stag at her feet.

"Okay, stop here." I jumped out and trotted up to the passenger side.

"What is this place?" the supervisor said.

As if by forest magic, a structure materialized from out of the shadows.

I pointed at the house. "Look."

Springer stood next to the vehicle, gawping at the optical

illusion. A bullet whizzed past and hit a tree trunk. Before we could move, a voice called out.

"Drop your weapons and lie on the ground."

Leaving the doctor in the Humvee, we followed orders and lay face-down on the wet earth. Approaching footsteps now. As I lifted my head, a thin, wizened man stepped out of the shadows, pointing an AR-15 at us. I recognized the long white beard and ponytail. Then there were the khaki cargo pants, Hawaiian shirt, and flip-flops. Crouching, he squinted at me and let out a high-pitched laugh.

"Dave Pulaski?" he said.

PART FOUR

FRIENDS IN NEED

FIFTY-TWO

uthrie Manson hung back, his ancient eyes sparkling. His wife, Caramel, was thin with flowing white hair. Expertly, she started a blood transfusion for Isaac, who lay on a twin bed in a guest bedroom. She had everything, including an IV pole.

The last time I saw these two, it was with my friends. We were on our way to Tres Marias to search for Holly. But it was too dangerous to go in without weapons, and Irwin Landry decided to pay his old pals a visit.

The quirky couple had dropped out years before, living alone in the forest with their two adult sons, Frank and Jerry. The family grew marijuana and collected guns—big guns. They were the poster children for aging, commune-tested hippies. Deeply in love, the old couple never hesitated to share what they had with worthy strangers. All they asked in return was to be left alone. Seeing them again made me long for the dead and gone.

"Not making any promises," Caramel said. "I'll do what I can."

I knelt next to the doctor. "How long will the transfusion take?"

"About four hours. In the meantime, let's get you boys something to eat."

We sat at the large, familiar, unfinished pine table in the kitchen, shaken by the day's events. Everything had collided —the plague, the cops, and now dangerous gray-suited agents in black Escalades. I didn't want to mention Landry, but I owed it to our hosts.

"Irwin is dead," I said.

He was Guthrie's oldest friend. The old man looked at his wife as she patted his hand.

"Figured as much since he wasn't with you," he said. "And the others?" He noted my expression. "Anyway, you're welcome to stay."

"Really kind of you," Pederman said. "I wasn't looking forward to driving through the forest at night."

"You're right about that. Besides, we got plenty o' room."

Leaning over, I gazed out the back door. "Where are your sons?"

Guthrie lowered his eyes. And that's when I knew the horror that was unleashed in my hometown had finally reached the isolated refuge.

"We lost 'em a few weeks ago."

"How did it happen?"

He didn't answer. Instead, he got up and put down place-mats for each of us. Warnick and Springer exchanged a look, then got up to help by setting out bowls, napkins, and flat-ware. The old man sat down again and rubbed his eyes.

"It's hard to talk about," he said. "More o' them ungodly creatures wandered over here from Tres Marias. Usually, they're dumb as spit and easy to kill. But these were different —cunning. Couple of 'em organized the others and surrounded Frank and Jerry like a pack o' wolves. Bit 'em up pretty good before the boys could shoot their way out."

He cleared his throat and squinted away a tear. "By the time they made it back, they were in bad shape."

"Sorry for your loss, Mr. Manson," the supervisor said.

"Call me Guthrie. And thanks. We keep 'em out in the garden. Come on, I'll show you."

Though I trusted him, I was hesitant to learn what he meant. I side-eyed the others as he led us out through the kitchen door.

Walking past rows of beautifully manicured apple, peach, and apricot trees, we continued towards a wood shelter where the old woman kept her gardening tools. His sons were chained to metal posts sunk deep in the ground. They seemed smaller than I remembered—and thinner. Their faces and arms were a leathery gray, and their clothes were torn and bloody.

They seemed listless and looked at us with mild interest as we approached. The old man checked the stakes to make sure they were secure.

"Caramel wouldn't let me put 'em down," he said.

Springer seemed fascinated. "Do you feed them?"

"We felt it was better to let 'em waste away. Shouldn't be too much longer now."

I remembered the draggers I'd seen over these past months—the ones who were too far gone to hunt. They would lie lethargically on the ground, waiting for a death that would never come. But something bothered me.

"Guthrie, you said you thought those draggers came from Tres Marias," I said. "How can you be sure?"

"Because Mt. Shasta has been clean for weeks."

"But how?" I turned to Pederman. "Black Dragon?"

He shook his head. "Our contract is with Tres Marias."

Tears like rain puddles welled in the old man's eyes. "We know it's crazy, keeping 'em here. But these were our boys. They were all we had."

As he approached them, Warnick reached for his weapon. Frank and Jerry stared at their father in mute fascination. Soon, matching sneers crept across their ravaged faces, and they snapped at him.

"It's okay," Guthrie said and started for the house. "I won't let 'em hurt you."

FIFTY-THREE

Guthrie placed a large bowl of stew on the table. It smelled unusual but appetizing.

"You did not just make this," Pederman said to the missus.

She blushed. "I like to keep a lot of food on hand."

She set out loaves of fresh homemade bread and butter, then handed everyone a beer—except me. I received a can of Mountain Dew.

"Thanks for remembering," I said.

Springer took a warm mouthful and immediately stopped chewing. Then he took a huge swig of beer and grinned at us stupidly.

"I thought it was beef."

"Nope, venison," the old man said. Then to me, "You workin' for the man now?"

Smiling, I glanced at the supervisor. "I like having unlimited access to awesome weapons."

"I heard that. Say, did you ever find your wife? Now, what was her name?"

Caramel patted my shoulder as she sat. "Holly."

"I did," I said. "It's a long story I'll share with you sometime."

Guthrie reached for some bread. "How about now?"

Thinking of my wife, I was desperate to let her know I was okay. Instead, I recounted everything that had happened since the last time I visited the Mansons. It made me sad talking about my dead friends, but it felt good to say their names.

"Helluva story," the old man said.

Springer wiped away the gravy dripping down his chin. "Turns out Holly's a way better shot than ol' Dave here."

"Hey, I'm pretty good with an axe." Then to our host, "We need to talk about Evie Champagne."

"Let's have coffee first," Guthrie said. "After that, there's somethin' I want to show you."

We sat on handcrafted furniture in the bizarre, colorful living room I remembered. Springer reached up between the hanging plants and played with one of the many calaveras hanging from the ceiling. It looked like an undertaker or maybe a politician.

I eased into a chair that, though irregularly shaped, was surprisingly comfortable. Outside, it was cold and windy. I was glad of the blackout curtains hanging across the windows. Soon, Caramel brought out a huge plate of brownies. At first, I was hesitant to try one, but she assured me they were cannabis free and handed me the plate.

"I'm going to check on your friend," she said. "Then I'll take a look at your boss's arm."

I passed the plate to the old man. "Was she a nurse in a former life?"

"We've learned to take care of ourselves over the years.

Those people you said were chasing you. Black Escalades, right?"

"Have you seen them before?" Warnick said.

"Evie tipped us off when she and her cameraman got lost in the forest. My boys found 'em and brought 'em here. She told us those guys had been pokin' around Tres Marias for some time. Not drawing attention to themselves, mind you."

"I wonder if they work for Robbin-Sear. And why didn't Evie ever mention them?"

"That's easy. She was scared."

Pederman looked at him intently. "Did she say who she thought they might be?"

"No."

"The first time I saw a black Escalade was in front of City Hall," I said. Then to the supervisor, "It was carrying Walt Freeman."

Guthrie bit into his brownie. "Follow the money."

Clueless, Warnick, Springer, and I turned to Pederman, who gave us a knowing smile. When he saw the dumb looks on our faces, he scoffed.

"Oh, for... Didn't you ever see *All the President's Men*? CREEP? Deep Throat? Ringing any bells?"

Springer raised his hand. "I saw *Teletubbies* once. Thought someone had slipped me a roofie."

"We're talking about Watergate," the supervisor said, giving Springer the stink eye. Then to the old man, "Are you suggesting this is about money?"

"What else?"

Warnick got to his feet. "Enough guessing. We seriously need to figure out what's going on."

"Well, I'm only a simple farmer," our host said. "And I don't claim to know the truth. But..."

Groaning, he got up. We swallowed our coffee and

followed him down a long hallway, past the bedrooms, to a storage room at the end. He unlocked the door, swung it open, and turned on the light.

An expensive Sony video camera lay on the bare floor next to a portable lighting kit and a tangle of black cables. But what got my attention was the box of memory cards. They must have contained hours of news footage.

Now I knew why Evie had mentioned Guthrie before leaving the command center. She'd asked him to store the evidence of her investigation for safekeeping. And she wanted me to find it. It was as if she were still here, guiding me to the truth.

Pederman picked up a memory card. "What is all this?"

"Something the mayor never wanted us to find," I said.

FIFTY-FOUR

We carried the camera and memory cards to the living room. Springer connected the device to Guthrie's massive TV using one of the cables. Warnick and I laid out the cards and arranged them in chronological order according to their labels.

Most contained the mundane reports we'd already seen on the local news—the violence, the fires, and the too few random acts of kindness. In one clip, Evie turned the camera on Jeff as he gnawed a Baby Ruth. He pretended to be a dragger and stomped towards her. She screamed like a horror queen, and they laughed as the shot went out of focus.

Warnick, Pederman, and I spent the night reviewing the recordings while Springer lay snoring in a corner. As I watched the progression of the plague, I thought about where I'd been at each point. There I was, working at Staples... Leaving Tres Marias to join Holly... Arriving in Mt. Shasta only to learn that she was missing, and her mother had turned.

We made it to the last of the memory cards sometime after

midnight. The reporter looked haggard. Unable to share newsworthy events, her entries became more personal—even confessional. There was a profound sadness in her voice.

She had grown up in Fresno, the child of an abusive, alcoholic father and a timid mother who was used to regular beatings. Evie lost count of the times she ran away. While a teenager, she finally left for good to live with an aunt in San Francisco. The move turned out to be her salvation.

Her aunt was single—a painter who hung out with poets, writers, and theater types. With the woman as her legal guardian, the girl attended high school in the city and spent all her free time at museums or with her aunt's friends. Everyone encouraged her to write, and they helped her form a picture of herself different from anything she could've imagined. Then, thanks to scholarships, she attended college, majoring in journalism.

Her father had died years before, choking on his own sick. Soon after, her mother succumbed to throat cancer. Though she'd never visited them, she managed to scrape together enough money for their funerals.

"We're taught that a reporter should never become the story," she said. "Screw that."

One memory card contained an interview with Ormand Ferry, the leader of the Red Militia. Seeing him on-screen brought back all the repulsion and pain I'd suffered as his prisoner. Even so, the recording provided us with valuable information.

When Evie brought up Robbin-Sear, Ferry confirmed that something fishy was happening in the forest. She and Jeff followed up, eventually encountering Dr. Larry Evans. I watched intently as the reporter asked him whether the virus had originated in their lab. His silent, shifty reaction was priceless—guilty as charged.

Because the internet was unavailable, Evie made her way to the public library where, using microfiche, she found old newspaper articles on Robbin-Sear. One contained a photograph taken in front of their offices in Virginia. As Jeff's camera zoomed in, we saw—standing next to Dr. Robbin and Dr. Sear—an Army general and another man who looked a lot like Bob Creasy, only younger. Both smiled, with the general's hand resting on his shoulder.

"It was a military operation from the get-go," the reporter said outside the library. "And there's another curious connection. We've learned that Black Dragon and Robbin-Sear are owned by the same parent company."

Warnick and I gawped at the supervisor. His eyebrows were raised, and his mouth hung open as she continued her story.

"There's someone else involved. In my research, I turned up articles about Plum Island. Supposedly, secret government experiments went on there for years. These same sources referenced another government facility in Mt. Shasta. I intend to find a way up there to learn the truth."

That was the last thing Evie Champagne would ever report.

Morning came, and my eyes were burning. Caramel had fixed us breakfast, which included plenty of hot coffee. Walking into the kitchen, I was surprised to find Isaac sitting there.

"How are you feeling?" I said.

"I'm alive thanks to this marvelous woman."

She set a steaming bowl of soup in front of him. "Nonsense. You're as strong as an ox."

Pederman took a seat. "We're taking you to the hospital."

"Learn anything from those recordings?" Guthrie said as we feasted on warm cinnamon rolls and eggs with sausage.

Warnick poured himself coffee. "Evie mentioned there might be another facility. It's like every time we try to get to the bottom—"

"There is no bottom," I said. "It's what Chavez told us, remember?"

The supervisor stared at his plate, his food untouched. "I can't believe our company is connected to Robbin-Sear."

I nodded. "We should take Guthrie's advice and follow the money."

The old man grinned like an evil elf. "How're you boys fixed for weapons?"

"We're good," my friend said.

Our host winked at me. "If you ever need any, you know where to find us."

Outside, we stood in the blue shafts of early morning light and said our goodbyes. Springer helped the doctor into the backseat and made sure he was comfortable.

"Keep an eye out for government agents," Pederman said.

Guthrie saluted him. "Don't you worry. Those idiots stick out like rabbis at a Klan meeting."

Caramel gave me a hug. "You take care of yourself. And Holly too."

"Friends in need," the old man said, shaking my hand. "In life, you can't ask for more than that."

Soon, we were on our way. A few draggers appeared as we followed the muddy road to Tres Marias. But there were no black Escalades. After watching Evie's recordings, I had a strange feeling it would be harder to protect my family now.

The supervisor's radio crackled to life as we neared the town. Someone was already speaking, but the first part was garbled. In another beat, I recognized Erzen's voice.

"Where have you guys been? It's crazy time. Over."

"Erzen? What's going on? Over."

"They're shutting us down," she said. "I repeat, they are shutting down the operation."

FIFTY-FIVE

When we arrived at the command center, Holly was waiting in front of the administration building with Griffin, Fabian, and Erzen. I held my wife close, our unspoken words declaring that we'd nearly lost each other again. But as I studied her face, I didn't see any anger over the violent episode at Robbin-Sear. Instead, there was a quiet acceptance of the horrific. A realization, maybe—life was never guaranteed for anyone.

"I was so worried," she said into my ear.

The interns greeted us, and Greta barked. As I hugged the girl, I noticed her holster and weapon.

"Look at you—you passed."

"I did! And so did Fabian."

The nineteen-year-old was also armed. Griffin touched his hand, which I decided to ignore. We had bigger problems. The other guards congratulated the interns. Then the supervisor shook their hands, but anyone could see he was distracted.

"Meet me in the conference room in one hour," he said.

Warnick waited for him to go inside. Gathering us together, he turned to Erzen. "Did the others make it back?"

She hesitated. "We lost four guards. And there are around twenty dead cops. It's a Charlie Foxtrot. And you guys?"

"Oh, we had a real nice time—thanks for asking," Springer said. "The cops took out the Vollmer twins and almost killed Dr. Fallow. And they would've gotten Warnick and Dave if Pederman hadn't—"

"Shut up, Springer," I said.

On the verge of tears, Holly punched me in the shoulder. "What were you thinking? Warnick, how could you—"

"Everyone's fine," he said. Then to Erzen, "What's this about the operation?"

She sighed. "They're moving up the timeline so they can end it."

"I thought the only way they could do that is if there's a breach of contract."

"Tell that to the mayor," she said.

Gunfire erupted near the fence surrounding the command center. Draggers were attempting to climb over. This was new —usually, fences confounded them. As civilians scattered, the hostiles dropped inside, overwhelming the guards. We grabbed our weapons and ran to assist.

They moved quickly, fanning out at the direction of a sly, skeletal female in a dirty, torn tracksuit. It was bald, except for a few strands of bright-orange hair crusted with blood. Like a general, it commanded the others through a series of short, piercing seal barks.

My friend directed us to spread out. The female let out a blood-chilling death shriek, and the others answered. Firing, I concentrated on the leader. But it eluded me, cleverly using the others as a shield.

Griffin was the first to take one out—a teenage boy wearing an In-N-Out uniform. Though its arms and legs were eaten away, the dragger made it to the top of the fence with the skill of a free solo climber. The bullet sent it falling back down on the other side. Lowering her weapon, the girl shuddered.

"Outstanding," I said and gave her shoulder a squeeze. "Shake it off."

By now, more guards carrying rifles joined us. Together we closed in. Incredibly, hostiles continued up the fence. One flopped forward over the top. My wife's bullet found its skull and stopped it mid-climb, its limbs twitching.

We continued firing till we'd finished them all. Some hung lifelessly from the fence, their bony fingers clutching the chain link. A sudden flock of crows went at them, voraciously picking at the eyes and what was left of their lips and tongues.

The female dragger I thought was dead shook itself like a wet dog and sprung to its feet. Fabian had it in his sights and could've easily taken it out. But he froze. Like a wounded sow, it let out an angry groan and tore out the throat of another guard standing nearby—a young woman whose name I didn't know.

Shoving aside the Latino, I jammed my weapon into the attacker's ear as it fed and squeezed the trigger. The blood spray covered the intern's shirt. The only sound now was the roar of the ATVs as guards moved up and down the length of the fence, searching for more hostiles. When I turned around, Fabian's eyes were glistening.

"You kill them, or they kill you," I said. "¿Comprendes?"

Clutching her neck, the injured guard writhed on the grass, the blood spurting brightly through her trembling fingers. She looked at me and the others in terror. No one said anything. I side-eyed Warnick, and he lowered his eyes.

All of us knew what had to be done. It was something we'd come to accept. And it wasn't written in any manual or taught in self-defense classes. It was the reality of the world we lived in. When you got bit, you turned. And the virus didn't care whether you were a sinner or a saint. You were destined to die and come back, a revenant without a conscience.

"Be still," I said as she whimpered, fighting death as best she could. "Shh."

I sent a bullet through her brain, laying her to rest. The Latino looked away in shame as I stood and holstered my weapon. Turning around, I found Holly and Griffin staring at me like I'd done something unspeakable.

"Way it is," I said and walked off.

FIFTY-SIX

I sat on the sofa, swilling a Dew to mask the taste of vomit. Holly had followed me into the trailer. We were alone. I started to ask where Griffin was and realized she'd probably gone off to comfort Fabian the Badass.

"You didn't have to be so hard on him," she said.

"Someone died needlessly because of him. Griffin took care of business out there. And she's *fifteen*."

"He was terrified, Dave. People don't always make the right choice when they're afraid. You should know that better than anybody."

I'd left a woman to die once because of a paralyzing fear. But this was different, wasn't it? Long ago, my friend Irwin Landry made a speech to a bunch of scared rookies after we banded together to fight the scourge.

Each of us has to be capable of doing this, either to save ourselves or someone else. This is not a movie or a video game—it's real life. There won't be time to think. You must respond quickly, which means being observant. We don't want innocent people getting shot. Remember. Observe, assess, and act. No hesitation. No remorse.

Those words haunted me every time I picked up a weapon. The Latino never had the benefit of that wisdom—not his fault.

"I'm sorry," she said. "You didn't deserve that."

I reached for her hand. "No, you were right. I'll talk to him."

"Maybe you should leave him be for now."

She removed her holster belt and sat beside me, her legs tucked under her. Cupping my chin in her hand, she gazed into my eyes.

"Why do you hate him so much?" she said.

A stiff drink would've gone good right about now. "I don't hate him."

"Really?"

"I'll admit I'm angry about a lot of things. But I do not hate Fabian."

"He's a good kid."

"Sure."

"He's just trying to help. Though I don't think he's a fighter. Not like you. He's—"

"Sensitive."

She touched my knee. I pressed her head to my chest and

held her close, wishing we were ten thousand miles from Tres Marias.

"You're a good man—the best," she said. "I get that you want to protect us and do what's right. I do too. But I feel like we're losing ourselves. Do you know what I mean? All this violence. I'm trying to hang on. But we weren't meant to live this way."

"There was a time when everyone did."

She sat up and looked at me. "That doesn't mean we have to. And what about the baby? I don't even want to think about what kind of world she'll live in."

"She?"

"I'm having a girl, and that's all there is to it."

"I see. No test required?"

"Nope."

"Perfect. Another woman telling me what to do."

"You know you love it," she said.

I was so tired—exhausted to my soul and fed up to here with the stinking rot of death and betrayal. No matter how hard we tried, everything stayed the same—or got worse. There was no cure for the plague, and everyone involved was corrupt. We were fighting people without faces—powers greater than ourselves. Where would it end?

Somehow, Guthrie and Caramel had found a way to survive in the forest without help from anyone. And although they'd suffered a profound loss, they were alive with their guns, dope, crazy furniture, and calaveras.

I couldn't see myself doing the same. For me, there was a long, deserted fire road in the middle of nowhere, strewn with bodies that led to the mouth of hell. And I could walk or run. But sooner or later, I knew where I would end up. It was where everyone went eventually.

My eyes welled with emotion. "I've lost hope."

"I have enough for both of us."

"I love you," I said. "I wish…"

She locked the door. In our bedroom, she laid me down and reminded me of what we used to have when life was good and right. I let go of the pain. Everything would work out, and we would raise our daughter together. We'd find a way to live again.

I kissed her and fell into the sweet nothingness of love-making, with the only person in the world who had the power to save me—my one true friend.

Later, we met in the conference room, where Pederman laid out the situation. I had to give it to him. Despite our predicament, he held it together. Everyone was there—Holly, Warnick, Springer, Erzen, and Griffin. And Fabian, who kept his distance.

"Here's what I know," the supervisor said. "Our plan to rehabilitate homes and apartment buildings is on hold. We're to focus on protecting citizens. That is our mission."

I couldn't believe what I was hearing. "What about the draggers?"

"If we encounter them, we take them out. Now, the mayor has called a meeting at City Hall tonight at 1900 hours. I'd like everyone to be there."

"Better make sure we come armed," I said. "I wouldn't want any surprises."

"For once, I agree with you. Everybody's on edge. I think it's reasonable that we take the appropriate precautions."

"Is it true they're ending the operation?" Warnick said.

"We'll find out tonight."

"Can they even do that?" my wife said.

"Our contract states that they have the right to exercise an early termination clause in cases of nonperformance or negligence. My guess is nonperformance won't fly, so they're going with negligence. Guaranteed, they'll bring up the incident at the checkpoint and say we needlessly endangered civilians."

Holly scoffed. "But they shot at us."

"And if we leave, what happens to Tres Marias?" I said. "And the people we're protecting?"

Springer snorted. "Didn't you hear the man?"

"We'll find out tonight," we said in unison.

"We want out," I said.

In the cafeteria, Holly held my hand as we waited for Warnick's reaction. As usual, his expression was inscrutable.

He took a swallow of coffee. "I'm listening."

"It's all going south fast. Pederman won't have a choice except to do what he's told. If we remain with Black Dragon, we'll be unable to protect ourselves."

He toyed with his cup. "Don't forget. As civilians, you'll be in an even worse position."

"All we need are guns."

"Dave, we've been over this. If you leave, you can't keep your weapons."

"I know where to get more."

Now my friend scoffed. "Guthrie? How will you get there without a vehicle?"

"I'll find a way."

"You mean the way Evie did? And what about Griffin?"

"We haven't told her yet."

He appealed to Holly. Though she and I had discussed

this before meeting with him, the thought of us on our own terrified her.

"I can't believe you're on board with this," he said.

She looked away. "We'll have to take our chances. I'm more afraid of the mayor."

Warnick drained his cup and brought his hands together. For a second, I thought he was going to pray over us.

"It's a bad plan," he said. "Here, you have resources at your disposal—weapons, medicine, everything. Out there, you've got nothing. Okay, some skills. But you've seen how even experienced people can die. No, it's a lousy plan, and I'm opposed to it."

I rolled my eyes. "You can't stop us." He muttered something. "I didn't get that."

"I don't want to lose you, okay?"

My wife gave him a warm smile. "Warnick, are you going soft?" She tried pinching his cheek, but he pushed away her hand.

"What about the mayor?" I said. "He murdered those researchers and tried to kill the rest of us."

"You're still better off sticking with the group. This is no different from Afghanistan. There, you have the legitimate government, warlords, and the Taliban. You can't trust anybody. But what you don't do is go off on your own. That's suicide."

Though I didn't like what my friend was saying, it made sense. Say we got ahold of a vehicle, avoided the draggers, and somehow made it to Guthrie's. Sure, we'd have weapons, but then what? Where could we go? And what about those gray ghosts in the black Escalades? Gripping the edge of the table, I waited for my anger to pass.

"So, we stay here and ride this out?"

"We've got your back."

"Appreciate it."

"Seriously, though," Holly said. "What about the mayor?"

Sighing, Warnick got to his feet. "It's an open question. Let's see what he says at the meeting."

"I hate your logic," I said.

FIFTY-SEVEN

Back in the day, downtown Tres Marias might have been described as charming. Little stores and restaurants used to line both sides of the main drag. On any Saturday night, teens in their parents' late-model cars cruised with their windows rolled down, blasting their music.

In those days, families went to the movies, then to the Tip Top Café for burgers and milkshakes. Meanwhile, in darkened alleys, the cops rousted stewbums and hookers out of sight of the general populace. It was California at its finest.

That was the Tres Marias I remembered as we drove past a dilapidated Dunkin' Donuts on our way to City Hall. But what I saw now was nothing like those rose-colored childhood memories. Shops were boarded up, their windows busted out. Trash lay strewn everywhere. Buildings were bullet-scarred and bloodstained. A torn banner hung from a streetlamp, announcing the mayor's annual prayer breakfast. It would take a crap-ton of money to make this place habitable again, let alone fit for a lifestyle magazine cover.

Warnick and Springer sat in the front seat of our Humvee. Holly, Griffin, Fabian, and I were behind them, tightly squeezed. Greta rode in the rear. We'd come appropriately armed. As we cruised past Staples, I avoided looking up. I still had nightmares about my last shift when Missy attacked us inside the store. That was the day I grabbed a cop's gun and shot my manager as he came at me, hellbent on tearing out my throat.

Unable to resist, I stole a glance. Everything was the same. The shattered windows, the building surrounded by a debris-filled parking lot. Outdoor lights illuminating the bloodstains on the sidewalks that even the rain couldn't wash away.

"It's so sad," my wife said.

The girl pressed her face against the window. "You guys worked there?"

"It's where Dave and I met."

Everything in this town was wrecked except for City Hall, which had been freshly painted. The grass was cut, the hedges trimmed, and landscape lights shone on the building, giving it the appearance of a white temple amid the rubble.

The sky had turned threatening, and the air smelled like rain. There were already several vehicles in the parking area behind the building. We climbed out and did a cursory sweep, looking for draggers. Pederman and Erzen were waiting outside the rear doors as we approached. Griffin insisted on taking Greta with us. She and the dog were inseparable.

"Why don't we meet at the Beehive after for drinks?" I said as Holly gave me the side-eye. "Kidding. Nobody gets me."

In truth, I wasn't kidding. The trauma of the last few days had brought on a nasty thirst. Each time I downed another Dew, I wished it was an ice-cold beer. The urge was always there—to drink and forget. Drunks never joke when it comes to alcohol.

"We've got a couple of minutes," the supervisor said.

"Remember, stay cool. This situation is tense enough as it is. We don't need any hothead shenanigans."

I knew that was meant for me. "I'm as reasonable as the next man." To prove my point, I turned to my left and found Springer cleaning his ear with a paper clip.

Pederman rolled his eyes. "Somehow, that doesn't give me a whole lot of comfort. Okay, let's keep it together, people."

He opened the door and held it for the women. A little civility never hurt. I made a mental note not to fart in my chair.

We marched through a dark hallway smelling of old wood and moldy carpeting. On the walls hung black-and-white photos of public events. I stopped at one of the Christmas parade from twelve or thirteen years back. In the shot, the crowd was visible between the floats.

There in the front stood a cocky kid with a huge grin, waving frantically. Next to him, his mother gazed off somewhere. The boy had on faded blue jeans and a black sweatshirt with a rendering of Arnold Schwarzenegger as the Terminator. Wearing wraparound sunglasses, the big guy was holding a massive gun. The words *I'll be back* were emblazoned across the top.

That kid was me—way before the drinking, when I played hockey like a skinny, crazed demon. My father had already passed, but I was happy. And though I gave my mother hell, she put up with me—I still don't know how. Tearing up, I moved on, saying nothing. Knowing my wife, she would've swiped the photo as a keepsake.

Distant chattering now as we approached the auditorium. I recognized the mayor's voice. He and Walt Freeman were going at it—not in a brawling way, though. When we passed through a final set of doors, the men fell silent.

The room was large enough to accommodate five hundred

people. Ancient wrought-iron chandeliers hung from the ceiling, their light sockets filled with energy-efficient bulbs that gave off an eerie, yellowish glow. Rows of old wood seats faced a curved, raised dais desk. That was where the mayor and the others sat in black leather chairs with high backs. Hizzoner was in the center, with the deputy mayor to his left. Two cops—O'Brien and Hannity—sat on his right.

On the floor in front were a table and chairs where, I assume, various aides might sit during city council meetings. Becky was there, ready to take the minutes on her laptop. Ahead of the first row in the center stood a podium for residents to complain about their water bill or the neighbor's crapping dog.

"Please make your way to the front," Walt said. He stood and gestured, his voice echoing. "The mics aren't working, and we don't want to yell."

Let the shitshow begin.

FIFTY-EIGHT

Pederman led us single file to the first row. The mayor rolled his eyes when Greta curled up next to Griffin. I did my best to contain my loathing for our elected official. As soon as our eyes met, he turned to the others. They conferred for a few seconds, then he struck his gavel and called the meeting to order. The girl tapped her foot repeatedly. Seeing her distress, Holly touched her knee.

"This special session will now come to order," the mayor said. "Let the record show that, in addition to those representing the City of Tres Marias, the following people are in attendance."

As soon as he'd recited the last name, I raised my hand. Reluctantly, he acknowledged me.

"You forgot the dog," I said. Then to Becky, "Let the record show her name is Greta."

Walt's assistant hid a smile with her hand. Springer snorted, and Erzen laughed. Warnick squirmed in his seat, and the supervisor narrowed his eyes at me. Ignoring the comedy routine, the mayor snapped open a manila folder containing a sheaf of papers.

"We had planned to hand out agendas," he said. "But there's a problem with the printers. The first order of business is to talk about the security breach."

I raised my hand again. This time, I didn't wait to be called on. "Are you referring to what happened at the checkpoint or Robbin-Sear?"

"Please don't interrupt. I'm talking about the checkpoint. We'll get to that other matter in due course."

He and O'Brien exchanged a look. The cop was probably imagining a new way to torture me. Thumbscrews maybe, or bad breath. Getting to his feet, he leaned on his hands and glowered. I tried picturing him as a bug—a fat, juicy one I could stomp on.

"Shut it, Pulaski, or—"

"Or what?" Now I was standing. "You'll beat me up again?"

"Let's stick to the business at hand," Walt said and signaled the angry cop to sit his ass down. "These folks were invited."

Covering his eyes, my boss shook his head. I did a quick sweep of the room. Police officers were posted at all the exits. I took my seat and turned to my wife, who gave me a sympathetic smile.

The mayor cleared his throat and jabbed his finger at the document. "Now then. We've conducted a thorough investigation and found that Black Dragon used excessive force in dealing with the trespassers. This is a clear violation of the contract and falls under the negligence clause. Mr. Pederman, care to comment for the record?"

The supervisor shot us an *I told you so* look and stood, his hands balled into fists. He was about to say something when the deputy mayor pointed at the podium. Pederman complied.

"Mr. Mayor, our response was in direct proportion to the threat. We were being fired on. Several of my people are dead as a result of the incursion."

"'Incursion'? I think the word you're searching for is *melee*."

The supervisor didn't take the bait. "In addition, we were dealing with a large number of undead who attacked us from the rear. We were in essence fighting on two fronts."

The mayor shook his head and turned to Walt. Squinting, the deputy mayor referred to his copy of the report.

"Kelly, we've done extensive interviews with the wounded civilians. Each of them—to a person—claims your people fired first."

I'd had enough and stood. "That's a load of crap. They—"

"Dave, sit down," Pederman said, pointing at my chair.

I complied immediately. But it was only because I didn't want him getting into any more trouble. Holly patted my hand. I thought I heard her say *Braver Hund*.

Walt cleared his throat. "Like-uh-said, we have sworn testimony to that effect."

The mayor glared at me, then redirected his wrath at the supervisor. I closed my eyes, willing the little weasel to die from a brain bleed.

"Although we acknowledge that there were undead present. And by the way, can we not use that term? It's degrading."

The rest of the assclowns mumbled their agreement. Satisfied, he went on.

"Our findings show your people engaged in…" He quoted from the report. "'Reckless and excessive violence, needlessly endangering civilians.' As a result, this committee concludes that you violated the terms of your contract and are therefore in breach."

Then, he raised the gavel. "The order assigning authority to the Tres Marias Police Department is now in effect. All in favor?"

"Aye," the others said, like a coin-operated Greek chorus.

"Black Dragon will continue reporting to Captain O'Brien until a transition plan can be implemented," the mayor said.

If this had been a hockey game, I would've wiped the ice with their faces. But it wasn't. Like it or not, that tool was in charge. These sons of bitches had decided the outcome way before we arrived. What was the point of us coming, then? Maybe they wanted to relish the looks on our faces as they destroyed the only hope Tres Marias had for a future.

"And there's your lunch," I said to my wife.

FIFTY-NINE

Zoning out for a sec, I imagined leaping onto the dais and putting a bullet into the head of each of those useless dicks. When I looked at Warnick and Erzen, their eyes were on the cops guarding the exits.

"Captain O'Brien will now go over the details of your new assignment," the mayor said.

The fat cop rolled back his chair and referred to his own set of documents. For the next few minutes, he bored the room with the mind-numbing minutiae of what we'd be doing till they could transition us out. It came down to protecting civilians, searching for survivors, and jerking off.

If we encountered any draggers, we were authorized to neutralize them and incinerate the bodies. Any humans we discovered were to be transported to the command center for testing. If they required anything more than basic medical care, we were instructed to drop them at the hospital.

O'Brien's last point made me want to scream. In case of another perimeter breach, we were forbidden to respond. Instead, Pederman would contact the police department and await instructions. Considering the last time when armed trespassers overran the checkpoint, it would be open season on Black Dragon guards.

"Any questions?" The cop's expression said he hoped there weren't.

The supervisor raised his hand. "Do our patrols extend to the forest?"

"Only if you suspect there are survivors or infected persons out there."

"Regarding the perimeter, what if our people are fired upon?"

"I've already told you. Contact us for instructions."

"Wait," I said. "Are you saying we're not allowed to defend ourselves?"

O'Brien pounded his fist on the desk, startling Becky. "You will wait for instructions. Is that understood?"

Ignoring the apoplectic theatrics, the mayor took over again. "Next item on the agenda. The isolation facility is to be shut down effective immediately."

"What about the patients?" Pederman said.

"That is no longer your concern. All in favor?"

I was on my feet again. "Hold on! What if we encounter a civilian who got bit but hasn't turned yet? Where are we supposed to take them?"

For once, they didn't have an answer. Looking uncomfortable, they conferred among themselves. Nodding, Hizzoner faced us again.

"To the police station," he said. "All in favor?"

"Aye."

Collectively, we scoffed at this, but there was nothing we could do. Someone would have to tell Isaac. We'd been at this for more than an hour. Finally, the mayor addressed the topic I'd brought up at the beginning.

"Now, regarding the incident at Robbin-Sear," he said.

"After looking into the matter, we've determined that the two slain police officers acted in self-defense."

The supervisor gripped the edge of the podium. "That, Mr. Mayor, is completely false. They killed two immunologists in cold blood. And they seriously wounded Dr. Fallow."

"And your people murdered twenty police officers!" the police captain said. "That's prison time, my friend."

Pederman shot a glance at Warnick. "So we're going to jail when it was your people who fired on us?"

"No one's going to jail," Walt said colorlessly.

The mayor organized his papers. "We're treating the incident as a case of friendly fire. All in favor?"

"Aye."

He brought down his gavel, the cracking sound echoing in the auditorium like a gunshot.

"This meeting is adjourned," he said.

They left the building before we could ask any more questions. The cops guarding the exits had vanished. Soon, we were alone in the auditorium, no wiser than when we arrived. They may as well have turned out the lights on us. I thought of that old joke about mushrooms—kept in the dark and fed shit twenty-four seven.

Springer walked up to the dais. "Hello? Can someone validate my parking?"

As I observed Pederman, I felt sick. Here was a man who'd served in the army—who lived and breathed the chain of command. Following orders without question while ignoring the daily crap that tended to roll downhill. Like the rest of us, he seemed confounded by the whole filthy business. Unable to understand what he could've done differently to effect a different outcome—one in which we would come out as heroes instead of borderline criminals.

"We'd better get back," he said.

Outside, the rain came down like broken glass. My breath was white in the chilled air. As we made our way to our vehicles, a dark figure approached us. Her eyes alert, Greta tugged at her leash, but Griffin held her tight. Fabian hovered protectively.

An Asian man stepped into a weak pool of light, pulling at his left arm. He was maybe thirty and slim. Though his clothes weren't shabby, they were bloodstained. He seemed disoriented. I looked hard for signs of infection but didn't see any.

"Why?" he said.

Great question. Why had the plague come down on this sleepy Northern California town and ravaged it mercilessly till the few survivors were beaten and hollow? Why were we cut off, out of reach of the rest of the world? And why had Evil decided to make Tres Marias its bitch? Only one possible answer—the mayor.

"Can I help you?" the supervisor said, his hand on his holster.

The stranger must not have heard. Rocking in the light, he touched his arm at the elbow like a kid who'd fallen off his bike. Something unseen had enraged him, and he tore at the limb as if trying to pull it out of its socket.

Springer held up his hand. "Take it easy, man."

Unholstering our weapons, we arranged ourselves in a half-circle. With guns at our sides, our trigger fingers were ready. The dog let out a low, steady growl. If she hadn't been on a leash, she would have laid into the unfortunate bastard like a chew toy.

The man gibbered now, pleading with the raindrops that fell on his face. I could barely make out what he was saying.

"F-first m-my wife. Then…then my s-sss—dammit—my son. Mah…my little girl…"

Shuddering, he fell to his knees. Holly wanted to help him, but I stopped her. Erzen went, holstering her weapon and gently touching the man's shoulder. Instantly, he snatched her wrist with his good hand. Then, letting out a low, chilling moan, he jumped to his feet and slipped his arm around her throat, cutting off her air. Raising our weapons, we aimed at his head.

"I'll snap her little neck like a twig!" he said.

Erzen struggled to reach her gun. He grabbed her hand and jerked her arm behind her, making her cry out.

"It's your fault," he said into her ear. "My wife. My son. My daughter! Why did you have to burn them? I could've saved them—I wanted to save them!"

"Calm down," Pederman said. "Tell me your name."

"Shut up—it's too late."

He retreated, dragging Erzen with him. There was nothing we could do. I thought about letting Greta go, but he might have time to kill the guard before the dog could hobble him. The loony continued moving backwards into the darkness. Cautiously, we followed.

A gunshot echoed in the stark, empty night. Erzen staggered into the light, coughing and rubbing her throat. She wasn't bleeding. Holly stayed with the guard while the rest of us hurried past.

The man lay twitching on the wet asphalt, the left side of his head torn away. Rivulets of bloody rainwater streamed away from his body. Another man stood nearby, holding a weapon at his side—Hannity.

"Still not safe," he said and disappeared around an inky corner.

SIXTY

No one wanted to tell Isaac the truth, so we faked smiles as he lay in his hospital bed. The room was pleasant. Morning light streamed through a large window, softened by grime from the old firepits. A plastic water pitcher and a stack of paper cups stood on the overbed table. A tray sat beside it with a half-eaten breakfast of weak-looking scrambled eggs and pale toast. Apocalypse or not, hospital food never changed.

"How was breakfast?" I said.

"If the disease doesn't kill you, the food will." He tried smiling, but I could see he was in pain. "They insisted on giving me morphine. Good luck with that."

"No wonder you're so grumpy."

He looked past me at Holly, Pederman, and Warnick. "Is this a social visit? I'm expecting my attorney any minute."

The supervisor moved past us. "Dr. Fallow, I've got some bad news. The mayor is shutting down the isolation facility."

"They can't do that."

"It's already in the works."

"But what about the patients? Our tests?"

"We don't have details yet, but the building is officially off-limits to everyone except the police."

"And here I was thinking you guys were in charge."

"They're ending the operation," Warnick said.

The doctor reached for his coffee cup, but it was empty. "I see. It makes sense after what happened at Robbin-Sear. Are they going to press charges?"

"That's the only good news," Pederman said. "They are not."

Isaac tried sitting up. He winced as my wife and I each took an arm to assist. There was a patch of dried blood on his patient gown—another reminder of how close we'd come to meeting our end.

"Thanks. Closing the facility is a death sentence for those patients."

"They'll use the incinerators," I said.

Holly's eyes widened. "They're going to kill all those people?"

The doctor folded his arms, a resigned look on his face. "Why not? They're contagious."

"But that's murder!"

"What if we placed guards at the facility so no one can get in or out?" Warnick said.

The supervisor shook his head. "You saw the bloodbath at Robbin-Sear. We can't risk it."

My friend persisted. "Isaac, what did you say the patients' mortality rate is?"

"Sixty percent, give or take."

"The mayor will argue that the others would die anyway," I said. "In the meantime, he can't risk infecting healthy people."

The doctor considered my comment. Then, "He's right."

"I get it now," my wife said. "Burning the bodies means no more evidence."

I decided to change the subject. "So, when are you getting out?"

"My doctor advised me to remain here another few days. I advised him that he's a horse's ass. I plan to leave tomorrow, with or without his damn permission."

Concerned, Holly stroked his arm. "Are you sure that's the best thing?"

"What would you prescribe, Doctor?"

She ignored his surliness. "Well, I think you should split the difference. Do some work in your office and sleep here at night. That way, if there's a problem, you'll be taken care of."

He scowled like a ten-year-old with a bedtime. "That's...a good idea. How are you feeling, by the way?"

"Other than a little dizziness, I'm fine."

"Taking your vitamins?"

"Yes, *Doctor.*"

"Good. Make sure she does, Dave."

"We should get going," the supervisor said. "Doc, let me know if you come up with any ideas for the isolation facility. Or the virus. They can't keep this town locked down forever."

"I'll be thinking long and hard on it. Thanks for stopping by."

"Do you think he's safe here?" I said to Pederman in the corridor. "They did try to kill him."

"I'll send over a couple of guards."

"Before we leave, can we take a walk?"

"What for?" my wife said.

"I want to check something out."

We made our way to the rear of the building, where the incinerators were located. There seemed to be many more bodies than the last time we visited.

"Do you think there are still a lot of draggers out there?" I said to Warnick.

"Could be. Unless…"

Holly turned to me, a strange look on her face. "Unless they're lowering the bar."

Two cops, their hands on their weapons, prevented us from getting any closer. I recognized them from the mayor's meeting.

"Can I help you?" one said to the supervisor. His expression didn't indicate helpfulness.

"This is Black Dragon equipment. We're checking to see how the disposal is coming along."

The officer side-eyed his pal. "All good here."

"Great. I'll enter that into my report."

The cop and his partner stood at ease, clearly wanting us to leave. These guys were no more police officers than I was.

My wife shook her head as we approached our vehicle. "Curiouser and curiouser."

"And weird too," I said.

SIXTY-ONE

A thought nagged at me as we pulled into the command center, but I couldn't bring it into focus. Probably all those years of drinking. Pederman had said something I couldn't remember, which only increased my frustration.

Before he could walk up the administration building steps, Holly stopped him. I knew that look. And I also knew it was best not to argue. Fortunately, her anger wasn't directed at me this time. I side-eyed him—poor bastard.

"This is wrong," she said.

He played it cool. "Which particular wrong are we discussing?"

"We can't let the mayor put down all those patients like stray dogs."

"She's right," my friend said. "We have to stop him."

The supervisor turned around to leave. "With everything that's happened, it's hard to know what's right."

"Protecting the innocent is always right," I said.

My wife took my hand. "Mr. Pederman, I can't have this on my conscience."

As he faced us, the look of defeat in his eyes turned to defiance. "Neither can I. Warnick, how many guards do you think we'll need?"

"One squad should do it."

"If I say no, you'll do it anyway, right?"

"No." My friend was dead serious. "I won't go against you."

The supervisor squinted at me. "Does that go for you too?"

"You should know by now—with me, there are no guarantees. But if we don't do something, those people are as good as dead."

He rubbed the back of his neck. "That's what I was thinking. Hell, who needs a pension anyway? Okay, let's do it. Warnick, assemble your team. I'll be joining you."

I turned to Holly. "Are you sure you—"

The look she gave me told me not to go there.

I couldn't stop worrying as we headed to the isolation facility. This had been my wife's idea. But she was carrying our *child*, dammit. And the body armor and helmets were of little comfort. Warnick, Springer, Holly, and I rode in a Humvee while Pederman and Erzen rode with the rest of the squad in an LMTV.

Nearing our destination, we passed a dozen or so Black Dragon guards making their way along the security fence. They carried AR-15s slung across their backs with the bayonets attached. I thought there was something peculiar about them as they continued single file. Using his radio, the supervisor told us to pull over ahead of them.

"Hey!" Pederman said as they approached. "Why haven't you reported in?"

They kept moving as if in a dream. That's when I knew they weren't right.

"I'm talking to you—"

The lead guard let out a death shriek. Then they came at us, surprising us with their speed. Before we could react, they grabbed one of our people and gutted him with their bayonets. The supervisor ordered us to take cover.

As the first few closed in, we ran behind our vehicles to get more weapons. I fired my rifle, catching one in the chest. In a red rage, the hostile tore the gun from my hands and tried eviscerating me. I saw my wife out of the corner of my eye. She fired at the attacker's head. Blood and brains coated the Humvee's windows behind me.

"You're welcome," she said.

"Nice shot." Then, "Holly!"

Another one tried grabbing her, and I yanked her back. As she fell, I retrieved my weapon and blasted the hostile's head in two. The body landed inches from where she was lying.

We put down the others, firing at their necks and heads. When the shooting was over, we examined the bodies. None were corrupt. I crouched beside the closest one and pulled back the eyelid with my thumb. The iris glowed iridescently.

"Hey, look at this," I said.

The others came over to see. As they gathered around me, the dead guard's eye went from purple to brown.

"Just like Ariel," Warnick said.

Erzen knelt next to another body. "Hey, guys? This one's warm. Call me crazy, but I don't think they were draggers."

Pederman crouched next to her. "It's as if the virus is making them more—"

"Human," I said.

SIXTY-TWO

After retrieving the weapons from the dead guards, we stood at the closed gate. The guard shack was empty—same as the parking lot. And no sounds came from inside the building. The fence was at least seven feet high, with three strands of razor wire running along the top.

I let out a tired laugh. "Don't tell me—we're climbing over."

"Patience," Warnick said.

There was a metal box mounted on a fence post with the words FIRE DEPT. Pulling something from his pocket, Springer flipped open the cover and inserted a key. As he turned it, a motor whirred, and the gate opened. Once we were in, the guard closed the gate using a switch inside the guard shack.

Warnick and Springer walked ahead of us. The front doors were locked. I tried peering through a window, but it was dark inside. Springer dug through his pants pocket and pulled out a set of keys.

"What are you, the Keymaster?" I said.

"Dr. Fallow hooked me up."

We raised our rifles as the guard unlocked the doors and swung them open. One by one, we went inside. Someone found the lights.

"What happened?" Holly said.

The building was deserted. Only the plexiglass cells remained. Wary, we cleared the area. As we made our way down a row, I checked to see if the patients' charts were there. Nothing. Eventually, we reached a row of offices along the rear wall.

Springer stepped into one and flicked on the lights. I recalled that each room had contained a desktop computer, monitor, and an external hard drive. Someone had taken everything.

"Let's check all the offices," Pederman said.

It took only a few minutes to hit every room. We didn't see a single piece of equipment, and we didn't find any physical patient records or other files. When we got to the conference room, we sat in the stainless steel and leather chairs. I wanted to shoot the mayor but kept my murderous thoughts to myself.

"You think they already killed the patients?" my wife said, laying her weapon on the table.

Springer leaned back and put his feet up. "Had to."

"And they took all the evidence."

Closing my eyes, I tried to bring into focus everything we'd learned. But there were so many rabbit holes and dead ends. I thought about Ariel. Up till now, I had assumed the patients were expendable. But that was before we encountered the infected guards.

"I don't think those patients are dead," I said.

The supervisor gazed out at the rows of empty cells. "What makes you say that?"

"Remember when we brought in Ariel? And her eyes turned purple?"

"That was right before she attacked us," Warnick said.

"When we found Steve Zimmer, those missing guards were eating his friend."

Pederman spun his finger like a hamster wheel. "And your point?"

"And what about those guards we put down?"

"That's it," Holly said. "I'm gonna smack him."

I gave her a tolerant smile. "The virus is different now."

"We already know that," my friend said.

"Don't you see? It's doing what they wanted it to all along. Erzen, you said it earlier. One of them was warm. That means the experiment is a success."

"Before, the virus would always kill the hosts," my wife said. "And they'd come back as draggers."

Getting to my feet, I addressed the room. "And now, they're no longer dying. But they are changing. Into what, I don't know."

"Are you saying those guards we put down were alive?" Erzen said.

"After Ariel's autopsy, Isaac said she wasn't a dragger. That's why they didn't incinerate the other patients. I think they moved them to another site for further study."

Springer jingled his keys at me. "Hello? Why didn't they take those janky guards?"

"Think about it. Those guys had just wandered out of the forest. Who knows where they were when the cops cleared this place."

"Well, that's just great," Warnick said. "How do we find out where they took the patients?"

"Evie mentioned another facility."

"Mt. Shasta," the supervisor said.

My friend rolled his eyes at me. "And I suppose you think we should go up there."

"You guys agree that everything that happened in Tres Marias was a controlled experiment, right?"

"Not at first. The dog infecting your friend was an accident."

"Sure, but they ran with it. I keep thinking about that little village in Guatemala. Bob Creasy planned to try the test again, probably in some other poor country where no one would ask questions."

"Then Tres Marias dropped into his lap," Pederman said. "Like a gift from heaven."

"And now they've gotten their breakthrough. They don't need our town anymore."

The supervisor brought down his hand on the table. "Dave, every morning, I'm grateful I hired you. And every night when I go to sleep, I regret it."

"Welcome to my world," Holly said.

I ignored the sarcasm. "We need to find that facility. And I might have an idea where to start."

"And just when I was starting not to be pissed off at you," Pederman said.

SIXTY-THREE

Evan kicked her feet as her mother held her. Steve sat next to Nina, holding her hand. He looked much better—nothing like the scared and bleeding victim we'd found in the forest. But he was nervous.

The conference room door was closed. There was no telling who in our organization might be spying for the mayor. Warnick, Holly, and I waited for Pederman to begin.

"How are you doing?" the supervisor said.

"Okay, I guess. The nightmares aren't as frequent."

"Glad to hear it. Understand that no one here is accusing you of anything. We're looking for information. What are they saying out there about Tres Marias?"

"Total news blackout. It's as if the town disappeared."

I jumped in. "What about the internet?"

"Are you kidding? I searched every day, trying to find something—anything. I'm telling you, it's like Tres Marias never existed."

"Tell us about the group you came here with," Warnick said.

Steve fiddled with a pen lying on the table. "When Nina and I were having our troubles, I left town and took a job with a startup in San Francisco. Found a studio apartment in the Mission District. It wasn't much of a life. Mostly, I buried myself in work. There was so much to do and not enough people. Usual story. The hours were long, but I didn't care.

"When the news broke about the sickness, I called Nina. We hadn't spoken in weeks and ended up fighting on the phone. I waited a few days and called again. I told her I wanted to come home. Thankfully, she agreed." He squeezed her hand.

"I saw on the news that they'd quarantined the town. No one knew what was going on. I brought my iPad to work and streamed the news all day while writing code. Everyone did. Eventually, management mounted TVs on the walls with the sound turned off. It was frightening to watch.

"There were so many stories. Evie Champagne seemed like the only credible reporter—the only one who made any sense. After she disappeared, the reports stopped. Pretty soon, everything went dark—newspapers, talk radio... When I couldn't reach Nina, I got scared.

"My team used to like to go to these dive bars after work. No one ever got drunk, though. It was a way to blow off steam. This time, it was Lucky 13. Do you know the place? Anyway, we came in around ten for a few beers after a long day.

"The conversation was always the same. We talked about work, our stock options, and what we'd do if someone acquired us. I overheard a group of men, and someone mentioned Tres Marias. It was the first time I'd heard the name in a couple of weeks. So I decided to talk to them. At first, they didn't want to tell me anything. They were probably afraid I was black ops or something."

"Why would they think that?" Pederman said.

"Early on, rumors were floating around that this endemic outbreak was the result of some kind of government-sanctioned experiment. Someone mentioned Mt. Shasta. Okay, so San Francisco has a lot of very smart tech people. But a few of these guys are big into conspiracy theories. I think Tres Marias fueled their imagination."

"What about you?" Holly said.

"Me? I was somewhere in the middle, thinking the outbreak was due to a virus like H1N1. I told these guys how much I needed to see my family. They asked me where I worked and wanted my address in Tres Marias. When I told them, somebody wrote it down and said they'd be in touch."

"Did they reveal any information about themselves?" the supervisor said.

"No. I had no idea who I was talking to. Looking back, I was pretty naive. I never should've given them my address. These guys could have been anybody. On my way home, I tried not to think about it."

Steve looked parched. As he shifted in his chair, wincing from the pain, I filled a cup with water from a plastic jug. Gratefully, he took it and gulped it down.

"A few days went by, and I hadn't heard anything. I went to that bar every night, but those guys never showed up again. Then I got a call at my desk. They said to meet me at this pub not far from our offices on Market Street.

"When I got there, I recognized one of the guys from that night. We walked down the street to the Yerba Buena Gardens, where we met the other guys who'd been at Lucky 13 and several women.

"I learned that some lived in Tres Marias and were out of town when the quarantine went into effect. Others had friends and family living there. Like me, they wanted to know what happened. And they planned to get in one way or another."

"And then, they armed themselves," Warnick said.

290

SIXTY-FOUR

Reddening, Steve gave Evan his finger to play with. He looked at his wife, who patted his arm encouragingly.

"There was this guy, Kevin—I never got his last name. He was our leader, the one I was with when you found us in the forest. The minute I heard they were planning to bring weapons, I walked. I promised I wouldn't say anything and told them I didn't want to be a part of any violence.

"You have to understand. None of these people were ex-military. And they weren't crazed vigilantes with some political agenda. They were gamers. People who'd only ever experienced warfare playing *Call of Duty* or paintball. But here's the thing—they were committed."

"And they were packing some pretty serious firepower," Pederman said. "Where did they get all those weapons?"

"You can find anything on Craig's List. Anyway, after a few days, Kevin showed up at my work. He claimed Black Dragon was a paramilitary group that had no right to hold the town hostage. He made it sound like we'd be liberating Tres

Marias. I didn't believe any of it. Then he showed me a video he'd discovered in a subreddit. Ever hear of Robbin-Sear?"

"Tell us," I said.

"It was an old marketing video. The quality was terrible. It showed soldiers going into combat. Despite taking direct hits, they killed the enemy and went home. I remember it was called *The Future of Combat*. He insisted it had something to do with the outbreak. Supposedly, Robbin-Sear had built a secret facility in Tres Marias. I didn't care—I just wanted to come home.

"The next weekend, I drove down to find out for myself. When I saw the barricades, the guards, and the helicopters, I began to think Kevin was right. What if this was some colossal government screw-up?

"It terrified me, the thought of going up against you guys. But by this time, I was desperate. All I could think about was Nina and the baby. Her phone kept going to voicemail, and I didn't know whether they were alive or dead. When I returned to San Francisco, I told Kevin I was in."

"When we found you, you didn't have a weapon," Warnick said.

"Kevin had sold me a handgun. He took me to a shooting range in South San Francisco. I was pretty good too. But those were paper targets."

"How did he decide when to attack?" the supervisor said.

"He friended a Black Dragon employee on Facebook, pretending to be a Giants fan. They even went to a game together. After a few beers, the guy let it slip that he was worried about sick people escaping from Tres Marias and infecting other cities. Kevin got him drunk, and he spilled everything—how Black Dragon rotates personnel in and out and when. He explained that during a shift change, there's a brief window when coverage is light."

"That guy is so fired," Pederman said, glaring at us.

"When we got to Tres Marias, I had my gun, but I couldn't bring myself to use it. So, I gave it to someone else. You guys shot at us—I was almost killed! Then the undead showed up, and the guards got distracted. I was with Kevin, and he instructed me to follow him.

"Somehow we made it through and ran, but I caught a bullet. Kevin said we'd go to the hospital once we were through the forest. Pretty soon, I couldn't walk anymore, and we ended up in a clearing. When those Black Dragon guards found us, I thought we were saved. But it was weird."

"What was?" I said.

"It was like they were in some kind of trance. One grunted at the others, and they surrounded us."

"Did they use their weapons?" my friend said.

"No. But they closed in. Their eyes, they... Never mind."

"What about their eyes?" Holly said.

"It was like they were *glowing*. It sounds insane, but I know what I saw. Kevin shot at them until he ran out of ammo. I didn't know what to do—I couldn't run."

Gripping the edge of the table, Steve choked up. "They grabbed Kevin and tore off his pants. I thought they were going to, you know, rape him. The one in charge grunted again. Others handed him the straps from their rifles. As they held Kevin down, the leader tied off his legs at the thigh. Then they used their bayonets to... To..."

Tears rolled down his cheeks. The fear he must've felt then was on his face. Though his mouth was open, no sound came out. His wife rubbed his shoulder and whispered something to him. He nodded and swallowed.

"Eventually, Kevin stopped screaming. He just—he laid there. Probably shock, I don't know. I can still hear them. Cutting his flesh... Eating him. Piece by piece."

The only sound in the room came from Steve, who was sobbing. Evan looked at her father and began crying too. Nina got up and walked around with the baby as her husband tried pulling himself together.

"I'd like to see that video," the supervisor said.

Wiping his eyes, Steve reached into his pocket and pulled out a thumb drive. "I downloaded it before we left San Francisco—I don't know why. I've kept it with me ever since."

Pederman left the room and returned with his laptop. After connecting it to the ceiling-mounted projector, he plugged in the drive. Though the video resolution was low, I could tell it had been professionally produced, with pounding rock music and slick visuals.

It opened with soldiers in a Humvee who were under attack. One got out and took a bullet in the chest. Marching on, he returned fire, killing all the hostiles. When the scene changed, he was home with his wife and baby daughter. The narration implied that, despite having been in combat, he was happy and healthy—no PTSD.

In the final shot, the soldier was asleep in bed. A tagline appeared on the screen: *No more nightmares.*

The supervisor killed the video and looked around the room. No one said anything. Evan reached for her father, and he took her in his arms.

"I think we're done here," Pederman said.

While the others went out for food, I remained alone in the conference room. I couldn't get that image out of my mind— Kevin lying on the ground as those cannibals carved up his legs like meat skewers at a Brazilian steakhouse. The wonders of science, next-gen soldiers who were invincible. But they were cunning too—like draggers—with the same hunger for human flesh. And though they were incapable of speech, that would come later.

What if the infected continued to evolve into something that looked and acted normal by society's standards? Cannibals in suits. How would we recognize them? Was killing one of these the same as killing draggers? Sure, they were alive—but were they human? Would eliminating them be considered murder?

I closed my eyes. A few minutes later, the door opened, and Holly walked in with Warnick and Pederman. Watching them eat made me nauseous. I poured myself a cup of tepid water.

"I brought you a sandwich," she said, handing me a PB&J and a juice box.

The smell made me want to hurl. "Thanks." Then to the supervisor, "We have to find that lab. What's the latest on internet access?"

Pederman took a swig of his Coke. "I did some checking. Someone outside of Black Dragon handles communications. I suspect those agents we encountered in the forest had something to do with the blackout."

"Did anyone check the school equipment to see if it's working?"

"Everything is blocked remotely."

My friend turned to him. "Someone needs to go to San Francisco. What about a special pass?"

"Negative. We're on full lockdown. No one goes in or out. There'll be agents watching the borders, I'm sure of it."

"What about the people we arrested at the checkpoint?" Holly said. "Weren't they supposed to be sent home?"

"Already been released. There's no one left except Steve Zimmer."

"We are so screwed," I said.

SIXTY-FIVE

My friend Jim eyed me like a bug under a microscope. He was dressed in white and reminded me of an old-timey bandleader—the name might have been Cab Calloway. And if you get that reference, I'll give you a dollar. Even his shoes were white. It took me a sec to notice the dark blood leaking from his starched collar.

"Why haven't you stopped this?" he said.

He petted Perro, who sat beside him wearing a white tuxedo and miniature top hat. The dog looked good, the way I remembered him before all the badness. But it was my friend's eyes—*Ariel's* eyes. Glowing purple like those carnivorous creeps who'd dined on Steve Zimmer's friend. Those spinning orbs saw right through me.

"I don't know what you mean."

But I did know. Like always, Jim wanted me to fix it— whatever it was. Of the two of us, he was the worse screw-up. I wouldn't say I was smart, but he was lazy-crazy. Always getting himself into shit and wanting me to dig him out.

What happened to my friend wasn't his fault, though. Not

this time. He died because of what the mayor, Robbin-Sear, and all the rest had brought down on Tres Marias. It was evil with a purpose. So many dead—countless numbers burned efficiently in the incinerators, leaving no evidence of crimes committed. Guthrie had advised us to follow the money. But was this only about riches?

"And you will know the truth, and the truth will set you free," Jim said and belched like in the old days.

He picked out a kidney worm from between his teeth. Incredibly, it was the size of a pickle. He held it up to the light to get a better look. Squirming, it emitted a squeaking noise. The whole business made me sick. Seeing my disgust, he made a frowny face and let the worm slip from his fingers. When it hit the ground, he stomped on it with his heel and stared at the tiny blood spray on his pant leg.

"Oops."

"I don't like these dreams," I said. "Seriously, they're not helpful."

"That's because you never listen. It's your biggest shortcoming."

"I'm listening now."

I realized I was sitting on the floor against a smooth white wall. And though I had on my Black Dragon uniform, I was unarmed. My friend approached me and looked me over. He kicked the soles of my polished boots as Perro sniffed my hand.

"Nice outfit," he said. "You look like a mall cop. Get up."

"Why? So you can start some shit?"

His eyes glowed fiercely, and his voice became a hurricane that pressed me against the wall. The force took away my breath.

"Get up!"

The floor liquefied. Suddenly, I was in the middle of a

twister—swirling—unable to touch the ground. As I tried focusing, I caught glimpses of Holly, Griffin, Warnick, and Springer. I felt like Dorothy. Pederman flew by, then the mayor. Now, O'Brien and Hannity. And finally, Walt Freeman. I was ready to puke when everything stopped. Now I was inside the fence at Robbin-Sear. Outside, a thousand old-school draggers moaned and raked their claws against the chain link, wanting to devour me. A part of me wished they would.

The front door opened, and Jim showed himself. He wore a patient gown printed with a field of lilacs. His unruly hair and days-old beard added to his unkempt appearance. He was three sheets to the wind and reeked of beer and vomit. This was my friend right before the car accident. Sloppily, he waved me inside.

"Where are you taking me?" I said.

"You'll see."

Instead of the reception area, there was a long plexiglass wall. And behind it, a massive warehouse where naked bodies floated vertically, end-to-end, as far as the eye could see. Their skin was dry and hairless, the muscles sinewy.

We continued downstairs to the lab where Dr. Royce was working. He was clean-shaven and wore a freshly laundered medical lab coat. I remembered shooting him in the face. The only evidence was a reddish-brown bullet hole above the bridge of his nose. When he spoke, he sounded English—like Ash from the movie *Alien*.

"Jim, where have you been?" he said.

"Dr. Royce, I brought my friend Dave. You'll have to forgive him—he's a little slow. I tried explaining the situation. Can you give it a go?"

The scientist gave him a pained sigh. "I suppose." Then to me, "Have a seat, young man."

Familiar faces appeared from the shadows—Holly, Griffin, Warnick, and many others. They lay on the ground, piling one on top of the other till they were the height of a low wall. Admiring his handiwork, he waited for me to do something.

"Sit down," he said. Then to Jim, "You're right, he's an imbecile."

My cheeks burning, I plopped on top of Springer. Blood seeped from the base as my weight settled.

"You see, Dave, it's like this."

He launched into a technical dissertation I couldn't follow. I put up with it, mainly because I knew the dream was a manifestation coming from my own mind. As he spoke, his skin decayed. His speech became thick, and he was starting to smell. I side-eyed my friend, whose head wagged like a metronome to Royce's technobabble.

The scientist went on for what seemed like hours. I struggled to comprehend, but it was no use. And the more he explained, the more he rotted. Finally, a shrunken eye popped out of its socket and hung lazily from the stalk.

"I can't make it any plainer than that," he said.

"I didn't understand a word of it."

Jim shrugged at Royce. "See what I mean?"

My friend stood close to me, smelling of smoke. I felt myself being absorbed into him. It was as if I was a part of whatever eternal damnation he was suffering.

"You already know how this ends," he said. "Do I have to spell it out?"

"You'll have to—I'm an imbecile."

"Everyone dies. Remember Guatemala?"

It was night now. Jim and I stood on a grassy slope at the mayor's house. His boys were playing football under the lights. They laughed as they chased each other around the yard. In the town below, flames licked the sky and smoke billowed. The human fire pits were back, filled to the brim with burning bodies.

Whoever did this was finished with Tres Marias. They would get rid of the evidence and start over somewhere else. They'd killed the innocent along with the rest, erasing every trace of what happened. And when it came time to explain—because someone always has to explain—they'd claim they eradicated the virus. But unfortunately, everyone was sacrificed.

Just like Guatemala.

SIXTY-SIX

Early blue light bled through the curtains. Shivering, I opened my eyes. I could still feel Jim's presence and smell the smoke from the burning bodies. Had my friend come to me in a dream for real? Or was it my mind putting a neat bow on a mystery that defied understanding?

"It's early," Holly said, stroking my hair. "Bad dream?"

"We need to get away from here."

"Why?"

"I know what the mayor is planning to do. He—"

Before I could finish, I heard the first screams. Greta trotted to our bedroom door and sat there, her ears forward. Rubbing the sleep from her eyes, Griffin appeared behind the dog.

"Get dressed," I said.

We armed ourselves and waited near the door. The dog was on her feet, ready to defend us. I pulled back the curtain and peered out. Guards and civilians ran in every direction. My radio crackled—it was my friend. A horde had breached the fence. I gave the women the signal to wait. When it was safe, I flung open the door and told them to remain behind me.

Across the way, Warnick, Springer, and others engaged the invaders. The girl tried bringing Greta. Worried the animal would be shot, I locked her in the trailer. We joined the fight, taking down draggers as we went.

"We need more guns," my friend said.

Seeing our chance, we raced towards the administration building. Behind it was a smaller structure we used as an armory. Pederman was already unlocking it when we arrived. After slipping inside, we bolted the door.

We put on body armor and helmets and went for the long guns. There was a bullpup similar to the one Guthrie had given me the first time we met. I grabbed it and plenty of ammo.

"How did they get in?" my wife said.

The supervisor checked his handgun. "Someone shot the sentries."

There was a loud banging on the door. Springer hurried over. "Who is it?"

"Erzen and Fabian!"

He let them in. "Did either of you get bit?"

She glared at him. "We're fine."

Griffin ran to her friend, and they embraced. Then she helped him with weapons.

"How many have we lost?" Warnick said to Pederman.

"Unknown. We've evacuated as many as possible from the trailers and put them in the gymnasium. I don't know how long they can hold out. I've already notified Captain O'Brien."

"This is not happening again," I said.

My friend and I knew the likely outcome. The last time the gym was used as an evac center, everyone inside was lost to draggers after the campus was overrun.

"Are there guards locked in with them?"

The supervisor nodded. "One squad."

"What are we waiting for?" Springer said.

Pederman gave Holly a serious look. He was about to say something when she cut him off.

"Don't even ask," she said.

I didn't want her to go, but it was pointless arguing.

The supervisor gave the interns a grim smile. "And you two. Each of us has to fight to survive. Copy?"

"Copy that," the girl said and reached for a helmet.

Springer brought body armor and a helmet for Fabian. There was terror in the Latino's eyes, and I recalled how he'd panicked the last time. The poor bastard was as good as dead. I hoped he wouldn't get anyone else killed in the process.

Griffin helped him suit up. "Come on, Fabio. Show 'em what you got."

"Mierda." He slung his AR-15 over his shoulder. "Okay, I'm ready."

On Pederman's signal, we exited the building. As expected, victims of the horde had turned. We fanned out to take care of as many as we could. If we found civilians who weren't infected, we'd take them to the administration building. We couldn't risk opening the gym again.

"Stay with your battle buddy," the supervisor said. "Now move it!"

As we marched forward, we took out everything we could. The gunfire was deafening. I fought to keep it from affecting my balance and thought of Steve and Nina Zimmer. Had they made it safely to the gym with Evan?

The horde seemed to swell despite our attempts to neutralize them. From their lumbering movements, I knew they weren't the cutters who'd used tools to dismember their prey. These were OG—and easier to kill. I never thought I'd find that comforting as they came at us from every direction.

I tried keeping an eye on my wife, but everything was moving too fast. Anyway, she could take care of herself. The interns were nearby. Griffin shot two draggers through the head with a single bullet. Fabian aimed his rifle. I'd observed him at the shooting range—he was good. But this was about overcoming your fear.

The girl whispered something to him and took a step back. Furious, he fired a stream of bullets that took down an entire line of draggers. They fell as if their movements were choreographed. It was a sight to behold.

"Nice work," I said as he lowered his weapon. "You good?"

As he marched off to find more hostiles, I squinted at Griffin. "What did you say to him?"

"I told him to get his fat Mexican ass in gear."

"Nice."

"I only said it to make him mad."

I tapped her helmet and signaled her to join her friend.

Once we made it to the ATVs, it was easier to get around. Holly and I rode in a four-seater between buildings, trailers, and vehicles, searching for more survivors. As we approached an MMU, I heard someone yelling for help and pulled up in front. Inside, we found a physician's assistant and a phlebotomist cowering behind a stack of boxes.

"Time to go," I said.

By ten, we had destroyed the horde. We sat on the administration building steps, surveying the damage. The command center had become a desolate landscape painted in blood. We'd lost an entire platoon—nearly a hundred men and women—and twenty or thirty civilians. Already, guards were loading up flatbed trucks to deliver the dead to the incinerators. By some miracle, everyone inside the gym and administration building had survived, including the Zimmers.

Fabian had proven himself, and I was proud of him. Griffin sat with him on a lower step, resting her head on his shoulder. Warnick and Springer were next to Holly and me. As we warmed ourselves in the late morning sun, Pederman walked out of the building. From his posture, I guessed more bad news was coming. He could barely get the words out.

"We lost Erzen," he said.

My wife got to her feet. "Where?"

"Last time I saw her, she was evacuating civilians from a trailer. We found her on the football field."

I'd been wrong about the horde. Unseen cutters were among them and had lashed her to the chain-link fence with rifle straps. And like Steve Zimmer's doomed friend, she'd been flayed alive and eaten, her face frozen in a rictus of terror. My stomach churned as Warnick and Springer took her down.

"This was deliberate," I said to Holly. "They wanted as many dead as possible."

"What are you talking about?"

"They're preparing to cleanse the town."

A burning rage consumed me. My hands shaking, I checked the ammo in my bullpup. Then I started off. The supervisor tried grabbing my arm, but I pulled free and kept going. Everyone shouted at me—I ignored them. The loudest was Pederman, demanding to know where I was going.

"To end this," I said.

SIXTY-SEVEN

Without judgment, Holly talked me off the ledge. She and Warnick had caught up with me as I stormed out of the command center. I didn't even know where I was going. All I knew was that I had to do something. She reminded me of the life our daughter would have without her father. Cheap shot.

After lunch, we met in the conference room. Thankfully, no one mentioned my earlier behavior. Outside, guards continued the grisly cleanup. The reek of blood and vomit hung thick in the air, even inside the air-conditioned building. Or maybe the smell was in my head.

"This was the mayor's doing," I said to Pederman.

He was a good man. Over these past weeks, I came to understand that. He'd tried to run a crisp operation by the book. But he was working against powers no one could control—not even Black Dragon. Hellish forces that were put in motion years earlier. Whoever it was—the military, a covert government agency, or Satan himself—they would not be stopped. And the soulless machine they'd created had one goal. What was it Creasy had called it? The Holy Grail. Funny thing for the Devil to search for.

"Dave, I know you don't think much of me."

My wife gave me a scalding stare. "That's not true."

Now with Erzen's death, I could barely keep my shit together. "I know none of this is your fault. You did your best. But we can't follow the rules anymore because no one else is."

"What did you mean about cleansing the town?" Warnick said.

"They'll get rid of the evidence. And that includes everyone who lives and breathes."

"And the draggers?" Springer said.

"Them too. Mr. Pederman, it was something you told Isaac before. You said they couldn't keep the town locked down forever. And you were right—they can't. Which means they'll raze it to the ground. Like Guatemala. We have to stop them."

Holly scoffed. "Stop the government? Listen to yourself."

"We need to try."

"What are we supposed to do?" Griffin said.

The girl had never spoken up in any of our meetings before. All eyes were on her now. Fabian nodded encouragingly. Her cheeks blazing, she pushed ahead.

"If what Dave says is right, we can't stay here." Then to me. "Or we're dead too, right?"

"Unless we take back control."

"There's a problem," my friend said. "The mayor put the police in charge."

I glanced around the room. "So let's arrest him."

"This is no time to be funny," my wife said.

"I'm dead serious."

Others joined in, and the exchanges got heated. Soon,

everyone was on their feet except the supervisor. As chaos reigned, he pushed back his chair and stood at attention.

"*Silence!*"

Now I knew what they meant by a "command voice." Meekly, everyone sat and stared at their hands. Pederman flipped open the folder sitting in front of him. Inside were printed pages filled with margin notes and yellow highlighting.

"Our mission is, and has always been, to protect the citizens of this town. But that also means protecting our people. Now, I've studied this contract. It states that the agreement can be terminated if Black Dragon engages in *willful or malicious injury to persons or property.*"

"If you're talking about the checkpoint—"

"Dave, I'm not finished," he said.

I wasn't sure if I liked the new Pederman.

"The contract also covers negligence." He turned to a new page. "In taking away our authority, the mayor put the responsibility of protecting civilians—and us—on the police. Anyone see them coming to our rescue? No, ladies and gentlemen. They were negligent. Therefore, the mayor is in breach."

Springer grinned like an imbecile. "Which means..."

"All authority over this town reverts to us," the supervisor said.

Early the next morning, two heavily armed squads headed out in Humvees and an LMTV with a flatbed and side rails. Everyone wore body armor and helmets. I tried imagining what it must have been like for the other guards, most of whom had deployed to war zones like Kandahar. Though Tres Marias wasn't like that awful place, the situation wasn't any less perilous. Always the joker, Springer reminded us not to forget about Walt Freeman's assistant, Becky.

"I might need to frisk her later," he said, picking at a hangnail.

Holly belted him on the arm. "You're disgusting, you know that?"

Like a scene from a movie, we arrived at the police station in force. Pederman ordered Griffin and Fabian to remain outside. Armed with AR-15s, the rest of us marched up the steps and burst in. No one was at the desk. We continued to the front office, where we found bored cops sitting or standing around shooting the shit. When they saw us, the place went quiet.

The men's room door creaked open, and Hannity walked out. "What the hell do you think you're doing?"

The supervisor stepped in front of us. "Arresting all of you."

The cop gave him a weak laugh. "Dumb sons of bitches— you can't arrest us. Captain O'Brien is in charge, remember? If anything, we can take *you* in." Then to the others, "Right, guys?"

Another officer drew his weapon and fired, missing Pederman by a hair. Warnick shot him. Screaming and clutching his knee, he keeled over. Hannity reached for his gun and froze as Springer pointed his rifle at the cop's head.

"I wouldn't try that," the supervisor said. "My people are highly trained and will without mercy drop you like last week's girlfriend."

It was official—I was in love with the new Pederman.

The supervisor instructed the officers to place their weapons on the floor and line up against the wall. My friend administered first aid to the injured cop. One squad swept through the premises and outside the building, looking for others. Meanwhile, the other team handcuffed the prisoners behind their backs using zip ties. They escorted them to the LMTV.

"You won't get away with this," Hannity said.

Springer scoffed. "Move your ass, shitbird."

After we loaded up the prisoners, Pederman did a quick headcount. He ordered the LMTV to head out with the other squad.

"How many?" I said.

"Twenty, not counting the injured cop."

"That can't be all of them."

The supervisor surveyed the parking lot. "You're right. We'll get the others eventually."

Our squad did another sweep to make sure no one was hiding in the building. We confiscated the weapons and went next door to City Hall. The only person we found was Becky. She was in her office, working on her laptop. Startled, she looked up with huge eyes.

"It's okay," my wife said. "We're not here to harm you. Where's the mayor?"

"At home, I think?"

Warnick came forward and took the assistant's arm. "You'd better come with us."

We escorted her out of the building and into our Humvee. Holly rode with Griffin in another vehicle, and Fabian rode with us. As we made our way to the command center, Springer leaned over from the front seat and smiled at Becky.

"You know, when this is over, we should hang out," he said.

Her ears turning crimson, she flipped open her laptop and pretended to work. Eventually, Romeo got the message. He didn't say another word the rest of the way.

At the command center, a waiting guard escorted Walt's

assistant into the administration building. As she disappeared inside, the Latino sauntered over to Springer.

"Smooth," he said, grinning. "Real smooth."

We decided to use the isolation facility since Tres Marias didn't have a jail. It was the only place we could think of that was big enough to house the prisoners. On the way, Springer blasted a song on his phone—"Seven Nation Army" by The White Stripes. That took me back.

The LMTV was empty when we arrived. One of our people manned the guard shack and opened the gate for us. Inside, the police officers stood in separate plexiglass cells with guards watching them. Nearby in an examination room, a doctor and nurse treated the injured cop.

Holly, Griffin, and Fabian went off to help with food and water distribution. As Warnick and I walked past Hannity's cell, the cop narrowed his eyes at me. Despite his predicament, he continued to be a royal asshole.

"You have no idea what you've done," he said. "I feel bad for you."

"Save the sympathy for yourself."

After locking the front doors, Pederman joined our squad. "Okay, let's head out."

"I wonder if the mayor knows we're coming," I said.

SIXTY-EIGHT

Springer used binoculars to scan the countryside from the Humvee's passenger window as Warnick drove. Sitting in the front, Pederman looked grim. Holly was next to me and held my hand. A slew of memories raced through my mind—images of everything that had happened since the start of the outbreak. And now, we were about to arrest the man responsible.

I craned my neck to look at the Black Dragon vehicles trailing us. Griffin sat up front in a Humvee. Fabian and Greta were behind her in the backseat. When she caught me spying, she smiled and waved. I loved that kid with all my heart.

"I can see six—no, eight—draggers," Springer said. "They're pretty far off, though."

The supervisor turned around. "Any cops?"

"Nada."

We turned onto a familiar winding road. It had been freshly paved, the divider line a brilliant white. At the bottom of the driveway, we stopped maybe twenty feet away from the black wrought-iron gates. The other vehicles lined up behind us. Pederman instructed us to wait in the Humvee as he and Warnick exited.

They examined the gate and squinted at the security cameras. The mayor had to have seen us by now. No matter—too late to call in reinforcements. The supervisor signaled the other drivers. Then he and my friend returned to our vehicle.

"Seatbelts, people," Warnick said.

Before we could respond, he floored it, springing open the gates. The other vehicles passed through and followed us to the top of the hill, where we found six or seven police cruisers parked in the driveway.

The shooting started before we could get out. Cautiously, we opened the doors and scooted behind our vehicles, using them as shields. Cops fired shotguns at us from the second floor. Fortunately, we'd thought ahead and brought riot guns equipped with CS gas canisters. Springer grabbed one and waited for the order.

My wife took Pederman's arm. "There might be children inside."

Nodding, he raised a bullhorn. "This is a warning. Move away from the windows." Waiting a beat, he pointed at Springer. "Fire!"

The guard shot a canister through an upper window and another through a first-floor window. As acrid smoke billowed out, someone screamed. In seconds, the front doors flew open. Two women and two children staggered out, choking and wiping their eyes. I recognized them as the mayor's family and their housekeeper. The younger boy vomited.

"Don't kill us!" the mayor's wife said.

Springer laid down his weapon and ran towards the frightened civilians. More blasts exploded from the open windows. The buckshot struck the guard in the chest. Hitting the ground, he reached for his handgun as the family huddled on the front porch.

I heard a familiar sound and was grateful this was a military-style operation. A high wind kicked up at my back as the intense drone of beating blades grew louder. I glanced over my shoulder. A Black Dragon helicopter swooped in and hovered ominously over the driveway.

The supervisor waved to Springer. "Get them out of there!"

Crouching, the guard scooted ahead and, taking each of the boys' hands, escorted them down the steps to our vehicles while the women followed. As they came closer, a hail of bullets rained down. Several struck the housekeeper in the back. Wailing, she hurtled forward and fell.

Springer shoved the boys and their mother into a Humvee. Pederman fired two more gas canisters as the guard went back for the housekeeper. Hugging the ground, he checked for a pulse and gave us a thumbs-down. Then he scrambled to rejoin the squad.

Screaming, the mayor's wife tried going to the dead woman. The supervisor restrained her. In a rage, she clawed at him and gaped at the body like it wasn't real.

"I don't understand what's happening!" she said.

He took her arm. "Where's your husband?"

"I don't know—we got separated. Why are you people doing this?"

Pederman raised the bullhorn again. "Lay down your weapons and come out with your hands up."

More gunfire and shotgun blasts. Above us, a gunner aimed the Browning M2. When the supervisor gave the signal, the helicopter moved into position.

"No!" the mayor's wife said.

We covered our ears as the gunner blasted a line of fire

across the second story. The deadly assault destroyed every-thing in its wake—windows, walls. All of it. He repeated the action along the first floor.

"Make them stop!"

After two more volleys, the helicopter pulled back. We listened for movement inside. Warnick and Springer aimed their rifles at the house and cautiously approached. The columns surrounding the front entrance had been sheared in two. Before the guards could enter, the porch roof collapsed.

Griffin pointed at the sky. "Look!"

A second helicopter lifted off from the lawn at the rear of the house. Shading her eyes, the mayor's wife watched it ascend. Her children left the vehicle to join her. The look of disbelief on their mother's face turned into burning hatred. She faced Pederman, her eyes pleading.

"How could he leave us here?" she said.

Breaking away, she stood in the middle of the driveway, incredulous, as the aircraft pulled away from the house. The supervisor guided the family to the Humvee.

"We came here to arrest your husband," he said. "Looks like he's trying to save himself."

"And he abandons his family?"

"You're safe now. We'll take you and your sons to the command center."

Pederman grabbed his radio and gave an order. Immedi-ately, our helicopter went after the mayor. The gunner fired a warning volley, which did nothing to stop the other aircraft's progress.

"Shoot them down," the supervisor said. "Do you copy? Over."

The mayor's wife stared at the sky, her face devoid of emotion.

"Copy," the pilot said.

As our people moved into position, a smoke trail appeared from the ground through the trees. Instantly, the Black Dragon helicopter exploded in a ball of flame, the sound reverberating. Spinning wildly, it fell like a dead bird.

"The hell?" Fabian said.

Pederman tapped my friend on the helmet and pointed. "Stinger missile. Came from that direction."

The other helicopter descended and landed at the spot where the missile had been fired. As it lifted off again, the forest swallowed it. The mayor was gone.

The supervisor turned to the mayor's wife. "Your husband is a criminal."

"My husband is a selfish prick," she said, gazing at the tree line.

Pederman ordered a squad to proceed to the crash site. He instructed an LMTV driver to transport the civilians to the command center. Meanwhile, another squad checked the house to search for survivors. The rest of us drove to the forest's edge to join the others.

Our helicopter's burning shell stood nose-down on the ground, its bent blades digging into the earth like grasping fingers. Thankfully, it had rained recently, so the fire hadn't spread. Six or seven draggers surrounded the twisted hulk. We dispatched them with bullets to the head and moved their miserable carcasses out of the way.

The passengers lay dead around the wreckage, probably killed instantly when the missile struck. Their faces and hands were gored. The supervisor unholstered his sidearm and shot each of them in the head. Springer kicked at something, then picked it up. It was a rabbit's foot.

"Guess the mayor knew we were coming."

"Right," I said. "But where is he going?"

PART FIVE

JUST LIKE GUATEMALA

SIXTY-NINE

The mayor's wife pushed the food around her plate with a plastic fork. She rubbed her eye with her little finger and stared off somewhere like a dayroom patient. Closed off and disheveled, she looked nothing like the polished, confident politician's wife I'd met that first time. We sat in the cafeteria at a table by the windows. Outside, her boys played touch football with Griffin, Fabian, and some other kids.

"Can I get you anything?" the supervisor said.

"No, thanks."

"Again, I want to express my deepest sympathies regarding your housekeeper."

"Why? You didn't shoot her." She looked up, her face defiant. "When all this started, we made it clear that she was free to go. But she insisted she couldn't leave me and the boys."

"How much did you know about your husband's affairs?"

"Are you talking about business or pleasure?"

Her voice rang with the bitterness of betrayal. I couldn't help wondering where a politician would get any action in a town under siege. Then, her face darkened as she focused on something across the room—Becky sitting alone, reading a library book. Really? The mayor and Walt's assistant?

"Did your husband ever discuss the town's business?" Pederman said. "The police and so forth."

"You're asking if I knew about a conspiracy, is that right?"

"I'd appreciate any details of what he was working on. And whether he may have been involved with another agency —possibly federal."

She picked up a French fry. After inspecting it, she flung it at a nearby table, where it landed on a chair.

"Guess that's detention for me," she said.

The supervisor didn't crack a smile. "Can we stick to the topic at hand?"

"The truth is my husband didn't tell me anything. He was always in meetings. For all I know, he was holed up with that brassy-haired skank."

"Are you suggesting that—"

"Besides, Walt Freeman handled all the important stuff."

Pederman side-eyed Warnick. "The deputy mayor?"

She stared at her hands. "It's kind of funny if you think about it. We never had a deputy mayor before. Then, one day in the middle of the shitstorm, this fat guy from who-knows-where waltzes in. After that, my husband always deferred to him."

"Did the mayor ever mention Robbin-Sear?"

"I told you, he never shared anything with me. Not that I was interested. I had my hands full with my sons. You ever try keeping two young boys occupied day after day? With no school, no friends, and no outside activities? Those...dead things always hanging around outside the gates?"

"It must have been very stressful."

"It was hell. I remember one time when Walt and that sad excuse for a police captain met at the house. I was in the kitchen fixing the boys a snack. The men were in the dining room, and I overheard them discussing a science experiment. Someone mentioned a name—sorry, I can't remember."

"Bob Creasy?" I said.

"That's the one. Walt said he'd already met with him. Creasy had convinced him they were ready to move on to the next phase."

The supervisor lowered his voice. "Do you have any clue what that might mean?"

"I went outside to feed the boys. Later, I told my husband what I'd heard. He said not to worry. Walt had everything under control, and soon, the plague would be history. I wanted to believe him."

"Did Creasy ever come to the house?" my friend said.

"No, it was always Walt. Come to think of it, he was there nearly every day."

Pederman wrote down something. "Ma'am, did your husband happen to mention when the quarantine would be lifted?"

"I used to ask him all the time. In fact, I begged him to let me take the boys down to my sister's in LA. But he kept insisting everything would be fine. He said he needed his family around him."

"Yet he took off without you," I said and immediately regretted it.

She shot me a hateful look. Then, her eyes welled up. My wife laid a comforting hand on her arm.

"I really can't explain it," she said. "I mean, who leaves their wife and children like that? Unless…"

The supervisor leaned in. "Ma'am?"

"Unless it's not my husband who's calling the shots," she said.

SEVENTY

The words the mayor's wife had spoken swirled in my head. What was she saying? Of course, the mayor was in charge. He was responsible for everything. Or was he? *We never had a deputy mayor before.* Walt Freeman had arrived in a black Escalade identical to the ones driven by those agents in gray suits. Coincidence?

She pushed aside her tray and stood. Everyone followed suit. The supervisor tried a smile, but any moron could see her words had shaken him too.

"We've set up a trailer for you and your sons," he said. "There's someone outside waiting to escort you. And please let us know if there's anything else we can do."

Though she was an attractive woman, she looked shopworn. There were dark circles under her eyes that no amount of makeup could hide. As the mayor's wife, she must've put up with all kinds of shit. I wondered whether she believed it was worth it.

"Thank you, Mr. Pederman," she said and shook his hand like someone with good breeding.

"If you need anything, just ask."

She walked towards the exit alone. We were about to sit when she stopped at Becky's table. With sudden fury, she grabbed the other woman's coffee cup and flung it at her.

"Bitch!"

Recovering her composure, the mayor's wife left the building amid stares and murmuring. The supervisor shrugged. I stole a glance at Holly—her expression was unreadable. Then...

"She doesn't deserve this," she said.

Pederman finished his coffee. "I've already questioned Becky. She insisted her sole function was to take care of administrative details for Walt."

"You're telling me she didn't sit in on any private meetings?" I said. "Didn't hear anything important being discussed?"

"She told me there were meetings. Everything they covered was routine business."

"She's lying," Warnick said.

"Possibly. But I don't think we'll get anything more out of her."

Springer appeared at the entrance. When Becky saw him, she dropped the napkins she'd used to dry herself and marched past him. Unfazed, the guard jogged over. He whispered something in the supervisor's ear.

Pederman seemed perplexed. "And you're sure?"

"Buddy of mine showed it to me," the guard said.

Exiting the command center, we drove to a nearby parking lot surrounded by a chain-link fence. Inside, there were rows of yellow school buses. As we made our way to the rear of the property, Pederman explained that Black Dragon maintained a private satellite-based data communications channel connected to our drones. Holly instructed Greta to wait outside while we entered a gray portable classroom.

The room was dark, filled with computers and other electronic equipment. The supervisor led the way as we walked single file down the middle aisle. We passed teams of guards seated in front of dual computer monitors, the glow illuminating their faces. One monitor displayed tabbed menus with scrolling data, while the second showed a live black-and-white video feed as the drone made its way around Tres Marias. The only sound in the room came from squeaking chairs.

I watched as a technician used a joystick to zoom in. On the screen, a dragger pack lumbered across an open field.

"Can't we arm the drones to take them out?" I said.

The young woman smiled appreciatively. "That would be awesome. But it's not in our contract."

A team lead named Keck walked up and, high-fiving Springer, shook hands with Pederman. He led us to a separate set of monitors, where another team sat. Here, they used only keyboards and mice—no joysticks.

"This is where we analyze the video recordings," he said. "We've gone through hours of it, trying to piece together how the attack happened. I think we got it."

He sat at the keyboard and used a mouse to navigate a list of time-stamped video files. Selecting one, he played the clip.

"That's the high school," the supervisor said and pointed at the timestamp. "Just before dawn."

"Notice that the surrounding streets are quiet." The team lead stopped the video and played another clip. "This was taken by a different drone ten minutes later. Keep your eye on the guard shack."

Pederman squinted at several dark figures approaching the command facility. "What are those, draggers?"

"Just watch," Springer said.

On-screen, the intruders closed in. Though there was no sound, bright muzzle flashes told us they'd fired on the shack. Seconds later, they loaded the guards' bodies into an unmarked van and drove off.

"Is there any more?" Warnick said.

Keck shook his head. "That's the end of the time period. These are autonomous drones, so they move independently from one place to another."

"Why the technicians then?"

"We can take over if necessary. Given the circumstances, we've set up extra surveillance around the command center."

My friend turned to the supervisor. "The attack was planned. They took out the guards, got rid of the evidence, and opened the gate."

"But it still doesn't explain where the horde came from," my wife said.

The team lead gave her a smile. "That's where things get interesting."

He navigated to a different folder. Scanning the screen, he found the file he was looking for and played it. Everyone moved closer.

"This was taken in the forest hours earlier," he said.

Though it was dark, I could make out faint lights and the outlines of low buildings. "That looks like Robbin-Sear."

A large gray mass made its way past the open gate. Ahead of it, a vehicle drove slowly away from the facility.

"Draggers," Warnick said. "And they're following that truck."

I pointed at the monitor. "Wait, you're saying this horde walked all the way from Robbin-Sear to the high school?"

Keck nodded. "This recording began around 0030. Other drones captured them at various points along the way. But it looks like they were headed for the command center. It took them a little over five hours."

"And you're certain this was the horde that attacked us?" Pederman said.

"We have video of them approaching the high school. I can dig it up if—"

"No, it's fine." The supervisor rubbed the back of his neck. "But how in hell do you get them to stay together all that way?"

The team lead got up and stretched. "That's easy. You use a carrot instead of a stick." He paused for effect. "This morning, one of our patrols spotted an abandoned pickup truck near the railroad tracks."

My friend rolled his eyes. "The suspense is killing me."

"They found a half-eaten body chained to the tailgate."

"The carrot," Holly said. "Any idea who it might be?"

"There was no ID, but they did take some photos." He flipped open a blue folder, revealing a grisly image of a middle-aged male. He was almost gored beyond recognition, except for the head. I recognized the dark curly hair and sallow complexion.

"That's Bob Creasy," I said.

SEVENTY-ONE

The next day, we returned to Robbin-Sear. We hoped to discover what the mayor, Walt Freeman, and the rest had in mind for Tres Marias. Me, I believed in my dream—the one where Jim laid it all out. Not that I shared it with anyone.

There was no way for Tres Marias to reopen without someone wiping the slate clean. Towns can be repopulated. And over time, people tend to forget. After a generation, guess what—it never happened. Or the story morphs into some new urban legend.

✓ Chemical spill devastates Tres Marias.
✓ Cleanup crew arrives—danger is neutralized.
✓ Medals are awarded.

The gate was open when we got there—not a good sign. Many of the buildings had sustained damage during the shootout with the cops. We would have to comb through each one. And I'd forgotten about the lingering effects of CS gas. This was going to be a treat.

Exploring the property, we found two incinerators behind the main building. I opened one. It was filled with fine ash and the partially burned remains of what might have been lab animals mixed with pieces of human bone. And still warm.

Something crunched underfoot. Crouching, I found a pair of horn-rimmed glasses like the ones Bob Creasy wore. This must've been where he met his end. But instead of inciner-ating him, they put his corpse to work. I couldn't say I felt sympathy for him—he had gallons of blood on his hands. Still, I couldn't help wondering if he'd felt any remorse for the monstrous things he did.

After a couple hours, someone from the other squad pulled Pederman aside to tell him they'd found something. The guard led us to a far building resembling a ranger's cabin. The front yard was beautifully manicured, with a green lawn and flowerbeds. A sign over the door read RECREATION ROOM.

"This grass isn't real," Holly said. "And neither are those flowers."

The supervisor walked up to the entrance and peered through a window. Then the guard forced open the door. Inside, there was a ping-pong table, a pool table, and a kitchen—all brand new and untouched. I recalled the sign posted on the fence—PROSPECT CORRECTIONAL FACILITY. This building was totally for show.

"We discovered something else," the guard said.

He and a companion got down on their hands and knees near the edge of the lawn and felt around. We moved closer to see what they were looking for.

"Here."

Pederman knelt and stuck in his hand. "It's metal, and there's a seam. Everyone spread out and look for a control box."

After a few minutes, Griffin jumped up and down, causing Greta to bark. "Over here!"

Fabian patted her playfully on the back. "Good job, güera."

A green plastic valve box was half-buried in a planter, and it was padlocked. Warnick waved everyone back. Using his handgun, he fired at the lock. Then he popped open the door, revealing a large red button.

"You might want to get off the lawn," he said.

When it was safe, he pressed the button. Somewhere, a motor whirred. The entire lawn lowered several inches and retracted underneath the ground we were standing on. The hole it left was dark—it looked around thirty feet deep. Another motor kicked in, and a square metal platform with rails ascended. As it reached the surface, it stopped with a clunk.

"Hydraulic," Springer said. "Nice."

Below, a series of lights snapped on in sequence. There was a metal post in the corner of the platform with three buttons—Down, Up, and Emergency Stop. The supervisor ordered our squad to get aboard.

"The rest of you continue searching the premises," he said. He pointed at a few guards nearby. "I want you four to remain here in case we're attacked. Use your radios."

Griffin tried leading the dog onto the platform, but she was skittish. Using her German, my wife put the fear of God into the animal, and she marched forward. When everyone was on, Springer hit the Down button, and we descended. I wondered if the lower level ran the entire length of the property. If it did, would draggers be waiting for us?

Once inside, the lingering odor of CS gas assaulted us. Coughing, we pushed through. There were offices, supply rooms, and labs. One room was hermetically sealed. Beyond the glass door, it was dark. Springer tried the door handle—locked. He raised his gun and drew a bead on the card reader.

"Hold it," I said, pointing.

Next to the keypad on the wall, a sign read STOP! PPE IS REQUIRED BEYOND THIS POINT. He put away his weapon. Pederman used a flashlight to explore the room. There were rows of metal racks labeled RS-6160. All the storage trays were empty.

It took us a while to make our way through. Up ahead, we discovered another area filled with plexiglass cells resembling the ones in the isolation facility. A strange-looking machine with a hole in the center stood against the wall. The opening looked big enough for a man's head. Computerized displays and controls surrounded the device. Next to those, there was a console. Though I'd never laid eyes on this contraption before, there was something familiar about it. I walked up and peered at the hole.

When Jim went missing, I searched for him at his house, only learning later that Creasy had made him a prisoner. After my friend escaped and found his way home, he built a bizarre-looking sculpture out of beer bottles and chicken wire. It resembled the machine I was now staring at. And then, it hit me—this was where the bastards had tortured him.

A memory flooded my brain. Right before the car accident, Jim had spoken to me. *I need to tell you something.* Maybe if we hadn't crashed, he might have revealed what happened to him. It took me till now to realize that he tried.

Continuing our search, we arrived at a locked steel door. I peered through the little window and recognized the lab where Dr. Royce had attacked me. The room was in shambles, with busted equipment and broken glass everywhere.

We found nothing else of interest at Robbin-Sear. If there

was another secret facility, we were no closer to finding it than when we started. As the sky darkened, we rode the platform up to the surface and secured the entrance to the facility. As we stood gazing at the vacant property, Holly rested her head against my shoulder.

"Another dead end," she said.

The supervisor pulled Warnick aside. "Our only option now is to talk to the cops."

"You can start with Hannity," I said. "I'm sure he's dying to tell us everything."

SEVENTY-TWO

It was no surprise that Hannity was uncooperative. Holly and I sat with Pederman in a conference room at the isolation facility. Warnick was on the cop's other side, gun in hand, in case the dipshit tried anything. The supervisor spoke in an even voice drizzled with honey instead of the acid I would've preferred.

"Why don't you tell me the plan?" he said.

Hannity wasn't buying today. Instead, he stared at his handcuffs. "Too late."

"Innocent lives are at risk."

"Everyone's life is, innocent or not."

The cop had an annoying habit of fidgeting whenever he responded. He was a born criminal, and I wanted to hit him in the face with a brick.

"The mayor and deputy mayor have disappeared," Pederman said. "I need you to tell me where they're headed."

"And I want a pony." Hannity glanced at Greta. "Nice dog."

"Dammit!" the supervisor said, apparently done with the good guy act. "Don't you care that people are in danger? Do you even have a shred of conscience? What kind of human being lets women and children die?"

Defensive, the cop glowered at us. I couldn't make heads or tails of this guy. Was he actually the cold-hearted prick he pretended to be? Or was this all an LA tough-guy act? After a beat, he deflated like someone let the air out.

"I'm dead anyway," he said.

Pederman touched his shoulder. "Then you might as well tell us the truth."

Lowering his head, Hannity exhaled. The next sound that came out of him made me think he was laughing. I was wrong. He'd broken down unexpectedly. Side-eyeing us, the supervisor gave him a minute.

"The experiment isn't over," he said, wiping his eyes. "They transferred everything and plan to start up again some-place else."

"Without Creasy."

"He'd become a liability. *Well done, good and faithful servant.*"

Pederman pressed him. "Tell us about Mt. Shasta."

"What you heard is true—there is another lab."

"Does Robbin-Sear own it?"

"It belongs to the Department of Defense."

"How do we find it?" Warnick said.

"Lake Shasta Caverns."

I scoffed. "What kind of crap are you selling, Hannity? That's a tourist destination."

He looked at me with eyes that were dead. "The Depart-ment of Agriculture owns part of the land."

"What are they planning to do?" the supervisor said.

"Keep going until they achieve what they set out to do."

"Which is?"

The cop shook his head. When he gave us that creepy

smile, I knew we were in for another one of his irritating monologues.

"Create the perfect soldier," he said. "It's what every nation on the planet wants, right? A combatant who won't die. Who'll kill on command and still be a nice guy who barbecues on the weekend. Who wouldn't want that?"

For a second, I thought I detected fear in Pederman's eyes. I felt it too. Thanks to Steve Zimmer, we already knew the story. And this shitbag had just confirmed it.

"Tres Marias was a testing ground," the supervisor said. "Isn't that right?"

"Wasn't supposed to be. Look, I don't pretend to know all the history. But I do know they'd been working on the project for years. We met with Creasy one time. You know, when he could put two words together without drooling.

"He told us about Guatemala. I dunno, some no-name village in the mountains. They infected the entire population —even the children—hoping they'd survive the transformation. They didn't. Young and old turned into what you see wandering around the forest here. And the crazy sonofabitch was proud of what they'd done."

"You mean murdering everybody," Holly said.

"Sure. The protocol has a contingency plan, though. Kill the infected and gas everyone else, including the livestock. After that, you burn the bodies. And most important, you dream up a cover story."

"What about Tres Marias?" Pederman said.

"Like-uh-said…"

Hannity waited for a reaction but didn't get one. The supervisor rolled his eyes.

"We don't have all day."

"Before the outbreak, they were planning another test in some godforsaken foreign hellhole. But the virus got into the wild, and you know the rest. While everyone else preached doom and gloom, Creasy acted like it was his damn birthday. Personally, I think he was batshit crazy. He still had the protocol from Guatemala and decided to go all in."

I'd already put together everything he was saying. But hearing the actual words made it real. I thought of all those lives lost—all the suffering. And I wanted to put a bullet into him—more to make someone pay than to punish him. As much as I hated the cop, I knew this wasn't his fault. Everything that happened to our town had been put into motion long before he and the other LA cops arrived on the scene. And there was something else. He was scared too.

"Creasy sold everyone on the idea," Hannity said. "He could be very persuasive when he was on joy juice."

My friend turned to Pederman. "This is why we were brought in instead of the National Guard."

The cop nodded. "The boss couldn't risk getting another government agency involved. Too many players already."

The supervisor caught the slip. "You said *the boss.* I thought the mayor was in charge."

Hannity shifted uncomfortably. "Yeah, that's what I meant."

"Creasy couldn't have done this alone," Warnick said. "Who did he report to?"

The cop began fidgeting again. "I can't tell you that."

"Give us a name."

"I said I can't tell you!" He was shaking now.

Pederman glanced at the clock on the wall. It was getting late. "I don't see what the mayor gets out of all this. What could be worth risking a town?"

"You don't know?" Hannity said. "They promised him the governorship."

SEVENTY-THREE

It took me a minute to absorb what Hannity had said. Now it all made sense. Guthrie was right—follow the *money*.

"I don't understand," Holly said. "Can they do that?"

The cop scoffed. "Money talks and bullshit walks. If Robbin-Sear gets the science right and offers it to every US military branch, they have a contract for life."

"How do you know all this?" Pederman said.

"I make it my business to know."

"You guys were brought in as extra muscle," I said. "To make sure everything went according to plan. And Black Dragon was a misdirection."

"More like a necessary evil. The mayor couldn't very well have the police department running the operation. And the National Guard was out because the mayor would lose control. Like the old song, it had to be you."

The supervisor bristled. "Which is why he took away our authority."

"I hate to be the one to break it to you," Hannity said, smirking. "You never *had* any authority, okay? It was all for

336

show."

The room went quiet. Pederman took a beat to regroup. From his expression, I thought he might hit someone. Instead, he relaxed and spoke in a measured tone.

"And you won't tell us who's really in charge. Fine. What about those guys in the black Escalades? How do they fit in?"

The cop's eyes darted around the room like he was being watched. "If I were you, I wouldn't mess with them."

"What made you decide to come clean all of a sudden?" I said.

"Everyone is expendable, me included."

"And you're hoping to save your own ass."

"Aren't you? Despite what you may think of me, I don't want to be responsible for any more lost lives. Believe it or not, I care about this country. And what these people are doing—it isn't right."

I laughed in his face, and it felt good. "Stop. You don't give two shits about this country or this town. Did they at least promise you stock options?"

Hannity was on his feet now, shaking his finger in my face. "I don't have to take this shit—I'm trying to help you!"

Warnick stepped between us. "That's enough." Then to the cop, "What happens to Tres Marias now?"

Giving me a sneer, Hannity took his seat. "Oh, I think you know."

"How will they do it?" I said, unable to look the miscreant in the eye.

"Nerve agent. It's like sarin, but this one is new—dissipates faster. It'll kill everyone who hasn't turned. After that, they'll bring in a crew to incinerate the bodies. Then they'll use your drones to find any remaining infected and neutralize them. The plan is to wrap up everything by Christmas."

My wife was in tears. "But how can they get away with that?"

He looked at her sideways, like she'd gone off her meds. "Are you kidding me right now? They already did. How do you think they cleaned up Shasta Lake?"

"But not everyone there was killed," the supervisor said.

"That's because the operation was targeted. They can dial it up or down. Whatever the situation calls for—you have no idea. Tres Marias will be a total reset. Not even a bird will survive. When it's over, they'll bus in the media and invite them to observe the cleanup."

Pederman nodded. "Makes sense. They'll need witnesses. The journalists will assume the dead were victims of the outbreak. They'll probably welcome the incineration."

The cop gave him an arrogant smile. "It's not hard to manipulate them. Those idiots will believe anything as long as it means more eyeballs."

A long silence hung in the air like low-lying smoke. Tres Marias was dying, and some dark power was about to deliver the coup de grâce. Hannity was right. Evie Champagne was dead, so no one was left to report the real story. Robbin-Sear would get away with it—again—and the media would lap it up.

"How much time do we have?" the supervisor said.

"Operation Guncotton is set to commence at midnight."

Pederman glanced at his watch. "That's twelve hours from now."

"Why *Guncotton*?" my friend said.

The cop waggled his fingers at us. "You ever see a magician use flash paper? It burns brightly for an instant. Then it's gone like magic. Along with the truth."

"What would you have done if we hadn't arrested you?" the supervisor said.

"We were supposed to bug out right before the operation started and return to LA."

The situation seemed impossible. We had twelve hours to save over six hundred people. I wasn't confident we could get it done. Then again, I wasn't ex-military. I decided to have a little faith. If anyone could pull it off, it was Black Dragon.

Pederman got to his feet. "We'd better get moving."

"What do we do with him and the others?" Warnick said.

The supervisor gripped Hannity's shoulder and bore down till the pain was visible on the cop's face.

"I'd like nothing better than to put a bullet in you. But I could use your help. I plan to save these people. Are you up for it?"

"Yeah," Hannity said. "I don't want to die here."

SEVENTY-FOUR

We planned to enlist Hannity and the other cops, then immediately begin evacuation preparations. Like the mayor and Walt Freeman, the police captain was MIA. Hannity convinced the others it was in their best interest to cooperate. A few grumbled till they realized we would leave them behind.

This was a precision operation—everyone had a job. Mine was to follow Warnick and Springer's lead. I made sure Holly and the interns stayed close. We now had less than twelve hours.

Pederman and Warnick turned the administration building conference room into a war room. From there, they worked the logistics as a nonstop parade of guards came and went. At first, everything looked like chaos, with people constantly talking over one another. In reality, the process was dizzyingly efficient. I was good with a gun but useless at tactical. I decided it was better to focus on helping the civilians.

We'd already lost one helicopter and would have to rely mostly on ground transportation. The plan called for us to prioritize children, the elderly, and the convalescing. We'd get them out of Tres Marias to a safe location. Isaac coordinated the medical side. He brought with him hospital personnel and any remaining patients.

After studying maps of the area, we agreed to take the civilians to the National Guard armory in Redding. Everyone would be safe there till they could be relocated to temporary housing, which Black Dragon would arrange out of San Francisco.

Our second priority was to evacuate our people before midnight. There was a risk that outsiders could breach the town's perimeter once our checkpoints were abandoned. Or worse—draggers could get out. But we had no choice.

I had a third priority. But when I asked about going to the Lake Shasta Caverns, the supervisor shut me down. It was no longer our concern. He believed investigations would be launched, and eventually, the truth would come out. His reasoning didn't sit well with me. I wanted the mayor and everyone associated with him to be punished.

Pederman decided to leave all the equipment and focus on saving lives. It was a good call. The doctor made sure we took only the medical supplies we needed for the short trip. We didn't have nearly enough vehicles to transport everyone and would have to commandeer civilian cars and trucks. There were plenty scattered around town.

Making multiple trips was out. As soon as we left Tres Marias, whoever was running Operation Guncotton would figure out what we were up to and try to stop us. The supervisor promised to keep our squad together. Once our transportation was locked in, a few guards and cops were to stay behind. They'd use police cruisers and any other remaining vehicles to evacuate the last group.

By 10 PM, we were ready to move out. Pederman radioed

the checkpoints to ensure no one was approaching. Everything was clear. For months, the freeway exits had been blocked for five miles in each direction. Detours had been set up for cars to use surface streets that would take them around the town.

We randomly assigned civilians to the vehicles, mindful that we should keep families together whenever possible. Out of respect, we placed the mayor's wife and sons in a Humvee at the front of the line. As we got them situated, Hannity walked over. I prepared myself for one of his dumbass speeches, but he surprised me.

"I'd like to drive the mayor's family," he said.

"We already have a driver. Stick to the plan."

He took my arm. "They were my responsibility—I messed up."

"How do I know I can trust you?"

"You don't. But, like you, I care about surviving. I'll protect them."

When the supervisor joined us, I relayed the cop's request. Pederman looked him in the eye as if trying to see into his soul.

"Fine," he said. "But you need to stay in formation. No breakout, got it?"

"I can handle it."

Isaac stood at the rear of an LMTV, making a final inspection of the medical supplies. I let him know it was time to board a vehicle.

"I'll ride with the supplies," he said.

"Fine by me. Don't steal anything."

"I need to tell you something."

"Are we breaking up?"

"I'm serious. This whole situation has been impossible. A lot of men wouldn't be up to it. I wanted you to know I appreciate everything you're doing. You're a good man, Dave. I'm proud of you."

I didn't know what to say. In some ways, Isaac was like a second father to me. Keeping my tears in check, I shook his hand.

"Thanks," I said. "Now get in the truck."

"Yes, sir." Laughing, he gave me a hug.

My wife was a short distance away, pointing at an SUV. "We have room for one more over here."

Griffin signaled my friend, Eddie Greely. I had visited him off and on, making sure he was being looked after. Unfortunately, his health had taken a nosedive due to emphysema, and I worried he might not make it.

"You done a good thing." He shook my hand and climbed in.

We were getting close to the deadline. When the Zimmers showed up, I placed them in a nearby vehicle.

"Thanks for everything," Steve said, gripping my shoulder.

I reached out and touched Evan's little hand. "The food must be good here. I think she's grown."

Nina put a hand on my arm, looking from Holly to me. "I hope we can stay in touch."

It was a nice thought. But I was pretty sure we'd never see them again. That's how life works. We're thrown together randomly under unusual circumstances, then blown apart by time and distance. Maybe it was for the best. So many of the people I had made friends with were dead. Better to say goodbye now.

I gave her a smile. "See you around."

She waved to my wife. "Can't wait to hear about the baby!"

We'd processed the last of the civilians when Springer

came running over and, out of breath, addressed the supervisor.

"We can't find Becky," he said.

Warnick rolled his eyes. "This obsession of yours has got to—"

"I'm being serious—she's missing."

"There's no way we're delaying this operation," Pederman said. "Dave. Warnick. Go with Springer and do another sweep. Make it fast."

We checked everywhere, but it seemed the woman had vanished. Our mission had always been to protect civilians. Waiting would put everyone at risk. The supervisor made the hard call, and we prepared to leave without Walt's assistant.

Pederman directed the vehicles to enter the on-ramp past the detour with their headlights off. He ordered them to leave in groups of six to reduce the chance they'd be spotted. After getting to the on-ramp, they would turn on their lights and proceed to Redding with the rest of the nighttime traffic.

I didn't know what would happen once we reached our destination. But soon, we were heading out—first, the line of Black Dragon vehicles, followed by the police cruisers, and finally, the helicopters. Nothing had been left to chance. We were careful, and we were armed. We had done everything right.

Then reality set in.

SEVENTY-FIVE

The first attack came as the vehicle carrying the mayor's family made its way to the on-ramp. I waited with the others at the checkpoint and saw it happen. The brutality of the dark forces controlling the narrative was never more evident than in that moment. And there was nothing we could do.

Out of the darkness, a black helicopter—not ours—hovered near the on-ramp over the Humvee carrying the mayor's wife and sons. Hannity was behind the wheel. At first, I thought he'd tipped off someone about our plan. But that reasoning evaporated as the aircraft, equipped with an Advanced Precision Kill Weapon System, launched a seventy-millimeter rocket that demolished the vehicle in one devastating burst. The Humvee exploded instantly, followed by angry flames that licked the interior and engulfed everyone inside in a white-hot hellfire. Nothing could have survived the strike.

Holly clutched my hand, and Fabian held Griffin. The five other vehicles stopped as the aircraft turned around, positioning itself for a fresh attack. As the other drivers accelerated past the wreckage, the helicopter from hell went in pursuit.

"Everyone move *now!*" Pederman said into his radio.

The lead Black Dragon helicopter ascended. The supervisor radioed instructions to stop the enemy by any means necessary. As it approached the hostile aircraft, a flash of machine-gun fire warned them off.

We boarded our helicopter and were soon airborne. The girl secured Greta in a harness and gripped my wife's hand. I was terrified I would lose my family, but this was no time to think of ourselves. Our job was to protect the civilians. I looked at the other passengers. Pederman, Warnick, and Springer's stoicism confirmed my conclusion—the mission came first.

The convoy picked up speed towards the final barrier, which was still a couple miles out. Banking away suddenly to avoid our aircraft, the enemy helicopter fired a second rocket that barely missed the first Humvee. As the explosion shook the ground, two lines of black Escalades appeared, straddling our vehicles.

Agents in gray suits fired automatic weapons. But they couldn't shatter the bulletproof glass, and the convoy held steady. We closed in behind our lead helicopter, whose gunner began firing at the enemy aircraft. The distraction was enough to keep the attackers from destroying another vehicle. Then, we caught a break.

Our gunner hit the enemy's main rotor, snapping off the blade. The force of the blast sent the helicopter's fuselage spinning wildly onto the road, where it crashed on its side. I worried the convoy would plow into it, but every driver expertly swerved to avoid the debris.

Below, two agents extricated themselves from the wreckage. As they stood upright, a speeding Escalade struck them, crushing their bodies under its wheels. It was hard to know what was happening, and my impatience was building. The pilot, Pederman, and Warnick wore aviation headsets. I heard them talking, but they couldn't hear me.

"We need to take out those Escalades," the supervisor said to my friend.

I tried getting his attention. "How do we shoot without hitting civilians?"

Pederman exposed an ear so I could repeat the question. "Not sure this will work, but it's all we've got."

He used the radio to communicate with the Black Dragon drivers. I couldn't believe what he was suggesting. Still, I had no better ideas. We'd only get one shot at this. If we failed, everyone on the ground would be lost. He and Warnick handed out industrial-grade earmuffs. Then, the supervisor gripped my shoulder.

"Son, if you know how to pray, do it," he said.

The lead helicopter pulled back and waited for Pederman's signal. Everything would have to be timed to avoid casualties. By now, we were less than a mile from the final barricade. I focused on our second helicopter, where the gunner manned the Browning M2. Taking Holly's hand, I closed my eyes.

"On my countdown," the supervisor said into the radio. "Three... Two... One... Brake!"

Working in perfect synchronization, every driver skidded to a precise stop, surprising the agents, who continued helplessly at seventy miles an hour. As we pulled back, the second helicopter zoomed straight ahead and hovered over the Escalades. What followed was Armageddon as the gunner opened fire.

Mercilessly, he peppered the vehicles from rear to front. The massive ordnance tore away the roofs and blasted out the windows as if the targets were Matchbox cars. Arms fell out of the broken glass, only to be severed by hot lead. Not a single agent survived. I had just witnessed the textbook definition of total annihilation.

"Go!" Pederman said into the radio.

The convoy started up again, accelerating past the line of wrecked Escalades burning from the inside out. At last, our lead vehicle took the on-ramp, and the convoy joined the rest of the late-night traffic. We continued on to Redding and the National Guard armory.

The Black Dragon helicopters were cleared to land. Using his radio, the supervisor continued monitoring the convoy's progress. As I watched the regular traffic below, I could hardly believe we'd escaped Tres Marias. I felt giddy and free, like someone who'd broken out of prison. We were miles away from the nightmare that had tormented us since that horrible night of July 5th. I turned to say something to my wife and found her crying.

But they were good tears.

SEVENTY-SIX

After setting down, we joined the civilians. National Guard soldiers greeted us and helped the shaken and injured into the armory. Incredibly, we'd lost only one vehicle—four passengers, including Hannity. I still didn't believe he was a cop. Now, we would never know.

Holly and I moved through the crowd, looking for the Zimmers. I spotted them near the side of the building. Nina cradled Evan. Steve stood with his arms protectively around them. They were praying. When Nina saw us, she hugged my wife. I put my hand on Steve's shoulder and felt him shaking.

"That's as close to death as I ever want to get," he said.

"So glad you made it."

A commotion got my attention. Guardsmen were taking the Tres Marias police officers into custody. The supervisor hadn't let them off the hook. One grumbled about wanting a lawyer, which made me smile. I found the LMTV Isaac had ridden in and went to check on him. He climbed out of the passenger side as I approached.

"You okay?" I said.

"Normally, I'd never say this in front of you—but, dammit, I could use a drink."

"You have my permission."

Pederman and Warnick signaled me to follow them into the armory. Before we could go inside, an armed guardsman blocked the doorway.

"I need you to surrender your weapons," he said.

We looked at each other. Though I had no reason not to trust the Guard, I felt nervous about being unarmed. The supervisor and my friend handed over their guns. Reluctantly, I followed suit.

"Thank you." He stepped aside so we could enter. "These will be returned to you when you leave."

Inside, the armory's commander awaited us. He looked to be in his forties. Fair and clean-shaven, with close-cropped hair and a trim build.

"Dave, this is Captain Louis Quincy," Pederman said, smiling.

We shook hands. "Good to meet you."

"Dave's been an important part of the team, along with his wife, Holly."

"This way," the captain said.

I didn't know whether these people were on heightened alert, but there seemed to be a lot of men and women in uniform. I'd assumed an armory wasn't this busy unless there was training going on. As we made our way past a large group, Springer caught up with us, bringing my wife and the interns.

We entered a conference room and found seats. There were already several other soldiers in the room who, out of courtesy, stood at ease against the wall so we could sit. Quincy moved to the head of the table.

"Kelly, when you radioed me, I was pretty stunned," the

captain said. "No one on the outside has been in communication with Tres Marias since the quarantine went into effect."

The supervisor scooted in his chair. "Other than our drone system, all internet and phone communications were blocked. We thought we were in charge. But we...uh... learned there was another agenda."

Quincy rubbed his chin. "We looked into that. I've already been in touch with my senior command. Everyone agreed that, for the safety of the civilians and your people, we should be involved."

"Glad to hear it."

"Captain?" Holly said. "What's going to happen to the civilians?"

"Great question. We've arranged for rooms at several hotels in the area. Our people will begin escorting them once they've been processed. I understand Black Dragon is working on a long-term solution."

Scanning the room, the captain lowered his voice. "Okay. Let's talk about the outbreak."

"Everyone who got out has been tested," Pederman said. "But we had to abandon the checkpoints, so there's the possibility the infected could escape."

"Why didn't you assign personnel to guard the perimeter?"

The supervisor's eyes wandered, settling on the guardsmen standing against the wall. Quincy seemed to understand and dismissed them. The last one out closed the door.

"Lou, there's something I need to ask you," Pederman said. "Are you familiar with Operation Guncotton?"

The supervisor ran down everything we knew about the mayor and the others, including the gray-suits in the black

Escalades. He provided a timeline up to the midnight deadline when the town would be gassed.

The color drained from the captain's face. "I'd better inform my CO. Where are the mayor and deputy mayor now?"

"We think they may be in Mt. Shasta," Warnick said.

Quincy didn't seem surprised. "At the facility."

"You know about that place?" I said.

"Only the location."

"We have information that there's a lab inside the Lake Shasta Caverns," Pederman said.

"Correct." The captain rose and went to the door. "I'm going to make a call. I'd like you folks to remain here until I return." Outside, he ordered drinks and snacks to be brought in.

"Sorry, could I get a bowl of water for our dog?" Griffin said, making Quincy chuckle.

When we were alone, the supervisor turned to my wife. "You look worried."

"Do you think the civilians will be safe?"

"They'll be fine. We're providing extra security at the hotels."

Someone returned with a cart loaded with bottled water, sodas, and snacks. He set out a bowl for Greta and filled it with water. We sat quietly munching on Cheez-Its, nuts, and candy bars. Soon, the captain returned and addressed Pederman.

"I spoke to my CO," he said. "He contacted Sacramento and let them know what happened. The governor was not pleased. He ordered us to take the mayor and deputy mayor into custody."

"What about local law enforcement?"

Quincy weighed his words carefully. "This is bigger than

anyone ever imagined. The governor isn't taking any chances."

I raised my hand. "How will you find them? I mean, we were only guessing they're at Mt. Shasta. What if—"

"I understand your concern, Dave," he said. "But our orders are to get up there and check it out asap."

The supervisor got to his feet. "I'll alert my people. When do we leave?"

"I'm afraid you're not going," the captain said. "This is a National Guard operation."

SEVENTY-SEVEN

Pederman and Quincy stood in a corner, inches apart. I tried not to stare. But the sight of two military men confronting each other was irresistible.

"It's vital that our people accompany you," the supervisor said. "If you're going after the mayor, we need to be there."

"No disrespect, Kelly, but the governor ordered *us* to carry out the mission."

"No disrespect, Lou. The mayor is responsible for the deaths of civilians and many of our people—on my watch. If it's all the same to you, we're heading up to Mt. Shasta."

Watching these guys go at it, it was clear no one wanted to give ground. I didn't know anything about the protocol. My guess was the National Guard trumped a private security firm any day of the week.

After going a few more rounds, the men stepped outside and closed the door. Judging by their muffled voices, the exchange wasn't heated. But it was intense. I had to hand it to Pederman. When it came to the mayor, he was like a dog with a bone. Before long, they returned. The captain gave us a sheepish smile.

"The governor didn't say specifically that Black Dragon shouldn't accompany us," he said. "Welcome aboard."

The supervisor shook his hand. "Appreciate the cooperation, Lou."

As Pederman took his seat, I leaned over. "You told me this wasn't our mission."

"Things change," he said. Then to Quincy, "Operation Guncotton commences at 0000."

The captain knitted his brow. "The governor was clear. My orders are to stay away from Tres Marias. Besides, we have neither the manpower nor the time. Our focus is on arresting the mayor and deputy mayor."

I raised my hand again. "Don't forget the police captain."

"Is he a part of this?"

"Like horns on the devil," I said.

We got back our weapons as promised. Outside, charter buses stood ready to take the civilians to their hotels. Considering what they'd been through, they were in good spirits. Mothers and fathers held sleeping children in their arms and waited with the others. We kept our goodbyes short as we helped the elderly board first. I thought I spotted a black Escalade across the busy highway. Then it was gone.

Quincy climbed aboard a military helicopter with a squad of eight privates and a staff sergeant. After they were airborne, a second helicopter carrying another group followed. Everyone was armed. Pederman had already decided the mission was too dangerous for Griffin and Fabian. Before boarding our helicopter, he ordered a Black Dragon guard to drive them to a hotel, where they'd remain till we returned.

"Please, I wanna go with you guys," the girl said. Her eyes, shiny with tears, darted from the supervisor to Holly and me.

My wife took both her hands. "It's for the best. Promise me you and Fabian will look after the civilians. We'll see you soon."

Griffin was an awesome guard with a strength of character I wish I had. She put on a smile and took her friend's hand.

"Let's go, Fabio," she said. Then they walked off with Greta.

By now, everyone else was on the Black Dragon helicopter. As my wife prepared to board, I took her aside.

"What is it, Dave?" she said. "We need to get moving."

"I don't want you to go."

"Don't start with that."

"*Listen* to me." It was hard to talk over the sound of the helicopter rotors. "It's too dangerous. We have no idea what we'll find up there—I want you to live. To have our baby."

When she hesitated, I thought I might be getting through to her. She was stubborn, but she was also practical.

"Please, Holly," I said. "Just this once, do as I ask. I can't..." I held her close and pressed my lips to her ear. "I can't lose you."

Pulling away, she stared at me. Everyone else was waiting in the helicopter, impatient to leave. I ignored them. No one in the world was more precious to me.

"Okay," she said.

Surprised and relieved, I held her and kissed her head. When I saw her face again, she was fighting tears.

"Don't die on me."

"I won't. I love you so much."

"Tell me something I don't know."

"I always wanted to see you in a sailor suit."

"Next Halloween. Now get outta here."

She kissed me one more time and pushed me away. I felt a hand on my shoulder and turned to find Warnick. I followed him onto the helicopter while Holly stood there alone. Soon, we were airborne. As we ascended, the wind scattered leaves and debris all around. I waved to my wife, and she blew me a last kiss.

Watching her becoming smaller and smaller, I worried I would never see her again. A terrible evil had caused the outbreak—an evil we were about to confront. Was I destined to walk away from this like all the other times with death at my heels? Or would there be another baby in the world who never knew her father?

No cold, ghostly hand touched my soul. No bone-deep dread washed over me like someone walking over my grave. If the devil is in the details, God is in the clues. And right now, He wasn't giving up anything.

"Don't let me die out there," I said.

SEVENTY-EIGHT

The moon shone bright through the trees as we touched down in a parking lot near Holiday Harbor. I detected the scent of pine and lilac. The military helicopters had already landed, and the guardsmen waved as we climbed down to join them.

The surrounding area was covered in a dense forest all the way to the lake. There was only one route we could take —Shasta Caverns Road—unless we wanted to go by boat. With everyone gathered together, Quincy went over the plan, emphasizing that he was in charge. Pederman didn't argue.

"What happens if we don't find the mayor?" Warnick said.

"A BOLO has already been issued. Local police and the highway patrol are on the lookout."

Supposedly, the lab was located in a separate compound away from the caverns. Our destination was around a mile from where we landed. When everyone's questions had been answered, the captain gave the order to move out.

It was past midnight, and Operation Guncotton was underway. Tres Marias, the town where I grew up, no longer existed. I was never sentimental about the place. But the thought of everyone and everything in it *dead* saddened me.

As we made our way down the paved road, I recalled that at the beginning of the outbreak, draggers had roamed this area like wolves. They bit my mother-in-law, turning her into a flesh-eater. I remembered what Hannity said about Creasy and his damn protocol. And I wondered how they'd eliminated the draggers without killing everyone else. Whatever their method, nobody was the wiser. Not even the media had caught wind of what went on up here.

No one spoke as we followed the road to the caverns. The only sound came from our boots hitting the ground. Every soldier carried a Rifleman Radio for secure communication. Although they weren't permitted to use them freely, the devices allowed Quincy to track each person's location in case we were separated.

I thought of Holly, Griffin, and Fabian. Thank God they were far away from the danger I knew we were about to face. Knowing my wife, she was pissed off that I'd talked her into staying behind. I recalled our conversation about moving to San Francisco and vowed to make that happen when this was over.

On hearing our approach, a colony of bats fled the trees. Circling high in the air, they disappeared. Dark thoughts swirled in my head like those crazy flying rodents. The enemy could be hiding—waiting for us to come into range. I wished Greta was with me.

Up ahead, the captain raised his hand, and everyone stopped. He directed one squad to go right and the other left. Then he signaled us to follow him into the shelter of the trees. We moved quietly, trying to avoid the pinecones and dead branches. Men's voices rode the chill breeze wafting through the trees. Again, Quincy signaled us to stop. We crouched near a chain-link fence topped with razor wire. Signs that read US DEPT. OF AGRICULTURE were posted all the way down.

The captain was about to signal us again when the sound of an approaching vehicle got his attention. A semi-trailer truck rolled up to the gate, its air brakes hissing. A sticker on the side of the cab read BASEBORN IDENTITY RESEARCH— LOS ANGELES, CA.

The gate opened. Men and women dressed in jeans and flannel work shirts poured out of the main building. They approached the truck as it pulled into the front yard. Forklift drivers followed with crates of what I assumed was lab equipment. It took a while for the vehicle to clear the entrance.

The crowd hurried to the rear, which faced us. A gray-suit unbolted the doors and swung them open. From inside, people in yellow hazmat suits with hoods appeared. Another gray-suit on the ground spoke to them. As they exited, the forklift drivers began loading the trailer.

Soon, a second semi showed up and parked inside. The doors to the building opened again. Using cattle prods, more hazmats herded a parade of draggers in chains towards the second trailer. Some wore Black Dragon uniforms. One by one, they loaded up the snarling, snapping captives. My gut had been right all along. Someone wanted these test subjects to survive so they could continue their hellish experiments.

We waited for the workers to load the last of the draggers. Then the first driver jumped into his cab. Carefully, he maneuvered the semi out of the compound and onto the road. Quincy texted something. Immediately, his squads received the secure message on their phones.

The captain gave the signal, and we rushed in before the gate could close. Panicked civilians ran towards the building, shouting for help. More gray-suits appeared from the sides and opened fire. Quincy's people shot them dead, including the second driver. We continued pushing our way inside while another squad engaged the hostiles.

We discovered a large foyer with a high ceiling and sparse furniture. Outside, the sounds of gunfire and shouting voices as the battle raged. Along the rear wall stood a massive photomural—an aerial view of the Pentagon. I pointed out the video surveillance cameras mounted in the ceiling corners.

More gray-suits burst in and fired on us. We took cover behind the furniture as bullets whizzed past. The captain was behind me when we entered the facility. I turned around and found him lying on the floor, shot in the face. He wasn't breathing.

We managed to kill the hostiles but lost three soldiers. There were no signs of the civilians we'd seen earlier. We hurried to the rear—there had to be a door. Springer and I felt around the edges of the photomural while others searched for a switch. The supervisor found a keypad mounted on a side wall.

"This might be it," he said. "You think we should shoot it?"

I pointed at the photomural. "Look at this."

The bottom was flush with the ground, which seemed odd. I pressed against the surface to test its strength. It felt solid.

"What do you think is behind it?"

"Let's find out," Warnick said. Then to the guardsmen, "Anyone bring C4?"

A young woman—Private Zelinski—opened her backpack and removed the explosive material and fuses. Expertly, she divided the C4 into smaller parts and mounted them in three spots on the photomural. Then she strung the pieces together with wire. We took cover as she connected the detonator.

"Fire in the hole!"

The deafening explosion shook the building. A fire alarm went off, and sprinklers rained water on us. As the smoke cleared, the interior became visible. Steel tread stairs spiraled down to another area. I got to my feet, my ears ringing. Struggling to keep my balance, I followed the others.

The soldiers took the stairs first. As they descended, semi-automatic gunfire killed most of them. Wounded but alive, the survivors returned fire as they retreated. Shouting another warning, Zelinski heaved a grenade past them. Screaming erupted as the detonation shook the floor. We checked the injured. Some couldn't walk, so we carried them into the foyer. I noticed that a bullet had grazed the woman's shoulder.

"You okay?" I said.

Rubbing it, she grimaced. "I've had worse."

There were only five of us now—Pederman, Warnick, Springer, Zelinski, and me. One after the next, we descended the stairs. At the bottom lay the mangled remains of guardsmen and half a dozen gray-suits. Behind the bodies stood steel double doors.

"Any last requests?" Springer said.

SEVENTY-NINE

The doors weren't locked. Weapon pointed, Pederman pulled on one. He was about to walk in when a bloody hand grabbed his ankle. Reacting, Warnick sent a bullet through the gray-suit's eye. The supervisor shook his foot free and continued through as we followed.

The interior was a vast cave. I realized the lab had been carved into the Lake Shasta Caverns. As a teenager, I came here once on a school field trip and didn't remember seeing anything like this. It was cold and damp inside. Our footsteps echoed as we walked on. A pungent odor hung in the air—one I'd smelled before. Bat guano.

A dirt path led us to a wood bridge that looked like something out of an adventure movie. Our weapons up, we cleared the area and approached the wood-and-rope structure. Below, rows of plexiglass cells crisscrossed the floor, surrounded by computers and other electronic equipment. Portable lights shone, bathing the area in an amber glow. Hazmats led the chained test subjects out of the facility. Lurching, the draggers let out ear-piercing death shrieks as their keepers cattle-prodded them.

Pederman was the first to cross. A gunshot screamed out of the darkness, and he stumbled from a bullet to the chest. Fortunately, his body armor had saved him. We tried retreating as more rounds zinged past us on either side. With no other option, we remained motionless. Then a bright light came on.

The mayor stood on a wide rock shelf, flanked by O'Brien and another cop armed with a high-powered rifle. Hizzoner looked bad. His suit was dirty and torn, and his normally perfect hair was a mess. I wondered if he knew about his wife and sons.

"Walk forward so I can see you better," he said, his voice echoing.

He sounded hoarse, like he'd spent the day at a playoff game. We stayed put. He nodded to the second cop, who aimed at Zelinski and, without hesitating, squeezed the trigger. The bullet hit her in the forehead. She collapsed on the bridge, stone-cold dead.

"Let's try this again. Walk. *Forward.*"

We continued to the other side, stopping around twenty feet from the enemy.

"Very good. Now, lay down your guns and raise your hands."

Everyone looked at the supervisor. With his jaw flexed, he nodded. The rest of us did as we were told. While the cop with the rifle covered him, the police captain stepped forward to meet us. He patted us down, then confiscated our weapons and returned to the platform.

"You can lower your hands now," the mayor said.

He ran his fingers through his hair and shook his head as if listening to some inner private joke. I couldn't help thinking the tool had completely lost his shit. He addressed all of us, but he was looking at me. Alarmed, I wondered why.

"You people have been in my way since the beginning. All you had to do was stay out of it."

"You broke the law," Pederman said.

The mayor was incredulous. "Did you think I hired you to enforce the *law*? You were there to protect the experiment. Why can't you see that?"

He side-eyed the second cop, who shot the supervisor in the head. I grabbed him as he fell onto me. Staring into my eyes, he crumpled on the bridge. Only three of us left now—Warnick, Springer, and me. My prayer hadn't been answered. We were going to die at the hands of a madman. I thanked God my wife wasn't here.

"I seem to have a dilemma," the mayor said, squinting into the lights. "You've disrupted my plans to the point where I can no longer move forward. What to do, what to do..."

He pretended to think over the matter. Smiling, he turned to the police captain, who snapped his fingers. From out of the shadows, two more cops with guns dragged three people onto the rock shelf.

"No!" someone said. It was me.

Holly, Griffin, and Fabian stood before us with their mouths gagged and their hands bound with zip ties. All had the same look of crippling fear. A cop held Greta on a leash with his free hand. Recognizing me, she barked and wagged her tail. The mayor smiled warmly as if they were his family.

"We received a tip that you were headed up here. Fortunately, a couple of the boys intercepted these three on their way to the hotel. I'm guessing they were looking forward to a nice hot shower and room service."

He pulled my wife away from the group. Tearing off her

gag, he gave her a shove. She stood there alone now, shivering. My blood turned to ice as his eyes met mine. I was desperate to make a move, but a rifle was pointed at my head. Griffin let out a muffled scream. I side-eyed my friends. The look on their faces told me it was over.

"Time to make things right," the mayor said.

EIGHTY

Holly stared into my eyes. Hands bound. Silent. Afraid. Behind her, Griffin and Fabian—their mouths covered—looked on in helpless horror. His fingers reached for hers. Then, defiant, they pulled down the gags.

"Stop this!" the girl said.

I tried going to my wife. The cop with the rifle fired once, striking me in the chest. Holly cried out. Though my body armor had stopped the bullet, the pain was crushing. Vaguely, I felt Warnick gripping my shoulder as balls of hot red light streaked across my eyes.

"You took everything away from me!" the mayor said. "My wife! My sons!" He sobbed. "My future."

Unafraid, my friend looked him in the eye. "We didn't kill them. Your friends attacked the convoy."

The mayor let out a pitiful wail that echoed throughout the cavern. The sound seemed to make the police captain uncomfortable. Then his voice became soft, as though he were in a private conference.

"If you hadn't come after me, they'd still be alive."

Despite the danger, Warnick wasn't finished. "Why did you leave them behind? You could've saved them."

"You don't understand." He sounded like a petulant child. "This was supposed to be my shot. It's bigger than you can imagine. They got me out of there so I could—"

"You abandoned your family."

"They promised me."

Cold sweat dripped into my eyes. The vague outlines of Holly, Griffin, and Fabian glimmered—ghosts in the harsh orange light. And like suffering spirits, they pleaded with me to do something. I glowered at the cop whose rifle was still pointed at me. When my wife screamed, I turned to find her on her knees.

"Dave!"

The mayor had O'Brien's weapon and pointed it at Holly's head. I couldn't breathe. There had to be a way to...

"Kill *me* instead!" I said, but he wasn't listening.

Desperately, my wife reached out to me. "I love you! I'll always love you!"

I was powerless. If only I could reason with him. "Please... Please don't do this."

"I've lost everything," he said. His voice was a cold, frightening monotone. "Let me show you what that feels like."

It was all a dream.

I saw the bullet leave the chamber—so slowly. Spiraling, it raced home to its target. Every conscious thought vanished as my mind focused on the deadly projectile. It struck Holly in the head, exploding out the other side in a burst of blood, brain, and bone. And I died for a little while.

That picture—my last memory of her—the impact of the hot lead twisting her sideways and down into the dirt in amber light—that photograph is burned in my memory forever like a firebrand on my soul. And always, it's accompanied by screaming—Griffin's maybe or mine—and Greta's frantic, urgent barking. It was all a dream—I knew it was—not real. A nightmare. But why couldn't I wake up?

Because it was real.

There was no escape—not this time. If I'd had a gun, I would have used it to join my wife. There wasn't any point in going on—not anymore. Nothing else mattered. And the baby? So blessed to have been conceived yet never to be born. I fell on my knees.

When I raised my eyes, the mayor was looking at what he had done—surprised that guns can kill. I sensed Warnick and Springer on either side of me. They slipped their hands under my arms and helped me to my feet.

Greta pulled at her leash. The cop holding her pointed his weapon at her head. Reacting, the dog sank her teeth into his hand. Then, lunging, she gored his neck. He screamed as blood squirted from an artery like a busted water main.

In the chaos, Fabian raised his arms and, driving them down against his body, burst the zip tie. He punched the other cop in the throat and took his weapon. As the hostile fell gasping, I bolted towards the mayor. The police captain tried to retrieve his gun. Pushing him aside, the mayor shot me in the arm and fled into the darkness.

Springer went for the rifle, but the other cop killed the guard before he could advance. Grabbing a handgun, Warnick dropped him. The cop Fabian had disarmed fled across the bridge. He didn't get far. The Latino sent three bullets into the hostile's back. Grunting, he fell over the side to his death.

O'Brien whimpered as Greta sank her teeth into his forearm. He was alone now. Retrieving my weapon, I glanced at Holly's body and marched towards him. Our eyes locked. No more tough cop—all I saw now was raw terror. When I touched Greta's head, she released him. He backed away, nursing his arm.

"Braves Mädchen," I said and patted the dog again.

I pointed my gun at the cop's face. But I didn't kill him—not yet. Instead, I shot out his kneecap. Screaming and swearing, he stumbled but managed to remain standing. Incredibly, he grinned at me—daring me. I destroyed his other knee.

This time, he fell. With my good hand, I grabbed him by the collar and forced him onto his shattered knees. With tears streaming, he cursed and babbled. The others made no move to help him.

"Pray," I said.

He gibbered like a lunatic as I pointed at Holly's body.

"Pray. For *them*."

He shook his head violently, incapable of understanding.

"You don't know how, do you? Want me to teach you?"

He closed his eyes, his lips trying to form the words. His garbled response was hard to understand. It sounded like *I'll kill you*.

"That's not a prayer worthy of my wife and child," I said.

I let go of his collar. He collapsed onto his back, moaning as blood gushed from his knees. Aiming at his face, I felt nothing—not even hate. As I squeezed the trigger, he never stopped staring at me, that same insolent sneer on his lips. Screaming, I mag-dumped him. When it was over, nothing was left of the cop's face except a crater.

Fabian stood next to me, looking at what I'd done. Disgusted, he spat into the meaty hole. "And there's your lunch."

My chest heaving, I went to Holly. Cradling her sweet head in my arms, I gently brushed the blonde hair from her face. Gazed into the unseeing green eyes I loved so much.

Bright red blood from my wound dripped onto her still body. Somewhere far away, I heard Warnick's voice.

"It's time to go," he said.

Blind with tears, I looked up and saw my friend. Greta trotted over. Whimpering, she nudged my wife's hand with her nose. Griffin tried embracing me, but I shook her off. Warnick reached out to help me to my feet—no! I wanted to remain here for all eternity. There was nowhere else I needed to be now.

"Come on, Dave. We need to find the mayor."

And like a dream, I felt myself moving as if on a cloud. Starting down a dark, rocky passageway, I turned around one last time to look at Holly. I kept hoping she'd call out to me. *Dave, wait!* As though she weren't really dead, only injured. But there was nothing. No voice. No movement. No miracle.

Only the sounds of our footsteps and Greta's soft panting as we made our way deeper into the mystery.

EIGHTY-ONE

LED strip lighting made it easier to see as we advanced through the passageway. Warnick and I took the lead, with Griffin and Fabian behind us. The smell of ammonia and uric acid from the bats was intense and gave me a headache. Up ahead, a body lay on the ground. It was the mayor.

He was on his side, his hand still gripping O'Brien's gun. Though I was elated he was dead, I felt cheated that I hadn't been the one to end him. A new rage burned in me, and I began kicking him in the chest. Why had God denied me the pleasure of sending the worthless piece of shit to hell? Again and again, I assaulted his body till there was nothing left in me but the ashes of my anger.

The girl touched my shoulder. "It's okay, he's dead."

My friend knelt beside the body and probed the gunshot wound. The bullet had entered through the back of the head.

"This man was executed," he said.

Far ahead, where the passageway crossed another tunnel, someone stepped into the light. It was hard to make out the person.

"Is that you, Dave?" Walt Freeman said.

"What do you want?"

"To go back in time and fix this."

I pictured Holly lying in a pool of her own blood. "Did you kill the mayor?"

"We removed him from the equation."

"*We?* Then I guess the deputy mayor thing was all for show."

"It was important I remain close to the project."

"Don't really give a shit right now," I said. Then to Warnick, "Get them out of here."

"We should all go."

"I'm staying."

"Don't be stupid. We can—"

"Dammit, Warnick, *go!*"

Griffin and Fabian gawped at me. My friend must've realized it was useless to argue. They retreated, with Greta whining as the girl led her away. When they were out of sight, I advanced a few yards and stopped, observing Walt's rotund frame in silhouette.

"They won't make it out," the fat man said.

"We'll see."

"I am sorry about your wife—truly. If only we'd gotten here sooner, we—"

"Woulda, coulda, shoulda."

"You have good instincts, Dave. I could use you on my team."

My injured arm was numb. With my other hand, I fired at the state-sponsored stooge, intentionally missing him. Flinching, he stood his ground. It was only then I noticed he had a gun.

"Don't make me kill you, son."

"I'm already dead."

Gunshots erupted behind me, and the dog started barking. Snapping out of my despair, I pivoted and ran. When I reached the open area near the bridge, I was alone.

"Warnick!"

Far off, Greta continued to bark, followed by more gunshots. I started for the bridge. But when I saw my wife, I stopped and knelt. Closing her eyes, I kissed her cold lips and freed her hands.

"I love you," I said. "Always and always."

When I reached the bridge, the scientists were almost done packing up. No sign of my friend or the others. Returning, I picked up Holly and slung her over my good shoulder. Soon, the lab would be shut down like a tomb. There was no way I would leave her here to rot.

Fighting the pain in my arm, I made my way across the bridge and up the steel stairs. Eventually, I reached the wrecked photomural and proceeded to the vast lobby. Someone had turned off the sprinklers—everything was drenched. The soldiers we'd rescued were dead. Warnick and the interns were nowhere in sight. I stopped near the exit.

Outside, scientists loaded the last of the equipment into the remaining semi-trailer. There were several black Escalades parked nearby. Maybe if I could get to one, I might be able to escape. But it was a long shot, like everything else in this endless nightmare.

Across the way, Walt chatted with a group of gray-suits. Another man stood in their midst. He was tall and gaunt, with close-cropped silver hair, and wearing a black suit. A hideous scar ran from his temple to his jawline. A chill went through me as I observed him.

A sudden death shriek echoed. A dragger had gotten free. Thrashing like a trapped animal, it reached out from its chains as hazmats used cattle prods to force it inside. It grabbed someone, pulled him close, and tore open the poor bastard's visor.

Seeing my chance, I darted across to the closest vehicle and squinted through the driver's side window. The key was hanging from the ignition. Quietly, I opened the rear passenger door and placed my wife in the backseat. Sliding in behind the wheel, I started the engine.

Walt and the others spun around as I hit the gas in reverse. Someone shouted, and the gray-suits came running. Immediately, they headed towards the open gate and planted themselves in a line in front of me, pointing their weapons at my windshield. Soon I would find out whether the glass was bulletproof.

I had no other purpose—no other mission—than to get Holly out of there. My heart was broken, and I couldn't unbreak it. But I could perform one act of kindness before they killed me. Taking a searing breath, I floored it as the gray-suits opened fire.

Round after round pinged off the protective glass as the Escalade picked up speed. Unwavering, the gray-suits continued to fire. I bore down on them, my eyes glazed over. Screaming, two of them leaped out of the way as I reached the gate. Gleefully, I hit one. His body flipped onto my hood with a loud thump and rolled off. The other I crushed under my wheels like a meat-filled piñata.

I knew this road—it led straight to the freeway. If I could make it away from the helicopters and other Escalades, I could continue south to our home, Holly's and mine. I checked the rearview mirror. No one followed me. I was free.

Traffic was light as I drove up the on-ramp and entered the freeway. I stayed in the middle lanes and drove the speed limit. When I was safely away from Mt. Shasta, I turned around to look at my wife.

The blood from her head wound had congealed. She seemed smaller, like a fairy I could put in my pocket. And I wanted to so much. A profound drowsiness overcame me. I felt like drifting away somewhere. But I still had work to do.

Focusing on the road, I tried to picture Tres Marias as it must look now. Would it be reborn in some new form? Would people return and start families? Open businesses?

Would anyone remember?

If Operation Guncotton had gone as planned, they would've already released the nerve agent. I had no way of knowing how long it would linger. Hannity had said the poison was short acting. It didn't matter now. It was like I told Walt.

I was already dead.

EIGHTY-TWO

I got off at the last possible exit. At the bottom of the ramp, I swung around under the freeway and continued to the checkpoint. The place was deserted—no people, no vehicles. Nothing. Only the stark, silent trees.

Earlier, I'd rolled up my windows and shut off the outside air, hoping that would be enough to protect me. I never said I was smart. Proceeding cautiously, I took the service road that would eventually bring me to a street leading into town.

Driving through the forest, my headlights shone on a deer lying on the shoulder. Soon there were more animals. Squirrels, raccoons, and a mountain lion. And thousands of birds —all dead. I wondered if anything would ever live here again.

The vacant streets filled me with a profound sadness. Vehicles stood askew along both sides of the road. Like any normal night, streetlights were lit, and traffic signals cycled. It wasn't too much farther. Though my plan was haphazard, I had faith that I could pull it off. If I succeeded, my death would be a blessing. But I'd forgotten something.

The nerve agent wouldn't have killed everything. Somewhere out there, draggers lurked. Biding their time till the last man on earth stumbled stupidly past so they could relieve him of his puny existence. A proper last supper before Walt Freeman's minions incinerated the wretches.

I needed a weapon. Somehow, I'd lost my handgun during my escape. For the next few minutes, I drove around, hoping to see a dead cop or a Black Dragon guard lying in the street. No luck. Turning at the next corner, I headed to the command center—my last hope.

The bodies of dogs, cats, and birds lay scattered on sidewalks and lawns like debris after a storm. The scene was like something out of a *Twilight Zone* episode but poorly written and devoid of humor. Up ahead, I spotted the familiar gate. Trash left behind during the bugout spun in little whirlwinds across the parking lot as I pulled in. Were the ghosts of the dead watching over this place?

Keeping an eye out for draggers, I continued to our trailer, half expecting Warnick and the others to be there. I could just picture them waiting on the steps. *Dude, where have you been? Pederman wants to meet.* The thought of seeing my friends again brought a smile to my face.

I stopped in front and remained still with the engine running. Like a ghostly invitation, the wind blew the trailer door open and closed. It knew what I wanted as it tried to lure me away from the safety of my vehicle. Afraid I would die here, I didn't budge.

Near the football field, something moved low to the ground through the darkness, making my nerve endings tingle. I waited a beat. It was a dog—a filthy, limping animal that resembled something born in hell. Whimpering, it zigzagged erratically across the parking lot. Maybe it was looking for a place to die. I could relate. Warily, I watched it disappear around the side of a building.

I was out of time. Taking a deep breath, I flung open the

car door and stared straight ahead. Then, I exhaled and sniffed the air. Nothing—not even a hint of poison. Breathing normally, I checked on Holly before entering the trailer.

Everything was the same. We'd only taken a few clothes and my wife's vitamins. There were no guns. I searched for a first-aid kit. A backpack lay next to our bed. Inside, I found an elastic bandage and wrapped my arm as best I could. Listening for draggers, I continued to the rear. I opened the utility closet and stuck in my hand. It was there, bloodstained and worn, patiently awaiting my return. My axe.

The blade was dull—that wouldn't do. I drove to the machine shop on the other side of campus and broke in. Fearing draggers, I left the lights off. Moonlight shone through the large windows. In no time, I found the bench grinder. I switched it on and carefully sharpened the blade, turning it as white sparks danced over my hands.

Using my good arm, I swung the weapon several times, my muscles remembering its heft. Hoisting it over my shoulder, I walked outside and peered into the darkness. I was alone. Tossing the axe on the floor of the passenger-side footwell, I climbed into the Escalade and headed out.

One final stop and my story would come to an end.

EIGHTY-THREE

We had survived, Holly and me. Traversed a landscape of terror that nearly destroyed us. Somehow, though, we found a way to live. Tres Marias was a way station. I knew that and was good with it. We had jobs and money. And for the first time in months, we had hope for the future. That was then.

When the nightmare was over, we would've found someplace new to live—San Francisco, probably. Wherever we ended up, we'd raise our daughter and be a family. While living in Tres Marias, my wife wanted to get pregnant. We'd imagined a baby girl named Jade. Often, I would think of her growing up. Marveling at her—seeing her thrive—this beautiful phantom child. But Holly was dead, along with our precious baby. And that meant hope was dead too.

Rage consumed me, and I realized it wasn't the mayor I was angry with. Though he had pulled the trigger, it was God who'd allowed my wife to die. He led me down the path, bringing me closer to my faith through Holly. He showed me a picture of a life much better than anything I could've imagined. With a woman who loved me and a little girl who held the promise of a brilliant future. Then, when I was at my happiest, He took it all away.

Forevermore, He crushed the one thing that had kept me going these past weeks and months. I'd read the Scripture and memorized the prayers. I was trying to live a good life. Maybe not holy, but good all the same. It was useless because my life partner was dead. And as much as I wanted to spit in His face, I knew being here now—at this moment—was all that mattered. Despite my wrenching anguish, I had to keep going somehow.

St. Monica's came into view and, with it, a new reality. Cruising slowly towards the church, I saw them milling outside like anxious, hungry vultures. Draggers—twenty or thirty of them. Only they stood in the way. But I was afraid for Holly, not me. And so, I continued past the church into the darkness, rolling to a stop on a lonely side street.

"Not much longer, babe," I said.

Reaching across, I grabbed my axe and exited the Escalade. Outside, the air was crisp. I turned my face to the sky. Gray clouds had rolled in, blotting out the moon. The wind chilled me, but I wasn't shivering. I was too numb. Gazing at my wife through the side window, I locked up the vehicle.

When you have something important to do, you do it. Nothing can distract you. Walking faster past the trash and the dead birds, I stepped into a pool of light thrown from a nearby streetlamp. I was maybe thirty yards away. Softly, I whistled, and they saw me. These were the crafty type—the kind who knew how to organize. All the better.

Their leader was a ratty teenager with stringy brown hair and black-hole eyes. I recognized him. He was my roommate in the police station holding cell. I remembered him telling me about the fun he and his buddies had setting draggers on fire. Now he was one of them. Oh, the irony. The thing tilted its head back and, its throat blowing up like a bullfrog, let out a death shriek that echoed up and down the block. That's when they came for me.

I waited in the middle of the street. Alone, unafraid, and gripping my beloved axe with both hands. Though I wasn't inclined to pray to a God who'd cut me so deeply, I did it anyway—for Holly. Wisely, their leader hung back while the others rushed me. As I suspected, they were organized, these disciples from hell. I stood my ground, my bad arm stiff from the gunshot wound.

As the first one came at me, I chopped off its hands in two swift strokes. Confused, it tried paddling me with the stumps. I took its head as a tribute. More grunting, more screeching. Then two more followed.

I hacked at their necks, throwing them off balance. Kicking each, I sent them sprawling into the others, who struggled to get ahold of me. These I stopped by cleaving their heads. Black sludge oozed out of busted craniums as they fell into a pile. Once they were down, I finished off the first two.

For one brief, shining moment, I was that confident kid with his hockey stick. Skating purposefully around the rink and taking on all comers. I was me at my best. The fatherless boy full of hopes and dreams.

I pushed through the oozing mass of hungry predators who thought they had a shot. Relentlessly, I separated arms and disarranged faces. I took their legs, leaving the ravenous attackers to army crawl. Squirming body parts lay all around, and I almost tripped going after the final few.

As one of them leaped at me, I side-stepped and watched it kiss the ground. I brought down my bloody axe on its spine, severing the last glitchy message its dead brain would ever send. Twisting its upper body, it raged at me. I gave it a pleased, icy smile. *You have no idea what rage is.*

Exhausted and aching, I faced the second to last—a woman dressed as a real estate agent in a ratty blazer and no shoes. It tried overtaking me, and I let it. As it got close, its raw, grinning mouth nearly on my neck, I jammed the axe handle under its jaw and drove it straight up through the head, liquefying everything in its path. Tumbling backwards, the hostile swung around—toothless—ready for another go. I sliced off its head, which rolled to the feet of the lone leader who'd witnessed everything. The kid with the stringy hair and black-hole eyes.

It stood there, studying me. I recognized a creeping intelligence as we faced off. The Billabong T-shirt and ripped jeans —and the flat eyes. And me in my bloody Black Dragon uniform, with a slug in my arm. All around me, everything— limbs, torsos, severed heads—were in motion. But not this predator. It was frozen in time.

"God, let me finish the mission," I said. "You owe me that."

EIGHTY-FOUR

The dragger gave me the once-over like it couldn't believe a nobody from a town no one ever heard of was praying. It might've chuckled. I turned the greasy axe in my hands. The handle was covered in black blood—same as my clothes. With all the patience in the world, the creature waited. I expected it to rush me. Instead, it ran away.

A distant death shriek echoed as I made my way to the Escalade. Once again, I was alone, my footsteps slapping the cold asphalt. The first raindrops fell. I tossed the axe aside and gently lifted Holly out of the backseat. Nothing moved—not even the gory remains of the other draggers. I was beyond tired—wasted to my soul. But I had to go on.

I marched up the church steps. When I reached the entrance, I heard a voice. Though it was faint, I was sure it wasn't my imagination. There was someone in there, and she was singing. The sound was high and reedy, like a little girl. Had she survived the gas attack? With my wife in my arms, I pulled open the doors and went inside.

The church was empty except for the child. I couldn't see her very well as she stood at the dimly lit altar. All alone in the church, she sang "Softly and Tenderly Jesus Is Calling." Her voice was the sweetest sound I'd ever heard. I wanted to listen to her forever.

My blood dripped on the carpet as I carried Holly up the aisle. All around, the saints portrayed in statues and stained glass windows watched me. On the walls, the Stations of the Cross depicted more suffering than I could ever know. In front of me, behind the altar, hung Jesus on the Cross. God had taken pity, and my wife was safe.

While the girl sang, I carried Holly to the altar and placed her on the marble floor as an offering. It was time to let go. Getting to my feet, I went to the baptismal font and dipped my fingers, fouling the water with dragger blood. I made the Sign of the Cross on my wife's forehead. Without a priest, it was the best I could do for her and the baby.

I knelt, gazing at her and recalling the sound of her voice. The way she scowled when she was mad. How she touched my face when she forgave me. All at once, the anger left me like a crow with its fill of carrion. A deep pain I knew would never heal wracked my body. And I wept.

"You once told me you couldn't wait for me to become the man you knew was inside me. I need to show you, but I'm not ready. Oh God, Holly! I'm not ready."

Someone touched me—it was the girl. Her small, waif-like body was dirty, in shorts and a bloody T-shirt with the words *L'il Princess* across the front. She couldn't have been more than ten, with blonde hair and hurt green eyes. There was something so familiar about her, but I couldn't... And then, I remembered.

This was the child I'd killed all those months ago on a

road near Shasta Lake. Because she had turned. I didn't understand how she could be here—*alive.*

She wiped away my tears with a soft child's finger. Grasping her hand, I stared at my wife's still body. It was done. I turned to the girl, exhausted and in pain. There was a peacefulness about her I couldn't quite understand. I felt myself floating away.

"What's your name?" I said.

"Holly. Do not be afraid, David. *Therefore, since God in his mercy has given us this new way, we never give up.*" Then she smiled. "I'll see you again."

Her little hand slipped from mine. Carrying her words with me, I left the church and stood on the steps, peering into the darkness. It didn't matter what happened to me now. I'd taken care of the mother and baby I loved and honored their memory the only way I could. There was nothing left to do except breathe in the scent of rain.

Sensing movement, I turned to the side. Someone approached from out of the predawn shadows—that same lone dragger. It had come looking for me, and I was ready. With determined steps, I walked down to meet it. I no longer had my axe—no gun and no knife. Weak from blood loss, I was defenseless.

What happens to the soul when you turn? Does it leave the body instantly? Or is it trapped inside, a silent witness to the atrocities you continue to inflict till someone puts you down? And why would God allow such an abomination to exist? Maybe when this was over, I'd finally learn the truth.

The hostile inched closer, still wary from our last encounter. Somehow, it seemed to understand I was unarmed and began moving faster. Soon, it would be on me. I felt no emotion. It was as if this were happening to someone else.

Grinning, it let out a triumphant death shriek and came at me. I closed my eyes and awaited the eternal darkness of unbeing.

Suddenly, gunfire erupted in the street. When I looked again, the dragger was slithering to the ground, its head blown to shit. Three people approached me, one aiming his AR-15—Warnick! Then Greta bounded towards me, yipping and whining. She covered me in dog slobber as I struggled to stay standing.

"Greta, how did you…"

Warnick and Fabian came closer. Griffin ran to me and fell into my arms, blessing me with her tears.

"Thank God you're alive!" she said.

After what happened that night, I was dead. I'd lost everything, including my will to live. I wanted to disappear forever. But after seeing the girl and the others, something changed. Breathing deeply, I took in the early morning air as the first rays of sunlight peeked over the buildings. Griffin was right— I was *alive*.

As the men embraced me, it began to rain, cold and steady. Washing away the poison that had killed most of the living in my town. Cleansing Tres Marias of all the bad and maybe offering a future for those who chose to accept it.

"There's a little girl in the church," I said. "She needs help."

The men went inside while Griffin and I sat on the steps. Like old times, I stroked Greta's ears. The girl clung to my good arm, her head resting against me. In another beat, my friends returned.

I stared at Warnick. "Where is she?"

"There was no one in there. Except Holly."

My wife was dead. My child was dead. But I was alive. I

couldn't figure out why or how. Maybe we're not supposed to know. I decided to accept what was. My friend held out his Bible and, taking my hands, placed it in them. I didn't sense anything—no healing power, nothing—but I took the book anyway.

"Come on," Warnick said. "It's been a long night."

EIGHTY-FIVE

When I was little and afraid of the dark, my mother would sing to me. An old song written way before I was born—"Catch the Wind" by Donovan. Though the song was about things that can never be, the words always comforted me. Maybe it was the sweetness of her voice or the way she gazed at me with kindness.

For my thirteenth birthday, Mom gave me an iPod. I don't know how she figured it out, but she managed to purchase and download the album. I hadn't heard "Catch the Wind" in a long time—skull-cracking hockey players don't need comforting. Yet there were many afternoons when I would stay in my room, listening to that silly song. And I remembered what it was like to be afraid. It's how I felt now without Holly.

During that last dangerous night, Warnick and the interns witnessed my escape in the stolen Escalade. In the chaos, they slipped out of the compound and ran. Eventually, they found their way to the waiting helicopter. Griffin had begged the pilot not to leave, convinced I was on my way to meet them. When I didn't show, they took off.

They waited for me at the armory. Warnick and Fabian thought the gray-suits might've overtaken my vehicle and killed me. But the girl insisted I was out there somewhere—her little woman had told her. She reasoned that there was only one place I would go, and that was Tres Marias. So despite the risk, they took off in a Humvee to find me.

My friends took turns watching me at the hospital, where I slept for two days straight. When I awoke, they made sure I was washed, dressed, and fed. Warnick delivered the news that Operation Guncotton had been a classified mission, which meant there would be no official investigation. Soon, a National Guard unit would deploy to Tres Marias to clear any remaining draggers and incinerate the bodies.

The cleanup would take weeks, but the Guard was confident they could make the town safe again. There was even talk of civilians returning. The idea sounded crazy. It only became real when my friend mentioned the banks and insurance companies were already sniffing around, eager to assess the damage and assign blame.

Emotionally, I was a mess. So Warnick saw to it that Holly's body was delivered to a morgue in Redding. While I drifted in and out of sleep, he enlisted Isaac's help in making the burial arrangements. An autopsy was required because she'd been murdered. The doctor performed it.

Even in death, Holly looked beautiful. I asked that she be laid to rest in her wedding dress and wearing her First Communion crucifix. Like me, she didn't have any other family. She was to be buried in Redding—not Tres Marias—because that town's only Catholic cemetery was full. Good thing. Too many bad memories.

Since my wife had died while employed with Black Dragon, the company paid for everything. We held the funeral Mass at St. Joseph Roman Catholic Church. Mostly, guards attended. Isaac, the Zimmers, and a few other civilians she'd helped also showed up.

At the graveside, the priest said the final prayers. Warnick had brought a CD player and blasted "Just Like Heaven" by the Cure. I had no idea how he found out—he wouldn't tell me. But it was Holly's all-time favorite song. I suspected Griffin had something to do with it.

After the service, a few of us met at Starbucks. I didn't want to, but the girl insisted, taking on the responsibility of preserving what was left of my family. The last time I was there, it was to convince Missy Soldado to leave me alone. That was a lifetime ago. The coffee line stretched across the store, and most tables were full. Waiting to order, I felt like a ghost.

We ended up outside, sipping our coffee as Greta lay at my feet. None of us were in uniform. Griffin looked confident in her jeans and yellow top. Fabian, dressed more like a cowboy than a guard, was a young man coming into his own. Warnick wore a black Weezer T-shirt. He wasn't just my friend—he was my brother.

"We have to report to the regional office for a debrief," he said. "They'll provide temporary housing, and eventually, we'll get our new assignments."

The girl cheered. "Awesome! I've never been to San Francisco. Where do you think they'll send us?"

"Could be anywhere. I heard there might be an interesting gig in Atlanta."

The Latino smirked. "Another plague?"

Warnick took a long swallow. "Let's hope not."

"And what about Walt Freeman?" I said.

My friend thought for a moment. Watching the traffic, he finished his coffee. "Looks like he got away with it."

Not surprised, I put a pin in it. "So when do we leave for San Francisco?"

"Tomorrow."

Griffin stroked Greta's ear while Fabian held her other hand. A warm feeling came over me when I realized those two belonged together. The thought made me smile.

"You make a nice couple," I said.

Blushing, the girl withdrew her hand. "I was... I mean, we..."

"You're fine." Then to her boyfriend, "Holly always liked you, dude."

Warnick gave me a suspicious smile. "And you?"

"He might be growing on me," I said.

It was a beautiful fall day. The air was crisp, the sky clear. Cars cruised past as parents pushed babies in strollers along the sidewalk. All around us, people went about their business as if everything were normal. And it was—for them. I was hungry to feel that. To be caught up in the everyday—not haunted by memories of the horror I'd witnessed. How could a person do that? Climb their way out of hell and return to a life where no one was trying to kill them? I wasn't sure I could.

"We should get going." I tossed my cup in the trash. "Not much to pack, and I'd like to take it easy."

Groaning, my friend stood. "Sounds good."

Griffin laid her hand on mine. "It's going to be okay."

In that magical moment, she sounded so much like Holly.

I wanted to close my eyes and see my wife alive and unharmed, wearing a summer dress and running into my arms. But a dream like that would tear me apart. So instead, I tried a smile.

"I know it will," I said.

EIGHTY-SIX

I was never good at endings, especially when I still cared about the people I was leaving behind. Setting Warnick's Bible on the nightstand, I headed out before dawn and made my way to a parking structure several blocks from the hotel. After returning from Starbucks the previous day, I went out to purchase clothes for the trip. Griffin and Fabian wanted to come. I told them I needed some alone time. First order of business—rent an SUV.

In the early-morning darkness, I climbed into the vehicle. The sound of the powerful engine revving echoed. My only weapon was the axe I'd hidden in the back. Where I was headed, I would need more than a blade. I sat awhile thinking about the girl, knowing she'd be okay. She had Warnick and Fabian to keep her safe. Leaving the parking structure, I stopped suddenly as a young coyote crossed my path. It stopped briefly, the bright headlights illuminating its yellow, questioning eyes. *I have doubts*, it seemed to say.

The animal wasn't alone. Reflecting on that horrible night, I'd decided to remain with the others. Wherever we ended up, whatever happened next, I would be there. But something buried in my unconscious ate at me. And then, when Warnick confirmed what I already knew to be true—that Walt Freeman had gotten away with it—my future was clear. God had spared me not to get on with life. I had a new mission—to right a wrong.

It didn't take long to reach Mt. Shasta. I found a fire road leading into the forest and followed it for several miles. The trees smelled wonderful. The birds and other wildlife reminded me of a different time. I turned onto an obscure road and headed to a clearing. Up ahead, I spotted the Diana birdbath. A warning shot zinged past the vehicle. Fearless, I climbed out, exposing myself to the wrath of Guthrie Manson. The old man emerged from the shadows, his bullpup aimed at my head. When he recognized me, he blew air through his lips and lowered the weapon.

"Next time, call first," he said.

"You don't own a phone."

"Good point. You alone?" He squinted at the vehicle. "Well, come on inside, I guess. I'll ask Caramel to put on some tea. I'm surprised to see you. Hungry?"

He always was a chatty old man. After giving me a hug, he led me inside. Laying the shotgun on a side table, he headed for the kitchen.

"Honey?" he said. "We got company."

The old woman with the flowing white hair stood in the doorway, holding a dishrag. Dropping it, she embraced me. "Goodness, you're alive!"

"Matter of opinion," I said.

Taking my hand, she sat me down and put on water for tea. Guthrie was about to ask me something when she cut him off.

"We heard about what happened in Tres Marias. We were

so worried you and your wife wouldn't..." She caught the look in my eyes.

"Holly's dead."

The words hung in the air like those little calaveras and brought back all the anguish. It felt like someone ripping the skin from my bones and feeding it to the dogs.

"Oh, honey, come here." She wrapped her thin arms around me.

"I'm on my way to kill the man responsible," I said. "Thought I'd stop by first."

The old man side-eyed his wife. "That's a dangerous game, Dave."

"I know, but I have no choice. They took everything from me. And the town."

"You do what you gotta do," he said. "But I'm gonna say my piece. More than likely, they'll kill you. People like that are way more skilled than a punk robbing a liquor store."

"Is that how you see me?"

Caramel rolled her eyes. "Boys, don't start."

"I need weapons," I said.

Guthrie scratched his beard and placed his hands flat on the table. "You can have whatever you want, you know that."

"I owe you both so much."

Caramel handed us mugs of steaming tea. Her husband blew on his and took a sip as she sat beside him.

"Any idea where you'll find the miscreants?" he said.

"I'm going to try LA."

"Got money?"

"Enough."

"Good," he said. "Most of our cash is tied up in ganja and guns. Stay the night, though. Looks like you could use the rest."

• • •

I left at dawn. Caramel begged me to be careful, and I promised her I would. Guthrie let me take the truck his sons used to drive. He agreed to return the SUV for me, even though it meant dealing with townies. After loading up weapons and ammo, the old man gave me some good advice. It was something I took to heart. *Don't trust anyone.*

It was hard for me to confide in people. I figured doing what he'd suggested wouldn't be a problem. But to live the rest of your life—however long that was—without letting anyone in was a damn lonely proposition. Instead of wallowing, I concentrated on the road ahead.

I had one abiding purpose, and I clung to it like a lifeline. As soon as I arrived in LA, I would hunt down Walt Freeman. But before killing him, I'd make him explain why he did this. And I would force him to tell me how many other towns he planned to ruin, how many more lives he was prepared to sacrifice. I would make him suffer till he admitted everything. Then, I'd make him pay.

In the early morning of a crisp fall day, I said my last goodbyes and drove away to a future with no name. Everything was behind me. I wanted nothing more than to move forward with no ties to the present and no past. It would be as if I'd come into the world anew, packing revenge.

I went by way of Tres Marias and stayed on the fire road going south. Eventually, I came to a small bridge that spanned a dry riverbed. It was a million years ago when I crossed over. I'd spotted a man being chased by what I came to learn were draggers. Unlike Mt. Shasta, there were no signs of wildlife. Up ahead, I noticed something in the road— possibly a dead raccoon. As I got closer, I recognized Jim's dog Perro. I pulled over and got out.

He lay in the dirt, a decaying mass, free of the evil that had poisoned him. A few feet away, my old friend observed me from the shadows. It didn't surprise me he was there. Often, I'd felt him watching as I struggled to survive the plague. I knew how much he had loved his dog—probably the only thing he ever cared about. In my dream, he said what happened to Perro wasn't fair. And it wasn't right what they did to him—or my wife. Or anyone else who was a victim of this terrifying hell of man's own making.

"I'm sorry, Jim," I said.

He nodded, finally accepting that I'd done everything I could. I climbed into the truck and fired up the engine. When I glanced back, my friend was gone. I noticed a CD lying on the passenger seat. Probably left there by one of Guthrie's boys. It was by a band I'd never heard of—The Chambers Brothers. I slipped it into the player and cranked it up, losing myself in the pounding, liberating rhythm of "Time Has Come Today."

As I picked up speed, I checked the rearview mirror and, for the last time, saw Perro's bloated body in the road. Newly arrived crows fought as they picked at the rotting remains. Eventually, he would return to the earth—maybe even nourish it. Circle of life.

I don't know where I'm going exactly, towards a future filled with uncertainty and danger. Anyway, it's what I'm used to. This time, though, there's a difference. No limits. I've got to find the people who did this. Even if it means dying alone with no one to pray for me. It's the only thing that matters now, and I must do it.

For Holly.

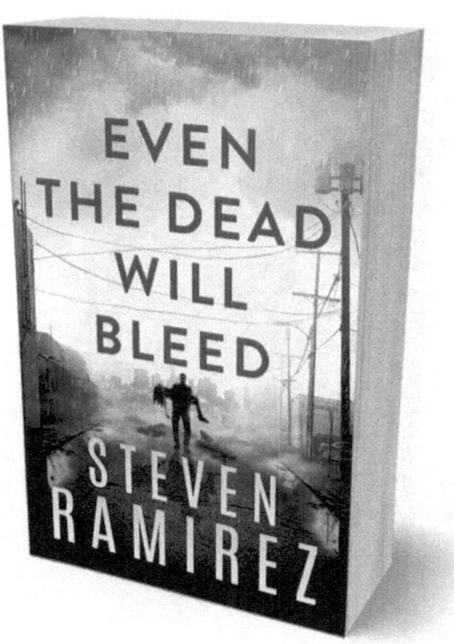

UP NEXT...

*Avoid the mutants. Save the girl.
Get revenge...*

In Los Angeles, Dave Pulaski tries to kill Walt Freeman, the man responsible for the outbreak in Tres Marias. But his mission is sidetracked when he chooses to rescue Sasha, a victim of another bioscience experiment.

AVAILABLE IN PAPERBACK

YOUR FREE BOOK IS WAITING...

When your boss pulls a gun on you, it might be time to quit.

Get your free copy of *Brandon's Last Words: A Jane Doe Thriller Prequel.*

BOOKS.STEVENRAMIREZ.COM/GET-THRILLER

ABOUT THE AUTHOR

Steven Ramirez is the award-winning American author of thriller, supernatural, and literary fiction. A former screenwriter, he's written about man-made plagues and idyllic towns infested with ghosts and demons. His latest novel is *Let's Get Lost*, a modern fairy tale. Steven lives in Los Angeles.

AUTHOR WEBSITE
stevenramirez.com

instagram.com/byStevenRamirez
goodreads.com/byStevenRamirez
bookbub.com/authors/steven-ramirez